DEATH
to the Rescue

RJ Huddy

A PEACE CORPS WRITERS BOOK

To:

Tom Sumner, a great friend before he became a great editor.

And to:

James Burgett, a great friend before he became a great photographer.

Acknowledgments

I would like to express my deepest gratitude to several people who have generously lent their time and expertise to this project: Mark Maynard, editor, and Lee Ward, lifestyles editor, *The Independent* (Ashland, KY); Mike Strange, *Knoxville News-Sentinel;* Anthony Davis, Sara Green, Teria Kiethley, Garry Lingerfelt, Darcy Meijer, and Fraser Thorburn.

Cover design by James Burgett
Book design by Tom Sumner

All proceeds from the sale of this book go towards research for a cure for CMT Neuropathy, a form of muscular dystrophy.

A Peace Corps Writers Book.
An imprint of Peace Corps Worldwide.

First Peace Corps Writers Edition, October 2012.

ISBN 978-1-935925-18-7

Mozambique, Southeast Africa. Four years ago . . .

Male grunts and a squeal of female delight cut through the somber Chopin prelude Owen Weeks was playing. His hands froze on the keyboard. He called, "Sabella?"

There was no answer.

Sabella Brooks was Owen Weeks' sixteen-year-old step-daughter. After the assassination of her mother by order of South Zambezi's President Abel Magwimbi, only Sabella and the servants lived with Weeks on his once-grand Portuguese tea plantation.

He called her name again, "Sabella?"

The only response was another happy squeal in the distance. He slammed his fists onto the keys, shouted for Jojo the houseboy, and ran onto the veranda. Out front he saw nothing more than a small herd of impala grazing in a field of matted grass under a sycamore fig, and beyond that the muddy Sabie River, still swollen from the year's good rains. Upriver the blue haze of the Bvumba mountains stretched from Mozambique to the border with South Zambezi.

A crowned hornbill shrieked from the fig tree. Weeks' chest surged and he tried to laugh. He thought, Was that all it was? A goddamn bird call? You see what you get? You let yourself get caught up in the antics of a young girl, and next thing you know your emotions run amok.

He calmed himself and walked back into the music room, where Jojo was waiting with a fresh gin and tonic on a tray of tarnished silver.

"This number four, baas."

"Where's Sabella? And who the hell are you to count my drinks?"

I

"You tell me, sah. And Miss outside."

"Well it's three, and I'm untelling you."

"Yes, sah baas. Maybe five."

"Go and find Sabella." He sat back down at the piano.

More shrieks from outside, this time mixed with laughter. Weeks hurried to the west veranda, toward the tourist bungalows, where this time he saw exactly what he had feared: his beautiful step-daughter on her knees at the edge of a makeshift wrestling ring where two teenaged South African boys were locked in a complicated embrace. The father looked on, shouting encouragement and insults in Afrikaans, while Sabella laughed and slapped the ground like a referee.

This was precisely the sort of sluttish behavior he had been expecting. She was her mother's daughter, through and through. Little tarts, the pair of them. This one even worse than her mother. Neither had ever showed him the respect he knew he deserved. Even when Linda was alive she'd acted like she was the rescuer, and now Sabella seldom noticed he was alive.

What kind of life would the little bitch have now if he hadn't saved her? He could tell you exactly: poor white trash, that's what. Just like her mother. A nanny to a family of blacks! Wiping *kaffir* backsides! A member of the despised white subclass in Abel Magwimbi's brave new South Zambezi. It was he, Owen Weeks, and he alone, who had plucked them from that life and placed them above their station in this fine old mansion. Granted, the tea plantation hadn't survived the Mozambican civil war, but the place came cheap and he'd resurrected it as a fishing lodge. Their home in exile. Their safe refuge.

He watched Sabella scrambling sideways around the wrestlers like some ecstatic crab, her perfect hips positioned up high, her face alive, her eyes transfixed on Boer muscle and sweat and strategy. She needed turning over his knee for a few well-aimed swats on that proffered backside, but it was far too late for that now. He called out, "Please take care out there, Sabella," but he was thinking, Someday you'll get yours, just like your worthless minx of a mother.

The South African father waved and called out, "I'm keeping

my eye on her." He seemed to say something to her, causing her to retreat a few inches from the struggle, then returned his full attention to his sons.

Weeks retreated to his piano and his Chopin. He knocked back half of his gin. Could this already be his fourth drink of the day? Maybe even fifth? But really, who cared? Things were falling apart before his eyes. His whole strategy, so meticulously implemented, beginning two years ago with his exile from South Zambezi and continuing right through to his wife's death, was now in free fall. He looked atop the piano to his wife's picture there, draped in black ribbon. The more he drank the uglier she got. Hard-looking bitch. Eyes like bits of gravel. At least in two more months the mourning period would end and he could take that ribbon down. He'd be happy to burn it and the photograph with it, only Sabella would act offended.

He turned his attention to Sabella's framed photo on the other side of the piano, thinking, Look at her, a whore born and bred. Her future—my future—is blindingly obvious. Soon she will abscond with one of these muscle-bound tourists, somebody much younger and better looking and a whole lot richer than I am. A man who can show her more of the world than smelly fishing holes and mud-caked river banks. And then who will I take into my bed and into my heart? Local chippies at five dollars a turn?

Can a white man be expected to live like that? Year after year of village girls smelling of wood smoke and onions, while the beautiful object of his every waking thought lies in the arms of some rugby player in Capetown?

"Jojo!"

The houseboy appeared with another drink. "Four or five or six, baas. Nobody counting."

Weeks felt his whole body starting to tremble. He couldn't be sure whether it was the gin, or the gruesome decision Sabella was forcing upon him. He looked up at old Jojo, everlastingly referred to as houseboy, even though his hair was a carpet of white and his gnarled bare feet had spread flat enough to overlap the wide teak boarding of the music room floor. "What do you think about it, Jojo? What would your people do with a girl who prefers to turn slut rather than cherish the man who sacrificed everything for her?"

Jojo averted his eyes, and did not speak.

This dumb silence sent an icy wave down Weeks' neck. "You will answer me when I ask you a question!"

"No, sah, baas. Old Jojo don't count no more, sah." He walked away.

Weeks laid his head against the keyboard, striking a sour and plaintive minor chord. Unresolved notes filled the room, and then faded away. Within the silence that followed he heard the voice of old Powerful, the Zambezi shaman he'd consulted before his wife's death. He recalled Powerful's simple advice: *To rid yourself of an enemy, create for your victim another enemy even more ruthless than you are.*

In that instant Owen saw what had to be done. There was no other answer for it. Now it didn't matter that Sabella was on her knees in the grass, moist reward for one victorious teenaged combatant. Her peals of delight no longer pierced his stomach. All of that was shut down. His mind was now an emergency committee of many conflicting thoughts, both rational and insane, of emotions tender and evil, all convened at this one defining instant to decide, with unbreakable unity of purpose, a course of action that would bring upheaval to countless lives on two continents.

Without Jojo's assistance he located pen and paper, and wrote:

To Lovemore Ngweyna,

I hope you still recall with some fondness your old piano teacher, just as I do my star pupil. I have an offer I think you should consider. Come here and be safe with us. We will be your shelter until our homeland is restored. You will have your own room here in our comfortable home. I will teach you to fish and to run tourists up the Sabie. The same person who delivers this note to you can arrange to bring you in.

Do you remember my daughter, Sabella? She once had a sort

of adolescent crush on you. Perhaps you never knew that. She's growing up fast, quite beautiful, with a developing wild streak. She refuses utterly to practice her piano. She needs a younger mentor, and I think you would be just the ticket for her. Sabella is a child of the modern age, even less race conscious than I am—if such a thing is possible.

Guardian Management History:

1882–1910 : Orval Shanley
1910–1923 : Rafael Shanley
1923–1934 : Nathan Shanley
1934–1946 : Roy Shanley
1946–1961 : Delmon Shanley
1961–1977 : Landon Shanley
1977–2010 : Woodrow Shanley
2010–   : Joshua Shanley

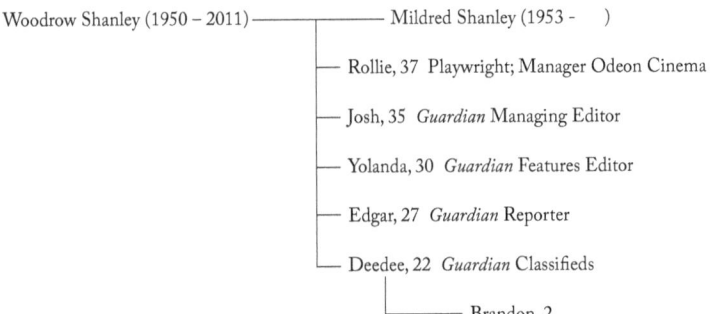

Woodrow Shanley (1950 – 2011) ——————— Mildred Shanley (1953 -   )

— Rollie, 37 Playwright; Manager Odeon Cinema

— Josh, 35 *Guardian* Managing Editor

— Yolanda, 30 *Guardian* Features Editor

— Edgar, 27 *Guardian* Reporter

— Deedee, 22 *Guardian* Classifieds

——— Brandon, 2

The Trial

The Twisting Creek Guardian

ESTABLISHED 1882 — Monday, September 20 — *The Voice of Reason in the Tri-State*

Murder Trial of Lovemore Ngwenya to Open This Week

DNA Evidence "Impossible to Rebut"—DA

CHAPTER 1: DEEDEE

THE NEW PAVED road leading up from the lake was just curvy enough to put her toddler to sleep. Deedee heard soft, stable breathing from the back seat, checked her rear view mirror, and saw Brandon already slumped forward in his car seat, his face almost buried inside a wet beach towel. With her troubled son momentarily at peace, she consciously relaxed the arc of muscles running from her neck to her shoulders, and allowed her thoughts to drift. The smell of lake water and plastic toys filled the car. She watched the clean asphalt slide under her, as silent as a gray cloud, and allowed her eyes to follow the fresh yellow of no-passing lines. For a few hypnotic seconds a slate-winged gull flew alongside her car, like a fender ornament.

This was Deedee's quiet time, her therapy session, the preserver of what was left of her sanity. For three harrowing years, since the day she'd decided against both abortion and adoption, she'd rarely had time to examine the chaos her life had nosedived into. Although the struggle seemed endless, an end to it was just what she'd planned to consider on the drive home from the lake, the one time when Brandon was guaranteed to be sound asleep.

But her attention snagged on a brand new road sign—*Archer's Bait and Boat*—and she turned impulsively, foolishly, down a dirt lane leading toward a gravel lot. There in front of her stood an old unstripped log house whose rain-blackened sides were peeling away in shreds of tangled bark. Wasp nests and tattered spider webs daubed the gaps between logs. Dead carcasses of spruce or fir trees littered the ground, like a graveyard of Christmas trees, their stumps standing nearby, not sawn clean, but hacked jagged with an axe. Protruding from the house at an odd angle was a wide porch covered by a roof that rippled with curled and disintegrating pine shingles. Above, dark shutters sealed the gable windows of the upper floor, and for a moment she wondered how a place this downcast and eerie, and so near the lake, could have for so long escaped her notice. It took her a minute to realize that before the new road went in, this place was buried deep in the backwoods. She was entering a secluded world.

At the sound of gravel against the bottom of the car, Brandon woke with a full hiccupping wail, the kind of anguish that most children have to achieve in stages. Deedee skidded to a stop and sat there amidst his convulsions, thinking, *Why not leave him strapped in right where he is?* She got out and closed the door, muffling him to a distant cry.

The lake water smell was gone now, replaced by a pungent mixture of humus, rotting wood, and an oppressive dog-days breeze trying to stir the forest canopy. For a moment, standing alone before this forlorn cottage, with nothing else in view but the green expanse of woods beyond, Deedee almost knew a sense of remove. The only sound now was Brandon's dampened screaming, from deep down a well, perhaps, or far back in a cave. It made her feel as though that faraway cry, that demand from some imperious and insatiable creature, might possibly be somebody else's problem. She could set herself free. What was to stop her? She thought, *What If I just lock all the doors and disappear into the woods?*

Through the rear window Brandon had his fierce eyes fixed on her, his mouth wide open and shuddering, his fists pounding his legs. He might have been some jungle primate demanding food from passing tourists. This rage, this caged and confused need to fill some dark hole in his soul, had led Deedee to the precipice. All she wanted was a normal child. Was that too much to ask? A regular, run-of-the-mill kid. Yet the child she saw through the car window, with his over-sized cranium and ferocious eyes, seemed to belong to a different world.

Deedee looked away from him when she glimpsed her mother's madness in his face; her mother, that is, before the Haldol and Thorazine, before her seclusion in Eastern State Hospital in Richmond. These days her mother, dozing and drooling in a wheelchair, more resembled the slumbering Brandon in his car seat, before the rattle of gravel had awakened the savage within him.

The sound of a screen door caused Deedee to look up a set of wooden steps, to where a large man walked to the near edge of the porch and stopped. He had a tanned, oblong face, with a hint of Cherokee in the cheekbones. His head was nearly shaved, although he showed no receding hair line, and he wore a ragged red goatee without a moustache. She guessed he hadn't yet turned thirty. He was dressed in a green camouflage t-shirt and black jeans. His bronze belt buckle had a big bas-relief fish on it. Not the Christian symbol, she noted, but a largemouth bass or something leaping for a baited hook. She supposed this was the Archer of Archer's Bait and Boat.

She remembered why she had turned onto the gravel lot, why she had transformed her son's slumber into rage: *This man knows knots, and he sells rope.*

She opened Brandon's door and his cries erupted as heat from a pizza oven. She fought through his flailing arms to release him from his car seat, picked him up and announced to the man watching her from the top of the stairs, "I need a noose."

The man put his hands on his hips and stared down at her, the classic showing off stance of a guy with wide shoulders and muscular arms. Deedee felt she knew a lot about him just from the way he stood there. You start to care for a guy like that, the next thing you know he thinks he's God Almighty. She'd seen his type many times before. In fact, it occurred to her she'd seen this very man before, casting for something in the shallows, a shirtless torso emerging from green waders in one of the streams that fed Lake Roosevelt.

He spoke. "So you need a noose? Let's see…you're too cute to be depressed."

She hated being cute. Being cute meant she wasn't beautiful in a way that made her not downright ugly. "Okay," Deedee said. "Now that we've established that…" Brandon twisted in her arms. She tried jostling him on her hip. The man on the porch seemed to be waiting for more. She asked him, "Are you Archer?"

"Travis."

For a while he didn't say anything else, just looked down at her with a smirk on his face that seemed to say, *If you could only see yourself from up here, you'd know what a hoot you are.*

Deedee gave him a few seconds to stand there all superior, then asked, "Will you sell me a noose or not?"

"What size you need?"

Brandon put his protests on hold and turned to look up the stairs.

"They come in sizes?"

"Depends on the size of the neck. Adult or child?"

"Oh, I see what you mean." She looked at her son, who had already grown bored with this and was flailing at her head.

Travis added, "Kid size might save you a couple of bucks. No sense wasting money these days."

She thought, *This is the most fun you've had all day, creep*—and was about to say just that, or something close to it, when a stab of burning pain in her scalp meant Brandon had grabbed a fistful of hair, and by the time she'd extricated herself she heard the screen door slam again, looked up, and Travis Archer was gone. It was one annoyance after another, and she scolded her son, "Don't you *ever* pull my hair again, you understand me?"

Brandon's scream doubled in intensity, then here came Travis again, onto the porch and on down the steps this time, carrying a rubbery toy-looking thing with streamers hanging from it.

"Hey kid," he said, dangling it in front of Brandon's eyes. Brandon looked at it. His hand darted for it, but Travis pulled it away. "You got some quick hands there." He teased him twice more, jerking it back each time.

Brandon cried and started to beat Deedee's head with his fists, but Travis managed to secure both Brandon's wrists in one hand, while with the other he held the fish lure right up under the child's nose. Brandon sniffed once, closed his eyes, and sniffed again. He opened them and laughed. Travis loosed his hands and let him hold the lure.

"Don't worry--it doesn't have a hook in it."

Brandon held the lure to his mother's nose. "Pee-*yoo!*" she said, and asked Travis, "What is *that?*"

"It's a fishing lure, with garlic and crawfish and salt, and I don't know what all."

"Fish like the smell, do they?"

He held his arms out and Brandon allowed himself to be transferred. "Don't you? I add pretty much the same thing to my spaghetti sauce. I bet you do too."

"Maybe not crawdads."

"Depends on my mood."

"How did you do that?"

"Do what?"

"Distract him like that."

"I guess that's why they call it a lure. I am one hell of a fisherman." Brandon was sniffing the lure again. He held it out for Travis to smell. "That's a very good sign, too. You notice that?"

"Notice what?"

"How he shared the interesting smell. That means he's not autistic."

"I never said he was."

"No. No, you sure didn't."

"Anyway, thank you...Archer...I'm sorry, I already forgot..."

"Travis."

"Travis," she repeated, and smiled. She hadn't meant to be short with him, and the fact was she *hadn't* noticed the sharing, or the revelation it carried with it.

He grabbed Brandon at the armpits and lifted him into the air. "Well, let's go inside and see what else we've got." He was saying this to the boy. "I know there's anise. And shad. And water moccasin." With each item on the list he pumped Brandon high in the air. "And crocodile. And shark." Brandon shrieked with each rise and fall.

Deedee said, "You're making this up as you go."

"Maybe some of it. Come inside and we'll find out what part's real and what part I made up."

The place looked better on the inside. It smelled of fresh paint and had bright lamps over racks of metal jigs that seemed designed to hook customers as much as bass or walleye. Rods were lined up like pool cues all along one wall. Deedee leaned over a locked glass case of expensive reels. This was unfamiliar ground to her. Her father had never taken any interest in either fishing or boating, nor now did any of her brothers, not counting Rollie and his kayak.

Travis took Brandon's hand and led him to a rotary rack of scented tube lures. "Here's one for your lunch," he told him. Brandon made a face and laughed. "Ha! He doesn't like anise! You don't have to worry about him stealing licorice from the candy store."

"You're just full of good news."

"As a new small business owner, I aim to please. You know, I should learn my customers' names."

"Sorry. I'm terrible about that. Deirdre. People call me Deedee. And that's Brandon."

"Hey there, Brandon. How old are you?"

"He's two-and-a-half. And he doesn't talk."

"The world could do with fewer loudmouths, right Brandon?"

In answer, Brandon held out his new lure.

"You won't get a word out of him. Not so much as a *mama*."

"Plenty of time left for that. How about Papa Brandon—is he a fisherman or a boater, by any chance?"

"Who? Oh, you mean Brandon's father? We don't mention him."

"You're too young to be a mom on your own."

"Tell me something I don't already know. I got pregnant before I could even take a sip of alcohol."

"That's so backwards! Most people have a couple of drinks first."

"Ha! I see what you mean. Let's say 'legal' sip, then." She walked toward Travis and the scented lures, put her arms out for her son. "You share my last name, don't you Brandy?"

"And that would be?"

"Shanley." She put out her hand. "Deedee Shanley."

"Travis Archer. As you know by now."

A moment of awkwardness took her by surprise. Brandon was so seldom quiet that Deedee was unaccustomed to stretches of strained silence. She put him down to play with his lures, and walked back over to the sales counter, where she noticed a copy of the local newspaper.

"Oh, good. You take the Guardian."

"Good, because…"

"Because I don't like to spend my money anywhere that doesn't take the paper."

"In that case I'm glad I do, but…"

"See, I work there." She was always disinclined to say, *We own it.* Even less so to add, *And we're going broke.* So she said, "You've never submitted an ad, or I'd know about it."

"Oh, I get it. You must be the bikini lady. Every boating ad has to have a beautiful young blond in a bikini."

"You are so wrong!" she laughed. "I'm the ad lady. People call me about whatever it is they want to advertise, and I do the rest."

"You like it?"

Briefly she considered telling him how much she hated her job and how eager she was to do almost anything else; how at twenty-two, an age when most women felt they could take on the world with their bare fists, at an age when others played tennis all day and partied all night, she had to plead with her body to get up each morning and place one weary foot in front of the other. But she couldn't say any of that, so she settled for, "Classifieds is not as easy as you might think. Customers usually just have an item and a price. I'm the one that has to put it in words and make it sell."

"Then you can expect to hear from me. As you can see, I'm not exactly overrun with customers."

"Anytime. The number's there in the paper. Right on top of the Classified Section."

Travis went around behind the counter and slid the paper over between them. The murder of Sarah Lester and impending trial of

17

Lovemore Ngwenya dominated the front page, as it had done for weeks now. The headline was *DNA Evidence Impossible to Rebut*.

Again an uncomfortable quiet intruded. The only sound was Brandon's energetic sniffing of lures. Deedee glanced down at the newspaper and said, "So…let me ask you the question everybody in town's asking everybody else. Do you think Lovemore's guilty?"

"Oh yeah, no question. Don't you?"

"Sure looks like it."

Travis said, "We'll soon learn what evidence Sheriff Greer has."

"Some people say Greer is a racist and you can't trust his evidence."

"I don't know where they get that. His main deputy is black."

Deedee didn't know how to read the man's tone. She didn't want to tripwire some pent up Aryan wrath, but she wanted to make it clear where she stood. "I don't think most people around here worry about race anymore."

"So you're saying you think Lovemore will get a fair trial."

Deedee saw that she may have crossed herself up. "Um, yes. Yes, I guess I am."

Travis didn't respond right away. She didn't know how to read his silence, either. Finally he said, "Then I guess we agree."

"I guess so," she said. But it sure didn't feel like it. It felt more like they'd dropped a subject to avoid disagreement.

"Sheriff Greer won't want to make a mess of his final case."

"His final case?" This was new information to Deedee. Her eyebrows pinched together as she looked at Travis.

"He was in here yesterday, just browsing. Said if anybody from the sheriff's department came in asking my opinion about a gift, recommend that tackle backpack right over there, that blue one. So my guess is he's hanging up his guns after the trial."

She looked over at the backpack, as at a clue. "If the sheriff has time to window shop, then it's all the more reason to say Lovemore's in the bag. The real question is, does he get life, or the needle?"

Travis said, "Big African comes into our town, strangles a Sunday school teacher to death with his bare hands, in her own back yard, and then robs her? Of course they'll execute him."

"Don't be too sure. They say he was tortured in his country, so when he finally escaped he might have been…you know." She tapped the side of her head.

"Nobody's going to cut him slack for that. More like the opposite: America gives him shelter and how does he repay us? Kills a woman. They'll fry him for sure."

"Lethal injection, you mean. For all crimes after 1998."

Travis looked at her funny, as though knowledge this precise had to indicate something.

She smiled. "Don't blame me. My brother's the main Guardian reporter on the story. It's all I hear, day in and day out."

Travis looked down at the newspaper and read out a name: "Edgar Shanley. He's your brother?"

"One of them."

"I read his stories all the time."

"He's really into it. He says it's the trial of the century."

"I'd say he's right. The whole town knew Sarah Lester. It was Sarah worked up my loan for me. I can't exactly say I owe this store to her, but she was right there every step of the way. At the beginning, anyway. She didn't live to see the results."

Deedee looked around at the merchandise and nodded, trying to appear impressed. "Sarah had a ton of friends. She was older than me, but she was friends with my sister Yolanda, and a couple of my brothers hung out with her."

"And now one's covering her murder trial. What a world. These outsiders. Who do they think they are? So it makes no difference to me how they do it. Lethal injection or electric chair or a good knock on the head with a poleax."

"Hanging, maybe?"

Travis looked in her eyes, as if trying to take the measure of a woman who takes her kid noose shopping on a Monday afternoon. "I think you're way out of date on that one."

She deflected his curiosity. "Here's one question that bothers me: people can't say his last name, so he's always 'Lovemore.' Will that sway the jury in some way? You couldn't ask for a more peaceful sounding name. And nobody can say 'Nag-wey-na…' See,

I can't say it myself." She pulled the paper to where she could read it. '*Ing-ween-ya*.' I guess that's how it goes. Even Edgar just refers to him as Lovemore."

"They say it's a common name where he comes from. Nobody going to be lenient on a killer just because he has a cute name. Did you ever see him around town, before…"

"Never. I heard there was a real African in town, but I never saw his face until it was in the paper."

"I saw him once—fishing. I went to one of my usual spots on Twisting Creek, about fifty yards from where it dumps into the lake. But he was already there. I'm pretty sure it was him."

"Really? Did you talk to him?"

"Naw. I just moved on up the creek."

"Was he with Sarah?"

"I didn't see anybody with him. What I did notice was he had nice gear—a reel just like this one." He pointed down through the glass counter top. "A Quantum Catalyst. From what we hear he was broke, should have been using a string tied to a cane pole, but the Catalyst isn't cheap. He knew how to handle it too—had a nice, light touch."

Deedee saw the price tag—$125.99—tried to think how that insight might affect the case, but couldn't see what difference it made. Unless maybe he stole it. Or Sarah bought it for him.

"One good thing to come from all this is newspaper circulation shot up by twenty percent. Same for my revenues. Not that anybody wants to make a dollar off other people's misfortunes, but newspapers are having a rough time of it these days."

"I've got an inventory of about fifty life vests just waiting for one person to drown in Lake Roosevelt."

Deedee smiled. "Sort of the same thing, I guess."

Brandon walked toward them in his odd gait, all trunk sway and stiff legs. He was holding a speckled lure in each hand, one a dull green, one more purple. "Brandy, can you put those back, please? Can you be mama's good little boy and put them back?" He dropped them on the floor and went back for more.

"So," Travis finally said, "You need some rope."

"Adult size."

"Ex-boyfriend size, is my guess. Would you consider drowning him instead?"

"Help you sell those life jackets?"

"You could write the ad. Say, *Don't drown like my ex.*"

"Sorry, it's got to be rope. Can you tie it too?"

"I tie hangman's knots all the time—not that I've ever hung anybody. They work great on fishhooks. I'll just make a big one, see how it comes out."

He left her standing there, weaved his way back through shelving stacked with spare boat parts, and through a door in the back. She heard him climbing some wooden stairs and then heard creaking footsteps overhead.

He'd done a nice job converting the inside of this old house into a shop. She wondered who had lived here before, why they'd let it go to ruin.

The longer she thought about it the more her curiosity was aroused. Wouldn't this have been a real haven at some time in the distant past, before termites and wood-borers infested the walls? Why had it been abandoned? Why would anyone ever want to leave this little place? She wondered if that side wall, now covered with fishing tackle, might hide a window that looked down onto the water. Surely upstairs there was a window with a view of the lake. Did kids grow up in this house and one day just get tired of it? Did they all run off to Lexington or Charlotte or Atlanta the first chance they got? Was that the normal way? And if so, why did she and her siblings try to hang on to the Guardian in an age when hardly anybody read newspapers anymore? Just because Daddy's heart and soul went into something, and he passes it on to you, doesn't mean you have to maintain it. It's perfectly okay to sell it off. Would that be the lesson of this homestead-turned-business? Was that why she had this sudden urge to know its story?

She could probably find out through old county directories, if she was really interested. Or just ask Edgar to inquire at the Register's office. He spent half his time down at the courthouse anyway.

She watched her son spinning the rack of lures, called to him "Easy now" as his spinning became energetic. She sensed that he wanted to see those colorful things go flying off their pegs, and to be honest she wouldn't have minded it herself, only she'd be the one to have to pick them back up. Brandy moderated his effort and looked up at her.

Travis made his way back through the dark aisles of his inventory. He already had the noose tied and was threading a larger loop through it. "How's that?"

"It looks perfect. Way too much extra rope, though. Can you cut it down to maybe…I don't know…ten feet?" She took out her purse.

"Oh, no you don't." he said. "This is a promotional effort on my part."

"You sure?"

"Absolutely."

"Then when you need an ad in the Guardian, I can return the favor."

"Deal," he said. He gave Brandon a garlic lure to take home.

Brandon used one hand to hold his lure to his nose, and allowed Deedee to take the other. She put the noose over her head and walked out with it that way, trailing the rope behind her like a bridal train.

As she walked down the stairs she heard herself repeating his words. There was something about them. *These outsiders come in here.* Outsiders? It was just one man, not a whole gang. And where the hell was Travis Archer from, anyway? She didn't know him as a local. Had he attended Twisting Creek High? Buford County High? Franklin College? Possibly. Still…something. Was it because he said "Sheriff Greer" where most people here just called him "the sheriff?" Or maybe it was the way he said "crawfish" for "crawdad." He couldn't be from around here. Could he? Didn't everybody around here call them "crawdads"? Or were they technically two different species? A fisherman might know that.

Yet—*Our town. Outsiders.* These *outsiders* come in here. He hadn't said, "*these niggers…*" He hadn't actually pronounced that word himself, but she'd bet anything that was what he meant.

And what gave him the right to comment on her son's mental

health, anyway, even in reassurance? There had to be something sneaky about a man who acted so nice.

His car might tell her something, but it wasn't out front. He must have parked it around back. She felt the impulse to drive around and take a look—she'd bet anything there was a rebel flag, CSA or Klan sticker, something—but she saw him watching her. He had followed her as far as the porch.

"Looks like another storm is brewing."

What did he mean by that? Her mind was still on *these outsiders*. She looked up at him. He pointed to the sky, where black clouds were already starting to gather for another evening storm.

She watched the tumbling edge of a thunderhead, shrugged. "They don't even break the heat." She turned her back and walked away.

"Hey!" he called out. "You never did tell me what you plan to do with that noose."

She didn't answer him immediately. She took her time getting Brandon into his car seat, then settled herself into the driver's seat, started the engine, and finally lowered her window. Travis was still standing there, so she called out, "You'll find out soon enough. Just keep reading the paper."

Auditions Tonight: 7:00 for
Death on Stage at the Odeon
See *Community Events*, B-9

Today's Weather:
Heat Advisory in Effect
Heat Index to top 100
More Evening Thunderstorms

The Twisting Creek Guardian

ESTABLISHED 1882   Tuesday, September 21   *The Voice of Reason in the Tri-State*

Defense Promises "Surprises Galore"

Jury Complete; Trial Starts Tomorrow

CHAPTER 2: EDGAR

A GIANT BILLBOARD said, *Welcome to the Pierce Addition. Starter homes from 270K.* Edgar Shanley drove through an arched entrance and stopped at the gatehouse. Humidity filled his car as soon as he lowered his window, but he needed to show Deedee's note to the guard, who read it and pointed straight ahead.

Deedee had written: *Meet Asst. DA Miller, 6:00pm this evening, 276 Chickasaw, Pierce Addition.* In parentheses Deedee had written *(6:00pm??? at his house???)*

Edgar considered Deedee's surprise. Didn't she connect Asst. DA James Miller with the Miller family who used to live a few houses up the street from them on Sycamore? Was she so naïve at the journalism game that she couldn't spot an attempt at news manipulation? Was she surprised that anybody would make such a bald play for her brother?

Edgar wasn't surprised. He didn't even much resent it. In a small town like Twisting Creek people had to scratch each other's backs. And anyway, he was cunning enough to play the game. Even though this was the first milestone story of his young career, he was confident he could hold his own with that courthouse crowd. After all, he was the son of Woodrow Shanley, and the grandson of Landon Shanley.

He parked on the street and could already feel himself start to sweat by the time he reached the door. He rang the bell, then looked up and down Chickasaw. He hadn't been in the Pierce Addition since the first houses were under construction. He'd done a story on the sale of the old Lyman Pierce farm and the plans to create a gated community there, then had come out once more to photograph a ceremony to showcase the first model home. That was over a year ago. Now, from the small front stoop of Jimmy Miller's house, he could see several rows of houses already occupied, landscaped with scrawny trees and evergreen shrubs that barely cleared a cinderblock foundation. Low houses and lack of trees made the air feel empty of everything, except the compressive damp.

In the other direction, the smell of raw cement was in the air, but there were no people, no sounds of hammers or electric saws. The completed houses gave way to wooden frames on scrappy plots of dirt, then beyond those, to metal supply sheds and strapped-up bales of bricks. The scene could have been a time-lapse photo essay of a civilization rising from nothing, or deteriorating into its component elements, depending on which end you started with.

Still no one came to the door. Edgar looked away to where the green hills were steep enough to halt the subdivision. The day was dimming, and dark clouds descended toward the mountaintops. The evening seemed to be preparing another thunderstorm.

He rang again. This felt so weird, waiting amid relative silence and emptiness for someone to come to the door of Jimmy Miller's house. He supposed that throughout his childhood he and his brother Josh and sometimes Rollie must have rung Jimmy Miller's doorbell a hundred times. Soon Jimmy's mom would greet them with, "He's waiting for you at the ping-pong table." Or at the Monopoly board. Or the horseshoe pit. Edgar had the feeling she might appear right now, and that when she did, great oak trees would fill the yard, and there would be a flower garden, and a red-tipped hedgerow bordering the lawn. And behind that people walking up and down sidewalks, and beyond them cars rolling down Sycamore.

But it was a Hispanic woman who opened the door and

showed him into "Mr. Miller's office," ushered him to a chair in front of the desk, and informed him that Mr. Miller would be delayed by ten minutes. As she left, she shut the door.

Okay, Edgar thought. A reporter has been given ten minutes alone in an attorney's home office. What am I supposed to find?

He didn't have to look far. It was on the desk directly in front of him: a manila envelope isolated front and center. Its top flap was open, with the corner of a photograph peeking out. Edgar glanced around for a security camera, didn't see one, and emptied the envelope into his lap.

Lovemore Ngwenya's face, immediately after his arrest. Even in a police photo he was handsome, with lively, angry eyes. He had a big scratch across his forehead. Around his neck he wore a gold crucifix with what looked like rubies set into the crossbeam.

Another photo: hands, wrists, arms. The hands were large, with elegant, long fingers, and carefully trimmed nails, but his wrists and forearms were streaked with raw, red gashes.

So, Edgar thought, what am I supposed to make of this? Lovemore wore gloves? Sarah fought back? She struggled like a wildcat to the very end?

He put the photos back inside the envelope, careful to slide them all the way down so Jimmy would know he'd got the message, and placed them back on the desk. He still had about seven minutes left, so he strolled around the room.

It was interesting to see how people turned out. As kids, they'd all seemed pretty much the same, riding their chopper bikes, playing Mortal Kombat and Road Rash, practicing whatever sport was in season. But here was Jimmy's adult self, with a red mahogany desk and brass-studded leather furniture, a fuzzy beige sofa, and above it a huge abstract painting of interlacing bamboo strips. It was about as standard climbing-class as you could get, and a world away from Edgar's own piled up mess of a room in the old house on Sycamore. He knew that a reporter could never afford a place like this, and suspected that an Assistant District Attorney couldn't either, if he didn't happen to have a pediatrician wife.

Finally Edgar spotted a framed photo of Jimmy's high school

football team. He looked for his brother Josh—there he was, his helmet tucked under his arm so his long hair could show.

Miller came in and said, "You never played, did you?"

He seemed taller here in his element than down at the courthouse.

"Not after I saw the hits you and Josh got."

They shook hands. "Great to see you. I hope you like looking at photos."

"They can be very informative."

"Sit down. Let's talk photography."

"I take it Sarah made those gashes?"

"They were fresh. And we found both blood and skin cells underneath her fingernails. Lovemore's DNA."

"Is any of this for publication? Can I take notes?"

"Sure. All the evidence will come out in court tomorrow anyway. Just don't mention the photos yet, which, by the way, I didn't show to you."

Edgar drew a pen and a slim notebook from his inside jacket pocket and wrote, *Lovemore blood/skin cells under SL fingernails.* "All right. Anymore?"

"We have a very credible witness to a screaming argument Lovemore had with Sarah after she fired him on the evening of her murder. The altercation ended with a death threat, and the next morning Lana Irwin discovered Sarah's body. And if that doesn't tie the whole case up in a bright red bow, when Lovemore was arrested he was in possession of a gold and ruby necklace valued at eight hundred dollars. And we know it was Sarah's. Confirmed not only by several of her friends, but by the guy at Bowman's who sold it to her. Plus we have the receipt and insurance photo. Sarah was very organized about her valuables."

"Lots of other jewelry missing, I understand."

"Loads. The jewelry box was empty and standing wide open. Guess whose prints were on it?"

Edgar smiled. This was what he loved about being a small town reporter. The negotiation, the scorpion dance. A little small talk. Half of the deal laid out—here's what I want you to run, you figure out why. Followed by more small talk, go through the family tree or relive some old times. The return on the deal is hinted at. If you're tempted, the signal doesn't have to be so subtle. This is not the big time. You don't have to stoop to finesse. This is a small town—there is honor among dealmakers.

"Any other suspects you may have overlooked? The first question the sheriff would have asked was: Who gains by her murder? Isn't that the usual starting point?"

"Yes, indeed. *Cui bono?* Only Sarah's older brother Ethan. He inherits the family home." Miller stood up and walked over to the photograph of the high school football team. "Ethan must be in here somewhere." He removed the frame from its hook and carried it across the room to Edgar. "Look at him—big jug-eared klutz. Couldn't catch a pass if it hit him in the mouth. We thought the guy was a total loser, and now he owns a nightclub in New Orleans and is richer than all of us."

"He sure didn't need that house. It's like our house, like all those houses in Bedford Woods—like your old place too, I guess. Once sort of stately and grand, still worth some money, but almost as expensive to keep up as to buy."

"A white elephant, my mother calls our place. Anyway, Ethan Lester was in New Orleans at the time of the murder. Deputy Victor Caraher checked it out. He will testify to it. And I'm pretty sure the jury will notice that Deputy Caraher is an African-American."

Edgar laughed. "You reckon?"

"I reckon."

"So you're sure it was Lovemore."

"Look Edgar, this case is not complicated. It's not one of those brain squeezers that keeps a team of forensic scientists toiling around the clock. As in most cases, the obvious perp is the guilty perp."

"So you want me to convict him in the Guardian before the jury is good and sequestered."

Miller smiled. "You want a drink?"

"I wouldn't turn down a cup of coffee."

Miller walked to the office door and called out something in Spanish.

"Hey, you're pretty good."

"I'm learning. Emilia gets a kick out of it. See, her command of the English language is at least as good as my own."

"Tell me something." Edgar tapped the picture of the football team, which still lay in his lap. "Back in high school, did people know Josh was gay? Teammates, I mean? You, Ethan Lester? Anybody?"

"I don't think so. I didn't, that's for sure. Why?"

"No reason. I never asked anybody, that's all."

"People seem okay with it now. I never hear anybody mention it, not even when he's out with Seth Estershear. Seth lives in the same house with the rest of you, right?"

"He's off and on. Nobody can figure them out."

"What about you? I figured you'd be married by now."

"I guess I just never met the right doctor."

Miller laughed. "Maybe you're gay, too. Does it run in the family, like the Guardian?

"I *am* married, Jimmy. Married to my job."

Miller shook his head. "I've heard my dad say, 'Those Shanleys and their newspaper.' With admiration, of course."

"Of course."

"So how's it doing these days? Financially, I mean. Are you guys to be the last generation of Guardian Shanleys?"

"Circulation's crept back up over the twenty-thousand mark. Half what it once was, but not bad these days for a town our size."

"I suppose the Lovemore story is good for business."

Edgar narrowed his eyes.

Miller smiled and let it slide. He seemed to count off something on one hand. "So are all five of you back living at home now?"

Edgar gave a short sigh. "We sure are."

"Deedee's back?"

"Yep, her and her devil child. Yolanda too. She's divorced now. You knew that, I guess."

"I ran into Yolanda recently. She still looks every inch the beauty queen."

"I guess she came out of that marriage okay."

"No worse for wear, from the looks of her. And with Rollie

back home…"

"That's the full set. Can you believe it?"

Miller laughed. "What year is this anyway? Somewhere in the 1990s?"

Edgar thought of his father, dying so young, and his hospitalized mother. No, he thought. The 1990s were a century ago.

Miller seemed to sense his misstep, and asked, "So has the prodigal son finally hung up his travelling shoes for good?"

"You mean Rollie?"

"The Shanley black sheep. Has he finally forsaken the bohemian life in France, or wherever it was?"

"With Rollie you never know for sure, but yeah—in some ways he seems to be settling back here now, finding his niche. He's still trying to revive the Odeon with old movies—excuse me—I mean 'classic films.' That's his gig these days."

"I go to one occasionally. I saw one of the Thin Mans there recently. Me and about five other people."

"For Rollie that's actually not a bad turnout."

"His problem is he doesn't have a ghost."

"What do you mean?"

"Every old theater needs a legend about a ghost, right? Or phantom or ogre or whatever. It's what pulls in the crowds."

"I'll pass on your suggestion."

"Is it true he's writing a play about the Lovemore case for your acting club?"

"It is absolutely true. He's finished a lot of it."

"I saw one of his earlier, um…shall we say…masterpieces?"

"Ha! Yes, I have no doubt. But so far this one's really good. I've read Act One. We'll open a week or so after the trial ends."

"No shit? That quick?"

"We need to strike while this iron is hot."

"I don't suppose I'm in it."

"Not in the scenes I've read. Your boss does all the talking for your side."

"Ah, yes. My own personal Cruella de Vil. How does our dear DA Reynolds come off?"

Edgar shrugged. "Depends on how the trial goes. Rollie plans to be there every day, and let it write itself."

"How is he handling the rest of it?"

"The first part is a romance between Lovemore and Sarah. You know the rumors about that. Rollie takes it and runs with it. Then there's the trial, however it plays out. It ends with Lovemore's execution."

"Very optimistic. From my perspective, anyway. Less so from Lovemore's."

Edgar laughed politely. "Do you think he'll get death?"

"Dead man walking, baby."

"Tell me seriously." To Edgar's own surprise he found himself growing impatient with the banter. He wanted to get to his end of the bargain.

"Seriously, then. Yes, I do. Everything is lined up for it, straight as a yardstick. Obviously he murdered her. That's number one. Then look at the jury—eleven salt-of-the-earth white folks. And the one African-American? A woman. Take my word, women of any color don't like men of any color who strangle women—of any color. She's as likely to identify with Sarah as with Lovemore. Simple as that. More likely, since Sarah is a hometown girl, and Lovemore is the alien. And the jewelry—you see the importance of that."

"I want to hear what you know, not demonstrate my own ignorance."

"It means he planned it."

"It might not. If he killed her in a lovers' quarrel, maybe he panicked and took some valuables, opportunistically. He needed some money to get the hell out of Twisting Creek."

"Nope. No jury will buy that. It was premeditated. And that's murder one. And that's the end of Lovemore Ngwenya."

"What about location data? Can you trace his movements that night?"

"He didn't use a cell phone."

Edgar tried to consider that from both sides. "So you'll say that strengthens your argument for premeditation."

"We probably won't even mention it, unless defense does,"

Miller said. "In which case we'll make them regret it."

Edgar wondered if he wasn't being used as a sort of batting practice pitcher, but he couldn't bring himself to resent it just yet. This was too much fun. "I can see a huge—a colossal—flaw in your case: There were no scratches on his hands. But if he wore gloves when he strangled her, why are his prints on the jewelry case?"

"They were gardening gloves. Way too clumsy to pick up jewels with."

"I don't know, Jim. You may have to do better than that."

"They're stiff as cardboard. We have them. We'll show the jury. Definitely not cat burglar equipment."

"And why would he wear gloves to strangle her with anyway? Can a killer be identified by the bruises his fingers make around the neck?"

"We can get the outlines of fingers and palms. If we're lucky we can now even detect latent fingerprints on human skin. Maybe he knew that. But anyway that's not how he did it. Remember, it was a cool evening, so she was wearing a neck scarf. He pulled on the ends of the scarf until she asphyxiated."

"But if premeditation is so important to your case, surely you can't expect a jury to believe he planned for her to wear her scarf a certain way. And he didn't need gloves."

"Probably he planned to choke her directly with his hands, but didn't want skin to skin contact. Then he saw the scarf and used that instead."

"Maybe," Edgar said. He looked down at his own hands and his scribbled notes. He thought of the perfection shown in Lovemore's pristine hands, in the elegantly tooled leather of his fingers, tipped in bright pink crescents. Edgar was more inclined to think that Lovemore was simply a man who cared about his hands. "Was he a musician?"

Miller gave him a look of sharp suspicion. "How did you come to guess that?"

"His hands, maybe? Plus, ever since Lovemore's arrest, Rollie has been playing South Zambezian music all over the house. Music seems to run deep in the culture."

"Well...I wouldn't know about that."

32

Now it was Miller's turn to look at his hands. Edgar realized that the Assistant DA didn't really enjoy being the one cross-examined. He started to push it, to find out exactly why Lovemore's musical ability, or lack of it, had created this anxiety, but he had other areas to explore before Jimmy put up his guard.

"Here's a puzzle the jury will expect you to solve," Edgar said. "On the night of the murder, Lovemore slept in his own room and didn't leave town until the next morning. When he finally did get around to absconding, he did it by hitchhiking openly in an illegal spot. Don't you think that indicates he didn't even know about the murder?"

"Don't you think he's clever enough to know that's exactly what people will say?"

"Maybe. So you don't see that as a problem for your case?"

"I don't think so. Reynolds isn't worried about it."

"There's one thing I bet sent a shiver up her ramrod spine— Leo Akers as defense attorney."

"You got that right. We figured the case would go to our poor old public defender, or maybe pro bono to some kid fresh out of UK. But guess what? Tomorrow when we look across the aisle we're going to see Twisting Creek's crafty old fox, possessed of jury charisma most of us would kill for. And suddenly the case isn't such a walkover anymore."

"You know, I can even remember hearing my dad say that if he ever got into trouble, Leo Akers was the one lawyer in town he'd want in his corner."

"Present company excluded, I presume."

"I think that's safe to say, since you were maybe thirteen years old at the time."

"Leo's still a local icon, no question. I happened to be with Reynolds when she learned he'd picked up the case. I was looking straight into her face. For one second, her cheek muscles flinched. It was like a sharp pain went through her. She really wants this one."

"Okay," Edgar said, drawing it out into a sort of question. "Where does that leave us?"

"Airtight. And it's becoming increasingly clear that Akers

himself is a spent force. Seating a nearly all-white jury. I mean, come on!"

"No, I mean us: you and me. Why didn't you just call me at work, let me come to your office downtown? You think I need to familiarize myself with the pleasures of suburban living?"

Miller hesitated. He slowly spun the envelope of photos on the smooth surface of his desk. "Do you know where my boss is now?"

"Sure. She's in Frankfort."

"Do you know why?"

"Of course I do. She's speaking to a legislative committee about the death penalty. I wrote the story from her press release."

Miller pressed his hands on the desk and leaned forward. "But do you know *why?*"

"No, but you think you do. And you think I need to know. You think if I know it, I will let you shape the Lovemore story I write for the morning paper."

"This is not for attribution."

"Then how the hell does it help me?"

"She's there because a private poll shows that sixty-seven percent of Republicans favor keeping the death penalty."

"So what? Everybody knows…"

"Five years ago it was seventy-eight percent, that's so what."

Edgar gave himself time to mull over the numbers before he spoke. "An eleven point fall in five years?"

"It's a massive fall. Among *Republicans*. Names taken straight from the primary lists. These aren't 'likely voters.' These are certain voters. Hardcore Republicans. Of course we all know that the Democrats would abolish the death penalty, but they don't matter anymore. It's Republican votes Reynolds cares about."

"Oh, I see," Edgar said, himself leaning forward. "Because she hopes to ride her new fame in the Lovemore case all the way to Frankfort."

"Twisting Creek's own June Elizabeth Reynolds, Kentucky's next attorney general."

"I get the impression you don't care much for her."

"She's a force of nature. It doesn't matter if you care for a tornado or not, you don't want to be in its way. You'd much rather be behind it, letting it clear a path for you."

"Of course! Now I'm starting to get you. Once she's safely out of the way, you're our next DA."

"I couldn't possibly say that. I'd have to leave speculation like that to you media guys. But right now there's still one more crucial connection you need to make, one more journalistic question to ask."

"What caused the massive drop in support of the death penalty?"

"Good question. Answer: DNA. Since DNA testing has started to be used to confirm old verdicts, it turns out we've been jailing god-knows-how-many innocent people. And with executed prisoners you can't just say, My bad, hand them a wad of cash, and turn them loose."

"Yet DNA evidence is a big part of your case against Lovemore."

"Bingo. Our beloved DA is in Frankfort right now, branding herself as the champion of the death penalty, the heroine who demonstrates that DNA testing should not destroy support for the death penalty. It should strengthen it."

"Provided that solid DNA proof is established. So that's why she contacted me on the weekend to say how solid her evidence was. I thought it was weird, a Sunday morning call from the DA with nothing more newsworthy than a science lesson. But it makes sense if DNA is her big weapon."

"Exactly. And what was yesterday's Guardian headline?"

"What the fuck!" Edgar said. He remembered it word for word. He'd written it himself.

"Not quite. It was '*DNA Evidence Impossible to Rebut.*'" Miller slapped his hands against the top of his desk, as though to say, *I rest my case.*

Edgar sat back to consider this new information. He didn't know exactly what to do with it, but he knew he didn't like it. "Will it work, Jimmy?"

"It sure might. If she can fry Lovemore, she'll be packing her bags for Frankfort."

Edgar looked away. A cold recognition of gullibility penetrated his flesh. He fought back the urge to cry foul—only a novice would do that. It would crown him as class dupe. Instead he needed to balance the equation by extracting some insider nugget.

He turned back to Jimmy and attempted a complicit grin. "So tell me—what's he like?"

"Lovemore?"

"Lovemore. I've never met the man."

"Old lady Crowell says he was as polite and quiet as any tenant she's ever had. Not a peep even from a radio turned up too loud. Paid his rent on time, helped with yard work and so on, not even asking for a discounted room rate. She says he never had a visitor, always kept to himself unless she needed him, and then he was friendly enough. Very low-keyed, unless the talk turned to so-called President-for-Life Magwimbi, whom he hates."

"That's understandable."

"No doubt about that. He doesn't talk about his own past. We know almost nothing about that. He says after Magwimbi's thugs torture you, you do your best to block it all out."

Edgar wondered what psychologists would make of that. He made a note for a possible sidebar on the long term effects of torture. "Do you think he's faking it?"

"More like it's too painful to go there. He simply says it's immaterial, and clams up."

"How does he handle himself under interrogation?"

"Very refined, articulate. He's not one of those English-speaking Africans you need subtitles for. To me he's got a posh British accent—real Masterpiece Theater stuff. He seems soft-spoken, but he does possess this big, booming voice—which is great for my side, because it's easy to believe that a neighbor overheard him shouting at Sarah."

"Maybe it's booming enough that somebody else heard the death threat and took the opportunity..."

"Get real, Edgar. Do you think murderers lurk in bushes, waiting for the chance to frame somebody?"

Edgar crinkled his forehead. "Maybe not, but if I thought of it, you can be sure Leo Akers has."

"We'll be ready for it."

"How about religion? Can he play the Jesus card?"

"He's nominally Christian—Anglican. They educated him, and very well, too. He quotes David Hume and Voltaire, believe it or not. Have they heard of those guys at...where was it you went to college?"

"Ah, here we go again. I thought maybe you'd outgrown this shit."

"Appalachian State, wasn't it? Where exactly is that again?"

Edgar's only response was a look of disgust.

"BOOOOONE," Jimmy said, stretching it out, wiggling his fingers, trying to make it sound spooky.

"Duke men never grow up. I think Voltaire said that."

"Maybe so. But according to Lovemore, it was quoting Hume that first got him in trouble. They caught him painting it on a wall in Tuvingu. Something like, *Human liberty is seldom lost all at once.* Magwimbi took offense. And Lovemore lost his liberty—all at once."

"And did so again in Twisting Creek. So much for David Hume."

On the way home, Edgar pondered the hierarchies of power. Magwimbi conquers Lovemore. Lovemore conquers Sarah. Reynolds conquers Lovemore. Was it really that simple? Shouldn't a whole town's anguish be born of almost unfathomable complexities? But isn't the simple explanation usually the best one? Somebody said that—maybe Voltaire or Hume. He tried to recall, but really, who the fuck cared who said it? It was still true, wasn't it? And anyway wasn't David Hume the great skeptic who said we can never be sure what's true and what isn't?

What's got you in such a crappy mood, anyway? Usually you love journalism's give and take. Only this time you got totally exploited by political operator? Is that it? Is it because so much is at stake? Because a guy who escaped Magwimbi gets nailed in Kentucky? Or is it merely because Jimmy Miller has grown up?

He didn't even wait until he got home. He found a place to pull off the road and phoned Leo Akers.

The Odeon Cinema's awning marquee was dark, its box office windows shuttered, but around the corner and almost half a block down a side street, Yolanda was taping a sign onto a sugar maple tree: AUDITIONS, with an arrow pointing to the service entrance. Inside the entranceway she placed an identical sign, only this one with its arrow angled down a dim flight of wooden stairs into a musty basement and toward a windowless and empty waiting room.

It seemed she was the first one there. She carried a jug of water through a set of stiff black curtains, moldy and threadbare, flicked on the light with her elbow, filled a coffee urn, and waited until she heard the hiss of heating elements before she pulled a jar of Kroger's instant from a low cabinet. Against the urn she leaned a note saying, "It's instant, but it's free." On a corner table she counted out a dozen forms for new arrivals: name, phone, address, stage experience, if any, and a check list for the parts in *Death on Stage* they might be interested in.

Yolanda was a good half-hour early for these small duties. She enjoyed the whole auditioning process and felt she was well-suited for it. She knew how to let people down gently, even the most ridiculously under-talented aspirants. She suspected that she even managed to impart to them some appreciation for their brave, foolish efforts.

She had heard no one follow her in, yet a terrified scream echoed from the auditorium, through the hallways and down into the basement. She scrambled up the stairs toward the stage.

Far to the back rafters of the unlit theater, someone else had heard the scream and was moving into position. The sound had penetrated even Rollie Shanley's secret hideaway beside the projection booth. He hurried to a wide slit in the wall, a lofty machine gun nest from where the followspot could rake the stage with light. He watched a grinning young man pretending to strangle a young woman with his bare hands, and thought, *Not with your hands, asshole. Use a scarf.*

Yolanda rushed onto the stage to inform the larking pair that the stage was off limits for now, that they could wait downstairs.

"We were just practicing," the young man said.

"Yeah," the young woman said. "I was taking advantage of the opportunity to practice my Sarah Lester scream on a real stage."

"Are you from the college?"

"Yes, ma'am," the boy said.

Yolanda had barely turned thirty, yet already she was *ma'am* to these kids.

"Professor Estershear recommended we should try out."

"You're Seth's students?" They both nodded. Yolanda smiled at the girl. "I have to say your scream was realistic enough to give my insides a little shiver."

Rollie, watching unseen from behind the upper window along the distant wall, was not inclined to such lightness of spirit. The girl might do. She was pretty enough, with her slender neck and gurgling scream. But not that geeky guy. No white frat boy was ever going to play his Lovemore Ngwenya.

Josh came rushing on stage as though playing a part. "They're flowing in downstairs, Yollie. Did you know that? Eight or ten people there already."

"Must have just happened. Maybe they all came together. Seth is pushing it."

"Still, who'd have thought that sleepy old Twisting Creek held so many Sarah Lester wannabees? Let's hope it also holds a few paying customers. If this thing fails…"

Yolanda said, "Aw, this town's more ga-ga over Sarah's murder than anything since the Civil War."

"And for once in his life our dear brother is on top of things and has a play about the case already written up."

"He says it's dead easy," Yolanda said. "It writes itself."

"Still," Josh said, "you've got to give him credit for the idea."

"I absolutely *ate up* the love scenes Professor Estershear let us read," the girl said, putting her hand out for Josh. "My name's Chea Hunnicutt."

"I'm Josh Shanley. I'm the director, sort of. And this is Yolanda Shanley. She's our casting director. Sort of. And we'll each play some subsidiary role in the play."

Chea turned to Yolanda. "Professor Estershear has told us so many wonderful things about your husband."

"I'll just bet. And he's my brother, not my husband."

"Oh! I just thought…you're so beautiful and he's so distinguished and handsome…"

Josh turned to the young man. "And you are?"

"Me? I'm Chea's boy…"

"He's my friend. He's just helping out. He's not even trying out for a part."

Josh said, "I only thought—he's so good-looking."

"Enough of that," Yolanda cut in. "We've got work to do. As soon as the trial ends we'll have this place packed to the rafters."

Josh said, "Or not."

"Josh, you said yourself there's a whole room full of people downstairs, ready to audition. That's a very good sign. We've never had a response like that to any of Rollie's flops."

"You're right. Print off some more pages of the script, let them all go over it. Tell them to practice their shrieks before they audition."

Chea shrieked.

Yolanda said, "Let's try waiting for a cue or something, ok?"

"I think that one was better," Chea said. "Don't you?"

"Possibly so. But still…"

Chea shrieked again. "See, I can really rattle them off."

"Jesus Christ Almighty!" Yolanda said. "Would you please stop that!"

Josh asked, "What do you think, Chea? Is there any sort of groundswell out there for this play?"

"All my friends at Franklin are talking about it. And I think there's a website."

"Casting Lovemore is the key." Josh said. "He needs to be both attractive and repulsive. Like opposing ends of a magnet. Chea, you've probably seen the real Lovemore often enough on news broadcasts. How did he strike you?"

"He's pretty good-looking, in a beaten down sort of way."

Yolanda said, "You never know what stirs people's loins."

"How about you, Chea?" Josh directed the conversation back to her. "Did our killer stir your loins?"

"He gave me the heebie-jeebies. But I have to say that the very first time I saw his face on TV....what happened was I switched on the TV and there he was but I missed the lead-in so I didn't know why he was on TV. So for those first few seconds, I thought, hmmmm. Interesting face—those eyes. They stop you in your tracks. Then I caught on that he'd been arrested for murdering a woman, and I just shuddered. Just the thought of what might have happened if I . . . "

"Quick now," Josh said. "Scream!" Chea released a truly blood-curdling shriek. "That's it! Hold on to that memory of what you might have done if you'd been in Sarah Lester's place. If you can summon that up on command, then you're well on your way to becoming a real actor."

"Don't you worry, Josh—it's not going anywhere. I'll hold on to it for dear life."

"In that case, Yollie, let's go downstairs and find ourselves a killer!"

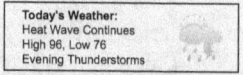

Swelter Shelter?	Today's Weather:
Cooling Centers Open:	Heat Wave Continues
Dunbar, Senior Center, Altwood	High 96, Low 76
All city pools reduced admission	Evening Thunderstorms

The Twisting Creek Guardian

| ESTABLISHED 1882 | Wednesday, September 22 | *The Voice of Reason in the Tri-State* |

Entire Region Captivated by "Trial of the Century"

Prosecution Case "Airtight"—Asst. DA

CHAPTER 4 : ROLLIE

THE PEACE OF mind Rollie Shanley found in the Odeon's janitorial closet was no ordinary peace of mind. It wasn't simply the isolated silence of a locked room within a locked floor, high above a locked and empty theater. It wasn't only an ironclad protection from anxiety or threat, with its skylight, its pull-down ladder to the lighting catwalks in the ceiling, and its escape route to the roof. It was more active than the soothing murmur of the fan circulating stale air, and the aroma of pine in bottles of floor polish and disinfectant. It was a living peace of mind, vital and alert. The moment he entered his closet and locked the door behind him, he felt the embrace of a universe beyond the peopled earth. Serenity seemed to caress the surface of his skin like a mysterious electro-magnetic field, connecting node with node, creating correspondences that no one had ever conceived, but which, once formed, could never be broken.

It was no ordinary janitor's closet either. He'd outfitted it with a small table for his laptop, and a chair on rollers. It had an Internet connection, a coffee pot and a toaster. In one corner sat a slate gray cast iron safe that great-grandfather Delmon Shanley had imported from Germany to protect the stacks of cash brought in by the likes of Cary Grant and Bette Davis.

The safe still had a purpose. It still protected a treasure. Not this week's sad little banded packet of dollar bills, but a crumple-edged King Edward Cigar containing Pops Woody's boyhood collection of baseball cards, and a tin-lidded Band-Aid container with a few joints in it, already rolled and ready.

In another corner were two cardboard Johnny Walker Black crates Rollie had picked up from the liquor store. One held sticks of beef jerky, packages of Oreos, Halloween-sized bags of Snickers, a box of Ritz crackers and a big jar of peanut butter. The other Johnny Walker Black box contained six bottles of Johnny Walker Black, three of them still full. He opened one now and poured an inch into a crystal glass. The weight of that glass felt just right with a bit of whisky in it. Its circumference fit his hand, and his fingertips notched perfectly into its cut divots. He didn't mind the smell of whisky residue in it, or the film of fingerprints all over it.

He lit a joint to accompany his drink, inhaled, and clamped his throat shut on a great lungful of smoke. He exhaled into his whisky glass and watched the smoke pour forth like steam from an amber pond. With that first hit he noticed, as always, how perfectly the peat in the whisky blended with the grassy taste of marijuana. The unity of this revelation seemed to lighten him, to raise him slightly in his chair, as though a breeze had kicked up and his inner self had the contour of a bird's wing. The weakened tug of gravity prompted him to stand up fully, to where he could reach a crank mechanism that opened the skylight a crack, to let the smoke escape. He noticed that the sky above was already gray with cloud, and with the end of another day. The evening thunderstorm would soon be upon Twisting Creek.

He sat back down and turned his attention to editing his day's output. He had spent most of the day in the courtroom, listening to Sheriff Greer testify about Lovemore Ngwenya's arrest, and then had passed most of the evening here in his secret closet, writing up the sheriff's testimony as a scene for *Death on Stage*. *Death on Stage* was the working title for Rollie's play about the Lovemore trial, which the Twisting Creek Players would debut precisely one week after the verdict of the actual trial.

He counted today's pages—nine—and calculated that as

written the scene would run for about fifteen minutes. That was just about right. He saw no need to cut it any further, so he started to read. He laughed as he reached the part where defense attorney Akers confronted the sheriff, "You think Twisting Creek can't home grow its own criminals? We have to import them all the way from South Zambezi?" And Greer snapped back, "It seems pretty unlikely that the same night one man threatened to kill her, lo and behold another one did!" The courtroom crowd loved it, and Rollie's audience would love it just as much—maybe more, with Lovemore's execution carried out right there in front of them, not years down the road, but on stage at the Odeon.

Yes, the scene worked. It was a good scene in a great play, a play that would rebrand Rollie Shanley as a valuable artistic force in the community, the local boy who had eschewed his newspaper birthright, transcended it to roam the world and return home in triumph. He directed a thought to his family and to his town: *Sneer now, fuckers!*

His mind drifted from the trial to the real reason why this play would exonerate him in the eyes of the town: Sarah Lester. That was his secret. He knew Sarah. During her celebratory visit to France as a brand new college graduate, Sarah had contacted him in Paris, and for two weeks they were constant companions. There, outside the social net of Twisting Creek, Sarah was not so much free, as freshly erased. When a street artist on Montmartre painted her portrait in eight minutes flat, he was filing a blank canvas with the new Sarah Lester.

Rollie felt privileged to witness her rebirth. He could hardly believe his eyes. Maybe it surprised Sarah herself. Surely the good folks back home had never dreamed their chaste and tee totaling good-girl was built around a core of pure desire. And now, as a playwright, he knew that the source of her fascination lay in her conflicted longings. Let everybody think it was the sensational trial that made his drama work. Let them point to the oddity of an African laborer in their small town, or to the heavyweight clash between old man Akers and old man Greer. Mix in the rising star DA Reynolds. Those elements had their place, but what made Rollie Shanley the man of the moment was his insider knowledge of the soul of Sarah Lester.

Rollie wasn't inclined to chastise himself for the Paris fling. She was so pretty, in a baton-twirling, sorority girl sort of way, with her short, blond hair cupping her face like devoted hands, and one eye hidden behind long bangs. How could anyone not fall for a woman like that, once she relaxed that Baptist pretense of hers and allowed herself to explore what nature had put there for a woman to enjoy?

And she—how could she ever return to a life of prohibitions once she'd experienced her sensual self? How could she walk around town wearing a long-sleeved white blouse, white gloves, carrying a white New Testament all zipped up, when she knew deep down that she wanted to break through the fence and be back in Paris again?

He sipped his drink, closed his eyes, and tried to call up the feel of her body beneath his fingers. He remembered the sounds she made at first, as she fought it, and then how they changed as the rush of events overcame her resistance and she surrendered herself. He could even smell her bitter, almost metallic breath when she spoke his name. "Rollie," she had said. "Rollie, no…"

A far less welcome memory intervened. It was the first time he'd seen her after his return from France. He'd glanced up as he was leaving a bakery, and there she was, across the street, coming out of a shop called Faith & Family Fashions. He had a bag of chocolate croissants, the closest he could find in Twisting Creek to the real thing. Sarah was carrying a shopping bag bulging with church-acceptable clothing. To Rollie's mind she had just bought a whole new line of strait-jackets. He stopped when he recognized her, in her oversized trousers and shoulder-padded jacket. She looked up too. He raised both hands to her, one as a greeting, one holding up the bag of pastries, an invitation to snack and reminisce. For an instant she looked at him, and in that instant he saw a decision cross her face. She tried to cover it with a wince and a snap of her fingers, gestures meant to convey that her eyes had not focused on him, that her mind had not registered his presence. The snapping fingers meant, "Oh, I'm mistaken—I must have parked around the other side."

Inside her knowledge. Rollie knew that look. It meant, I don't know you and you don't know me. It made him feel like a stalker. Yes! That's what she was saying. *Stalker!* I am a Christian woman and you are a wicked, wicked man! Don't come near me with your chocolate or anything else. Not unless you want the police on you.

Thunder sounded through the open skylight and Rollie felt a splatter of rain on his arms, so he quickly cranked the window shut, emailed the Sheriff Greer scene to his brother Josh, and shut down his computer. He said good night to his little office and walked out onto the dark stairs that led to the top row of cinema seats. Guided by nothing more than beads of light from strips of emergency lamps, he felt his way down the aisle, touching backs of chairs as he descended, until he reached his second favorite spot on earth: the front row of the balcony in the Odeon.

From this dark perch he enjoyed rare access to that most precious secret: what others say about us when we're not around. Many nights Rollie had sat in his balcony and overheard the backbiting of his siblings. He'd heard that sometimes they were embarrassed to stage his plays, that doing so was more mercy than performance, that the real acting was in pretending his stuff was any good. He'd heard Josh…the same Josh he'd walked to school all those years; the same Josh he'd practiced grounder after grounder with in the back yard . . . that very Josh had sat there on the stage and told the others, "One more embarrassment like this and we'll have to refuse, even if it does put his titties in a twist."

Yolanda had asked, "But what else has he got? *Who* else has he got?"

And Josh had said, "Still…can you bear to read this crap?" And they'd all laughed.

Not all, Rollie reminded himself. Not Deedee. She wasn't a part of the troupe or the sniping.

For some odd reason that Rollie couldn't decipher, he had a stronger connection with Deedee, fifteen years his junior, than with the other three. But how could that be? They shared no common childhood experiences. All he remembered was a kid in diapers running around the house … then he finished high school, left home, and that was that. He had only a dim idea of who Deedee really was, but she seemed to like him, and he liked her.

No, Deedee didn't sneer at his plays, but to the other three—the core three, as he thought of them—Rollie was the family loser. He would soon change that. *Death on Stage* would change it. This was quality drama. The dialogue seemed to pour into his ear, flow straight through his arms and fingers, and then spill onto the keyboard. It was like one of those Renaissance paintings where an angel whispers holy text into the ear of a frantically scribbling St. Matthew.

The love scenes set it all up just right. He knew the words to have his Lovemore speak, and in what tone, to make Sarah's face go soft, her breath catch. He knew the words she liked to hear when her resistance fragmented into surrender.

No one in the family, not even hot-shot Josh, would make fun of this one. Maybe they'd staged his other dramas simply because they were a group of amateurs and he was their brother. Not this time. This time he had what people wanted to see. In a crime as heinous as this one, people didn't want to wait through months of investigation and criminal proceedings, then certainly years of appeals, before the execution finally took place. There was no satisfaction in that. That wasn't how the human psyche worked. People wanted the accused to get a fair trial, and, if found guilty, to be hauled straight from the courtroom to the execution chamber. That's how true justice should work. The Old Testament prophets understood that. An eye for an eye. Quick, simple, done. They didn't say an eye, followed by a decade of legal wrangling and petitions, and then an eye. The average person needed to *feel* justice, needed to emotionally experience the reordering of the universal soul after its disruption by evil. The courts couldn't give people that satisfaction. In the legal system, cooler heads must prevail, but cool reason doesn't compensate the outraged. There is no community catharsis in year after year on death row. But there would be here, on stage at the Odeon. Rollie Shanley was the one who would supply it. And in their hundreds the good people of eastern Kentucky would purchase tickets to share in it.

This evening he waited contentedly in his balcony for the Players to arrive and read his new scene. He sat there thinking how much he had come to love the Odeon, how he loved it in darkness, as now, with only the green exit signs interrupting total blindness, and how he loved it when the screen lit up or the stage lights came on to stun the eyes with the heightened reality of make believe. When the theater was being used as a cinema, he liked to sit high up here under the projector and watch the well-defined tube of light pass overhead, illuminating the swirls of dust around it as a meteoroid streams its trail of ions. He would sit there, not watching the screen at all, but staring up at that expanding tube of light and knowing that within it, somehow, Atlanta was burning and Clark Gable was leaving Vivian Leigh, or Humphrey Bogart was speaking for every single one of us when he told Ingrid Bergman to go ahead and shoot, she'd be doing him a favor.

As his eyes adjusted he began to make out the broad-shouldered proscenium arch over the closed burgundy curtains, and atop it a coppery glint that would, when the lights came up, reveal itself to be a series of puffy-cheeked angels blowing into long trumpets. High up along the side walls he saw the heads of red-eyed eagles that protruded from a *trompe l'oeil* barrel vault ceiling of the heavens, a ceiling of cottony clouds in blue skies streaked in golden rays, all now in total darkness, but long since memorized and in fact made more beautiful by Rollie's imagination, where the years of soot, dust and grime had never collected.

Josh, Yolanda and Edgar would be here any minute. Josh's love interest, Seth Estershear, a Fine Arts instructor at Franklin College, was supposed to come by with his ideas for the stage set. Yolanda might even have scheduled another audition. And he would hear his Greer scene read for the first time. That's what Rollie was perched up here to witness, and his skin prickled at the thought of it unfolding below.

A rim of light appeared around the stage curtain. He heard some scraping sounds, felt a familiar but always fresh thrill as the curtains opened, and saw Yolanda arranging a triangle of folding chairs. Edgar followed her, placing papers in each seat. Seth, carrying a camera and a sketch pad, walked onto the stage with Josh, who gestured to the empty stage right, said something Rollie couldn't make out, greeted the others and sat down. Yolanda found another chair for Seth, who sat and began to draw.

Josh said, "All right. This is today's testimony: the sheriff's. I'll read his part, until we decide on our Greer. Edgar, you're defense, right?"

"Makes sense. Akers is a man. Yollie can be Prosecutor Reynolds, since she's a woman. Not that it makes any difference to me. I'm happy either way."

"I suppose that's the way to play it. Otherwise it might confuse the audience. What do you think, Yolanda?"

She shrugged, and asked, "Where's Rollie?"

Josh said, "Home, I guess. Probably stoned in the basement, by now. He emailed me this about twenty minutes ago."

"How is it?" Edgar asked.

"Don't know. Haven't had a chance to read it. You'll be the one to judge that. You were at the trial. Shall we? I'll cue."

ACT 2, SCENE 1: COURTROOM. SHERIFF GREER TAKES THE STAND.

Reynolds: Everybody here knows you well, sheriff, but for the record...

Greer: I'm Allard Dale Greer, sheriff for the town of Twisting Creek.

Reynolds: And could you tell the court what transpired on the morning of October 31 last?

Greer: I hadn't been in my office more than ten minutes when I got a call from Lana Irwin of the First Security bank. It seems she and the deceased had their own little car pool, and when she showed up at Sarah's house, Sarah didn't come out to the car.

Reynolds: That was her usual habit, was it?

Greer: Yes. Lana would pull over to the curb and usually Sarah was there on the porch waiting for her, or in bad weather she'd be watching from a window. Lana waited a couple of minutes, tooted her horn, and finally walked up to Sarah's front door. Through the big picture window she could see Sarah stretched out on the floor. So she used her cell phone to call 911. The 911 operator dispatched an ambulance and

	notified me.
Reynolds:	Was the rescue squad there when you arrived?
Greer:	Yes, they were inside. They had broken a window in the door to get at the lock, but of course it was way too late.
Reynolds:	Police photos show the victim fully clothed. Did you notice anything unusual about the way she was dressed?
Greer:	She was dressed for going outdoors, but not to her office. She had on blue jeans, one of those ribbed turtle-neck sweaters, a cream colored one, but the striking thing was that she had a wool scarf cinched tight around her neck. I mean, real tight. That's what he used to strangle her.
Defense:	Objection!
Reynolds:	You mean to say that's what someone had used to strangle her.
Greer:	Yes. The scarf was the murder weapon. It was knotted so tight that her face was the color of an eggplant. The blood couldn't even drain down from her head.
Reynolds:	And what tipped you off to the defendant, Lovemore Ngwenya?
Greer:	In response to a radio and TV appeal for clues, a neighbor, a Mr. Evans, phoned to say he'd heard her in a bitter argument with her handyman the previous evening. He clearly remembered that Ngwenya had threatened to murder her. Then my patrolman picked up a hitchhiker out by the entrance ramp to I-64, brought him in. He gave his name as Lovemore Ngwenya and admitted to being a man who recently had done some work for Sarah. We searched him and found he was wearing a ruby crucifix. He claimed Sarah had given it to him.
Reynolds:	Did you uncover any other evidence?
Greer:	Oh yes. His fingerprints were all over the house, inside and out. On his jacket he had bits of poplar leaves like those on the tree in Sarah's back yard.

Reynolds: Sheriff Greer, you've indicated that the murder weapon was a neck scarf that the killer used to strangle Sarah Lester with. Anyone, even a woman much smaller than her assailant, might be expected to put up a fight in that circumstance. Her arms would be free."

Defense: Objection. Calls for speculation.

Reynolds: I'll rephrase the question.

Defense: Rephrase what question? It was a statement."

(JUDGE USES GAVEL)

Reynolds: Were there any marks on the deceased's wrists that would indicate they had been bound in any way?

Greer: Her wrists were not marked or bruised.

Reynolds: And how about the hands, wrists and face of the defendant? Did they show any signs of injury?

Greer: He had scratches on his wrists and one big gash on his face.

Reynolds: Would these scratches have been consistent with a recent struggle?

Greer: They could have been inflicted by fingernails.

Defense: Objection!

Judge: Sustained. Witness will refrain from speculation. The jury is instructed to ignore that remark.

Reynolds: Were any traces of human residue found beneath the fingernails of the deceased?

Greer: Yes. DNA traced it to the defendant.

Reynolds: Let's just clarify—the DNA beneath Sarah's fingernails matched identically with that of the defendant?

Greer: That's correct. A perfect match.

Reynolds: Thank you. And according to the coroner, what was the time of death?

Greer: Between 6:00 and 8:00.

Reynolds: And from your reconstruction of the crime scene, how did it appear the murder had taken place?

Greer: Judging from the heated conversation in the back

yard, as reported by the neighbor, and the tracks leading from the pile of leaves into the house, I'd say the murder took place back there. The murderer dragged the body of Miss Lester into the house, picked up some of her most marketable jewelry, and left through the front door, locking it behind him.

Reynolds: No further questions, your honor.

Judge: Your witness, Mr. Akers.

Defense: So, Sheriff Greer, let's get rid of a few things right off the bat. You'd absolutely expect to find evidence like fingerprints and poplar leaves, wouldn't you? The man had been working in the house and yard.

Greer: That's true enough. The category of evidence we call Evidence of Presence—fingerprints, footprints, and the like—is of no benefit at all in cases of insider murder. Cases where the killer had legal prior access to the murder scene, however...

Defense: So you admit it's irrelevant.

Greer: However, most murder victims are killed by insiders. The fact that his fingerprints should have been there doesn't make him innocent.

Defense: I don't think you need to insult the jury by stating the obvious. Now tell me, when your patrolman picked up Ngwenya out by the highway, did he know who he was?

Greer: No, he just knew it was a hitchhiker where hitchhiking is illegal. And he knew we were looking for a murderer.

Defense: Did Ngwenya make any attempt to flee?

Greer: No.

Defense: To resist arrest?

Greer: No, he came quietly.

Defense: Did he try to conceal his identity?

Greer: That would be pretty hard to...

Defense: Didn't he in fact quite willingly tell you that he had been working for Sarah Lester for some weeks, and had been there on the evening in question.

Greer: He didn't put up much of a fight, no.

Defense: Let's be even clearer than that. Did he in any way act like a man who was trying to hide a murder?

Reynolds: Objection! Suddenly counsel encourages the witness to make wild guesses.

Defense: I'll withdraw the question. About those scratches on Mr. Ngwenya's face and wrists—did you ask him what had caused them?

Greer: I did.

Defense: His answer?

Greer: He said he'd got them doing yard work.

Defense: Specifically, he said he'd been pulling old brush and leaves from underneath forsythia bushes, isn't that right?

Greer: That's what he said.

Defense: I will not ask you whether you found that answer plausible. Any home gardener amongst us who's ever pruned a tree or dug out old yard debris from underneath shrubbery can answer that question for themselves. Now tell us about this necklace. Did he try to conceal that?

Greer: No, he wore it openly around his neck.

Defense: And why did that seem suspicious to you?

Greer: *(laughing)* What kind of man wears a ruby crucifix necklace?

SFX: SOUNDS OF CHUCKLES AROUND THE
COURTROOM

Defense: Did he say how he came by it?

Greer: He said she gave it to him.

Defense: As payment for his labor?

Greer: Just as a gift.

Defense: Well, Sheriff, I have to tell you that somewhere I still may have a green jade Buddha that a very pretty young redhead gave me when I was a sophomore at UT.

53

Well lookie here! I happen to be wearing it right now. What crime can you charge me with?

Greer: Oh, I don't know, Leo. Criminal taste in accessories, maybe?

But my guess is that your fiery redhead is the current Mrs. Akers, so I'll just shut up before we have another murder in Twisting Creek.

Defense: Wise decision. My point is that it may have been a gift from Sarah Lester, as my client contends.

Reynolds: Objection! The parallel is irrelevant. No such relationship between the deceased and the defendant has been established.

Judge: Was such a parallel your intent, Mr. Akers?

Defense: It was, your honor, and it will be established.

Judge: Until that point, objection sustained.

Defense: In any case, Sheriff Greer, colorful jewelry is not evidence, is it?

Greer: It is if, and only if, it fits into an overall pattern of evidence.

Defense: Defense stipulates that other costly items were missing from Sarah Lester's jewelry case. But tell me, sir, was the defendant in possession of those items at the time of his arrest?

Greer: Only the ruby crucifix.

Defense: So where are the others?

Greer: We haven't been able to locate them.

Defense: You've said that my client was very forthcoming with other facts. Did you ask him about the other items of jewelry?

Greer: We did.

Defense: And?

Greer:	He says he knows nothing about them.
Defense:	As, indeed, he says he knows nothing about the murder itself.
Greer:	Correct.
Defense:	Did you check with the jewelry stores in town, the pawnbroker, and any other dealers of second hand goods where jewels could be quickly converted into cash?
Greer:	Of course we did, but…nothing.
Defense:	Given your theory that Miss Lester was murdered Tuesday evening, you must have asked him why he waited until Wednesday morning to try to leave town, am I right?
Greer:	He said he never murdered anybody. He was leaving town because Sarah Lester was both his girlfriend and his only source of income, and she'd just jilted him.
Defense:	And did you investigate the possibility that he was telling the truth?
Greer:	How do you mean?
Defense:	If, as he claims, at about 6:30pm Lovemore Ngwenya left Sarah Lester alive and well at her home, and, as the coroner's report indicates she could have been murdered as many as two hours later, that leaves plenty of time for a genuine jewel thief to break into her home, kill her and take all those valuables that you cannot account for. Did you take any action to eliminate that possibility?
Greer:	We have a witness who will testify that the defendant threatened her that very evening. It seems pretty unlikely that the same evening one man threatened to kill her, lo and behold another one did!

SFX: WILD LAUGHTER IN COURTROOM

Defense:	In other words, no, you didn't even consider that possibility.
Greer:	We've had no reports of suspicious strangers….

Defense:	Twisting Creek can't home grow its own criminals, I guess. We have to import them from South Zambezi? We don't have our own crackheads, Oxycontin addicts, crystal meth addicts, who'd be happy to strangle a defenseless young woman to finance their next fix?
Reynolds:	Objection! This is from way out in left field.
Defense:	On the contrary, your honor, I submit that this gets to the very heart of the matter.
Judge:	I'll allow the question, but Mr. Akers, stay within limits.
Defense:	Thank you, your honor. So Sheriff Greer, I repeat my question: Can you assure this court beyond reasonable doubt that there is not one resident of Buford County who could have murdered Sarah Lester and stolen her jewels—jewels that I remind the court have yet to be found?
Greer:	Well, no, I guess it's within the realm of possibility, but what likelihood….
Defense:	And you will recall that last summer a Hollywood film crew came to Twisting Creek to shoot a movie.
Greer:	I do…
Defense:	Can you recall off the top of your head how many people there were in that film crew?
Greer:	Maybe a hundred. But what…
Defense:	About a hundred. One hundred strangers running all over our little hometown. And can you recall if any local people became involved as extras, or providing supplies to the crew, or in any other way?
Greer:	A lot of people did.
Defense:	Was Sarah Lester among the participants?
Greer:	I have no idea.
Defense:	Do you happen to have any idea when that large contingent of out-of-town workers broke camp?
Greer:	Early fall, I think. They wanted summer scenes, so they had to finish before the trees started to change color.

Defense:	They left the week before the murder, to be precise.
Greer:	*Before* the murder being the key point.
Defense:	Did you investigate whether Sarah Lester might have known any of them?
Greer:	That would be nearly impossible.
Defense:	And how about this? For reasons unknown, one of those hundred strangers turned right around and returned to Twisting Creek. Would that be impossible?
Greer:	It's hard to rule out everybody who ever set foot in town.
Defense:	Did you try? That's my question.
Greer:	We had no way…
Defense:	Did you even contact the Personnel Office responsible for hiring these people to ask if they'd all made it back to California?
Greer:	We've had no contact with them.
Defense:	No contact at all?
Greer:	No.
Defense:	And did you know that thirteen Franklin College students left town the week after the murder?
Greer:	Who told you that?
Defense:	The college registrar. He will testify to it.
Greer:	No, I didn't know that.
Defense:	And a person in Miss Lester's position as loan officer at a bank—did you look into any enemies she might have made there?
Greer:	We asked around if she had any enemies. She seemed to be well liked by one and all.
Defense:	Do you mean to say that every loan foreclosure she had to make, every loan denied to any weirdo who walked in off the street hoping for some cash, not a one of these walked out of her office harboring any resentment toward her at all?
Greer:	Not as we could find.
Defense:	How far back did you check her transactions?
Greer:	We didn't see that as a useful way to spend our limited

	resources.
Defense:	I see. And what about this supposed death threat? Did you find anyone to corroborate the testimony of the one neighbor who believes he heard such a threat?
Greer:	No, nobody else seems to have heard it.
Defense:	No one in the whole neighborhood heard an argument loud enough that a seventy-eight year old retired factory line worker could hear it from inside his garage?
Greer:	People were cocooned inside their houses. It was a cold evening.
Defense:	The temperature was above freezing, sheriff. In fact, the Weather Service says it was thirty-eight degrees at 6:00. You're telling me that in this town nobody walks a dog when the thermometer hits thirty-eight? No kids play basketball in a lit driveway? Indeed, nobody else but Lovemore Ngwenya was hardy enough to be out raking leaves?
Greer:	I don't know where they were. I'm just saying nobody heard the threat, that's all.
Defense:	Maybe they didn't hear it because it didn't happen.
Reynolds:	Objection. We will produce a witness under oath.
Defense:	I'll withdraw the comment.
Judge:	Jury is instructed to ignore defense's last comment. And I'm warning you, Sam.
Akers:	No need, your honor. No further questions.

As they finished, Deedee appeared from behind the curtain and applauded. "Once more, with feeling!" She didn't normally turn up for these rehearsals. She was carrying something wrapped up in brown paper.

"What did you think?" Josh asked her.

"It all made sense to me. How does it stack up with what you heard in court, Edgar. You were there, right?"

"It's close to the way it went. Rollie's distilled it, combined the coroner and Lana Irwin's testimony with Greer's to eliminate the need for bit parts. He's cut out all the boring shit."

"Was Greer that rattled?" Yolanda asked.

"He was kind of pissed off. Whoever does him should try to get that sarcastic edge in his voice. And that antique southern accent of his. Like, *It seems puhty onlikely 'at one man threatened huh, and lo and bee-hold anothuh one did kill huh.'* Like you can almost hear him saying *heh-heh-heh* under his breath."

"He could be a tough one to pull off convincingly," Josh said. "Any ideas who could do him?"

"I have an idea," Deedee said. "Get Greer to play himself."

They all looked at her. Even Seth stopped making sketches and looked up at her.

Josh asked, "What do you mean by that?"

"I have a feeling he might soon be out of a job."

"Where did you hear that?" Edgar asked.

"Oh," she said, swinging her package like a baseball bat. "I have my sources. Speaking of which, where's Rollie?"

"We think he's home getting stoned," Yolanda said.

"Oh, okay. I have something for him." She turned to leave.

"Sources?" Edgar called after her. "What the hell kind of sources do you have in the sheriff's department?"

Deedee glanced back at him, smiled, and kept on walking.

Her cheeky exit was ruined, though, when she remembered something. She turned back toward Edgar and asked, "You know how that new road down to the lake has exposed some old cabins that used to be way the hell out in the backwoods?"

"Uh…okay."

"Doesn't matter. If I give you the name of the current owner, can you check out the history of the property?"

"You want me to trace a deed? It's a pretty big job, and I'm not exactly a trained title examiner. What do you need it for?"

"More curious than anything. Seems to me there might be a story in it for you."

Rollie had heard all he wanted to hear. He wasn't interested in cabins in the sticks. He followed the beaded strips of light back up the stairs to his closet, and gently closed the door behind him before switching on the overhead light. He took another joint from his Band-Aid can.

"At home getting stoned in the basement," he said aloud. He had to laugh at that. He lit the joint, carefully picked off a hardened bit of white ash from the twisted end, and blew gently on a sparking seed to coax the tip into an even burn. Deliberately he filled his lungs, noticing the way the neurons of his mind also seemed to relax and expand, like a man just home from work, like the celestial bodies of the universe. "At home getting stoned in the basement," he repeated, laughing exactly as before. "Try upstairs at the Odeon writing a masterpiece. And saving the family from bankruptcy."

The Twisting Creek Guardian

Prosecution's Prime Witness "Heard the whole thing"

Neighbor Evans Next Up for Reynolds

CHAPTER 5: JOSH

THE LIGHTS IN Josh's office flickered. He heard thunder and knew it was time to switch off his computer. He'd had about enough for today anyhow. No matter what he tried, he couldn't tip the Guardian's ledger into the black. Eighty-five percent of his expenses went for two items: salaries and printing. He couldn't bring himself to gut his staff the way media conglomerates did, so that left newsprint, which kept skyrocketing in price. The day the Guardian's death rattle sounded was the day First Security blocked his attempt to make two life-saving purchases: Lombard Paper Mill and a Coghlan Digital ImagePress. If he could sell himself newsprint at cost, and replace his out-of-date printing plant, the paper would be more secure. Nobody might not even have to lose a job.

As it stood now, however, nothing worked. He didn't know how many spreadsheets he had open. Out of curiosity he counted: seven. One thing he did know without so much as a glance was that every one of those seven financial scenarios ended with a big red number staring him in the face. The one calculation that resulted in a nice, fat, positive number wasn't on his screen, but in an envelope on his desk. It was a letter from somebody named Lawrence P. Kavanaugh at Independent Community Newspapers of America, inviting him to their headquarters in Dallas, where, it was implied, he would be offered an eye-popping sum for the Guardian.

Mr. Kavanaugh wrote, "It has long been ICNA's vision to build upon the tireless efforts of the great media empires of our illustrious forebears, and forge ahead with their work into the awe-inspiring digital age of the twenty-first century—and beyond."

Josh's initial impulse was to edit Kavanaugh's overwrought prose and send it back to him with a note to contact him if he ever got a degree in journalism. His second impulse was to discredit ICNA's very name, saying that, like the Holy Roman Empire, which was neither holy nor Roman nor an empire, ICNA's empire had nothing at all to do with independence, community, or with newspapers, or at any rate not with any newspaper worthy of the name. The "A" might hold up. It might actually be America, but an America that not one of our illustrious forbears ever dreamed their great media empires would contribute to.

However... He sighed and pushed back his chair. He needed to be sensible. Of all the family, Josh was the one who best understood the financial and social forces they were up against. It was one thing to get up on his hind legs and proclaim that the legacy of five generations of Shanleys was currently in the safe-keeping of Joshua Shanley and would one day be passed on to ... here he had to pull up short, as in fact there was no little Josh Jr. to pass anything on to, and there wouldn't be one unless he started having sex with someone other than Seth. But that technicality didn't alter the principle. He wouldn't be the one to break the chain. He would pass the Guardian on to somebody who cherished it. But he couldn't do it with high-minded pronouncements. He had to do it with dollars.

He knew all about ICNA and how they turned their profits. ICNA had invaded the south like kudzu, paying over the odds for every struggling newspaper that had fallen under the control of a new era of ownership, a generation that didn't know a newspaper with character and backbone from an AutoMart ad sheet. Then ICNA fired the existing staff and made everybody reapply for their positions. They could hire young college graduates and save at least one hundred dollars a week on every salaried employee. Josh didn't need a spreadsheet to tell him that right there was nearly half-a-million dollars a year off his labor costs. Then ICNA changed the news-to-ad ratio to the point that every page was basically one story surrounded by advertisements. They would dictate whether the front page needed more features or fewer, how many pages for sports, how many for business. They would compile whole sections centrally and simply send them to you, with nationwide ads already embedded, and holes for local ads. They would require so many column inches of celebrity news, take revenue from the paper and put it into website development, dictate special sections that somebody in Dallas thought would make money. They'd force you to run their movie and book reviews, and forbid any others. They'd reduce the number of pages and try to move everything online. This saved a bundle on newsprint, and allowed them to cut the press staff, mailroom staff, circulation and composing staff. There were no workers in ICNA's vision of the awe-inspiring twenty-first century. A person with a job was an affront to shareholder value.

ICNA would fly Josh to Dallas. They seemed to think that every man's dream was a free trip to Dallas. They asked him to set a date. This was meant to excite his imagination. ICNA would hand over such a stack of cash that all five Shanleys would be set for life. No longer would they need to share one deteriorating old house on Sycamore Street, with a temperamental furnace and no central air-conditioning. A house that required a team of acrobats for exterior painting and roof repair. They could all move out and start whatever life they wanted. With no more ties to Twisting Creek, they could offload the Odeon, too. Somebody with a lot more business sense than poor Rollie could knock it down, replace it with one of those pretentious town malls, with a Starbucks, an Apple store, a panini shop, and a weight loss clinic.

Josh read the letter again. When would it be convenient, it asked? If he could make it on a football weekend, they said, he could use their corporate tickets for a Cowboys game.

He looked above his monitor to a bulletin board, and to a Christmas card he kept tacked up there. It was from Samuel

Hoggarty, former owner of the Tri-City Times in Bragg County, West Virginia, and an old friend of Pops Woody. It had been addressed to Mrs. Carol Shanley and Family, on Sycamore Street, which just showed how out of touch with them Hoggarty was, because by then Mom had been hospitalized in Eastern State for nearly a year.

The card came from some place called Sugar Sand Beach, Florida. It showed two splayed bare feet propped up on a redwood railing. Evidently it was meant to be humorous. Between the feet you could see a sandy beach and the ocean beyond. It was captioned, "My View of Retirement."

It could have been captioned, "Look what ICNA did for me." Hoggarty had swapped the Tri-City Times for a patch of Florida sand. Josh could hardly stand to look at that picture, which was why he kept it front and center. The view of two knotty, purple feet framing emptiness to the horizon was not the view Josh aspired to. He wanted to go like Pops Woody, not from some unpeopled back deck, but out on the front porch, exchanging pleasantries with passing neighbors, talking about the weather, the score of the game on the radio, the results of an election, somebody's old gall bladder or somebody's new granddaughter. And every morning on that front porch, a fresh Guardian all rolled up.

Josh had a drawer full of no-hoper job applications from laid off Tri-City journalists, and he knew that even those that ICNA hadn't fired had been forced to take an extra week of furlough this year. That made a full month without pay, consistent with ICNA's corporate policy. Another quick mental calculation told him there went another two hundred thousand from his labor costs. That was the Guardian spreadsheet done the ICNA way. Take the numbers from the red column, put them in the black column. Pick your workers' pockets for a few hundred grand, stick it in your bank account. Problem solved. Let the suckers pay their mortgages the best way they could. Let them flip burgers and deliver pizzas. They had a month off, didn't they?

He put ICNA's letter back in the envelope and thought, *Screw the Cowboys. I gave up football when I grew up.*

A new email arrived from Rollie. The attachment was titled,

64

Scene with Witness. A sharp crack of thunder and a flash of light through his office window told him the town was about to receive its now-accustomed evening storm. Stories on drought relief would soon give way to accounts of flooded neighborhoods. He printed Rollie's scene and shut down. Within the percussion of rain on the roof, he did not hear the silencing of his machine.

He pushed aside his heavy glass office door and walked out through the newsroom toward the photocopiers. The sound of the storm barely penetrated this far, and at this time of evening the office was pretty subdued. All the reporters and secretaries had gone home. As he moved through the main office he looked it over as though he had already decided to sell, as though he were saying goodbye. He loved the way the air blowing from air-conditioning vents seemed to hum through stacks of files. He loved the smell of electrons carrying human thought through copper arteries and plastic tubing, the sight of desks cluttered with clippings, plants, and family photos. The effect on Josh was not of a still life painting, but of a paused film that could bounce back to life at any time.

Walking past the kitchenette he smelled cinnamon and knew that Mindy, the on-line editor, was making yet another cup of the tea that she believed would ward off diabetes. Further along the corridor he saw a light on in the composing room, and a silhouette on the wall. That was probably Jeremy, who tried to stay at the office until his wife had gone to bed. Over the divider in Sports he could see the top of Rod Mussnell's head, now almost completely white. As he neared the copier he heard a radio tuned to some sports talk show. Rod sat motionless, listening. He didn't have much to do on a Thursday night. Wait for a few baseball summaries to come in, that was about it. The sound of the photocopier caused Rod to turn. He made a sort of hand pistol with his thumb and forefinger, shot it at Josh. It was Rod's way of waving hello.

On his way back to his office, Josh checked the big clock on the central pillar. It was seven-thirty. He still had half an hour before the Twisting Creek Players meeting at the Odeon. The new cleaning woman named LaRhonda something had bent over to pick up a wastebasket. As she stood up she saw him and said, "You're working late."

"You are too," he said.

How he loved this place. Loved it full of bustle, and loved it quiet. How could he let ICNA come in here and fire all these people? Where would Jeremy go when his wife was on the warpath? What did ICNA care about Mindy's two diabetic grandmothers? Did those Cowboy supporters care that Rod Mussnell had done the game story and photos for every Twisting Creek High School football and basketball game for the past thirty years? Would they notice that one of the pix over the sports desk was of a young man catching a football and maintaining a balletic foot in bounds? Would they care that the photographer was Rod Mussnell, or recognize the young wide receiver as Josh Shanley?

He couldn't accept a deal like that. His view of retirement couldn't accommodate a betrayal of that magnitude. He'd keep running spreadsheets until the numbers came out right.

Sarah Lester's murder helped his numbers. It didn't provide a permanent boost, but for now it helped. No sense denying that. The more ways he could parley that interest, the better. *A survey*, he thought. Readers love surveys: it puts them in the process, makes them feel rational. Let's canvass the public on Lovemore's guilt or innocence. Specify race. Are local blacks and whites more or less in agreement on that point, or is there a racial angle here?

Yolanda would be the one to handle this. Like nobody else on the staff, better even than Edgar, Yolanda could breathe life into those statistical stories. He'd get her on it for the Sunday edition.

"LaRhonda?" he called back to the cleaning girl. She turned to look at him. When she smiled, her soft, chestnut cheeks pulled back into bright round knots. Josh knew she had left high school when she learned she was pregnant. ICNA would put her on part-time, minimum wage, no health insurance.

"You need something?"

Josh noticed the absence of distinction in her response. No *Mr. Shanley*. No *sir*. Just a dignified eagerness to be of use. It touched him that southern society had come so far, so soon. The Guardian, he knew, as an early and steadfast promoter of civil rights, had played a role in the transformation, perhaps had deleted a few *sirs* and *misters* from everyday human discourse. The proud past would suffocate him, if he allowed it to end here. He consciously took a deep breath. "Only…can I ask you something?"

Her smile didn't fade, but her eyes narrowed. "Sure."

"Do you think Lovemore is guilty?"

"You mean, because I'm black?"

"No, no. Not specifically. Well, yes. I guess so." He laughed.

"Lovemore didn't kill that woman. All that time in prison over there, you think he want more of it over here?"

"I take your point. But you know the whole town disagrees with you."

"I know the white part do."

He thought, *See? That's why we need that survey.* He wrote a note and stuck it to his monitor.

He had already changed his shoes, located an umbrella, and was walking the two blocks to the Odeon, mostly concentrating on avoiding the puddles forming in sinkholes in the concrete, thinking of nothing more substantial than the need for an editorial on sidewalk repair, when the import of LaRhonda's response combined in his head with Sheriff Greer's rickety testimony. When it finally did, it stopped him in his tracks.

This changed everything. If the Guardian took up the cause of Lovemore Ngwenya, they would lose nearly every subscriber they had. But if his young janitor had it right, and the authorities had it wrong, yet the Guardian remained silent, it wouldn't be the Guardian any more. Either way, he'd just lost his newspaper.

<table>
<tr>
<td>
Tops in Sports:
Heat or No Heat, Rain or Shine, Undefeated Pirates
host 3-1 Sullivan South River Rats Field, 7:30
Game Preview, C-1
</td>
<td>
Don't know your adiabatic
lapse rate from your
orographic lift?
See Meteorology 101, B-2
</td>
<td>
Today's Weather:
Today's Weather:
Just make it the usual:
Hot, Humid, Rain later
</td>
</tr>
</table>

The Twisting Creek Guardian

Hottest Autumn Opening in 65 years

Autumn Heat Wave Fluke or Global Warming?

CHAPTER 6: SHERIFF GREER

THE ONE GREAT advantage of being with the piss-ant local newspaper, and not with the *Louisville Courier-Journal* or the *Cincinnati Enquirer* or even the mighty AP, is that you are much more likely to know where the sheriff hides out in the evenings, what he does there, and what he drinks while he does it. With the whole herd of out-of-town reporters nosing around all the usual places without picking up any scent whatsoever, Edgar made sure no one was trailing him, stopped at a Roadrunner for a six-pack of Sam Adams, and drove the old road out to Lake Roosevelt. When he saw the hand-lettered "No trespassing" sign, he slowed his old GMC Jimmy to a crawl, shifted into four-wheel drive, and aimed it between two yellow pines. It didn't look enough like a road to merit such a warning, but a road it was, or at least a trail, and it led to a cabin where the sheriff, and sometimes his deputies, liked to do some quiet fishing and loud drinking.

The rain clouds moving in made it feel later in the evening, but by the clock there was still plenty of daylight left. Edgar drove over a mound and soon saw just what he'd been expecting: the ancient green Scout that Greer had driven for about as long as anybody in Twisting Creek could remember.

Edgar grabbed the bag with the beer in it, hopped out of his truck calling, "Anybody to home?" He wanted to sound as sociable as any reporter could sound while approaching a high sheriff in hiding from the biggest trial of his life. "You out here catchin' bass when you should be back home catchin' crooks?"

Greer stuck his head around the corner of his back deck. His salt-and-pepper hair looked out of place with his crew cut and his aviator glasses. He'd traded his tan uniform for a plaid lumberjack shirt and brown corduroys. One thing you couldn't accuse Allard Greer of was changing with the times.

"The fuck you want, Shanley?"

"Looks like a pretty good-sized storm brewing."

Greer looked out over the blackening lake, to where it narrowed at the mouth of the meandering stream that gave Twisting Creek its name. He squinted into the wind. "If I want to hear the weather, I got a radio. What do you really want?"

"I want to drink some decent American beer and talk to you about your future."

"Can't you pick up signals that say a man wants to be left alone?"

"You mean like he goes into hiding miles out in the wilderness?"

"Too subtle for you?"

"I'm a reporter."

"I got half-a-dozen weapons I could get my hands on in about three seconds. Maybe a load of buckshot in your dumb ass would send a message."

"I did bring beer. American beer."

"If you brought a pizza with it I won't shoot you—'til I done eat me some."

"Sorry. Just beer."

"What's this about my future?"

"Since you're going to have a lot more free time…"

"Who says I'm going to have a lot more free time?"

"Nobody. I'm just doing the math."

"I'm nowheres near sixty-five, if that's what you're driving at."

"I'm nowhere near thirty, either."

"How old are you?"

"Twenty-eight."

The sheriff laughed. He accepted a beer, popped off the cap with a blade on his pocket knife. "I bet you always got good grades in arithmetic."

"Straight F's. Why do you think I'm a reporter instead of a nuclear engineer?"

"Because your good daddy raised you to be a reporter, is why."

Edgar laughed. "I guess I did get it drilled into me. But that doesn't mean I can't go down some new road some day."

"Look, I'm a widower. My kids are all grown up and high-tailed it out of here. Now suppose you tell me just why in the world I'd want to retire. So I can run all over the world and take pictures of myself at the Eiffel Tower and Taj Mahal?"

"That's not what I think at all. I think there's a lot more to you than the redneck act you put on for the benefit of voters, and if I'm right, you've been playing a role for years. Which makes you a pretty damn good actor. So why not join our theater group?"

Greer looked at the bottle cap still in his hand, seemed on the verge of sailing it into the lake, then let it drop to the floor. "You mean that thing of your brother's?"

"You know about it?"

"Everybody down at the courthouse knows about it. It's supposed to make us all famous."

"We know we might have to change the names."

"Go ahead and use mine, if you want to. I couldn't care less."

"We need somebody to play you. Why not you yourself? It might be fun."

The sheriff looked around at him. "You mean it might help you gets lots of free publicity."

"Wouldn't hurt. You've seen the turn-out we normally get."

Greer stared down at his beer bottle for a while, then took a long drink. "Aren't you drinking?"

"I'm driving."

"Ha! That's rich." He opened a bottle for Edgar and handed it to him. "I'll fix your fucking ticket."

"Well?"

"Yes, I surely have seen your turn-out. I donated my five dollars to one of Rollie's little masterpieces. A truck driver picks up a pretty young hitchhiker, only she turns out to be a transvestite."

"Which is fine, because the truck driver turns out to be gay. It was supposed to be a comedy."

"I laughed my ass off. Maybe not always in the right places."

"This one's quality—I swear to God. And in the end Lovemore is executed, right on stage. Vengeance is mine. Everybody goes home happy."

"Look, Edgar." Greer stopped, looked out over the lake. He seemed to be struggling not only to get his words right, but to judge whether simply pronouncing them might not be a grave mistake. "I know why you really drove all the way out here. And I'm going to lay it on the line for you, personally, but not for the paper. Okay? Is that clearly understood?"

"Got it."

"I know my testimony may have seemed...haphazard. Leo Akers just gets in my craw. He's as sneaky as a copperhead and twice as dangerous. Just like yesterday he made old man Evans look silly. That honest and good-hearted old man, looking the fool. But here's my position and you can't print it. You can't even breathe it. But I know, in my heart, in my gut, that Lovemore killed Sarah Lester. I saw the killer in his eyes. He had all the rest of it too—motive, opportunity, means, plus some of the stolen goods in his possession at the time of arrest. But it was in his eyes that I saw cold-blooded killer. That dead stare, the fish-eye glaze he gets when he replays the murder in his mind. I saw it in him just like I saw it in Vietnam, and like I've seen it in law enforcement. He killed Sarah Lester. I'd say he enjoyed it. I'd even say she's not his first—nor his last, if we don't put him away."

"You don't think maybe Reynolds pushed it too far going for Murder One? Maybe wanted to make a name for herself as one tough-assed bitch?"

"She is one tough-assed bitch. We all knew that."

"And now the whole state knows it."

Greer stared at him, the question already taking shape on his lips, but he let it fade. "The charge wasn't my call. I just bring 'em in."

"But let's suppose Reynolds has overreached, and the jury isn't

71

convinced Lovemore deserves to die…"

"All I know is what I know. He looked Sarah Lester in the face and strangled her to death, drug her body up the steps into the house, cleaned out her jewels, and headed out of town. So when the verdict comes in guilty, and the sentence comes down death, I can retire a happy man."

They looked away from each other and out to the trees beyond the water, where a veil of rain was forming. For a transitional moment the landscape was a silvery green gauze. They sat quietly for a while, drinking, watching it darken and lose its green as it came near.

Edgar said, "So why not retire happily to the stage? You might enjoy it. You might even be good at it. And you can fry the bastard every night."

"What if I stink?"

"Then you'll fit right in."

By the time they reached the Odeon, it was raining hard. Josh had just arrived, and Yolanda followed them in. Everybody stood in the side vestibule, flipping umbrellas, slapping rain from their jackets and smoothing back their hair.

Rollie, though, was already dry. He'd been there all along, waiting for them. "Sheriff!" he said. "What a surprise!" He was thinking through all his pockets, if he was clean or not.

"The sheriff wants to sit through a rehearsal," Edgar said. "Maybe he'll even join in."

"Excellent," Rollie said. "Welcome to the Twisting Creek Players, sheriff."

"Yes," Yolanda said. "Feel free to join in. None of has read today's scene, except Rollie of course. Who never joins us. The playwright with stage fright. Very sad."

Rollie shuffled his feet and bit his thumb in a parody of a bashful child. With the ice broken, everybody relaxed and laughed. Clearly Greer wasn't there to frisk anybody.

"So," Yolanda said. "Shall we get started? I'm doing Prosecutor Reynolds. Edgar is Defense. Josh will be Evans, I guess?"

Josh nodded. "Until we cast. Anybody else in the scene?" He

looked at Rollie.

"Only a couple of lines each for a judge and court clerk. Maybe the sheriff will take those? Get his feet wet?"

"I'm game."

"Great," Josh said, passing around the scripts. "I'll cue."

ACT 2, SCENE 2: COURTROOM.

THE WITNESS, MR. EVANS, TAKES THE STAND.

Court Clerk: "Do you swear to tell the truth, the whole truth, and nothing but the truth, so help you God?"

Evans: I do.

Court Clerk: You may be seated.

Reynolds: Could you tell the court your name and address, please, sir?

Evans: My name is Ambrose Walker Evans. I live at 1260 Jackson Circle, here in Twisting Creek.

Reynolds: As you probably know, Mr. Evans, I am Elizabeth Reynolds, the prosecuting attorney for Buford County. I know this must be stressful, so I just want you to relax and tell the court exactly what you know about the case in question, no more and no less. First of all, how is the location of your residence situated in relation to that of the deceased, Sarah Lester?

Evans: Our back yard butts up against Sarah's back yard.

Reynolds: By "our" back yard, whose back yard do you mean?

Evans: Mine and my wife's. Just the two of us now. The children are all grown up and gone away.

Reynolds: And could you tell us your profession?

Evans: I'm retired from Pecco.

Reynolds: That would be the Pecco Electronics plant that is one of the main employers in Twisting Creek?

Evans: Pretty much the only one.

Reynolds: Yes, and what did you do at Pecco?

Evans: I worked the line for years, until my hand-vision coordination started to slip, when they put me in shipping.

Reynolds: And how old are you now?

Evans:	I'm 78 years young.
Reynolds:	And Mrs. Evans?
Evans:	Same as me.
Reynolds:	I'm guessing you were high school sweethearts.
Evans:	We were grade school sweethearts. Married sixty years. I guess they don't hardly make couples like that these days.
Reynolds:	And poorer is our society for it.
Defense:	Objection. Irrelevant.
Judge:	I'm sorry, counselor, but I will not be the judge who goes down in history as sustaining an objection to a sixty-year marriage.
Defense:	Just wanted the court to know I was paying attention. I'll overrule myself.
Reynolds:	Even pro bono humor is out of place at a trial like this, your honor.
Judge:	We'll get there, Liz. Continue.
Reynolds:	Fine. So now Mr. Evans, could you tell us in your own words what you know about the events of the evening of last October 30?
Evans:	I was doing some work back in our garage, which is in a separate building that extends to just a few feet from the back of our property. Now that we have just the one car, I put a workbench and keep my tools in half the garage. I was back there in the evening. I can be pretty sure what time it was, because I remember it was just getting dark, so the time must have been around 6:00 or 6:30.
Reynolds:	Could you see into Miss Lester's back yard?
Evans:	No. I was inside the garage, with the only window pointing out to the west.
Reynolds:	In other words it faces away from Miss Lester's?
Evans:	No, it faces at a right angle to it. It looks towards our next door neighbor, but not to the back. I guess if I stood over toward the very edge I could get a glimpse of her back fence, but not straight on.
Reynolds:	I see. So you have no eyewitness account of the events

of that evening.

Evans: No, ma'am, I don't. I've got an earwitness account, if there's such a word. I could hear their conversation from my workbench.

Reynolds: But if you couldn't see the participants in that conversation, how could you possibly be certain they were Sarah Lester and the defendant?

Evans: I often heard the two of them out back, working in the yard. I've known Sarah since she was little, and nobody could mistake Lovemore's voice and accent for anybody else.

Reynolds: So you are sure the conversation you heard was between Sarah Lester and Lovemore Ngwenya.

Evans: No question about it.

Reynolds: And how would you characterize this conversation?

Evans: Well, it was an argument, is what it was. First I could hear somebody raking leaves, and then Sarah came out of the house complaining that he had made a mess of the paint job in her bedroom. He said he'd take care of it, and anyway he was doing a lot of free work in the bedroom and she should take that into account. She said she would have no more work for him and he could just lay his rake down right then and there and take his leave.

Reynolds: How did he respond to being fired?

Evans: At first he was upset, kind of pleading, saying she was his only source of income at the moment. She said that was his lookout, that his work didn't qualify as professional. Then he started shouting at her.

Reynolds: How much of this conversation can you recall word for word?

Evans: Maybe none of it, word for word. Except the last sentence he spoke. That one I'll never forget.

Reynolds: Could you tell the court exactly what he said to end their exchange?

Evans: He said, "You're a dead woman, Sarah. You're a dead woman." Then she screamed, and there was not another sound out of her.

Reynolds: Your witness.

Defense: Now Mr. Evans, there are a few details that maybe I missed out on in your testimony. How can you be so sure it was 6:00 or 6:30?

Evans: Because when I left the house for the garage, I didn't need a flashlight, and on the way back I wished I had one.

Defense: I think by that time of year it gets dark earlier than that, doesn't it?

Evans: Daylight savings time didn't change until the next weekend.

Defense: Yes, that could explain it. You didn't tell us about the weather of the evening in question.

Evans: It was chilly. I was wearing a flannel work shirt and a University of Kentucky sweatshirt. A gift from my granddaughter. See, I'm good with details like these.

Defense: I'm beginning to see that. So tell me, if it was cold enough to require a flannel shirt and a sweatshirt, you must have had the windows closed there in your workshop.

Evans: Wrong again. The job I was doing was adding a coat of varnish to a nightstand I had made for my wife. See, that's my hobby—woodworking. So of course I opened the window to let the smell of varnish escape. And no, I didn't have any circle saw or drill or any other machinery going. Just varnish on a brush, so I could hear just fine.

Defense: And while you were listening to this loud exchange between Miss Lester and my client, weren't you tempted to peek out the edge of that window to see what little piece of her back yard you could, or, better yet, walk outside and look straight over the back fence?

Evans: I might have, but it's a big tall redwood fence that she had put up there to preserve her privacy. I'd have to climb a ladder to look into her back yard.

Defense:	One last question, Mr. Evans: When you thought you heard my client saying "You're a dead woman," why didn't you call the police immediately?
Evans:	Well, that's because…it's complicated. I mean, it's not all that easy to explain. My wife, you see, we talked it over after I went back into the house, and… she's in poor health, you know. She's a shut-in, you might say, an invalid. She was afraid I might have to go down to the police station, and get all involved and everything. We can't leave her alone. She needs a caregiver if I leave her alone.
Defense:	Yet you felt free to leave her alone while you varnished a nightstand in the garage?
Evans:	Oh, I'm pretty sure I could hear her call me from the house.
Defense:	You could hear your invalid wife's frail voice calling from within a house closed up for a chill fall evening? Through that house sealed up against the weather and across the back lawn and through the small garage window facing not your house, but the house next door.
Evans:	It's not a small window.
Defense:	It's 12" x 18". And when slid open, the maximum aperture is 4 inches. You really should repair that sticky window sill, Mr. Evans, wood-working being your hobby and all.
Evans:	Well, her voice isn't frail. She can still blast you…
Defense:	If she had a stroke and fell facing the carpet…let's face it, Mr. Evans, your grade school sweetheart is in reasonable health, and thank God for that. You could have gone to the police station just as safely as you could have gone out to the garage to varnish a table. And you could certainly have phoned the police.
Evans:	At the time…
Defense:	The fact is, you didn't take any action because the conversation my client had with Miss Lester didn't sound all that threatening, isn't that right? You

	returned to your house and did nothing because there seemed no need to.
Evans:	The more I thought about it....
Defense:	You thought more about it the next...
Reynolds:	Objection! He's clearly badgering the witness.
Judge:	I'll allow it. Ask your question, counselor.
Defense:	Isn't it correct to say that it was actually the next morning, after you heard that Miss Lester's body had been found dead in her living room, that's when you recalled the conversation and it was then, and only then, that it started to seem worthy of a call to the police?
Evans:	When I heard on the radio that she was dead, I thought back.
Defense:	Thank you. No more questions.
Evans:	I thought, "You're a dead woman." And then she was.
Defense:	No more questions, your honor.
Judge:	The witness is excused. You may step down now, Mr. Evans.
Evans:	As dead as dead can be.

The Twisting Creek Guardian

Weekend Break Allows Both Sides to Assess Strategy

Defense Confident of Victory—Akers

CHAPTER 7: YOLANDA

YOLANDA WOKE UP grouchy and couldn't figure out why until she noticed that the stupid ceiling fan had stopped working. Sometime during the night she'd kicked off her sheet, yet she was covered in a thin layer of something that didn't seem so much like sweat as a film of shortening, as though somebody had basted her with Crisco before shoving her in the oven. Sticky nights like this in late September simply weren't fair. The week's evening storms had done nothing to break the heat wave. In fact they had simply dumped more water into the cauldron that soon after dawn the sun would bring to a rolling boil. Refreshing rainfall during one of these eastern Kentucky hot spells amounted to nothing more than the prelude to a steam bath.

The only thing to do with a mood like this was to grab a quick shower, throw on a pair of ripped jeans, an old Vols t-shirt and matching orange crocs, and get the hell out of the house before Brandon woke up. She didn't even slow down for coffee and a peanut butter waffle. Instead she defied every norm of civilized behavior and on the way to work stopped for a drive-through Egg McMuffin and a cardboard mug of coffee.

She watched the damp asphalt of McDonald's parking lot shimmer behind a vapor of rising steam, but it troubled her no longer. Yolanda had prevailed in her rare bout with foul spirits. She tended to picture the human condition as a small clique of Nazis who wouldn't be satisfied until she was thoroughly miserable, so she stayed happy just to spite them. Her motto was *Happiness is the Best Revenge*, and, true to form, she was starting to relish the day ahead. She was in an air-conditioned car, on her way to an air-conditioned office, where a real journalistic task awaited her: a county-wide survey on the guilt or innocence of Lovemore Ngwenya.

Saturday was the perfect day for a telephone survey because most people would be home, and they might not be in such a rush to end a phone call. It also meant that the story would be fresh for the Sunday *Guardian*, the best day for newsstand sales, as well as the edition with the most regular subscribers. Yolanda needed an eye-catching front page story above the fold. She envisioned a graph, in color, spanning three columns, atop her story. Page one, top left. This was where most people's eyes fell immediately after a glance at the headline. She would balance it with a smaller photo on the right side. She didn't yet know what it would be. With the trial recessed for the weekend, maybe a non-Lovemore story would be refreshing. Perhaps the wire services would break some big international story. If not, maybe something regional on last night's storm damage and the current heat wave.

She thought through all this at her desk while she finished her breakfast. With her free hand she checked her inbox and found eight new job applications, all from Beckley, West Virginia. The Ledger, an ICNA property, was going through another round of layoffs. She moved the files to a folder she'd created for the purpose: *doomapps*, short for Doomed Applications. She could just as easily have deleted them, for all the chance these applicants had of finding a job. But it seemed disrespectful to summarily delete the hopes of good journalists, to send their livelihoods into the trash file, so these eight joined a hundred of their brothers and sisters in *doomapps*, and she reminded herself that her role in the struggle was to help keep the Guardian out of ICNA's portfolio.

She opened yesterday's submissions to the Letters to the Editor section. As usual, the prime topic was Lovemore. Every day a couple of people wrote that a murder like this was the consequence of allowing foreigners into their midst. Yolanda ran one or two of these a week, confident that they would trigger an opposing response. Someone was sure to point out that they were all immigrants, except for the Cherokees, and if you went back far enough they were too. Today she selected the least wacko argument from either side, pasted them into the op-ed holes, and headed them *The Risks of Cultural Mixing* and *We All Came from Africa*.

She turned her attention to styles of graphs, looking for the clearest form to display contrasting bi-polar views. She took her time with the coffee, wishing she'd popped for a fried apple pie to go with it.

It was much too early to phone anybody, but that didn't dim her enthusiasm. First she had to figure out this new survey software with its random autodialer, then import the residential numbers into its database, and set some statistical parameters. She had to produce a script that, without sounding intrusive, explicitly asked people to identify themselves as to race. Then she would assign portions of the database, by alphabet, to various people in the office. Deedee would help out, if she wasn't swamped in classifieds. The Saturday part-timers and the Franklin College interns could handle the job, too, providing the script was self-explanatory enough.

More enticing than any of this, though—the thing that made the early morning minutes seem to ooze past like refrigerated molasses—was her own cunning and perhaps even unethical scheme to use the random calling system as a pretense for allowing a simple twist of fate to put her in touch with Victor Caraher, Twisting Creek's Chief Deputy Sheriff. Part of the plan's allure was the way it intruded onto Edgar's holy turf and allowed her to do a little investigative reporting of her own, and the attraction was doubled—at least doubled, maybe more—because earlier that month, at the annual Labor Day Antique Car Show at the Kiwanis Park, Yolanda had caught Victor staring at her across the hood of his precious "candy-apple red"—his description—1965 Barracuda fastback. He was giving her the look that recently divorced people recognize to mean, "Me too. I'm one of you now." They'd spoken for only a minute, mostly about his car, but every day since then she'd been trying to devise a method of bumping into him, and here it was: random autodialing.

She spent a couple of quiet hours engrossed in her task. At nine-thirty she decided it was late enough to give the survey system a trial run, and to her surprise it worked fine. She took any successful first attempt with new software to be a modern spin-off of some ancient augury, like chicken entrails or the direction of a vulture's flight, predicting a bright day ahead. Her mood continued the rise that had started with her reckless choice of breakfast food, and intensified further when she walked into Deedee's office and was greeted with one of those sparkling smiles that were once so typical of her little sister, but which recently seemed to be no more than a distant memory from a lost past.

"New customer," Deedee said, turning her screen for Yolanda to see the ad layout she was designing. "He's asked for a quarter page, but he's got so many items featured that you can barely see them, so I think I'll recommend a half-page, discount the difference, and see if it brings him some business. It's either that, or cut some items. What do you think?"

Yolanda moved in for a closer look. It was all fishing reels, lures, bits of tackle, and boating accessories. "Sure—new customer—comp him the difference. I'll also give him a plug on the front page."

"He's just opened his store. I met him out by the lake. This sale is on me."

"So. Lookie here who's saving the Guardian single-handed."

Deedee laughed, bent her arm to flex her bicep.

Yolanda said, "My guess is it wasn't the muscle in your arm that got his attention, but we won't go into that."

"We can if you want!"

Yolanda smiled. "Awwright! Is he good looking and single?"

"He's got more hair on his chin than on his head, but he's buff and not exactly oogly. And no mention of a significant other. No ring either. I haven't quite decided what to make of him."

"How do you mean?"

"I mean, he could be either super-nice, or way creepy."

"With our luck, you know which way that'll turn out."

Deedee smiled. "To me he's just, like, whatever. But he was so incredible with Brandon. It's amazing." She paused and shook her head—not for the first time—at the magic Travis had worked on her son. "Have you noticed how quiet he's been this week?"

"Are you kidding me? I've already made an appointment to get my hearing tested." They laughed. Yolanda noticed how pleasurable it was to engage in sisterly banter. The difference in their ages meant they'd never had the chance as teenagers, then soon enough her own marriage and Deedee's pregnancy pre-empted it altogether. Now, though, they were both back in the game, and here was a surprising side-benefit. "Hey listen…how busy are you?"

"Once I get this fishing ad done I'm all caught up. Why?"

"I could use some help with a poll we're doing. We've got a computer program that randomly calls people. All you have to do is read a script to whoever answers, then note their response. I've made it very friendly and informal." She handed Deedee a sheet of paper:

Good _____ (morning) (afternoon). My name is _____ and I work for the Twisting Creek Guardian newspaper. I'm not trying to sell you anything. We would very much like to know your opinion on a subject I'm sure you've thought about a lot: the trial of Lovemore Ngwenya. {*pronounced "ung-way-nya"*} We won't use your name or anything, only record your opinion. Do you think that's okay with you?

{*If they don't agree, thank them and wish them a good day.*}

{*If they agree, continue with….*}

Thanks for helping out. The question is, Do you think Lovemore Ngwenya should be found guilty or not guilty of the murder of Sarah Lester?

{*Record answer on the accompanying tally sheet…*}

{If they say they're not sure, ask them if they lean one way or the other. Record answer.}

{If they insist they have no opinion, thank them and wish them a good day.}

{If they have a response, continue...}

Okay. Now one last question, and you certainly don't have to answer this, but if you do it will help give a clear picture of our community's opinions: Would you identify yourself as Caucasian/white, African-American, Hispanic, or other?

{Record answer.}

"What I didn't write out," Yolanda added, "is what to do if they refuse to identify their race, but you can tell it by how they talk. I say, note it anyway. Nobody's name gets used. It's just a bit of data, and the more bits, the more reliable the results will be. What do you think?"

"I don't see who it'd hurt. It's just going to be a graph and percentages, right?"

"Yep. Plus what I write. It's not scientific, but pretty accurate if we get a reasonable sample. Oh, one more thing. If somebody seems unusually willing, or perceptive, or interested, ask them why they feel the way they do, and note their response. Then ask them if we can use their name for attribution. Make sure they understand that if they give their name, it'll be printed in the paper alongside what they had to say. Okay?"

"Does that usually switch people on or off?"

"It can work both ways, but we've never surveyed an issue this hot before. We'll see. The article will be fine with no quotes at all, but better with some."

Yolanda left Deedee to get on with it. She had reserved for herself the portion of the phone register that contained family names beginning with "C". She had a plan for Chief Deputy Victor Caraher and his candy apple red 1965 Barracuda.

He answered on the first ring. Yolanda supposed that meant he was working on something and had a phone on his desk. Yolanda read:

"Good morning. My name is Yolanda Shanley and I work for the Twisting Creek Guardian newspaper. I'm not trying to sell you anything. We would very much like to know your opinion on a subject I'm sure you've thought about a lot..."

"Yolanda? Hi! What's all this about?"

She paused, allowing him to think she was processing this surprise response. "Hey! I think I recognize that voice! Is that you, Victor?"

"You should know—you dialed my number."

"Actually a computer dialed your number. We're doing a random survey."

"I should be disappointed that you didn't call me on purpose."

"But you're not?"

"Not really. Maybe it's fate."

"Good way to look at it. I probably can't ask you the survey question, though."

"Ask me anyway. I've got opinions on everything—especially stuff I don't know anything about."

"No, it's not that you don't know anything. I mean you're too involved. We're canvassing public opinion on whether Lovemore is guilty or innocent."

"Oh, I see what you mean. You need a simple thumbs up or down, where my answer would take pages and pages."

"Yeah, I guess so. I'm sorry to have bothered you. I hope you weren't busy."

"Oh, you know—paperwork. Nothing that has to be finished this minute. You always work on Saturday?"

"Oh yes. That beast we call the *Sunday* Guardian has to be fed constantly. We do most of it in advance, but the front page is my baby." She waited for him to comment, but he made no reply. "Of course that's the last one to compose. Along with sports." Still he said nothing. "In case there's some breaking news." The man had gone completely silent. Either the line was dead, or he was trying, and failing, to work up the nerve to ask her out. Finally she added, "I usually finish by five o'clock," and left the rest up to him.

"So...pretty full day, then. By that time are you exhausted, just want to go home and put your feet up?"

"Usually a cup of coffee puts me back on track." *Jesus,* she thought. *I've told you what time and I've told you what. You want me to tell you where?*

"I have an idea! Let's have that coffee together. How about that?"

"Oh, wow. Okay. That way you'll have plenty of time to answer my survey question."

"Can I pick you up at the paper? Say five? If you should finish earlier, call me. I'm really pretty free all day."

DEEDEE TURNED HER portion of the polling results over to Yolanda, printed out the finished design for the *Archer's Bait and Boat* ad, then drove home to pick up Brandon for an afternoon at the lake. On the ride out there he was quiet. He held his lure right up against his nose the whole way. It had become for him what a teddy bear was for some kids. He even slept with the damn thing. For five nights running he'd held it pressed to his face in his right hand, stuck the thumb of that same hand in his mouth, and slept through the night without so much as a whimper. This afternoon as they drove by Travis Archer's store he grunted and pointed, but didn't protest when they continued past it.

At the lake the only near-fit he threw was when he found that the odor of his lure intensified when immersed in water. He celebrated his discovery by flinging it into the air with a great burst of laughter, only to lose it when it splashed into the shallow water a good six feet behind him. The cry that followed showed that the old Brandon was still there below the surface, ready and willing to pierce eardrums if need be, but Deedee laughed and within seconds had retrieved his lure, restoring the little strip of manmade beach to its happy, kid-filled commotion.

On the way back when they neared Travis' store, Brandon began to shriek. Deedee said, "Don't worry. He's on our itinerary." She turned onto the gravel lot, but this time instead of stopping in front of the main entrance she drove around back. She wondered if Travis could hear her from inside the cabin. She hoped not. She wanted to do some snooping.

The place looked a little better this time. The dead evergreens were gone, and somehow the log walls appeared less infested than they had. She drove past an exterior window, but recalled that from the inside it was covered by a display of merchandise.

Out back Deedee discovered an unpainted, obviously homemade wooden structure, big enough to hold a car. She'd convinced herself that his car would provide clues to Travis' personality, and she was determined to have a look at it, even if she had to skulk to do it.

The garage door was closed and from a distance she could see a shiny new padlock on it. She parked, told Brandon to be real quiet, closed her door as softly as she could, and walked the last few steps. The gravel crunching under her feet sounded like firecrackers popping. She placed her hands and then her face onto the rough timber of the garage door. She put an eye to a wide crack between boards and peered inside as best she could.

With interior sunlight slanting through gaps, illuminated panels of swirling dust revealed that Travis Archer drove a black Jeep Wrangler, one of those with a removable roof, also black. It was possibly a bit rugged for her taste, but she reminded herself that an outdoorsman might need a car that could withstand some abuse. She was more interested in finding something—perhaps a rebel flag, a Jesus fish—anything that would help her define the owner, but she found nothing more than a plain, black Jeep. She could see no tribal markers on the rear bumper. That did not mean, she noted, that there were none, because the whole rear of the Jeep was covered in dried mud. She'd learned at least one thing about him: he'd been driving off-road after the recent storms.

The sight of all that mud on his Jeep caused her to survey the ground near the garage door, and sure enough she saw deep ruts leading off the gravel drive into a gap in a stand of hemlock that seemed to mark the border of his property. Fallen needles from the hemlocks obscured the tire tracks where they penetrated the dark shade of dense foliage along what was probably the beginning of an old logging trail. Deedee was tempted to follow it, but feared Travis had heard her drive past the cottage, so she didn't dare. What was in there, she wondered, worthy of a trip in such weather? A shortcut to the lake? A swampy area for gigging frogs? Apparently the man liked cooking. Maybe frog legs were on his menu. Now it even seemed to her that she could smell a swamp, a dank effusion of stagnant slime and rot. A movement inside the car caught her eye, and she saw that Brandon, too, was looking in the same direction, sniffing the air and crooking a chubby finger up and down toward the gap into the dim woods. She attempted an internal laugh meant to signify, Now you've got me doing it too. She knew it was pure fantasy, yet she couldn't quite shake the thought that there was something more sinister about Travis Archer than she'd first imagined, back when the worst she could come up with was that he was a simple redneck. The temptation came over her to walk straight into those woods. What could she find in there that spooked her so? A cemetery? An Aryan Nation weapons cache? Some Satan-worshiping shrine? She ached to know, but now wasn't the time. *Later,* she thought. *When I can be sure he's not here...*

She retrieved Brandon and by the time she reached the side of the porch, she saw Travis standing there with his hands on his hips, just like the first time she'd ever seen him, only now surveying the empty gravel lot and the empty road beyond. He looked her way when he heard Brandon's yelp.

"I thought I heard somebody."

"I parked around to the side, since I'm not really here as a customer."

He gave her a puzzled look. "Yeah. Like it's so packed."

She smiled up at him, but said nothing.

He came over to the side of the porch and squatted to receive Brandon, whose arms were reaching for him. "Come here, little buddy. I see your lure is still doing its job."

Deedee continued around and climbed up the steps. She held out the printed version of the newspaper advertisement she'd created for him. "I thought you might want to see this before we run it. We've decided to give it a half-page, no extra charge for the difference. If that's okay with you. I owe you one anyway." With a nod she indicated the lure.

"Nah," he dismissed such a thought. "We don't worry about little things. My old uncle always said not to worry about big things, because you can't fix big things, and don't worry about little things, because they're little."

"That doesn't leave much, does it?"

"Medium things, I guess. But I don't think he had a category for medium."

"Smart man," she said, noting that he'd cited an uncle, not a father. She cupped the back of Brandon's head. "This here's my big thing."

"Aw," Travis said as he lifted Brandon overhead, "he ain't all that big."

Deedee looked way up there at her smiling son, his arms spread wide, like a soaring angel. She allowed her eyes to descend the cut lines of muscles in the arms that held him up there, down shoulders and torso, finally to the printed copy of the newspaper ad she held in her hand. She started to mention it. It was the only topic of conversation she'd prepared for this meeting. She had planned to say that they would run it in tomorrow's sports section and that she'd already asked Rod Mussnell to find a fishing story to run alongside it. She knew she should stick to that topic, but instead she asked, "How did you know?"

"How did I know what?"

"I mean, ever since we stopped here that first time, Brandy's been less cranky and more…I don't know…at peace with himself… than he ever was before. It's somehow connected with you and that lure. How did you know?"

"That was easy. I had a little brother who wouldn't speak one word and screamed just like this little monster here." He rubbed the rough whiskers of his chin against Brandon's neck. "How'd you like a good bearding, you little monster?" Brandon yipped a spasmodic laugh. "My brother was one miserable kid. One day I saw him walk out in the back yard and stick his nose right down in a pile of warm dog poo. I swear it! I thought, *Holy shit!* Excuse my language, but that's exactly what I thought. *Holy shit!* This kid's bound for the loony bin! But then I remembered how he was always sticking garlic up his nose, or a piece of onion. Or a dead fish off the creek bank. He reminded me of our dogs, never happier than when his nose was down in something disgusting. And then it hit me: he *was* a dog. Not really a dog, I mean, but maybe he had something in common with them. For whatever reason, his sense of smell occupied such a large part of his brain that he had to keep it stimulated."

"Wow." She needed to think this one through before she commented further. It sounded nutty, but then again, Brandy really had calmed down. Clearly she needed to learn more about this. She would research the hell out of this one when she got home. But there was one thing she needed to know right now. "So what happened with your little brother?"

"He's at Wayne State."

Deedee looked away from Travis, out across the empty gravel lot and onto the empty road. She felt a heat in her chest, and the taste of something sour rose to the back of her throat.

So it was true. Her worst fear for her baby had not been the frenzied imagination of a silly young mom. He really was abnormal. A nightmare future awaited him. The insanity in her mother's eyes had pierced right through to the second generation, and, like her mother, her son would end up in an institution.

"I guess," Deedee said quietly, "that Wayne State is a sort of... mental home?"

"A mental home?" Travis laughed and gave her a light slap on the back of her head. "Hell no, it's not a mental home. You're the one needs a mental home. Wayne State is a university in Michigan. My brother's in law school there."

She could have wept. *A university!* All her suspicions about Travis Archer vanished, and she had to fight off the impulse to give him the sweetest hug he'd ever had in his life. This man, only minutes earlier a potential Klan member or Satan worshiper, had turned out to be an angel. She took Brandon and held him close to her. She smelled the sweet skin of his belly as she blew a wet raspberry there. She thought, Maybe you like stinky things, but you still smell like my sweet little baby boy. She said, "A lawyer, huh? You mean to tell me I'm raising a lawyer?"

"Could very well happen."

"Then I guess I'd better quit giving away ads, and go sell a few."

Even as Travis watched Deedee drive across the gravel lot and turn onto the road, even as he was waving goodbye, he realized he may have made a tactical error. A dumb, needless blunder. *Stupid! Stupid!*, he cursed, slapping his forehead. Did Wayne State University even have a law school? Why hadn't he said Michigan State? Surely they had one. Or Notre Dame? Fucking Harvard, for that matter? Any goddamn place. He hurried to the back of his store, logged on to the Internet, googled "law school wayne state" and read: *Wayne State University Law School.*

He laughed aloud and said to the empty room, "You always had balls, old son. Now you got luck."

CHAPTER 9: ELIMINATING THE IMPOSSIBLE IS THE EASY PART.

LONG BEFORE THE others had submitted their survey results, Yolanda knew what they would show. Twenty-five calls into her own section of the alphabet and it was clear that public opinion in Buford County on Lovemore's guilt or innocence was sharply divided by race. It was almost as simple as: if you're white, he killed her; if you're black, he didn't. The final numbers indicated that 91% of all Caucasians either leaned strongly toward or were convinced of his guilt, while 96% of African-Americans believed just the opposite.

At three-thirty she phoned Josh with the final results. She knew he'd want to work up an editorial for the Sunday edition. An hour later she'd written her story and devised what she thought was a pretty clever graphic: a blindfolded Justice held out her two hands to weigh the evidence. Her left hand was white. It held a tall stack of ninety-one red coins, indicating guilt. In her black right hand a stack of ninety-six green coins indicated innocence. Yolanda headlined the story *Polls Apart*, hoping a little levity would temper the impact of her findings.

Josh's editorial pulled no such punches. He wanted it run front page and headed *A COMMUNITY DIVIDED*. It decried the lack of commonality between the races even after all the efforts of the last decades. He did manage to trumpet the Guardian's frontline stance in the push for racial harmony, and even got in a plug for the Odeon by citing uncle Delmon Shanley's 1949 desegregation, a good fifteen years in advance of most southern theaters. But he made no attempt to prettify the ugly fact that, three generations later, blacks and whites could look at the same evidence in a landmark murder trial and draw completely opposing conclusions.

Yolanda admired her new front page, sent it to the printers, and immediately called Victor Caraher to tell him she was running just a few minutes late and to ask him to pick her up at her house on Sycamore instead of at the Guardian office. She knew that made it sound more like a date than an interview, but she wanted to change out of her jeans and crocs into something nicer. Interview or date or some mix of the two, she still didn't want to look like a woman he'd be more likely to arrest than invite to coffee.

The house on Sycamore, oversized as it was even when Orval Shanley built it in 1902, was separated from the sidewalk by only a red-tip hedge and shallow front yard. As soon as Yolanda opened the wooden gate, which by habit everyone lifted by the handle to keep it from dragging, she sensed something strange. It was an odd feeling, one that she almost dismissed without even thinking about it. It was a recognition of something missing.

When she reached the porch she noticed the quiet.

Brandon. Brandon wasn't screaming. Deedee must have taken him swimming.

Was that it? Did that explain her odd…but her eye was drawn to the empty rocking chair where her father had passed most of his final days, the stroke-diminished coda to his vigorous life, and she heard him say, with his sad, brave, lop-sided smile, "Kind of quiet round here today."

Yolanda stopped there, her hand on the knob of the screen door. The need to fight back a tear seemed to require all her energy. She had thought she was long past this response to Pops Woody's absence from their lives, but now she found herself unable to pass his chair. There must be a reason for that. She had sufficiently mourned his death.

This moment of immobility, however, wasn't about his death. It was about his last months. It was because "Kind of quiet round here today" meant so much more than it said. It meant that Mom was up in her room in a Haldol-induced stupor. It meant that a hammer blow from modern medicine had finally conquered her months of screeching agony. It meant Pops Woody had outlived his allotted happiness, and, for the time left to him, his only contentment would consist of a moderated sorrow.

Yolanda shook herself loose from it. She thought, Is this connected with meeting Victor Caraher? Will the teensiest little glimmer of beginning a relationship send me straight to the memory of how even enduring ones end?

No, was the answer to that. *No!* Pops Woody himself would have counseled her otherwise. Once you outgrow fairly tales, he had told his children, there are no happy endings. The end is always tragic, so get on with the beginning and enjoy the hell out of the middle.

This beginning had to start with a quick shower and a change of clothes. She debated between a white, medium-short, pleated skirt with white strappy high heels—an outfit that highlighted her long, tanned legs—or blue jeans with cowgirl boots. She finally decided on the jeans and boots, because if Victor was a leg man it would be cruel to drive him bazookas with absolutely zero chance of relief in the near future. Anyway, maybe cops preferred the allure of tooled leather. For a top she added a simple white t-shirt Rollie had brought her from one of his foreign trips. The writing on the front would give Victor something to read while he stared at her boobs.

Do NOT, she reminded herself, get so caught up in sexing up the dude that you lose sight of your main goal, which is to find out if the sheriff's chief deputy is as convinced of Lovemore's guilt as the sheriff is. You're doing exactly what Edgar would do, if he had the legs and breasts for the job.

She was on the porch waiting when Caraher drove up, not in the Barracuda, but in his imposing black-on-silver police cruiser, because, he explained, the Barracuda's air-conditioning wasn't really up to the job, and on top of that if she needed her coffee fast he could siren people out of the way and do eighty or ninety.

He too wore jeans. Not fashion ones—clean, but probably also worn for yard work. His sport shoes had a green tinge to them, reminding Yolanda that Victor lived on a small farm just out of town. She found herself imagining him weeding the garden with his little girl, the one now lost, with her mother, to California.

They decided on Fifi's French Press, out to the west of town near Franklin College. More students than townies hung out there, and Yolanda liked it that way. Victor said he'd never been there except once, to quell a disturbance. She assured him that no police presence would be required today, unless his response to every question was "No comment." As they left the car he smiled at her and pulled a Guardian from the door pocket. She felt her heart give way a little.

Fifi's was in a converted Depression-era house. They found a table tucked away in an alcove. Tracy Chapman was on the stereo. There were enough people to create a pleasant background buzz and to muffle any private conversations. She ordered an iced mocha. He asked for "a plain old cup of coffee."

"They call it an *Americano* here. It's all very pretentious."

"And how's the coffee?"

"*Delicioso.*"

"Then they can call it whatever they want."

She watched his eyes flick towards her breasts and then quickly back to her face, where they seemed to try to lock on. Again they went back to her breasts. She inhaled.

"I've never seen a t-shirt like that."

"My brother picked it up somewhere. You know Rollie?"

"Sure I know him. I like his movies. *Hesburger,*" he read from the shirt. "What does it mean? A hamburger joint?"

"I guess so."

"Where is it?"

"Maybe it says on the back." She stood up and turned her back to him. That was a side benefit of this shirt—it gave him an excuse to check out her butt. She gave him plenty of time, then, over her shoulder, asked, "Does it say?"

"*Four locations in Vilnius.* Where the hell's that?"

"Beats me. You know Rollie."

"You sure do have an interesting family."

What seemed like a platform for conversation actually stopped them both for a while. Did he mean Josh's homosexuality? Deedee's single motherhood? Rollie's....Rollie-hood? He couldn't possibly mean Edgar. There was nothing interesting about him. Edgar was your basic guy guy. She was tempted to say, "Yours is the interesting one," since Victor Caraher's wife had run away to Hollywood. Not, it had to be said, to pursue an acting career, or even to live lavishly with some actor or director. She had left Victor for a make-up man from the crew of *No Senator's Son,* which had been filmed in Twisting Creek the previous year.

Finally she asked, "What's so interesting about my family?"

"Oh, the history of it, I guess. Founding the newspaper. Building the Odeon. Sticking up for civil rights in spite of the enemies created. All the way back for how many generations now?"

"I don't think I know. Five or six? *Established 1882.* Says so on top of every paper."

"See. That's what I mean. I came here alone after finishing UK. Greer hired me, and that was that. My people are from way out west, in Paducah. I'm more river rat than mountain boy."

"Still…here you are."

"Alone again."

"Yes. I was sorry to hear what happened. I knew Shelley a little bit. We went to high school together."

"So you know what happened."

"Well…small town."

"The thing that kills me…"

Victor paused there; paused so long that Yolanda went way past wondering what killed him, and focused on what a nice face he had when he tried to phrase something just right. The flesh tone was more sandalwood than mahogany. His eyes were on his hands; his lips, normally full and pillowy, were pressed hard together. His hair was trimmed almost to the scalp, yet managed to look rebellious thanks to a sharp angle shaved into the temple. Yolanda wondered whether the point was style, or was he hiding hair loss at the temples? He had the look of a man trying to phrase a loss for the thousandth time, knowing full well it was beyond the limits of language. Yolanda wanted to take his hand and assure him that it was okay, he didn't need to say what killed him. Sometimes stuff just kills us and we have to keep silent about it.

Victor exploded in a laugh. "A cosmetologist! And he's not gay! Aren't all Hollywood cosmetologists supposed to be gay? I thought there was a union rule. My wife finds the only straight make-up artist in the history of cinema, and runs off with him."

"Maybe she gets free mascara."

"All a cop gets is doughnuts. You know why she said she left me? Because I'm boring."

"I don't see where she gets that. You could come home at any time with multiple gunshot wounds. That should liven things up right there."

He laughed. "I wish I'd thought to tell her that."

"You should have pulled a gun on her. That would be exciting. Or simply place her under arrest."

"Handcuffs. Some people go for those. Got lots of those. Not the fluffy pink ones, though. Just steel."

A college girl brought their coffee and left without a word. Yolanda asked Victor, "Take sugar?"

He made a small nasal sound that seemed to be a negative. Clearly he did not want an interruption. "I blame it on the farm. She hated living out in the country. She thought it was for hicks. My daughter Sasha loved it, but Shelley hated it."

"She could have suggested a move into town."

"She never did. She just called me a bore." They let the word hang there in the air. Somebody needed to say something witty, but no one did. Instead, Victor said, "It's true, though. I am boring. I'm a man of regular habits. I don't throw fits or get roaring drunk and overturn tables."

"One woman's boring might be another's stability."

He smiled. "How about you? Were you boring too?

"No. I was just stupid. I married the wrong guy for the wrong reasons."

"He didn't get nasty, did he? I could have used those handcuffs on him."

She stirred her ice cubes, then thought she caught his meaning and looked up at him. "Boring, my foot," she said.

"No, really. Did he hit you?"

"No, he just stupided me to a pulp. I'll tell you the truth, Victor. I honestly believe the only reason I married him was to show that one of us, one of the five Shanley kids, I mean, could make a commitment to the future. You know? None of us looked like we'd ever get married. We were dead end kids. No future generation was on the way, or ever would be, it seemed like. So I wanted to buck the trend."

"Then along comes Deedee."

"The exception that proves the rule. Probably got pregnant the only time she ever had sex."

"Like I say—interesting family."

She'd never thought of her family that way. It was a nice way of looking at it, but she knew she was on the verge of allowing the conversational balance to tip the wrong way. She wasn't here to be interviewed; she was here to interview him.

"So listen—this all started with a survey question: is Lovemore guilty? What's your opinion?"

"Look, Yolanda..." he said, the first time he'd spoken her name. "Two points. One: I'm not allowed an opinion. Two: if I had one, I sure couldn't tell a reporter about it." When she shrugged and gave him a little smile of resignation, he added, "Not even one in cowgirl boots."

"I thought you might have a quick thumbs up or down opinion."

"At this point only one man knows the sure up or down on this one, and that's Lovemore himself. I'm afraid I can't help you much there."

"Hey, I totally understand. The survey numbers are already in. The story's written, the front page is done, the paper is at the printer's. Let me lay out what I need and you can see if there's any room for you to help me, without in any way crossing lines you shouldn't. And you should know that anything you tell me will be in the deepest of deep backgrounds. The Mariana Trench of backgrounds. Wild horses, etcetera, etcetera."

"I still can't say anything."

"I know. But you can listen. We are getting worried..."

"We? Meaning?"

"We at the paper. Mainly Josh and I. We've followed this case since the beginning and like everybody else...or, according to our poll, every white person...we assumed he was guilty, open and shut. But now—let's you and me be frank about this—the sheriff's testimony seemed a tad underwhelming, and old man Evans may not be the most credible witness ever. One piece of jewelry..."

"One man leaving town the next day."

"One suddenly unemployed man leaving a good twelve hours after the crime. Plus..." Victor started to interrupt but she lifted

99

her hand. "Plus I've just uncovered the stark numerical fact that almost every black person in this county thinks this trial is a miscarriage of justice. Okay, they're giving him the benefit of the doubt, but they see the same evidence as we do. Can they all be wrong?" She sat forward, put her elbows on the table and her chin in her hands.

Victor turned his coffee cup around and around. He looked around the café, then leaned closer to her. "Have you noticed that except for me and a couple of Asian students, everybody in this room is white?"

"So what?"

"So what? So I don't know what. We're two cultures apart, I guess is what. Does it surprise you that there are big disagreements?"

"This big, yes. We're not *that* divided. At least I don't think we are."

"Look...I owe my career to Allard Greer."

"I like him too. He's even joining the Players. He's going to play himself."

"You're shitting me."

"This is no time for shitting people, deputy." She gave him a grin, hoping it had come out funny, even though she hadn't intended it as a joke. "My newspaper has been sitting on its hands while a possibly innocent man is railroaded to death row. We've played it up from day one. We've profited from it in the form of increased sales. Not once have we introduced questions into the public dialogue. The questions Leo Akers asked Greer: Did Sarah have enemies from mortgages she foreclosed on? Why can't a woman give a man a necklace? Where was the rest of the stolen jewelry? What about that huge film crew that left town just before the murder? And what about those students who left Franklin College that week? The Guardian never once asked our readers these questions. Have we pandered to white opinion because that's where our sales are? The Guardian has a history of standing up for the oppressed. The press in this whole country is supposed to do exactly that. My family as far back as anybody can remember has stood against racism. Yet now we've laid the groundwork for executing this African because...because why? Because we need the revenue? Here's all I ask of you: Are we doing the right thing? If you truly believe we have covered the case in as honest and objective a manner as we should, then don't say a word. I'll interpret your silence as affirmation that we don't need to change our course."

He sat there silently. Yolanda didn't know how long to give him. She hadn't thought the least bit about using this tactic. Maybe it had been a big mistake. Maybe better to wheedle a little at a time. The guy was quick to sull in conversation anyway. She knew that much about him. She should have taken it into consideration before she put herself in a corner. She tried to think of a way out.

Victor spoke. "Those thirteen students left that week because it was the last day to withdraw and get a full tuition refund. This is straight from the registrar."

He had broken the silence, but to support the prosecution's case. Was he simply rejecting her tactic, or did it mean…? His face gave away nothing.

"Why didn't Greer say that in court? He looked foolish."

"Ill-prepared is how he looked. I was the one who spoke with the registrar. After the sheriff's testimony. But at least we hadn't overlooked a suspect."

"How about the movie people?"

"They broke camp a week before the murder. I remember the date with punishing clarity." Again those sad eyes stared at his hands, and his lips nearly disappeared under the strain.

Yolanda prodded him, "There might have been stragglers. Or somebody could have returned."

"Absolutely impossible to know the answer to that. You can't rule out everybody. Who's to say a passing motorist didn't exit the Interstate at random, pick her house at random, rob her, kill her, then get back on the Interstate? It's possible, isn't it? Remember Sherlock Holmes? Once you eliminate the impossible, what's left is true? That's why he's fiction and not a policeman. Eliminating the impossible is the easy part. Finding the guilty among all the possibilities is where a detective earns his keep. And the possibilities are infinite. That's what my life has come to: eliminating the infinite."

They let their silence speak for itself within the happy college chatter. They didn't look at each other, but both faces had the same solemn look. If any students had glanced their way, they might have thought them an older couple having a fight.

"Another thing…" Victor said, then restarted, "A minute ago I told you wrong. I said that right now only Lovemore knows if he's guilty or innocent. There might be a second man who knows the answer to that. If there is, he's out there, somewhere. As this town's next sheriff, I could inherit an innocent man on death row, and a killer roaming free. And nothing I can do about either one."

Yolanda needed to intervene somehow in this admission of futility. This man's wife had broken his heart, and now his career was breaking his spirit. She took her hands from her chin and placed them gently over his hands. There was nothing she could say.

Victor tried to smile. Yolanda thought again of her father, in his porch rocker. Kind of quiet round here today.

Finally she said, "It'll soon be suppertime. Are you getting hungry?"

"Ah. I almost forgot. That's why I brought the paper. Let's see what Rollie has on this weekend." He took his hands from hers and opened the newspaper to the movie guide. "Maybe we can eat there, too. They sell hot dogs now, you know. With just about the best hot dog chili I've ever tasted."

"It was my mother's recipe." Of course he knew what that meant. He looked up at her, but she let it drop. She would save Mom for another day. She asked, "Find it?"

"*Scarlet Street*," he read. "Edward G. Robinson stars in a psychological drama in which a woman's lover is hanged for her murder while the real murderer is slowly destroyed by guilt."

"Whoa!" Yolanda said. "Those hot dogs better be pretty frickin' good."

When they stepped outside Fifi's French Press, Victor opened the newspaper and held it overhead as Yolanda leaned in toward him. Drops of rain splattered their faces, and storm clouds obscured the sky.

Driving home later that night, after the movie, and after a glass of wine at a damp table on the back terrace of the Lakeside Grill, Yolanda couldn't understand why Victor turned onto a side street that led, not toward Sycamore, but down Spruce and then over to Dogwood. She didn't ask. She just let him drive. They were driving down the street where Sarah Lester had lived, and died.

Victor said, "Some of the residents complained of unfamiliar cars parked along this street about the time of Sarah's murder."

Yolanda considered this, didn't say anything.

Victor continued, "You and Sarah are about the same age and you lived in the same neighborhood. I suppose you knew her well."

"Ever since grade school. Our whole family knew her whole family."

"Was anybody especially close to her?"

"Me, I guess. Even then not like best friends. Josh was a good friend of her brother, Ethan. Maybe you met him?"

"Only briefly, at the funeral. I've called him several times down in New Orleans."

"I hear he owns some kind of club down there."

Victor looked over at her. "He wasn't a suspect, if that's what you're thinking."

She laughed and held her hands up innocently. "Hey, I hardly knew the guy."

"So Josh would have known her. How about Rollie?"

"I don't think they had much contact. Flaky Rollie and Sunday School Sarah. They would have made quite a pair. Oh—except..." she said, and stopped. She felt Victor's gaze move from the empty street toward her face. "There was that one time in Paris."

"They went to Paris together?"

"God no. He was already there. A sort of hometown tour guide for her, already in place."

"And after that?"

"After that, nothing. They didn't seem to pick it up when he returned."

"I wonder why not?"

"Who knows? I suppose here she could read a menu without his help."

With Sarah's house in sight, Victor slowed the patrol car to an idle and pointed across the intersection to another of Twisting Creek's fading mansions. Beyond broken lattices and a collapsing trellis, Yolanda could make out light rimming a crinkled window shade.

Victor said, "There's a crazy old woman lives there. She talks in riddles. You should interview her. For your survey."

Tops in Sports: UK stops Hoosiers 27-14; Morehead loses to Dayton EKU rolls over UT-Martin *Details C-1*	A **HUGE** Twisting Creek welcome to the newest member of our business community: *Archer's Bait and Boat*, on New Lake Road.	Today's Weather: Will it never end? High 94, Low 78 Evening Storms

The Twisting Creek Guardian

ESTABLISHED 1882   Sunday, September 26   *The Voice of Reason in the Tri-State*

Race apparently the overriding opinion-maker

Guilty or Not? Local Residents Polls Apart

CHAPTER 10: MOTHER IN THE MIRROR

SUNDAY MORNING WAS Rollie's favorite time to visit Mom at Eastern State. The church crowd hadn't turned up yet, so getting a parking space wasn't an issue, but the parking lot wasn't as empty as on weekday mornings, when nearly everyone he saw was either paid or paying to be there. On Sundays Rollie was not all alone with white-nyloned nurses and a hundred and fifty patients hiding or hidden from the world outside.

He found Mom in her usual place, in a wheelchair an orderly had parked in a corner under a blaring TV. How could any doctor think anyone would find sanity in a ward of screaming TVs? Yet if he complained, the reply was always, "But the old people can't hear it if we turn the sound down," which, Rollie thought, might have been a step in the right direction. His mom didn't seem bothered by it. In fact, showing irritation, or recognition, or any other response, would have marked a breakthrough for her, but when Rollie greeted her she showed nothing. Her only movement was an inertia-fed jostle when he started to push her chair from the rackety hallway into her room.

A nurse came by and smiled. By now she knew that if it was Sunday, one of Mrs. Shanley's five children would visit. "Not a bit of change this week," she said, without being asked. "Oh, I figured out she likes it when people brush her hair. Or she seems to. Here," she took a hairbrush from a nightstand drawer, handed it to him, and left. The closing of the wide hospital door choked the television sound down to a murmur.

Rollie positioned his mother in front of her dresser mirror. He felt like a hairdresser. He wanted to say, *How would you like it today, Mrs. Shanley?* But he knew there would be no response, and what in this world is sadder than silence where there should be laughter?

He watched her face in the mirror as he started to smooth back her hair. He could see no sign of the nurse's predicted enjoyment. Or was there a twitch of relaxation in her neck? He said nothing for a long time. If Mom didn't want to talk, he saw no reason to push it. This wasn't like Brandon, where a little encouragement could conceivably produce results. Brandy was merely a late talker. Wasn't he? Or could this disdain for the spoken word somehow reach across generations?

Still, maybe talking was better than silence. He asked her, "Do you remember your grandson? He's named Brandon. That's right. You're a grandma now. Brandon lives at the old house now. I guess you knew that. Deedee's back, with Brandon. All five of your children are back at the old place. Plus the newest generation. Brandon doesn't talk either. Takes after his grandma, I guess."

He watched her eyes in the mirror. She rarely even blinked. He watched his fingers as they picked out silver strands of his mother's hair and exposed lines of clean, pink, healthy scalp. It was hard to think that only one layer down from there something had gone horribly wrong. There were secrets buried down there, secrets he needed to know.

"Let me ask you this, Mom." The face in the mirror showed nothing. She might have been deaf. How could they even check for that? "Before your…before you came in here, did you have times when you were too happy for it to be real? When it seemed like you had transcended this world and you felt so good you knew it was off-limits?" He realized he wasn't simply making conversation now. He needed answers, answers that this woman, half of his genetic base, might have supplied. He watched for a sign from the mute eyes in the mirror. None came, but he continued talking into the vacuum. "And then you soon grew wary of this happiness, because just when you started to feel that your own life and the whole universe were merging, you knew that soon the underpinning would collapse and you'd fall into a vacancy without any bottom? Did you sometimes feel that way, even back home, even when I was still small? Like even while you were planting a flower or stirring a pot of soup, you suddenly felt the approach of a destructive force so powerful that all it would leave behind was a void?"

He looked down at his hands and only now saw he'd bunched a strip of her hair into a tight fist. He released it and found strands of loose hairs in his hand. "Oh jeez, Mom. I'm so sorry. Did that hurt?"

The eyes in the mirror registered no pain.

CHAPTER 11: HOLD STILL. I'VE GOT BLOOD ON YOUR NECK.

It was Deedee's turn to cook Sunday Supper. The Shanley's Sunday evening meal was such an established institution that when they mentioned it in writing, as in emails or notes, they capitalized it. It had developed into a forum for discussing any family or business matters that arose. With Mom out of the picture, each sibling was essentially a twenty-percent shareholder in their father's legacy, so at times Sunday Supper took on the tone of a board meeting. Since they all shared a house, sometimes it was more of a condo committee meeting. One of the unwritten rules was that, barring extreme circumstances, all five of them needed to be present. Another was: no guests allowed. The exception was Brandon, who, as a Shanley, slipped through on a technicality. He could sit there until he grew belligerent, whereupon his poor nanny-of-the-month would be summoned to take him away. But that was it—the five of them, plus Brandon. During Yolanda's brief marriage, she came to Sunday Supper alone. Even Seth knew to make himself scarce.

Another institutionalized twist to Sunday Supper was the cooking rotation. Each sibling cooked every fifth week. The agreement was that you prepared whatever menu you wanted, and nobody should complain much if it went wrong. Ordering pizzas or a bucket of chicken was entirely acceptable. Edgar did that all the time. You could go with standards like meat loaf or pot roast (Yolanda's routine). You could experiment with recipes that called for exotic spices available only by online order (Josh). Or you could be as unpredictable as you wanted, switching from grilled cheese sandwiches one turn to chicken Kiev the next to sushi the next (Rollie, Deedee). The cook also set the table and set out drinks. Nobody else needed to help with anything. The idea was that each week's four non-cooks could completely relax before supper. It was perfectly fine to just show up, sit down and eat. The corollary was that once they sat down to eat, the cook's job was over. He or she could relax and enjoy the meal, in the certain knowledge that the workday had ended. This system required a secondary worker, the dessert-and-coffee- server/busboy/dishwasher, a job that also went in rotation. This position, which the Shanleys called the "afters", would be next week's cook, then for the next three weeks that person could simply show up, eat, and leave.

They all liked this plan. Josh had revised it from the system their father had devised some years earlier, when their mother had wearied of household tasks, and had alienated every possible domestic helper in eastern Kentucky. Originally it had been a daily plan, with each child preparing one supper in turn, Pops Woody on Saturday, a restaurant for Sunday lunch—or "Sunday dinner", as it was known—and a free-for-all on Sunday evenings. Although now it was a free-for-all every meal of the week except for Sunday Suppers, the system still carried with it the ghostly imprimatur of Pops Woody.

With this rotation schedule, the same cook and "afters" were always paired. Rollie always did afters when Deedee cooked, and usually he was there with her even before the meal, because he liked doing homemade desserts, especially fruit pies. Tonight, though, Deedee didn't expect to see him before dinner—it was just too damn hot. He would probably dish out ice cream with some special topping. One of his successes was made from raspberries, black walnuts and a mint chocolate liqueur imported from Holland. That was another thing she had in common with her oldest brother: they were the true dessert lovers of the family.

Standing at the stove with the exhaust fan running, she didn't hear him climb the steps from the back garden and cross the wooden floor of the deck.

He stopped just inside the kitchen door, set a dark-stained paper bag on the floor, and began to peel off a pair of long rubber gloves whose fingertips had been cut out. His own fingertips were bright red, with beads of blood. Brandon didn't look up at him. He was sitting in his playpen trying to stick a spring onion up his nose, and Deedee was stirring a deep pot of spaghetti sauce. Its steam added mass to the aroma of garlic and tomato sauce in the heavy kitchen air. The scent of yeast, too, permeated everything.

Rollie glanced at the bread machine, saw the red light on. A tall fan by the open window to the rear garden brought the smell of cut grass into the mix as it swept back and forth across the room, like a searchlight. He watched the breeze ruffle the hem of his sister's apron and lift strands of blond hair from her damp neck. He thought of his mother—not the husk of a woman now immured in Eastern State—but the mother of his early childhood, who at Deedee's age had stood in that same spot, stirring perhaps the same pot with the same spoon, maybe even wearing the same ruffled apron, certainly constricted within the same oppressive heat. Rollie, as the oldest child, had more vivid memories of his mother than the others did, and those memories always surfaced whenever he found Deedee leaning over the stove. Seen from the rear they could have been twins. At Brandon's age he had sat right there on the kitchen floor and watched the same scene. Was this like one of his classic films? You watch it again and again and it always comes out the same way? Or was it like one of his plays, where he could revise the ending?

Within the whir of the fans, Deedee didn't hear Rollie sneaking up behind her. He put his hands around her throat.

She screamed. Brandon looked up and laughed. Rollie laughed and clapped her on the shoulder. "What's cookin', sister?"

"God*damn* you!" Her spoon hand splattered tomato sauce over the counter. "I should smack you with this."

"No need for violence. I'm helping you rehearse for the part of Sarah Lester." He turned away from her to wash his hands in the sink.

"Don't even joke. You couldn't get me on that stage for love or money." She looked around at him. "My god, are your hands bleeding?"

"Mostly it's red stain, but I did stick myself a couple of times. I've been picking raspberries." He washed his hands, retrieved the paper bag and showed Deedee the contents. "Mom's Autumn Bliss are bearing up well in this late heat."

Neither said anything for a moment. They thought of their mother, not bearing up at all well in the late heat of her life, even as her handiwork thrived in the back garden.

"Uh-oh," Rollie said. "Hold still. I've got blood on your neck." He rinsed a cloth in cool water, wrung it out, and drew it down her neck where the apron fell open, then around her throat.

She eased her head back and sighed. "Wow, that feels nice. Why don't you stand there and do that while I cook."

"You really are flushed. I hope you're not getting overheated." He refreshed the cloth in cool water, wiped it across her shoulders and down her arms. "You know, though—I wasn't joking about you playing Sarah. You'd be perfect. You're beautiful, graceful in your movements. You've got Sarah's blond hair. You have a mellifluous voice."

"Mellifluous? Listen to Dr. Vocabulary."

"It means honeyed. In Italian honey is *miele*. Did you know that?"

"Of course."

"Liar."

"Maybe so, but here's one thing that's honest to god: I wouldn't get on that stage if my life depended on it. I've got worse stage fright than you do."

"In that case," he said, "you've got it bad."

"What a family. Two shrinking violets and three hams."

"The irony is that one of the shrinking violets is a playwright. A failed playwright, at that."

"Not for much longer!" she said, and held his gaze to watch him smile with his eyes. "How was the movie? Humphrey Bogart, right?"

"Edward G. Robinson. It was good. Great actress playing the femme fatale. Joan Bennett. Looked a lot like you."

"Yeah, right. Did she get murdered?"

"Of course."

"How was the house?"

"Nice little crowd last night. Seth made it an assignment for one of his classes, so that sold about twenty tickets. Today though, only a handful of customers. Oh—guess who showed up last night?" Deedee shrugged. "Deputy Victor Caraher with none other than...drum roll...Yolanda."

"No way!"

"Trust me."

"Like on a date?"

"I suppose so. She wasn't in handcuffs."

"Cool! More family scandal."

"Exactly what we need."

"She didn't mention him to me. Just yesterday morning I was telling her about this new guy I met, but not a word from her about her man in uniform."

Rollie gave her a big-eyed stare. "What new guy?"

"Oh...not yet. It's way early. It may come to nothing." She stopped at that.

Rollie let it drop. "What would you like for dessert?"

"I thought maybe it was too hot to bake."

"Nah. If you don't sweat in the kitchen, you're not a real chef. I was thinking raspberry tart with *pâte sablée*." Deedee gave him her one-raised-eyebrow look. He explained, "It just means a sweet, crumbly crust, almost like shortbread."

"Sounds good to me. I guess we'd better use up those raspberries."

"I've got a couple of pie shells already pressed out in the freezer. What are you making? Smells good."

"Tomato sauce for spaghetti."

"Smells different."

"I've put a secret ingredient in it. You'll have to guess." He moved toward her for a taste, but again she threatened him with her spoon. "Later! It's not ready yet."

"I bet I can identify it."

"Don't be so sure. Hey!" She recalled something. "I have a surprise for you. And an idea to go along with it. Here, stir this a minute—no fair tasting. I have to run up to my room."

Deedee hurried away. Rollie watched Brandon's reaction, expected a gamma-ray shriek, but...nothing. He was busy twisting the stem of his onion back and forth, looking for a configuration to fit both nostrils. When Deedee returned he held it up to show her the design he'd come up with.

"He's been very quiet lately," Rollie said.

"He likes stinky things. Apparently if we can keep him busy

sniffing stinky things until he matures, he'll go to law school."

"Is that some kind of lawyer joke I don't understand?"

"Maybe. I don't really understand it myself. But more to the point…here." She handed him a brown paper bag.

"What's this?"

"Open it."

Rollie put his hand into the bag and began to unroll a long strand of rope. When the noose end appeared he recoiled. "What the hell is this for?"

"You mean *who* the hell is it for."

"Deedee, not *him*!"

"No, not *him*, you booby. He's going to be a lawyer. It's for Lovemore!"

"What are you…?"

"I said there's an idea that goes with it. We were talking about how to end your play, right? Some kind of cheesy knock-off of an electric chair or whatever. Then a couple of days ago I came across this new store that sells boating supplies, and suddenly it hit me: Hang him! Nothing spooks people like a hanging. The noose, the gallows, the hangman's knot. They even hung Saddam Hussein, right?"

"But…"

"But nothing. Let me finish. There hasn't been a hanging in Kentucky since 1936. That's what you were going to say, right?"

"Well…"

"Only you didn't know the 1936 part, but I do. I looked it up. It's way anachronistic to use a noose. So here's my companion idea: change the setting to 1936. Have all the characters in 1936 clothing, all the men wearing felt hats, the women in those high waists and button shoes. Put Sarah Lester in a bonnet. Whatever they wore. I don't actually know that part. You'd know better than me, with all those old movies you watch."

It was fine rope. Rollie held the tight hangman's knot--a thick, velvet-skinned snake, coiled thirteen times. Gripping it was like holding a silk cylinder, or a woman's braided hair. It carried a message of mercy, a hint of purity, as though the designer didn't want to contaminate a human being's final moment with something as common as a neck burn.

"Good god. A costume drama."

"Listen—it'll have a more ominous atmosphere that way. Because they were lynching black men all the time back then. Put Greer in one of those old sheriff's uniforms and everybody will know he's classic racist right from the moment he walks on stage. It's got possibilities. Will you at least consider it?"

There was nothing to consider. At a flush Rollie was overcome. He had to fight back tears. Nobody had ever taken such an interest in his work. No one had ever believed it worth thinking about. And she was absolutely right. This was the ending the play was crying out for. He and Deedee were collaborators now. He walked toward her, put his arms around her and held her that way for a long time.

She put the side of her face to his chest and said, "I was thinking maybe at the end he can put the noose around his own neck and swing himself out over the stage. I'm sure there's some kind of rope contraption we can rig up to make that possible." She pulled her face away from her brother and looked up at him. "And I think I know just the man to do it."

Just then Edgar came in. "Jesus!" he said. "So this is what you two get up to in the kitchen."

"Don't worry, little bro," Rollie said. "If you come up with any great suggestions for my plays, I'll give you a big squeeze too."

"Thanks for the warning. What's for supper?"

Deedee listed, "Spaghetti with a surprise sauce, arugula salad, and fresh garlic bread."

"And raspberry tart."

"Sounds great to me," Edgar said. Edgar never met a food he didn't like. "Did you know real Italians don't eat bread with spaghetti?"

"And yet they have the nerve to call themselves Italians," Deedee said.

"Well, apparently. But hey, I'm not really here to discuss the menu. I wanted to tell you I checked on that land title for you. The new bait store. Remember you asked me?"

"Of course I remember."

"Sorry—no big sensational story. The same family has owned it for the past thirty years. Some guy named Marvin Archer bought it as soon as the state put it up for sale, and now a Travis Archer owns it. He took title last year. I guess the old man died. That's all I know. Did you think there was more to it than that?"

"Maybe. I don't know." She turned back to look down into the pot she was stirring. "It just seemed so odd. You step inside this spooky old half-way falling down log cabin, and all of a sudden you're in a shiny new world. It's just weird, that's all."

"I guess it isn't so weird after all. Sorry."

"No need for sorry. I'm fine with everything being exactly as it appears."

CHAPTER 12: "MY MOMMA SAYS IT'S NOT NICE TO CALL YOU A NIGGER."

YOLANDA HEARD THEM talking in the kitchen but didn't take the time to join in. She was on her way to Dogwood, the street where Sarah Lester had been born and where, thirty years later, she died. She wanted to visit Victor's crazy old woman who talks in riddles, and she planned to walk the five blocks—screw the heat—because a strolling neighbor who stops for a chat seems less threatening than a stranger who parks a car and heads up the front walk.

Nearing the corner of Dogwood and Spruce, she saw a sugar maple that had already started to change color. The sight of that tree, stubbornly demanding its right to follow the calendar into fall, no matter what the temperature was, seemed to be a message that Yolanda was doing the right thing, that certain procedures had to be followed even if the prevailing attitude was to ignore them. Under the maple, a middle-aged black woman in a folding chair was reading the Guardian. This, too, seemed a sign.

"Hi there," Yolanda called.

The woman lowered her newspaper. "Hello."

"How do you like that front page?" A glimmer of suspicion crossed the woman's face. Yolanda widened her smile to indicate that she would make it all clear. "I work for the Guardian. I happened to design that front page, and that graphic."

The woman looked down at blindfolded Lady Justice holding the balance of public opinion in her bi-racial hands. "Is this your name here? Yolanda Shanley?"

"Yes, ma'am. I work there. I took that survey. Does it surprise you that opinion is so divided?"

"Not really. All my friends think he's getting sold down the river. You know what that means, don't you?"

"Yes ma'am, I do." It was an expression from the days of slavery. A slave shipped down the Mississippi River was sent from a bad situation—tobacco field slavery in Kentucky or Tennessee—into a worse one—cotton field slavery in Alabama or Mississippi. "My paper wants to find out what people think, and get it out in the open."

"I can't see anything wrong with that." She stood up and put out her hand. "I'm Felicia Lewis. Let's go up on the porch. I'll get you a glass of ice tea. If you've got a minute."

Alone for a moment on the porch, Yolanda looked through a screened window into a living room that seemed to have been furnished a century earlier—all cushions, fringes, heavy mahogany furniture and musty drapery. In the space that in most homes would hold a television, there was a big wooden chest-style radio that collectors would eagerly bid for. She was still peeking through the window when Felicia came out with two glasses of tea. "I was admiring your radio. Does it work?"

"Hasn't worked for years. It's not really mine, anyway. I just stay here and take care of Odessa. Odessa Dean. This is her house."

"Is she getting on in years?"

"Older than Methuselah. And you know how old that was."

"Not exactly. But I know it was *old* old."

They laughed. "She's sick, poor old thing. She's got the Alzheimer's. Most of the time doesn't know her own name."

"Where is she now?"

"Taking a nap. I just looked in on her. I have to check every five minutes or she'll be trying to set fire to a box of corn flakes or something."

"So she won't be any help in my survey."

"You mean about Lovemore? I can answer that for her. She thinks he's the berries."

"She knows him?"

"He worked right over there, you know." She pointed catty-cornered across the street. "That's where Sarah Lester lived. I guess you know that."

"Oh, yes. I visited her there many times. We were classmates all through school."

"And you know he was working there for her. One day the wind brought down a big limb in that pin oak right there, over our sidewalk. I asked him if he would help me pick it up just to lay it out of the way until the city could haul it away. While we were doing that Odessa came out and saw him, and didn't she come *bounding* down those steps like a young girl! She hugged him and started into kissing him all over his face. The poor man was mortified. I bet he never had such a reception from a strange old white woman in all his born days. She kept calling him 'Tim.' Must have been some kid she knew way back."

"How did he react?"

"He was nice about it. She says, 'I been missing you, Tim' and he says 'Me too, madam.' He smiled at me over her shoulder, where she couldn't see. He understood she wasn't right in the head."

Just then the screen door opened and Odessa Dean stepped onto the porch. Her hair was long and white, but still mottled with dark streaks. A tortoiseshell comb had fallen out and was hanging from the ruffled collar of her dressing gown, which in turn was hanging from her shoulders by one button about three holes away from where it belonged. The hem of the misshapen gown revealed two wrinkled legs no bigger around than icicles, and the same blue-tinged shade of white. All her color seemed to have pooled in her bare feet, which were as purple as petunias, streaked with black veins.

"Look, Odessa—we've got company. This is Yolanda Shanley."

"Miss Shanley!" the old woman said, approaching Yolanda for a hug. "It's been much too long."

Felicia stepped between them. "Let's go get you fixed up."

"I want to talk a while to Harriet. Doesn't she look as pretty as a picture?"

"Let's pretty you up some, too. She'll wait, won't you Miss Shanley?"

"Sure. I'll be right here." When Odessa Dean turned toward the door, Yolanda noticed that she tucked her eyes down and toward the welcome mat on the floor, away from the direction of Sarah Lester's house. Yolanda stopped her. "Just a moment, please. Do you remember Sarah Lester?"

"No, don't..." Felicia tried to prevent the question, but Odessa Dean's body had already started a pattern of spasms, a sort of rapid stuttering between wild jerks and rigidity. "Oh," Felicia said, "I wish you hadn't done that. Ever since the police and ambulance sirens, she has been terrified of that house." She took the old trembling body in her arms.

Then came the sobs, and the incoherent screams that Victor Caraher had alluded to. "Smoking black soldiers' willies! Smoking black soldiers' willies! I hear with my ears! I see with my eyes! I smell with my nose! I taste with my tongue! Smoking black soldiers' willies!"

Felicia led her toward the door. Again Odessa Dean went through the hear-see-smell-taste litany, this time pointing with each phrase to her ear, eye, nose and mouth. "It's a memory exercise the visiting nurse teaches her," Felicia explained.

It seemed to calm her down. Yolanda stood watching at the porch window while Felicia led Odessa Dean through the living room and into an internal corridor. By that time the sobs had already subsided into whimpers. It seemed Alzheimer's limited the memory of everything, even terror.

Uninvited, Yolanda entered the house. The living room was a museum piece for gracious pre-World-War-Two southern life, a world now dimly remembered, and then only by the very old. And, thought Yolanda, as the very mass of the furniture confined her curiosity to a set path, Good riddance to it. She strolled through the living room as at an antique dealer's exhibit, her mind barely registering the dingy silk shade of a brass reading lamp, or the inlaid swans under the glass cover of a coffee table. Most of her thoughts went to *Smoking black soldiers' willies!* What the *fuck* was that all about? Was that the riddle Victor was trying to puzzle out? Why would he even think it had anything to do with Sarah's murder? Simply because one poor demented creature screamed it out every time she looked across the street toward Sarah's house?

Now it fell to Yolanda to make sense of it. Smoking black soldiers' willies! The only possible literal meaning had to be... but no, she couldn't mean that. Could she? Could the "Tim" she saw in Lovemore have been a black soldier she'd once loved? A very far-fetched notion. Could she even have ever heard the word 'willy" used to mean a penis? Wasn't it mostly British? For Americans didn't it come from...I don't know...Monty Python or somewhere? A venerable southern lady couldn't possibly mean that, not even ten miles deep in Alzheimer's.

But it was a hilarious phrase to hear issue from a woman with Odessa Dean's background. *Smoking black soldiers' willies!*

Yolanda was mostly thinking about that. She was in front of that huge radio, as imposing as a butcher's block, when Felicia returned with Odessa just behind her. Odessa now looked utterly composed, her momentary panic as forgotten as every other event in her life for the past fifty years. Had this ancient lady of standing, even in her most delirious, Freudian dreams, ever smoked a black soldier's willy? Good god, no. It was too absurd.

Odessa told Yolanda, "Amos and Andy are my favorites."

She's reading my mind! Yolanda thought. But then she realized that the old radio, and not black willies, had occasioned the remark. "They were white," Yolanda said. "Did you know that?" It was the one and only tidbit she knew about old-time radio.

"No, dear," Odessa laughed at such a lapse. "They were colored men. You're thinking of Lum and Abner."

Yolanda sent a quick glance toward Felicia to see if the "colored men" had offended her, but she showed no reaction until she noticed Yolanda looking at her. Then Felicia said, "She thinks she's being polite. One day she told me big as you please, 'My momma says it's not nice to call you a nigger. I'm supposed to call you colored.'"

"Well, yes, I guess in her time…"

"You want to hear something funny? One day I was talking to Lovemore on this very subject."

"You *knew* him?"

"After that tree limb, he helped out with a few other odd jobs. He said over there where he comes from, even with as much trouble as they had with white people, *nigger* doesn't bother people so much. They have another word. *Kaffir*, he said. That's what gets people riled up over there. Now it's illegal in his country to even say the word *kaffir*." She chuckled. "I guess I could be arrested right now. Isn't it funny what gets people's goat, and what doesn't?"

"My dad used to say, 'Call me anything you want, just don't call me late for dinner.'"

"He was a good man, your daddy. A friend to all."

There was always a moment of silence after such a statement, then Yolanda asked, "So tell me about Lovemore. Did he seem like a violent man?"

"Exactly the opposite. He was the gentlest, sweetest thing you could ever hope to meet. Soft-spoken, polite. In Africa he studied in a missionary school and could quote the Bible. It's not possible he killed anybody."

"But that's what you always hear when they catch some madman. You know what I mean? A neighbor says he always seemed like a polite, quiet man, even though the guy has fifty human livers in his basement freezer."

Felicia laughed and Odessa copied her, clapping her hands.

"Amos and Andy," Odessa said. "Jaw sugar buzzy! Lum & Abner! Jaw sugar buzzy!"

Felicia Lewis shrugged her shoulders.

"RCA Victor," Yolanda said, nodding at the radio. "I bet it's worth a lot of money. Who'll get all this when…when the time comes?"

"You've asked a million dollar question there. I have no idea."

"Doesn't she have any family?"

"She's got a brother, Lucius Dean. But he's older than she is."

"Where does he live?"

"Right here in Twisting Creek. Over at Presbyterian Assisted Living."

"So if he only needs assisted living, that means he's not as bad off as…his sister. Does he visit?"

"Not hardly. Once in a blue moon. She doesn't recognize him, so what's the point?"

Yolanda nodded. Seeing sick old people always forced her to consider her ultimate philosophy. What, indeed, was the point? What was the point of anything? What's the point may *be* the point. We're all heading for Presbyterian Homes or dementia or Eastern State or a wheelchair on the front porch. Or something equally unthinkable. Then an eternity of nothing. What would happen in that blink of an eye between now and then? Lovemore would be convicted and executed. Newspapers would go the way of RCA Victor radios. Smoking willies riddles would prove meaningless. Victor Caraher would satisfy himself as to Sarah Lester's true murderer, whether Lovemore or someone else. Or else he would not. In any case, they would all grow old, die, and be forgotten.

She needed to shake loose from this mood. From somewhere far back in the house came the faint ringing of a cell phone.

Odessa popped out with, "By grannies! By grannies!"

"She always says that when the phone rings," Felicia said. "God knows why. Did I leave my purse upstairs? I'm getting as bad as her. Excuse me."

Alone now with Odessa, Yolanda watched a wide smile cross her face. "I hear with my ear," she said, pointing. "I see with my eye."

By the time Yolanda got home, Deedee had the dining room in order. All the food was laid out on a golden oak sideboard that had been sitting in the same spot through four or five generations of Shanleys. Its drawers and bottom doors had warped shut, and its mirror had clouded into a sort of avant-garde abstract slab, but it admirably held Sunday Supper buffets, and no one would have dreamed of replacing it. It had two side shelves, each at the perfect pouring height for wine from a box. It was as though the original purchaser, perhaps even the great progenitor Orval Shanley himself, had foreseen hard times for his descendants and knew that good Kentucky bourbon and French cognac would one bleak day give way to cheap Chilean box wine.

Josh and Edgar were already seated, Deedee was loading Brandon onto a booster seat, and Rollie was heaping salad onto his plate. Yolanda lined up behind him, loaded her plate and helped herself to a glass of white.

Brandon made a preliminary yelp, a test probe into the enemies' defenses, but Deedee was ready with a peeled clove of garlic, which she stuck up his nose. She placed a back-up clove on his tray, which he promptly inserted into his other nostril.

"No, take that one out," Deedee said.

"Parenting tip," Edgar announced. "Children should only stick garlic up one nostril at a time."

Brandon started to protest, but Deedee produced his new lure, which she had kept hidden in her apron pocket for just such a moment. Brandon gleefully grabbed it and banged it a few times against his forehead.

Deedee announced. "There. He'll be fine now. Don't make me explain."

"If you say so," Josh said. He raised his glass. "Cheers, everybody."

They dug in.

"Holey moley," Yolanda said. "There's something funny in this sauce."

"Not bad," Edgar said. "But what is it?"

"We're supposed to guess," Rollie said.

"Something sea-foody," Josh said.

"Beats me," Edgar said. "I give up."

Deedee asked "Anybody want to take a stab at it?"

Yolanda tried, "That fake crab—what's it called?"

"I don't know what it's called, but that's not it."

Rollie guessed, "Canned lobster?"

"No. It's crawdads!"

Everybody stopped eating for a moment, then Yolanda asked, "What gave you the idea of putting crawdads in spaghetti sauce, anyway?"

"I don't know—the mood just struck me, I guess. What do we call them, anyway?"

Yolanda shrugged and glanced around the table. "Crawdads, I guess. If I call them anything"

That was the consensus.

Rollie said, "I think that *crayfish* is the, like, official name. I remember in France I looked up *écrevisse* and found *crayfish*. Then I had to find an English dictionary and look up *crayfish*."

"So who calls them *crawfish*?" Deedee asked.

"They're crawfish in Louisiana," Josh said, and sang, "*Jambalaya, a crawfish pie and filet gumbo*. Up north, too, I think."

"Michigan, maybe?"

Josh said, "I'm guessing yes. Why do you ask?"

"No real reason," she said. "Mostly curiosity."

Edgar looked up. "You know what that did to the cat."

Deedee looked down at her plate, but everyone saw that her face had turned bright red.

Yolanda jumped in, "Then it's a damn good thing a cat has nine lives. Don't we have anything better to talk about than linguistic trivia?"

"In fact we have a huge decision to make," Josh said, "but I'm waiting until after we've enjoyed a nice meal."

This announcement assured that no one would enjoy a nice meal. Nobody said anything else until Josh asked, "Whose Sunday was it to visit Mom?"

Rollie had his mouth full, so he raised his hand.

"Any change?"

He shook his head, swallowed, took a sip of wine. "Not one bit. Didn't say a word. She might have enjoyed it when I brushed her hair. At least she kept her head up instead of letting it droop. Her eyes followed me around the room. Modified catatonic state, they called it." This was hardly news. One of them had delivered much the same report for several months. "Oh, her hair's turned bright silver, just in the five weeks since I saw her last. You think somebody put a rinse on it?"

Yolanda said, "I doubt it. It was starting that way when I saw her last."

Josh said, "Does that mean in thirty years the five of us will be sitting here around this table with our heads shining like streetlights?"

Again they all fell to silent eating.

Finally Rollie said, "Oh, I have better news. I've changed the title of *Death on Stage* to *Stage Death*, and Deedee's come up with a brilliant ending for it." He reached under his chair for the brown paper bag. "Remember I was struggling with the finale? A lethal injection isn't dramatic enough, and can we reasonably expect to find an actor who can fake an electric chair sizzle every night? So...how about this?" He showed them the noose.

Josh jumped, almost stood straight up. "You're not going to lynch him!"

"Of course not. We're going to move the trial to the 1930s, when the death penalty meant hanging. It'll be a period drama. How about that?"

"You're going to hang a black man? In Twisting Creek?" Josh said. "You *cannot* do that. It's a hideous idea."

"Come on, Josh. It's a play. It's theater."

"It's ludicrous. Every news outlet in the country will pick up on it."

"I can see it now," Edgar said, framing a headline in the air with his fingers. *Lynching in Twisting Creek.* The name Twisting Creek alone will guarantee nationwide publicity. And you know what they say about bad publicity."

"Yes, Edgar," Josh said, "but not everybody is as cynical as you are."

Edgar said, "Some might call me a realist, but you're the managing editor."

Rollie stepped in, "I'll tell you what, let's none of us pass judgment until we see how it plays out. If it's tasteful and effective, we'll keep it. It could even be seen as a condemnation of the death penalty. After all, the state really is proposing to kill Lovemore. Kill him really dead. But after our actor is hanged, he gets up and takes a bow."

"It was my idea," Deedee said, "so bawl me out, not him. But he's right. This whole modern system of hiding the condemned in a little room and injecting him might look less grisly, but it only allows society to hide from the awful truth. The dude's just as dead."

They all seemed to consider these points. There was a common, unvoiced agreement to let the matter rest there until they could see how the scene unfolded. They finished their meal, hardly breaking the silence. Yolanda did mention that she liked Brandon a lot better with garlic up his nose.

Deedee's work was done. Rollie brought in dessert on a cart, along with coffee and several types of liqueur he liked to keep on hand, in spite of the cost. No one had said much since the rumpus about the noose.

This time Josh really did stand up. It was a gesture that said, This is big.

"So," he said. "Where to start? We all know that we have to find a solution to our cash flow situation. The only strategy I thought might work, didn't. To explain to Deedee, who wasn't here at the time, we had hoped that by buying our own paper mill and installing a digital printing system—running it not only for the Guardian, but also as an outsource for other regional publications—we could turn things around. With the estimated cost in the millions, we needed a bank loan. But when First Security refused to take the risk, we had to rethink.

"At the moment, in fact, we've caught a little updraft, mainly thanks to the Lovemore trial, and I'd like to think that many of our new subscribers will stay with us when the trial ends. But here's what we need to discuss tonight: have we been pandering to the conventional view that Lovemore is a cruel and wicked beast? I mean, we haven't gone that far, but we certainly haven't raised any big questions about the handling of the investigation, have we? And now that we've heard courtroom testimony that is, to my mind anyway, unconvincing, should we not take a more courageous stand?

"I know what you're thinking: Too late now. The jury is sequestered and the trial is about over. But my point concerns the death sentence. If he is sentenced to death, should we stake out a position against it? It would mean asking a lot of questions that will raise hackles all over our distribution area. You saw yesterday's survey stats. We'd have to brace ourselves for the loss of many, many subscribers."

Josh paused to let that part sink in, but held out his hand to indicate that he hadn't yet finished.

"There's more. We all know what ICNA is. Well, Rollie might not. They call themselves the Independent Community Newspapers of America, but it is in fact one big corporation that has purchased more than a hundred small-to-medium-sized papers like ours. There aren't many family-owned newspapers left. We've become the oddity. Now ICNA wants us too. I can't give you an exact dollar amount right now, but I calculate that if we sell up, lock, stock and barrel—the Guardian, the Odeon, this house, everything that ties us to Twisting Creek—we'll walk away with over two million dollars apiece."

"Apiece?" Deedee asked.

"Each and every one of us. After taxes. Over two million each. Probably well over. However, we have to choose—and we have to choose right now: do we oppose a Lovemore execution, or do we sell?"

"We can't do both?" Again it was only Deedee who spoke up.

"No, we can't, and here's why. If by supporting Lovemore we lose as much revenue as I think we will, our value to ICNA will drop proportionally."

"And there goes our cool two mil," Edgar said.

Josh gave everybody time to ponder the choice they were facing, then suggested, "One thing we can be sure of—an ICNA run Guardian will never challenge the DA or public opinion on a case like this. If we sell, and Lovemore goes on Death Row, he'll get no help from ICNA. So, shall we go around the table and have our say, one by one?"

"I'll go first," Rollie said. "I wouldn't mind two cool mil, as Edgar puts it, and I'm not even in the newspaper biz. I'd miss the Odeon, but it's not my life. So selling up doesn't sound all that horrible to me. However, I will offer my two cents on the Lovemore issue. There's one thing I know—I can't tell you how I know this, and even this much cannot leave this room—but Sarah Lester was not the saintly Sunday school teacher she's cracked up to be."

Deedee looked at her oldest brother. Of all the family, he had the least to lose by selling to ICNA, and the most to gain, not to mention the stake he had in Lovemore receiving the death sentence. Without a dramatic conclusion, *Stage Death*, the work that was supposed to make him famous, would end with a whimper. Yet here he was, voting to forego his millions and to neuter his play, all because something wasn't quite right with the investigation. She reached out to take his hand.

Deedee didn't release his hand as she spoke next. "I guess I was too young to get the full force of Pops Woody's sermons on the First Amendment. To be honest, I see newspapers as any other product that has its day and then dies. I've thought a lot about this. Imagine if we owned a factory that made cassette tapes or typewriters or something, how would we react if somebody offered us big money for it? We'd be skipping to the bank. Cassette tapes get replaced by CDs and then they lose out to iPods and so on. It happens. People get their news on TV and the Internet. Maybe it's their loss, but it's their choice."

"It's the community's loss…"

"Wait, Josh. I'm not finished. So I'm not wedded to journalism like you three are. God knows being the Guardian ad lady is about as rewarding as digging turnips for a living. But if a man in our town is getting railroaded, we can't sit back and watch it happen. Now, that's my say."

Josh said, "Thank you, Deedee. Edgar, what's your take on it?"

"Hey, I think he's guilty. The sheriff certainly thinks so."

Deedee interrupted. "Edgar—sorry to butt in, but this needs to be cleared up before anything else. Some people say Greer's a flat out racist. What do you all think about that?"

Yolanda said, "A racist sheriff wouldn't have a black chief deputy."

"That's the second time this week I've heard that argument," Deedee said. "Couldn't it be a convenient shield against charges just like this?

"Victor Caraher seems to respect him." Yolanda said. "Maybe we're wrong to buy the stereotype."

Edgar said, "Most people are wrong about Greer. I think I know him pretty well. He's old school. He's a born hillbilly and still talks like one. Still *tawks lack* one."

"Maybe playing the yokel is good for votes," Yolanda said.

"Exactly," Edgar continued. "The sheriff is the last of those cops who could make it to the top with no more than a high school diploma, experience, and slapping a lot of voters on the back. But my take on him is he's a conscientious and honorable lawman. He's no racist. Plus, I happen to agree with his basic logic: a man threatens a woman's life at 6:00 and she's dead by 8:00. *Duh!*"

"So you say sell?" Josh asked.

"I don't say that at all. The whisper in my ear is that DA Reynolds is trying to parley a death sentence into statewide office. She sees this trial as part of her political campaign. First of all, to me, that sucks. Second, it's not just her. A whole bunch of other people can't believe the luck this case has brought. The sheriff gets to end his career under the spotlights. Leo Akers gets a very public encore. Why else did he take it *pro bono*? Almost everybody in Twisting Creek, black and white both, can enjoy righteous indignation over this. And look at us, sitting here counting up our bottom line. About the only person without a piece of the windfall is Lovemore himself."

Nobody challenged him on that, so Edgar continued, "And

third, I think Lovemore plays the piano."

"You what?"

"A janitor down at the courthouse tells me that they've just carried one of those little pianos into the evidence room by the courtroom."

"And this tells you…"

"The gloves! Prosecution says Lovemore wore gloves to keep his prints off Sarah's skin. It backs up their claim of premeditation, which they need for the death penalty. I suspect he wore gloves because he values his hands."

Rollie said, "He was gardening, wasn't he? Most people wear gloves when they garden."

"Wrong. He told Greer he was gardening, but according to the eavesdropping neighbor the argument was about painting the bedroom. And do you remember what old man Evans heard him say about it? That he also did a lot of unpaid work in the bedroom. That means sex, right? They really were lovers. That wasn't just some nasty rumor the defense put out."

"Trust me," Rollie said. "Sarah was no vestal virgin."

Edgar said, "But that's not even my main point. Leo Akers hinted to me that their strategy isn't to try the case on the evidence. He wants the trial itself to be on trial. He wants this to be a test case against racial verdicts in modern Kentucky." Edgar held up his hand. "Bear with me. Therefore, he wants to show the jury that Lovemore is a refined, educated man. Not some feckless, half-steppin' immigrant freeloader. You know Akers and his dramatic flair—you wait and see. He'll have Lovemore playing Beethoven in court before this trial is over."

"So," Josh persisted. "Did I miss a yea or nay in there?"

"Screw ICNA," Edgar said. "Lovemore may be guilty, but this thing is being stage-managed for all its worth. Let's say so."

"I'm not going to disagree with that," Yolanda said. "Mainly because I didn't follow much of it."

They all laughed. Even Brandon celebrated the comic relief by sneezing. His garlic shot onto his tray and bounced onto the table. This was funny enough to merit a good fling of his lure across the table at Josh. Deedee quickly shoved her spare clove of garlic up his nose.

Rollie addressed Yolanda. "Aren't you going to mention last night? Because if you don't, I will."

"I thought you might. So yes, last night I suppose I went out on a date. It didn't start out as a date, but it sort of morphed into one. Thanks to your stupid movie, in fact."

"I accept full credit."

"This date was with none other than Victor Caraher."

"Oooh," Edgar said. "And did you uncover any...police secrets?".

"Ignoring your smutty double entendre, no, I didn't pick up much. Apparently some residents along Dogwood reported strange cars parked there. But that doesn't mean much."

"A lot of people park there," Josh said. "From Main Street, it's either the first or second street after the paid parking zone ends. It's only a short walk to the post office and library. I park there myself sometimes, if I'm not in a hurry and don't want to feed the meters."

"Me, too," Yolanda said. "Also, there's an old neighbor of Sarah's who goes absolutely ballistic every time the murder is mentioned, and she's not the least bit afraid of Lovemore. But she's got Alzheimer's and if she knows anything at all, nobody can decipher it. So...what can I say? Victor was scrupulous in saying nothing to discredit the investigation. But still I picked up little vibes that he isn't one hundred percent convinced of Lovemore's guilt. In short, I agree with what Edgar put so succinctly: screw ICNA. We need to ask some questions."

Nobody said anything to adjourn the meeting, momentous as it was. They all sat there a while longer, scraping remnants of raspberries and cream from their plates and draining the dregs of their drinks. Soon Rollie said, "I'm on afters," and started collecting plates.

"Can I help?" Yolanda asked.

"No, I've got it."

Everyone started to stir. Only Yolanda remained seated. Before anyone left the dining room, Josh told them all, "I'm proud to be part of this family."

Indeed that was the general sense, but it was a quiet, almost gloomy pride. Five people had just voted to kiss off several million dollars, and they all knew they'd never in their lives have the opportunity to undo that vote.

Rollie didn't mind doing afters. He liked it when all the others went off to read or watch TV, or whatever they did with the weekend's waning minutes, and left him alone in the big kitchen with just the one light on over the sink. He enjoyed the solitude of the whirring fan and the backyard crickets, so when, for the second time, Yolanda offered a hand, and Rollie said he was fine, he meant it, and thought that was that. However, a good forty-five minutes later, after he'd finished with the kitchen and locked up the back of the house, and was heading through to the dining room to check the rest of the house, when he found her still sitting there just as he'd left her, all alone at the dining room table, he understood.

He sat down opposite her. "I thought you'd gone upstairs."

"Nah. Too much going on upstairs. Upstairs here, I'm talking about," She tapped her temple.

"About the paper?"

"That's just one thing."

"About Victor Caraher?"

She looked up at him and smiled. "Seems silly, doesn't it? Your thirty-year-old divorced sister sitting at the dinner table stewing over a possible new boyfriend."

"It doesn't seem silly at all."

Yolanda laughed, and he joined her, because, in fact, it did seem silly. Rollie added, "Well, kinda, maybe, a little."

She cut her laughter short and sat up straight. "But the thing is, it all ties together. The Guardian, Victor, the trial."

"Our cool two mil."

Yolanda twisted her mouth. "Our ticket out of here."

"Apparently we don't want out all that badly."

"Apparently not. Though it's hard to say why."

"Maybe we'd miss the spaghetti à la crawdad."

She gave a little laughing sigh that died quickly. Her mouth registered something between pain and resignation. It was unusual to see Yolanda this way, yet as Rollie thought about it he realized that her mood was but a portion of the creeping frailty that seemed to be infecting the whole family, with Pops Woody's stroke and Mom's breakdown only its most visible expressions. Was frailty itself a family legacy? Was their strength of purpose, so recently displayed, already streaked with brittle fault lines of surrender?

Yolanda said, "I know what ties it all together—one demented old woman. That's exactly the link I've been trying to make."

"You don't mean Mom?"

"No. Or, yes—maybe in a way I do. For both of them, for all of us, no matter what you do for your whole life, as you near the end you always arrive at some shit-hole ending. No wonder people came up with the idea of an afterlife in paradise. No wonder belief outsells non-belief by a blue million to one."

"Thirty to one, to be precise."

"What do you mean?" Yolanda asked.

"Believers outnumber atheists thirty to one. In America, anyway."

"Where did you hear that?"

"I read it in the Guardian. You probably wrote it."

"Sounds more like some of Edgar's mischief."

"And that's what's got you like this? Some distant threat of senile dementia?"

"No. What's got me like this is one very specific and very present old woman with Alzheimer's. It's just that…she's trapped. She's desperate to reveal something important, but she doesn't even know she knows it, or that she can't explain it. She can only sense that something evil has taken control. It's so eerie. It's like there's this woman in there, still alive, her mind and emotions functioning fine, to a peak, even, yet she's forced to try to communicate through the mouth of this corpse, and the words come out as words all right, but the message is totally garbled." She paused there, said, "Aw, hell, Rollie, I don't know," and made darting looks around the room. Rollie thought she was about to give it up and go to bed, but then a new energy took control and she said, "Listen—tell me what this means to you: *jaw sugar buzzy.*"

Rollie shrugged.

"How about *smoking black soldiers' willies.*"

"Um…did we just toke up on some shit so good I don't remember smoking it?"

"See? There's only one possible meaning in those words, and that meaning can't mean anything. And the way she says it, it's like inside her there's this oracle screaming cryptic warnings through her own mouth, and even she can't decipher them. I can hear her bewilderment. It's the force behind the scream."

When Yolanda sat still, she simply sat still. She didn't twitch, hardly blinked an eye. Rollie rearranged himself in his chair a couple of times, then went into the kitchen and returned with two glasses and a bottle of cognac. He showed it to Yolanda, who put up her hand. He put the bottle and glasses on the table.

"So," he said. "Aren't you sleepy?"

She didn't even acknowledge the question. "I'll tell you who it is and why maybe it matters." Rollie poured them each a drink after all. She accepted hers. "Her name's Odessa Dean and she was a neighbor of Sarah's ever since before there was a Sarah. She was so spooked by the murder that even today she can't so much as glance at Sarah's house without getting hysterical. I think she knows something."

"Maybe you just want to think she knows something. It would be understandable, given how little we really do know."

"I get the feeling that Victor also thinks…no, *thinks* is probably too strong a word. He intuits she witnessed something. That's all. Her nursing aide says it was simply the ambulance and all the police activity that traumatized Odessa."

"That would explain it."

"Listen—you know some people out at Presbyterian Homes, right?"

"They run a mini-bus to the Odeon on Tuesday afternoons. Some of the residents remember these movies from their childhood. I worked out group rates with the management."

"Tomorrow, let's go over there together. Odessa has a brother living there. He visits her on Dogwood occasionally. Maybe he can decipher her hieroglyphics. Or maybe he saw what she saw, and didn't know what he saw."

Bengals defeat Denver, run record to 3-0	Today's Weather:
Carolina outlasts Jaguars 10-9	Fall Weather at last???
Atlanta-Tampa Bay tonight 8:30, ESPN	High 70, Low 58
Full NFL Report, C-2	Goodbye humidity!!!

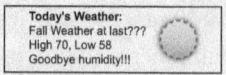

The Twisting Creek Guardian

| ESTABLISHED 1882 | Monday, September 27 | *The Voice of Reason in the Tri-State* |

Does he plan to put Lovemore Ngwenya on the stand?

Trial In Recess; What's Up Akers' Sleeve?

CHAPTER 15: "GO DER!"

ROLLIE WOKE BEFORE dawn and lay in bed thinking about Deedee. How was it that she, his near-stranger little sister, who had returned to Sycamore in such desperation—people of another day might have said in such disgrace—how could she now be the dearest person in his life?

He wasn't one to analyze his isolated approach to life, and didn't dwell on it now. He was dimly aware that even during childhood, when having a best friend was almost a requirement, he had a new one every few weeks. Later it was the same with girlfriends. His two-week stint with Sarah Lester was at the shorter extreme, yet wasn't his shortest, and even his longest could be counted in months.

When he thought about it, he saw no need for a complex explanation. The world was full of traitors who would slice your neck in the name of love and friendship. Why would anybody expose themselves to that? People rejected you, and even though really it was their loss, it felt like your loss. In fact, it felt like someone was dipping your brain into a vat of boiling acid. So Rollie operated quite happily as the lone wolf, thank you. Yet here comes Deedee, first commandeering the house, and now his play, perhaps even his heart, and certainly today's pre-dawn thoughts. A collaborator—that's what she was. Better than a friend. In her case it included friendship, and extended it.

He shouldn't be thinking so clearly, so early. He shouldn't even be awake. He had stayed up last night even after Yolanda went to bed. Past midnight he'd worked on Deedee's idea of placing *Stage Death* in the nineteen-thirties. It had so many possibilities, yet he ran into one obstacle after another. He could eliminate references to television and so on. That part was easy. South Zambezi itself could become South Rhodesia—although how many black men in Kentucky a hundred years ago were willing immigrants from Africa? But the real sticking point was Abel Magwimbi. An African escaping persecution in 1930 would have been escaping white persecution. Even ignoring the absurdity that they would seek refuge in the American South, for Rollie to replace a black tyrant with a white one would seem cowardly, even condescending. Rollie had noted that when utopian liberators—Marxists, Maoists, Zionists, nationalists, medieval popes or modern African Presidents for Life—when any of them finally took power, they turned out to be just like everybody else. To substitute Cecil Rhodes for Abel Magwimbi would be cowardly, and unfair to the human reality.

After thinking all this through, he was surprised to notice that his window shade had turned a dull yellow, and even more surprised to notice that sometime during the night he had pulled a sheet over himself. He got up, switched off the ceiling fan, and opened the shade. A refreshing breeze lifted the curtains and he heard a catbird squawk at something in the poplar outside his bedroom window. In the blue-black sky above the outline of the tree he saw the stable beam of Venus. Nearby was a quarter moon so bright as to be almost translucent, like a wedge of lemon fashioned from white quartz.

He left the window open, got back into bed, and soon drifted into a state of nervous half-sleep in which he seemed to see, belatedly, as though after a slow clearing of deep shadows, little Brandon standing beside the bed. Not the real Brandon, but a spectral Brandon, with oversized cranium, unblinking eyes, and a calm, wise face, all surrounded by an accusing aurora of clairvoyance. Rollie froze on the jostling mattress as Brandon nestled the crown of that cranium against his spine.

The illusion of Brandon lying there was so strong that, even as Rollie emerged from his small dream, he hesitated to roll onto his back for fear of smothering him. When he finally did manage to shake off the dream, he knew that it was not one of the meaningless garbage dreams that experts of late assure us we can delete without a second thought. This was a visitation, an old-fashioned omen-bearing vision of the power resident in Deedee's strange son.

Rollie accepted without analysis the implied responsibility. He knew what had to be done.

He got up, crossed the hall to Deedee's room and put an ear to her door. Apparently she was still asleep. He returned to his room and wrote her a note: *Don't worry. I'll take care of the boy.*

He opened her bedroom door a crack and peeked in to find Brandon standing on the mattress beside his sleeping mother, already staring at him. He stood with perfect balance, his arms down at his sides. He didn't move or make a sound. It was as if he had known someone would soon open the door, and he was waiting for them. Rollie's first thought was to put a finger to his lips, but Brandon's eyes told him this was unnecessary.

Sunlight streamed through the curtains. The room was already nearly midday bright. Rollie hadn't known that the windows in this room were unshaded. Not that it bothered Deedee—she was sleeping away. The thin line of drool stretching from the corner of her mouth, down a tangle of blond hair and onto her pillow, reminded Rollie of a story he'd once heard, that from the moment a young Prince Siddhartha wakened early on the morning following his wedding night, and noticed that his beautiful bride drooled in her sleep, he knew that even the most perfect of human visions is spoiled by imperfection, so he left home and founded Buddhism. Rollie had to laugh at that. He had an important mission that day, but founding a world religion was not it.

He moved with his note toward Deedee's nightstand. Brandon, his eyes not on the note, but on Rollie's, extended an open hand across his sleeping mother. Rollie obediently handed the note over—it seemed he had no choice—and moved toward the door. Just before he pulled it shut he looked back into the room. Brandon still stood there, as rigid as ever, staring back at him. He allowed the note to fall onto his sleeping mother's body.

With Brandon in his car seat on one side, and the inflatable kayak in its pack on the other, Rollie's back seat was loaded. Nearing Archer's Bait and Boat, Brandon started to make throaty sounds and to shake his purple fishing lure. Rollie adjusted the rearview mirror so he could observe him. He was acting like some kind of Bantu witch doctor doing an incantation. It grew louder when the Archer's sign came in sight, and reached a shriek when they passed it.

"You got to tell me in words what you want, dude. I don't understand this baby talk." Brandon started to beat his fists on his thighs. "Won't do you any good. Tell me in words." Rollie watched him go crimson in the face. His cheeks started to bulge from a pent-up explosion. Rollie prepared himself for a seismic blast.

"*Go!*" Brandon emitted, as though some powerful Heimlich thrust had blown a bone from his windpipe. "*Go der!*" He was pointing back over his shoulder.

"That's it!" Rollie hit his brakes and steered the car into a gravel-scattering U-turn. "Yes, yes, my good man! You can talk! You hear that kiddo? You just talked! Wait 'til your momma hears about this."

"*Go der!*" He was pointing now through the side window, toward Travis Archer's log cabin shop.

"We're going, li'l dude. Don't you worry about that. You just talked, so you get to call the shots. How does that feel?"

There were three other vehicles in the parking lot—two SUVs and a Harley. Brandon was laughing as he walked from the car. Once inside the store, they heard a man say, "Be right with you."

Travis Archer was demonstrating the use of a casting reel to a young woman whose neck had a turtle tattooed on it. He glanced up at the new arrivals, looked away, then back again. He said nothing more, but walked over to take Brandon in his arms, then carried him over to where the customer was still fiddling with the reel. He looked no more toward Rollie, but Rollie was almost sure he'd noticed some censure, some expression of malice, on his face.

Sure, he thought. You gave him a fishing lure and he likes you. Fair enough. But that doesn't make you his daddy. Who just made him say his first words?

It took forever. Three other customers tested all sorts of merchandise, and asked question after question, and finally made their purchases and moved on. All the while Brandon had been sniffing his lure and resting on Travis' arm. Finally Travis moved around to the side counter where Rollie waited.

"You need something?"

"Doesn't your arm get tired?"

He looked at Brandon, seemed to heft him lightly. "Not really. You here to shop?"

"Maybe. I wonder if you sell children's life vests. I'm thinking my nephew here might enjoy kayaking with me."

"Your nephew?"

"This little monkey belongs to my sister, Deedee. I think you met her. Well, obviously you did, since you knew Brandy already."

"You bet I know her. And you're her brother. Nice to meet you. I'm Travis Archer. Are you Edgar?" He put out his hand.

"No, I'm Rollie. Rollie Shanley."

"Oh, you're the one that writes plays, yeah?"

"How in the world did you know that?"

"I read about it in the Guardian. How else does anybody know anything in this town?"

They laughed about that.

"So…PFDs for children?"

"Yeah, I got some, but I don't think it's such a good idea just yet. Has he had any swimming lessons?"

"Not that I know of. But he loves the water."

"Make sure he's a good strong swimmer first. Kayaks are too unsteady. If you can't roll one, you're in deep trouble."

"That's kind of what I figured, but I wanted to hear your thoughts on it."

"I'd advise against it. Totally."

"Hey! I just realized something. Are you the guy that knows ropes?"

"I'm not sure…"

Rollie looked around to make sure the shop was still empty. "Deedee said she knew a guy who could rig up a gallows if we need to hang somebody. That must be you."

"I wouldn't be surprised," Travis said. "If somebody asks me real nice I'm capable of almost anything."

Brandon allowed Rollie to hold his hand as they walked down the steps of the porch, but then broke free. In his odd run, almost as if he were on a horse, he cantered away, but not toward the car. He turned to look at Rollie. "Go der!" he said, pointing around back. He seemed determined to get somewhere, whether Rollie followed or not, so Rollie hustled to catch up.

He lost sight of him. At first he thought he might have gone into the old plank garage or storage building or whatever it was, but then he noticed a padlock on the door. He stopped, listened, and heard a rustling of weeds.

Brandon crossed the grassy field behind the *Bait and Boat* and plunged headlong into the secondary undergrowth of a wild, once-logged section of forest. He did not feel the wet, grit-covered leaves of low bushes on his face. He did not hear the drumming of woodpeckers against rotting oak stumps, or the cicadas' shrill ring. He was captive to a force as powerful as a sucking undertow. It pulled him forward, deeper now into dark woods, past the last logging trail and into virgin forest of white oaks and sycamores that had escaped the hand of man. Some had stood witness as the Cherokee drove out the Creek, and as the white man drove out the Cherokee. As irresistible as gravity, it attracted him further and further into its heart. It overpowered him. He abandoned himself to the quest. He was one with it.

When Rollie finally caught up, he found Brandon buried arm-deep in mud. "Jesus, you little scamp." He pulled him up by the shoulders. "Look at you! We just got you clean down at the lake, and now you're nothing but a mud pie. I should call you that. If you ever play baseball your nickname's ready." He had hold of his arm, directing him back toward the car. "I can see it on a baseball card: Mudpie Shanley. We may have to go back to the lake for another wash."

A water hose was coiled up at the corner of the cabin. Rollie stood Brandon in the grass and sprayed him down. He heard gravel crunch and looked around to see a police patrol car pulling in. It gave him a start. He thought through his pockets and his car. No, he was clean. Somebody closed a car door and started laughing. Victor Caraher came around the car and asked, "What have you dug up, Rollie? The swamp monster?"

"Meet Mudpie Shanley. Don't you think we should call him that on his baseball card?" Brandon reached for something in his pocket, brought it close to his nose. "For cat's sake, Brandy, what did you dig up this time? A chicken bone? Throw it into the weeds. It's yucky."

Brandon gave it a heave. From the porch Travis said, "The kid's got an arm."

Victor looked up at him. "That's Mudpie Shanley. Soon be on the mound for the Reds."

Rollie asked, "What brings you out here, Victor? You investigating?"

"I'm shopping." He walked over to the porch, where Travis handed him down a large box. "Is this the blue one?"

"It's what he said he wanted."

"Oh," Rollie said. "Now I know. Our newest Twisting Creek Player." Victor smiled, said nothing. Rollie continued, "Hey, thanks for coming to the Odeon Saturday night."

"I enjoyed every minute of it. Who'd ever imagined Edward G. Robinson as a chump."

"Talk about casting against type."

"What are you guys talking about?" Travis asked.

"Rollie's weekend movie. I went with his sister."

"With Deedee?"

There was no hiding the alarm in his voice. Rollie recalled how huffy Travis had been until he realized Brandy was his nephew, not his son.

Victor said, "With Yolanda. It was a newspaper interview that turned into a movie. Great movie, too. It helped me make my point. I had just been telling her how hard it is to get at the truth.

How easy it would be to execute an innocent man, and let a guilty man go scot-free."

Brandon put his hand in his pocket, and left it there.

THE FRESHENING NORTHEASTERLY draft down the Big Sandy Valley gave Yolanda ideas of cancelling her appointment with Lucius Dean, in favor of a leisurely bike ride out Lindy Mill, past the country club and the Franklin College campus, up around Mt. Horeb and the old cemetery, maybe down to that new winery on Bard's Hollow, to see whether the grapes were in, or if the vineyard was still active with the harvest. There might even have been a story in that—what effect the late hot spell would have on this year's production. Maybe in a more settled time the afternoon would have been the perfect occasion to learn if Victor Caraher owned a bicycle, and, if so, to throw some of Deedee's leftover bread and a can of deviled ham or maybe some liverwurst and gherkins into a little backpack, and cycle over there for a quick interview, some pix, and a bottle of syrah. If she remembered correctly, Bard's had a few picnic tables on a platform overlooking the vineyard, where she and Victor could laugh about next to nothing in that lightness of spirit that always results from a session of outdoor exercise, followed by a glass of wine.

That, she told herself, is how relationships should start. Not with a possibly innocent man headed for death row, his fate in your hands. Or out of your hands. Not with signs all around that for all of us truth is every bit as elusive as it is for victims of Alzheimer's, only we pretend to be unperturbed by it while the Odessa Deans of the world rail against it.

She picked Rollie up at the Odeon and together they drove out to Presbyterian Homes, where a teenaged receptionist told them, "I think Mr. Dean is waiting for you in the music room." Her eyes followed something tucked under a shelf at her desk, apparently a series of security monitors, for she smiled and said, "Oh look, he's playing the organ." Her hand moved toward the monitor and the volume came up. They heard the organ playing, and then a phlegmy-throated voice singing *Shadows are gathering, deathbeds are coming, coming for you and for me.*

"Deathbeds a-plenty in this place, I suppose," Rollie said to the receptionist.

She laughed and said, "You're right about that."

"Jesus," Yolanda said. "This may be worse than I thought."

"Don't you worry," the receptionist told her, "he's a sweetheart."

He had dressed for the occasion—or was he one of those ancients who would never be seen in public without a coat and tie? Maybe the onset of cooler weather wasn't so welcome here at Presbyterian Homes. He was wearing a wool gray herringbone sport coat with dark gray wool trousers.

Like his sister, Lucius was tall and angular, an aspect magnified in profile as he sat perched there on the organ stool, with the amateur's exaggerated bend of the back and head over the keyboard. Unlike his sister's hair, his had turned blindingly white. It was combed back smooth and flat from a sharp peak that started, it seemed, nearly at the bridge of his crooked nose, giving him the profile of an osprey as he concentrated over his sheet music. When the door opened, he stopped playing and looked up. His laborious focus relaxed into a broad smile.

"Don't stop on our account," Rollie said, but Lucius rose from the organ stool.

"No, that's enough of that. What I used to dislike most about hymns is how they make you think about death all the time. And now it's what I like most. They remind you what a commonplace occurrence it is." He put his hand out to Rollie. "Roland, how nice to see you outside the theater. And you must be Yolanda."

He did not extend a hand to her until she remembered that a gentleman wouldn't, unless she offered hers first, so she did, and he took it, not with a shake, but with a slight pressure on her palm.

"Yes, we spoke on the phone," she said, hoping to lead directly to the topic of Sarah Lester's murder.

"I knew not only your father and grandfather, but your *great-*grandfather."

"That's amazing," Yolanda said, and resigned herself to the inevitable genealogy that formed the prelude to any conversation with any older person in this town.

"In fact, I had a Guardian route when I was a boy. I covered all of Bedford Woods, starting from Dogwood right down to Birch. Which was where it ended in those days. A month's subscription cost seventy-five cents, if I remember correctly, and I got to keep fifteen cents for every one I collected. My oh my, I felt rich at the end of the month when my pockets bulging with dimes and nickels."

"That's great," Yolanda said. "Since you have such a good memory..."

"Wonderful memories. And Roland, I must say you've done a splendid thing for this community by reopening the Odeon and bringing in all those great movies. Hollywood at its finest. I keep wondering why, with all the interest in the Lovemore trial, you haven't shown *Inherit the Wind*."

"Crap!" Rollie shook his head. "Why didn't I think of that? Man, my brain is nothing more than dead weight for my neck to lug around."

"I should think it was an obvious choice." Lucius turned to Yolanda. "Its subject was the Scopes Monkey Trial in the 1920s, when the world's attention was focused not all that far from here, down in east Tennessee. The trial of the century. It is said that more words were transmitted through the transatlantic cable about that trial than the total of all the words ever sent, combined, to that point."

"I've read about that," Yolanda said.

"It would be most timely. Help me convince your brother to schedule it."

"Hey, you don't need to convince me. I'll email my film booker as soon as I get home. Maybe we can have it here by the weekend."

"You don't actually remember that trial, do you, Mr. Dean?" Yolanda asked.

"I'm afraid not. I was about four or five years old. I hope that isn't what you're here to discuss."

Yolanda looked at Rollie, then back at Lucius. "No, not that trial. But maybe this trial."

"You want to know if I think Lovemore is guilty. Yes, of course I do. Do you want to know why?"

"Yes, I do."

"Because I'm white, of course." He winked at Rollie. "You see, I read your sister's excellent article in yesterday's paper."

Yolanda said, "Thank you, but that's not…I'm really here to talk about your sister." She'd caught him unprepared. The playfulness disappeared from his face. "Do you visit her often?"

"Not so often, I guess. Sometimes I go from a sense of duty, but she doesn't recognize me, and it breaks my heart."

"But you were once neighbors of the Lesters, I take it. And you knew the child Sarah?"

"Indeed. And not only as a child. I saw Sarah perhaps once a month right up until the time of her murder."

"You knew her recently?" asked Yolanda.

"But of course. She came here regularly to donate her services to us old codgers."

"What do you mean by 'donate her services'?"

"Tax help, investment advice. Or so she called it."

"You didn't call it that?"

"Personally…" Here Lucius Dean paused. "They say we shouldn't speak ill of the dead."

"I've never understood that rule," Rollie chipped in. "Why the heck not, is my question."

Lucius Dean laughed. "Indeed. Dying shouldn't let you off the hook. That's way too easy."

"And with Sarah?" Yolanda pressed.

"Well, it was always *listed* on our bulletin board as a donation of services, but frankly I saw it more as marketing for First Security. Every session would include investment brochures—from you-know-where. There would be no brochures from Wachovia or First National, you can bet your bottom dollar."

Yolanda thought about that. On first consideration it didn't seem any more self-serving than most other marketing these days. "Maybe it was a simple matter of give and take. I scratched your back, now you scratch mine."

"Sarah Lester didn't seem to me like a back-scratching kind of woman."

"The Guardian often plugs our advertisers. Not to mention the Odeon. Isn't that the same thing?"

"If all your readers are gullible old folks, and instead of five dollars, Roland here wants their life savings, then yes, it's about the same thing."

"Four bucks for you guys," Rollie said. "And you don't eat enough popcorn to keep a bird alive."

Yolanda said, "But your sister, Odessa—she was fond of Sarah."

"Odessa was fond of everyone. I'm not saying Sarah was preying on old people. Not exactly. And there's nothing wrong with First Security, as far as I know. I just don't like it when somebody pretends to do you a good turn when what they're really doing is commerce, plain and simple."

"Do you have any idea why Odessa gets so upset when Sarah is mentioned?"

"I suppose the commotion was too much for her."

"Did you witness any of it?"

"I went over later, when her care giver phoned me, but by that time she was quiet."

"She says strange sentences, over and over," Yolanda said. "Do you know what she's talking about?"

"Like what?"

"Like—forgive me—she says, 'smoking black soldiers' willies.' Does that hold any meaning you can decipher?"

He slowly shook his head. "None at all."

"How about 'jaw sugar buzzy'?"

"Ah! That one, yes. I'm Buzzy. When she was little she couldn't say 'brother'. It came out 'buzzy'. So to her I was Buzzy all throughout our childhood. 'Jaw sugar' means a kiss on the cheek. So when she said 'Jaw sugar, Buzzy,' she wanted me to kiss her on the cheek."

"So it's got nothing to do with Sarah."

"No, but I do say, you bring back some delightful memories. Oh, and on that earlier one, the Willys company made a kind of military vehicle, like a convertible Jeep. They were well known during the war."

"Oh, I see. Soldiers' Willys. That's a relief." She gave a sidelong glance toward Rollie, who was ready to burst out laughing, but managed to restrain himself. Later he would certainly entertain the whole family with this story, but for now Yolanda enjoyed a private laugh at what her imagination had run to.

"Yes. Her memory of the wartime era, and before, is still sound. Old memories die later, they say."

"How about this one: every time the phone rings she says, 'By grannies'. That doesn't sound like much of a clue to anything either."

"It sounds familiar. I think it's from an old radio comedy. Every time the phone would ring a character would say 'by grannies'."

"Oh, okay." Yolanda realized she was wasting her time. She looked at her watch. It was too late to contact Victor with that bike ride idea, and without him and the ride over to Bard's Hollow, any story on the winery lost its appeal. She sat back in her chair, and noticed that as she did so, Rollie did the same.

"How about some more organ music, Lucius," Rollie said. "I've been thinking that the Odeon needs an organist. Care to audition?"

As Lucius laughed he tossed back his head and spun around on his stool. "You give me far too much credit, Roland. Let's try something easier." He began to play *Kentucky Waltz*. He called out over his shoulder, "Feel free to dance, if the mood strikes."

Two women residents heard the music and came in to do just that. They stood poised for a beat, cheek firmly to cheek, arms out stiff, then bent their knees and stepped into the waltz.

"Oh my god!" Rollie was on his feet in an instant. "Yollie, we've got to go. We've got to go right now."

With the merest of goodbyes they were out the door and to the car. "Drive like a bat out of hell. I need to get to Leo Akers' office—now."

The Twisting Creek Guardian

ESTABLISHED 1882   Tuesday, September 28   *The Voice of Reason in the Tri-State*

Risky move to "humanize"enigmatic defendant

Ngwenya to Testify on Own Behalf

CHAPTER 17: "YOU ARE DEAD, WOMAN!"

IN THE AFTERNOON, a sour-faced man on a motorbike eased his way down Sycamore, looking at house numbers. He stopped at the Shanleys' front gate, pulled his bike onto the sidewalk, and checked something on a cardboard packet he carried. Still he seemed uncertain until he noticed Rollie sitting in a wicker swing on the porch.

Rollie was eating a pastrami sandwich and reading his notes on the morning's trial proceedings. Against the opinion of most legal experts, Lovemore himself had been put on the stand. It was the most sensational day yet of a most sensational legal battle, and Rollie's focus was on transforming it into sensational drama. He'd vaguely noticed the sound of a motorcycle engine as it eased to an idle, and didn't see the man approach until he was on top of him.

"I'm looking for Roland Shanley," the man said.

"Oh. You startled me."

"Sorry. Is this the residence of Roland Shanley?"

"That's me."

"You have been served." He placed the envelope on the swing beside Rollie, but did not leave.

Rollie opened the envelope. It was a subpoena from Leo

Akers. Rollie was to appear in court the next morning.

"Yes. I was expecting it," Rollie said. The man still stood there. "Do I need to sign something?" Now Rollie noticed he held two more envelopes.

"How about Joshua Shanley and Yolanda Shanley? They here too?"

"Are you joking? Akers wants them too?"

"No. Akers wants Yolanda. The DA wants Joshua."

Rollie directed the guy to the Guardian office and as the whine of the motorbike grew faint he thought, OK. It's still cool. At least they didn't arrest you. Forget for now this latest mess you've dicked your way into. You didn't mean to involve those two in it, but you did. It's probably for the best, so remain calm. Finish your sandwich, go to the Odeon, write the Lovemore scene, smoke a joint. Then, and only then, will you need to own up to the truth.

ACT 2, SCENE 3: COURTROOM. LOVEMORE TAKES THE STAND

Akers: Defense calls the defendant, Lovemore Ngwenya, to the stand.

Court Clerk: Do you swear to tell the truth, the whole truth, and nothing but the truth, so help you God?

Lovemore: I do.

Akers: Tell us, Mr. Ngwenya, how long ago did you come to Twisting Creek?

Lovemore: I came at the end of August, last year. I had been a political prisoner in South Zambezi for supporting the democratically elected Movement for African Democracy and opposing the Magwimbi dictatorship. With the assistance of many courageous Anglican church members, I was able to escape from Sisimutsa Prison in Tuvingu, and was smuggled to safety in South Africa. I was offered political asylum in this country and resided for some weeks in Falls Church, Virginia with a church sponsor. Someone there heard that Pecco Electronics was hiring. I have always been strong, good with my hands, good with machines. So I hitched down here to try my luck.

Akers: How did your luck turn out?

Lovemore: (GIVES IRONIC LAUGH) How does it look like my luck turned out?

Akers: Good point. But I mean when you first came to Twisting Creek.

Lovemore: It started almost okay. I found a cheap room that I could rent for a week with the seed money the church had given me. The next morning I went to Pecco Electronics' front office, but they told me there were no jobs at all, that there was a waiting list of twenty people for any job that might open up. Mrs. Crowell—my landlady—suggested I list myself on a website to do yard work and so on for people, since I had already paid her for a week. She was kind enough to do the listing for me, and right away Sarah called up. She said she had lived alone in a large house since the death of her mother, and it needed a lot of work.

Akers: Could you be more specific about the work you did for Sarah?

Lovemore: Painting, both inside and outside. Some simple carpentry. General gardening jobs.

Akers: It was while doing yard work that you contend an event happened that has a special bearing on the prosecution's evidence in this case, is that right?

Lovemore: Yes. That is right.

Akers: And this relates to the skin cells found under Sarah's fingernails during the post-mortem medical examination, is that right.

Lovemore: Yes, it is.

Akers: Could you tell the jury what happened?

Lovemore: I had crawled far under her forsythia bushes to clear out dead bits of plant material, when I felt spiders or some other biting insect attack my bare back. It began to itch horribly. I retreated quickly and Sarah saw my distress. She cleansed my back with a lotion, and helped me to scratch the itching I could not reach. It provided a great relief. The incident was that

	simple.
Akers:	Thank you. Now please tell the court how many days that week you worked for Sarah Lester.
Lovemore:	Every day. Sunday too. And it was not as though I was the hired hand and she sat around drinking iced tea or something. She worked right alongside me. She had all kinds of long delayed projects, owing to the illness of her mother. That is another thing. My mother had not been dead so long either—she died in a Magwimbi prison—so sometimes we stopped in the middle of a job to talk about how empty you feel when you don't have your mother any more. I do not think anybody is ever ready to live without a mother. It always comes as a shock, no matter how sick she has been. Or, in my case, how much better off she was to be out of the reach of those monsters who held her captive. Since I worked with Sarah from morning until dark and I did not have any kitchen at my rooming house, she would make lunch for us both, and we would discuss our lives.
Akers:	Could you be more specific as to the topics you discussed?
Lovemore:	South Zambezi's ruthless dictator, for one thing. She was very interested in that. She seemed moved by our struggle for democracy. Also, personal topics, such as still being single at our age, about how odd it was that she, the woman, had a good job, and I, the man, did not. She said that a generation or two ago it would have been the opposite. I told her not to be so sure about that, because my people have been poor for generations. She could laugh about things. About normal human things. I never heard her tell a joke, but she loved to laugh.
Akers:	Could you indicate for the jury why you sensed that the relationship was moving in a particular direction?
Lovemore:	You can probably see already that it was not just homeowner and handyman. Then one day in early

October—I can tell you exactly when it was, because it was the Saturday when the University of Kentucky had a football game against the University of Georgia. She wanted us to hurry and finish our work so we could watch the game together. Of course I know next to nothing about American football. At the mission school I attended in South Zambezi I played rugby, which is a bit like American football. Even so, I only pretended to be interested because it was important to Sarah. It is my belief that if something is important to people you care for, it becomes important to you as well. By association, as we might say. I also knew nothing about the state of Georgia, except that Martin Luther King was from there. Every South Zambezian admires him. So I told Sarah I planned to support Georgia to defeat Kentucky. I vividly recall her words to me that day: "Today we will have our first fight." These are not the words of an employer to a gardener. These are the words of young lovers.

(PAUSE, STRUGGLING NOT TO GET TOO EMOTIONAL)

In my worst nightmares I never dreamed I would be sitting here now telling you about our last fight.

Akers: Did you fight a lot?

Lovemore: No, never. That is what makes it so horrible.

Akers: Then back to the day of the football game...

Lovemore: I do not feel right about telling you all this. I am not the Boer who kisses and tells. It is not a gentlemanly way of behavior.

Akers: Mr. Ngwenya, you are on trial for your life. The jury will understand that you are forced to reveal things against your nature. You must be entirely honest and open.

Lovemore: Well...this was Saturday afternoon, and it was still more like a summer day. She referred to it as Indian summer. I was cutting dead branches from her trees and then sawing them up to stack and cure for firewood. I was sweating heavily, and had my shirt off. I heard Sarah moving something so I looked around and saw her standing on some little stool, stretching way up to hook the top of a bird feeder across a tree limb. I could see she had the stool placed unsteadily over some tree roots, and she was likely to lose her balance, so I hurried over and put my hands on her waist, to steady her. Only that. My touch surprised her, and made her jump a little, so she started laughing and spilled bird seed all over me, so we both had to laugh about that, and she started brushing it off my shoulders and hair and so on. Then suddenly she just looked me straight in the eyes, stopped laughing, stopped cleaning me up, picked her feet up off of that stool and wrapped her legs around my waist. Then she kissed me. I do not think she even thought about it; we just moved together. She said, "You know, working side by side like this makes me feel that we are a couple of newlyweds." I knew exactly what she meant. I felt the same way but never dreamed she would too. I did not even put her down on the ground. I carried her up her back steps and straight to the bedroom.

Akers: But things changed between then and the evening of October 30. Can you explain why?

Lovemore: No, sir, I cannot. I have been considering this subject all the time I have been imprisoned, and I still cannot work it out. Maybe she thought it was a sin, what we were doing. Maybe she was afraid people would find out. But what I keep turning over in my mind is how she said we had reversed the old way couples worked out, which should have been a man with a good job taking up with a good-looking sweetheart without a penny to her name. One thing I came to realize, sitting there in my prison cell, was that what usually happened in earlier days was the man would soon enough meet someone of his own class, or his people would demand he stop raising a scandal with such as that, and then suddenly the poor girl did not look so good. In fact, he could not bear the sight of her. So he would give her a few gold coins, and send her away. As I see it, that is what happened to me.

Akers: Did she offer you money?

Lovemore: She gave me that ruby cross. She claimed it was worth several hundred dollars.

Akers: And you accepted it?

Lovemore: Sir, I am very nearly broke. But I swear before you and this court and before my almighty God: when I left her I did not steal any jewelry, and she was as alive as you and I are right now. I would like to get my hands on whoever did it. I still miss her so much.

Akers: And the last sentence you spoke to her—the sentence that some in this courtroom have characterized as a death threat—how can you explain that?

Lovemore: The words are pretty close, but the meaning that the gentleman attributed to them was well wide of the mark. I said, "You are dead, woman." I meant to convey, "Your heart is cold and dead." And anybody in this room, if they knew the truth of our relationship, would have said the same thing.

Sound Familiar?	Today's Weather:
A trial in a small mountain town captures the nation's attention.	Pleasantly cool and breezy
Coming Soon to the Odeon	High 71, Low 58
Spencer Tracy in *Inherit the Wind*	

The Twisting Creek Guardian

Eleventh hour revelation "will stand this case on its head"—Akers

Trial Shocker—Defense Calls Surprise Witnesses

CHAPTER 18: SWEET BREEZE FROM THE GRAVEYARD

IN FORTHRIGHT BUT unemotional tones, Edgar's front page article said that two of the three surprise witnesses were connected with the Guardian, while the third was their brother. For the purpose of full disclosure he noted that all three were his siblings. Although he knew the gist of Rollie's testimony—it was all they'd talked about since the subpoenas arrived—his article gave no hint. This was one instance where a journalist guarded insider information as though it were a family secret.

The courtroom was packed when Deedee got there. She spotted Rollie, Yolanda and Josh—but no Seth—seated together against the far wall, on the window aisle. Edgar was down in front with the press contingent. She tried to spot an empty seat, but the place seemed full. She thought she might have to stand at the back of the room, if they even allowed her to stay, but then a man stood up and waved in her direction. It was Travis Archer.

"I knew you'd be here," he called across the rows of spectators, "so I saved you a seat."

She excused her way past reluctant knees and finally sat down beside him. She picked up the scent of some musky after shave, and noticed that he had dressed up for the occasion, in pressed sandstone khakis and a blue polo shirt. His ugly red paintbrush of a beard had been trimmed down to a...well, she had to admit that now it looked less like facial hair than a painful skin rash, but at least he had tried. Everything about him, including his eager smile and nervous glances, said he was a man on a date. It almost made Deedee feel that way too—taking her seat as at a movie theater. She wondered if he might not try to hold her hand.

That whole scenario was forgotten as soon as her sister took the stand.

Akers: The defense calls Yolanda Shanley to the stand.

Court Clerk: Do you swear to tell the truth, the whole truth, and nothing but the truth?

Yolanda: I do.

Court Clerk: Be seated.

Akers: Miss Shanley, some eight years ago, in approximately June, 2004, did you give Sarah Lester the email address of your brother, Roland Shanley?

Yolanda: Yes, I did.

Akers: Would you tell the court what circumstances led to that event?

Yolanda: Sarah was one of my friends—we were in the same year at Twisting Creek High—and even though we went away to different colleges we often saw each other during summer vacations. The summer of 2004, after her graduation from Transy...that's Transylvania University...we met up at a coffee shop and she told me that as a graduation gift her father was giving her a two-week holiday in the destination of her choice. She said she'd like to go to Paris, because she was really interested in art, especially the Impressionists, and wanted to see it firsthand. But she said the problem was she had never been outside the US, didn't speak French, and was worried about basic things like getting around town, ordering food, getting cheated, and so on.

Akers: And you had a solution for these concerns?

Yolanda: Rollie–he's my oldest brother—he has always been the traveler in the family, and it happened that at that time he was taking cooking lessons in Paris. So I told her to contact him and he'd show her the ropes. I wrote his email address out for her, and that was the end of it.

Akers: Prior to that conversation, was Sarah Lester aware that your brother was in Paris?

Yolanda: No, I don't think so. She seemed surprised.

Akers: Did you have any contact with her during her visit to Paris?

Yolanda: No.

Akers: Or with your brother?

Yolanda: None. I'm pretty sure I wrote him soon after I gave out his email, just to tell him to expect a message from her, but other than that, no.

Akers: And did you speak with Sarah following her return from Paris?

Yolanda: Oh, yes. She said she'd had a great trip. Said Rollie was a great guide, really knew his way around town, and around a French menu. She thanked me for hooking them up.

Akers: She used those words? "Hooking them up?"

Yolanda: Yes, I'm almost certain she did.

Akers: And by "hooking them up" you mean...

Yolanda: It just means putting someone in touch with someone.

Akers: Does it carry sexual connotations?

Yolanda: Not necessarily.

Akers: But it can?

Yolanda: I suppose it could, in its extended meaning, but then again...

Akers: Then again, what?

Yolanda: Then again almost everything does, if you take it that way.

Akers: And when you heard from your brother again, how did he describe Sarah's visit?

Yolanda: He said they had a good time. That was about it. He's not one to go on and on about things.

Akers: Did he have anything to say about Sarah personally?

Yolanda:	Oh...he said Sarah seemed different abroad than here at home.
Akers:	And what did he mean by that?
Prosecutor:	Objection!
Judge:	Sustained.
Akers:	How would you yourself characterize Sarah, at home?
Yolanda:	Pretty straight-laced. Church-going. I never knew her to drink, for example. She could laugh at an off-color joke, but would never tell one. I guess that sums it up.
Akers:	No more questions.
Reynolds:	Miss Shanley, how close would you describe your friendship with Sarah Lester?
Yolanda:	Maybe second-level friends. Meaning we didn't do much together just the two of us, but if there was a group outing of some kind, she would be included.
Reynolds:	Do you have any explanation of why you weren't "first-level friends"?
Yolanda:	Not so much in common, I guess. Our parents and Sarah's had been close friends, back in our country club days. Much of Sarah's socializing continued to revolve around the club, while we dropped away from it.
Reynolds:	And why was that?
Yolanda:	Financial reasons, as far as I know. The newspaper business doesn't pay like it used to. Plus both my parents developed health problems.
Reynolds:	But you say the main reason was financial?
Yolanda:	We were cutting back on luxuries before either of them got sick.
Reynolds:	Your brother now runs The Twisting Creek Guardian, the local newspaper, isn't that correct.
Yolanda:	Yes. But not Rollie, not the one in Paris with Sarah. My brother Josh is managing editor.
Reynolds:	And isn't it true that in an attempt to rescue your failing enterprise, your family tried to borrow money

	from First Security Bank? And that Sarah was the loan official who denied you the loan?
Yolanda:	Oh, wow. I have no idea about loans. Josh is always trying to work things out, but…
Reynolds:	Can you assure the court that this last-minute family assault is not an attempt to besmirch the deceased woman's reputation in revenge for the denial of that loan?
Akers:	Objection! Is this a question or a baseless allegation?
Judge:	Sustained. The deceased's name has by no means been besmirched in this court.
Reynolds:	Oh, it will, your honor. You just wait and see.

"She looked good up there, didn't she?" Travis put it like a question, but to Deedee it didn't sound like one.

"She's very beautiful. I've always envied her long legs and that oval face."

"Naw. You don't have to envy anybody anything like that. They probably envy you. I just mean she looked cool and collected. Confident in her ways."

"She's pretty steady. But that was the easy part."

"I just wonder why she's got it in for Sarah."

"What do you mean by that?"

"Saying she was different away from home. Bringing sex into it."

"Akers brought in sex. Not Yolanda."

"But why's your family mixed up in this? What's this all about? Do you know?"

"No, I guess I don't. Not exactly. I only know I'm worried about them."

It was the brothers who worried Deedee. Rollie could easily walk face-first into a two-by-four, and Josh was so earnest and volatile she could imagine him tying himself in knots. At least Prosecutor Reynolds's question about the Guardian's finances tipped her hand as to why they wanted Josh on the stand. With Rollie next, Josh would have a few minutes to think it through.

Rollie moved toward the stand, leaving the seat beside Josh free. Deedee thought maybe she should grab it, as a demonstration of moral support for Josh. But it might offend Travis, and anyway Yolanda quickly took that seat. Where the hell was Seth? That's what Deedee wanted to know.

All that was forgotten when Rollie took the oath.

Akers: Mr. Roland Richard Shanley. Is that right?

Rollie: Correct.

Akers: You've heard testimony that you met with Sarah Lester in Paris, in the summer of 2004. Can you confirm the accuracy of that testimony?

Rollie: Yes. It's correct.

Akers: And can you tell the court how that meeting came about?

Rollie: It was almost exactly as my sister described. I was living in Paris, got an email from Sarah saying she was coming, could we get together. She was a little worried about being alone in a foreign country. So I said sure. She gave me her flight details and I met her at the airport.

Akers: You said your sister's testimony was "almost" accurate. Can you clarify?

Rollie: Yolanda said I was in cooking school. In fact I had finished my course and was helping out in a little *patisserie*—a pastry shop—near my apartment.

Akers: Does that detail matter to the substance of the case?

Rollie: In a way, yes. I wasn't really working, see. I volunteered, just for the experience. So it was easy for me to free up more time for Sarah.

Akers: And did you?

Rollie: Oh, yes. For two weeks we were constant companions.

Akers: If you had no job, what did you live on?

Rollie: When I turned twenty-one I got an allowance from our family holdings. All five of us did.

Akers: You mean you, plus your two sisters and two brothers.

Rollie: Yes. Well, I should say we were supposed to. As the years went on the funding dried up. As the oldest, I was lucky.

Akers: How substantial was your allowance?

Rollie:	Meager. I wasn't some trust fund kid. I had just enough for a shabby little two-room flat, with a few euros left over for food. But, you know…I was young, in France. It was cool.
Akers:	Did your limited funds affect Sarah's visit?
Rollie:	In a weird way, yes. She had a good-sized stack of traveler's checks, and she wanted to enjoy herself, which meant good food and wine. But I couldn't afford to dine out like that every day, and she couldn't afford to pick up my tabs. Not if she also paid her hotel bill. So we decided she should stay at my place and spend the hotel money on entertainment. My spare room had a little *banquette*—like a sofa with no arm rests. She could have that.
Akers:	Who first had this idea?
Rollie:	Honestly I don't remember who said the words first. It just seemed kind of…you know…obvious.
Akers:	How long did it take for you to come to this arrangement?
Rollie:	I think she spent the first two nights in a hotel. After that she was at my place.
Akers:	And did she in fact sleep on your sofa for the rest of her stay in Paris?
Rollie:	She did for a couple of nights. But then one night we came home after a great day—we'd been out to Monet's garden at Giverny. Beautiful weather, great supper, nice bottle of wine. Just one of those days you'd relive over and over if you could. And then when we got home she said, "Kiss me goodnight." Then she slept with me after that.
Akers:	Wine, Mr. Shanley? We've heard from a previous witness that Sarah was a non-drinker. How do you square your testimony with that?
Rollie:	I thought she was a teetotaler too. I certainly never knew her to drink here, either before or after. But she sure did in Paris. We had wine with every dinner, and she tried cognac. As I said, she was a different person

	over there.
Akers:	How did the affair end?
Rollie:	Her two weeks were up. Simple as that. We'd both had a great time, and parted as friends.
Akers:	Did this Parisian liaison revive once both of you returned to Twisting Creek?
Rollie:	Not at all. Even in Paris she told me more than once that it was a temporary fling. I was her "hometown foreign affair" as she put it.
Akers:	And how did that sit with you?
Rollie:	I was fine with it. We never had any future together. It was a relationship specific to its time and place. Like some wines, it didn't travel.
Akers:	Mr. Shanley, two days ago you came into my office with what you took to be information most relevant to the case against my client, Mr. Lovemore Ngwenya. Can you tell the court how Sarah Lester's visit with you in Paris all those years ago has any bearing on this case?
Rollie:	It has to do with Mr. Ngwenya's skin and blood cells found under Sarah's fingernails. The prosecution uses it as proof that she was scratching at him while trying to fight off his attack. But I don't think that's it. Sarah was a wildcat. She would cat-scratch you.
Akers:	Please explain what you mean by that.
Rollie:	During sex. When she was ready to…let's say as the most thrilling moment approached, she scratched my back, hard, with her fingernails. She drew blood.
Akers:	You know this from firsthand experience?
Rollie:	I do. She scraped my back, more than once. If her fingernails had been tested that time in Paris, you'd have found my DNA there.
Akers:	No more questions.
Reynolds:	Mr. Shanley, please explain to the court—indeed to the whole world whose attention is focused on your testimony right now—just why is it that you

waited until the last moment to make your dramatic announcement.

Rollie: Believe it or not, I just remembered.

Reynolds: Believe it, he asks the jury—or not.

Rollie: I guess it sounds hard to swallow, but I swear to this court that I simply never made the connection between that incident and the medical evidence in this case.

Reynolds: Do you seriously ask this court to believe that in a frenzy of ecstasy a beautiful young woman scraped the blood from your back, and it slipped your mind?

Rollie: Well, yes. It's the truth. I mean…I don't sit around and relive old sexual exploits. It's over and done. It's in the past. I just kind of let the past go its own way.

Reynolds: But suddenly this week you decided to relive your sexual exploits, as you say, and, Oh! What a surprise! One of them is pertinent in a first degree murder trial. A trial that, by the way, you have followed avidly from the beginning.

Rollie: Let me explain the circum….

Reynolds: Is it not true that you have been in attendance every day this court has been in session?

Akers: Objection. Badgering.

Judge: We'll allow the witness to explain the circumstances.

Rollie: I heard Sheriff Greer mention the cell samples, and I thought, Whoa, that's damning evidence. I saw the photographs of his scraped wrists and face, along with the explanation that Sarah had scraped him with her fingernails during a struggle. It all sounded plausible, so I didn't think about it anymore. I certainly didn't connect it with that Paris fling. But then this past Monday I overheard an old man say that Sarah Lester didn't seem to him to be a back-scratching kind of woman. What he meant—I know this from the context—what he meant was that she wasn't accommodating, like you scratch my back, and I'll scratch yours. But the phrase "back-scratching kind of woman" ran around in my head a few times and I realized, *No!* That's exactly the kind of woman she *was*. The back-scratching kind. So I went straight to Lovemore's attorney.

Reynolds: Mr. Shanley, are you not a local playwright of some sort?

Rollie: I do my best. I write dramas for our amateur theatrical company.

Reynolds: How successful is your company?

Rollie: We mostly do it for our own amusement.

Reynolds: You also manage the local Odeon Cinema, is that not right?

Rollie: Yes. We're a revival house.

Reynolds: Does that mean you're some kind of preacher?

Rollie: {Laughing} It means a theater that runs old movies. Classics, perhaps.

Reynolds: And how is business there?

Rollie: We're surviving.

Reynolds: That's good to know. Occasionally my husband and I have stopped by.

Rollie: Welcome anytime. Maybe you saw *To Kill a Mockingbird*.

Reynolds: *{Taken aback}* No…no. It was…I can't recall right now what it was.

Rollie: Don't let it worry you. I've been known to forget things too.

{GENERAL LAUGHTER IN COURTROOM}

Judge: *{Uses gavel}* Order!

Reynolds: My point is, when my husband and I went to the Odeon, there were perhaps a dozen other people in the audience. Is that a typical turnout?

Rollie: There is no typical number. As I said, we scrape by.

Reynolds: And the newspaper that is the basis of your family's wealth—how is it doing, financially?

Rollie: Not my department.

Reynolds: I didn't think so. That's why we've subpoenaed your

166

	brother. But back to the Odeon and your acting troupe—are you not, in fact, currently working on a drama about this very trial?
Rollie:	Well, yes, as a matter of fact…
Reynolds:	And would you not say that the publicity garnered by your sensational last-minute allegations—headlined today, by the way, in the very newspaper your family owns—wouldn't you say that all the sexed-up news reports around the country will create a great deal of interest in your little play?
Rollie:	I hadn't thought about …
Reynolds:	How could anybody as desperate for income as you say you are, not, I repeat NOT, think about the box office receipts that might follow just such a fortuitous "memory" as you claim to have had?
Rollie:	I don't know, but trust me. This has nothing to do with money.
Reynolds:	Must not the very idea of making a fortune from the brutal death of a well-loved young woman—a woman who in this courtroom you dared to call your friend—must not that idea come from a man who circles death like a vulture?
Akers:	Your honor! Let's limit the grandstanding to the political arena.
Reynolds:	I withdraw it. No more questions.

Deedee leaned toward Travis' ear. "He did just fine, don't you think?"

"Just fine? He's killing the case. Reynolds couldn't even faze him."

"Didn't faze him one bit." Deedee said and sat up straight again. "I just think he's so wonderful."

"I met him, you know. He came into the store. Did he tell you?"

She moved closer to him again. "No! What did you think about him?"

"Nice enough guy. At first I gave him the cold shoulder. I thought he was your…Brandon's father. Later I learned he was

167

your brother. Even then I didn't know he was a witness."

"He didn't either until Monday evening. What was he doing at *Bait & Boat*?"

"He wanted a PFD to take Brandon kayaking. That's what he said, anyway. I said wait. Too early for that."

"That's just like him. I love him to death." When the court clerk called Josh's name she whispered to Travis, "Another one of my brothers," and turned her attention to the witness stand.

Reynolds: Mr. Shanley, you are the owner and Managing Editor of the town's only newspaper, the Guardian, isn't that right?

Josh: My family owns it and I'm Managing Editor.

Reynolds: How many family-owned newspapers are there left in America? Would you happen to know?

Josh: Not very many. Big media conglomerates scoop them up, strip them down, and treat them as cash cows.

Reynolds: And how's the Guardian doing, financially?

Josh: We're surviving.

Reynolds: It seems to me that your brother said the same thing about the Odeon Theater. Is business at the Guardian any better than at the Odeon?

Josh: Maybe a little.

Reynolds: I remember reading it when I was a little girl. I do believe that my grandparents and maybe my great-grandparents were customers, too. It's been in your family a long time, am I right?

Josh: A hundred and thirty years.

Reynolds: With such a distinguished history, I suppose it would be painful for you to be the one to lose it.

Josh: It would hurt.

Reynolds: Maybe even be humiliating?

Akers: Objection.

Judge: Elizabeth…

Reynolds: I'll rephrase. Is it fair to say that saving the Guardian is a priority for you?

Josh: Of course.

Reynolds: Isn't it true that you applied to First Security Bank

	for a commercial loan that you hoped would rescue it?
Josh:	Yes. But I also…
Reynolds:	And can you recall the name of the person who compiled the data regarding your application?
Josh:	It was Sarah.
Reynolds:	That would be the murder victim, Sarah Lester.
Josh:	These snide innuendos are unworthy…
Reynolds:	And who at First Security informed you that your application had been rejected?
Josh:	Also Sarah.
Reynolds:	Sarah Lester refused to lend you the money that might have saved your family's failing fortunes?
Josh:	Not her alone, surely…
Reynolds:	Yet you ask the jury to believe that this full-court family assault on the dignity of a murdered woman is entirely unrelated to the humiliation you felt when your request was denied.
Josh:	You've got it all wrong. It's not like that at all.
Reynolds:	Let's let the jury decide that, shall we? Luckily in this country the media can't dictate what we think.
Akers:	Objection!
Reynolds:	No further questions.
Akers:	So, Josh … you must be quite surprised to find yourself a witness in a trial that has nothing to do with you.
Josh:	It does seem odd. Seven years ago and four thousand miles away my brother has a fling I didn't even know about, and suddenly I'm in court.
Akers:	The Justice system can take some ugly turns, but luckily my job is to put it back on the right road. So let's make this quick and clear: Did you harbor any ill feelings at all toward Sarah Lester in light of First Security's refusal of your loan?
Josh:	Of course not.
Akers:	Explain to the court why not.

Josh:	It was a company decision. I'm sure Sarah didn't do it personally. One person doesn't decide on a loan of that size.
Akers:	Did you apply at other lending institutions?
Josh:	Sure. Several.
Akers:	And they all denied the loan?
Josh:	They did.
Akers:	Do you harbor resentment toward all of them?
Josh:	I don't harbor resentment toward any of them.
Akers:	Then how can you explain the rejections?
Josh:	I suppose it's all down to an under-capitalized banking system, or the low savings rate in this country. Changing habits of the reading public. Economic woes. Big issue like that, bigger than any one individual. Certainly nothing personal.
Akers:	No more questions.

When the judge called recess, the crowd rose, reluctantly, it seemed, as though stiff from sitting and stunned by the day's whipsawing allegations. Men idly patted their pockets for wallets and keys, while women felt around for purses. The torpid movement and dazed eyes seemed to mean that people were waiting for some super-sleuth to round everybody up on stage and disclose the truth. Travis and Deedee remained in their seats longer than they might have, not yet willing to speak. With the crowd finally on its feet and shuffling toward the door, when they alone were seated in their row, Travis said, "That brother held the line, too."

"Yeah. I was worried he'd feel the pressure, but that seemed pretty easy."

"It makes the prosecution look desperate. Why does your family want Lovemore off the hook?"

"Nobody wants that at all. They're just telling everybody what they know."

"What they *think* they know, you mean. And what they *think* they know is helping a vicious killer slip the noose."

"We don't know that. And speaking of the noose, Rollie loved his gift."

"That noose was for *him*?"

"That's all I'm saying on the subject." She zipped her lips.

"When are you going to tell me…"

"Tick-a-lock," she said.

That made Travis laugh. "So…see you here tomorrow?"

"Oh, I don't think it's…don't you need to open your store?"

"Not really. I don't have many customers."

"You will, now that you've starting advertising. And if they show up and find you closed, you'll lose them for sure."

"Probably I lost some today, but it's been worth it."

"Today you're here because my brothers and sister were getting grilled. And I really appreciate it. But tomorrow's just the summations, and we already know what they're going to say anyway. You're needed at the store."

"On the other hand…" He left it there.

She knew what he didn't want to say, that the courtroom was a chance to spend the day with her. "If you want to see me, there are other ways."

He smiled and scratched his chin. "Like dinner?"

"Like dinner and a movie. Maybe I can get you past the rope line at the Odeon, if you ask me real nice."

It didn't occur to Deedee that she was missing a great chance. If she'd simply said, "Sure, see you tomorrow," Travis would certainly have closed the store, affording the perfect chance to search Travis' property while he was guaranteed to be away. She could easily have managed it—just show up a little late at court, make up some reason for her delay—but by now she wasn't thinking that way. By now she'd forgotten that Brandon had sniffed the wind and pointed to the rutted trail between the hemlocks, and that at the time she'd felt an almost mystical union with her son, a determination to locate the odor coming from the swamp, identify it, expose it. Now, however, her instincts were telling her that this man should make a success of his business. For a single mom, a man worthy of dinner and a movie needs to be a good provider. You stay home and keep the store open, she told him, for the faint smell of wet death had wafted past, and now the wind was sweet.

The Twisting Creek Guardian

ESTABLISHED 1882 | Thursday, September 30 | *The Voice of Reason in the Tri-State*

Region Holds its Breath as Life or Death Decision Nears
Summations Due Today, Then Jury Takes Over

CHAPTER 19: AUDITIONS TONIGHT

FOR SUCH A day as this, when the town's long drama would finally draw to a close, the Guardian office was oddly calm. There wasn't much left to do now, except wait for the jury. At eleven o'clock that morning, Edgar sent in his story on the closing arguments. Yolanda composed the next day's front page, leaving a twenty-seven inch hole, center top, three columns wide. If the jury returned its verdict that afternoon, she would put Edgar's concluding story there. If the judge imposed the death penalty, Josh had an editorial ready. The headline would be "A TRAVESTY OF JUSTICE." If the jury remained out, Yolanda would shift Edgar's first story into the center space, and fill the resulting hole with something national.

So by early afternoon there wasn't much left to do. Josh sat alone at the long table in the editorial office, stewing. He twirled his cell phone on the table. Yolanda brought in a cup of coffee and joined him. She repeated her plans for the front page. He nodded. Deedee came in, said the ads were up to date, went out to get some coffee, and came back in. Nobody said anything for a while.

"Well…." Deedee said. "I think I'll walk over to see how things are at the Odeon. I've got a guy coming later to rig up gallows."

"I'll join you," Yolanda told her. "I need to set things up for tonight's audition."

Josh looked at his watch. "I might as well go with you. Seth will probably be there already. If anything happens down at the courthouse, Edgar will phone."

Rollie had left the door to his broom closet open so he could hear when people started to arrive. He walked out to peer down at the stage through the gun-turret of his followspot. His play was starting to come alive. He loved the buzz that came exactly now, with the first self-sustaining life moment of a creature that had begun as an embryo of an idea, a single-cell fetus in his mind, but he hated with nearly equal vehemence the creature's abrupt independence. He'd been mother and father to a child that all of a sudden was a willful adolescent, unaware of his existence. The ungrateful brat was running wild on stage, hammering at infrastructure, painting panels, adding or removing weight from sandbags that would fly scenery, pacing back and forth with script held at eye-level, repeating lines, posturing, measuring steps.

Deedee came on stage with Brandon, who ran straight over to the far wall where a college student was painting a mural of the jury, stuck both hands into a tray of black paint, and smeared it all over his face. Josh and Yolanda appeared behind her. They called out their greetings. Josh held his phone up and said, "No word yet."

Chea Hunnicutt was sitting on the edge of the stage, silently mouthing Sarah's lines. There was Seth, reading aloud, striding purposefully, all knee jerks and head bobs, and gesticulating for the back rows of the balcony. He'd "volunteered his services"—not to Rollie, but to Josh—for the part of Lovemore, in case nobody more suitable came along. Lobbied, more precisely. In bed, no doubt.

Rollie watched him prancing around, and thought: Nobody more suitable? Tell me one male on this planet *less* suited for my Lovemore than Seth Estershear. A blond, nelly, whispering, woman-slaying African the likes of which Riverbend Maximum Security can't even imagine. It was ludicrous. It made a mockery of the triumph that Rollie had imagined for himself, that by right should be his. Maybe Brandon would paint Seth's face too. Rollie tried to laugh at the thought.

But then...the choice was either Seth or some college boy. At least Seth looked weathered enough to know what heartache feels like. And he was a gifted artist in many fields—including the piano.

The judge had not allowed Leo Akers' clever ploy. The jury never learned of the real Lovemore Ngwenya's musical ability. But Rollie's audience would. That was his next task—choosing music for Seth to play. Certainly Chopin's *Marche Funèbre* would be in there. That should shiver a few spines throughout the house.

What else could he play? Rollie wondered vaguely about that as he leaned on the ledge, high up the rear wall of the theater, equally out of sight and out of mind to the enterprising people below. What music would go down well with an audience? A little ragtime for comic relief? Or maybe he should aim to soften the hearts of his audience with a stirring version of God Bless Africa. Maybe the cast could close with it, as a choir. Franklin College Chorale might get in on it.

He thought about this as he watched the on-stage energy and experienced the impossible combination of unity with the living organism as it changed and grew before his eyes, and the great divide between him and this alien thing with a life of its own. He watched Deedee take a phone call, hurry through the aisle of the main theater toward the lobby, then return, walking slowly this time, with Travis Archer at her side. Archer carried a homemade tool box in one hand, and several loops of rope in the other.

Rollie watched, powerless to prevent the transformation of his offspring into a hybrid organism, a foreign species. Ever since his own involvement in the trial, everything had gone out of control. The sight of it unfolding on his stage seemed to corrode his eyes. He needed a joint like never before. He moved away from his viewpoint and toward his closet.

"Hey! Quiet!" Josh's voice brought him straight back. He heard the clipped ringtone of a cell phone, then heard Josh say, "Is this a fucking joke?" He closed his phone, turned away from Rollie and announced to the stage, "Not guilty. He's free."

Josh and Yolanda ran from the theater. Rollie slouched into his office. He didn't light that joint. He poured a glass of whisky, but couldn't find the energy to drink it. He held his head in his hands.

Tomorrow's paper was done. Yolanda had used Josh's initial reaction as her headline: *Not Guilty; He's Free.* Edgar's article filled the central hole. The main photo showed a glowing Lovemore saluting the American flag outside the courthouse. It was a good front page. It was a classic, a union of event and print media that people would purchase as a souvenir. Framed copies of that front page would hang in offices and rec rooms for years to come. She was proud of it, and the role her family had played in the trial.

He's free, she thought. The execution of a quite-possibly-innocent man is not going to cleanse the town of its outrage, or further the career of a prosecutor.

It was long after dark when Yolanda walked down the narrow street by the theater. She needed to collect those *Auditions Tonight* signs and make sure somebody had locked the side door. Unplug the coffee urn and put away the cookies. The little things she always did on audition nights.

She kept thinking, *He's free.* As free as you or me. If he wants, he can walk into a bar this very night and order a beer. He might be drinking one right now. Or he could already be on a bus heading back to Falls Church. Or on his way to California. Or anywhere he wants. He's a free man in a free country.

Just along the street she saw something she almost missed: a black Jeep parked a few feet from the side door. She slowed to look at it more closely. It had a removable canvas roof.

She quickened her step until she reached the door to the Odeon. Had Rollie remembered to lock up? She turned the knob—it opened without a sound. The hallway light was off but a faint light penetrated from down a set of stairs.

She called out, "Is anybody there?"

No one answered. She walked down the stairs toward the light, which came from the waiting room. From the corridor she heard the quiet hiss of the coffee urn, and then a shadow fell across the doorway. A large black man approached her, his arm extended.

"I understand you are searching for an actor to portray

Lovemore Ngwenya. I have a great deal of experience in that capacity. I am Lovemore Ngwenya."

PART TWO

The Drama

A HOMELESS MAN squatted solidly on his haunches, his back supported by the frame of the basement door of the Odeon. He seemed to be asleep, with his arms curled snugly around his knees and his head bent into the open space at his elbows. A gray felt hat concealed his identity and the position of his arms nearly concealed the rolled-up paper bag he held wedged against his torso. Rollie noticed him as soon as he steered his bicycle down the side street, but only long enough to wonder if it wouldn't be wise to turn back, enter the theater through the main door, and store his bike in the coatroom off the lobby. A second look, however, told him his bike cable and U-lock would deter this guy. It was probably only a drunk sleeping one off.

It didn't occur to him to fear for his own safety. The man's frame didn't appear all that outsized, wrapped up, as it was, within itself, but the sleeping man stirred at the sound of a key in the lock, and when he rose, he just kept on rising. Rollie took a step back, first because of the size of this African-American, and then another step because it wasn't an African-American at all. It was an African.

Lovemore saw that Rollie had finally arrived. Immediately the slumber left his face, and his whole bearing seemed to crackle with the fire of the new day. He saw that he had startled Rollie, held out his hand, and said, "It's me. I am Lovemore Ngwenya, and I come to offer you my deepest gratitude."

"Wow, I was...you took me by surprise." He shook the offered hand, noticing that his own seemed a child's inside Lovemore's grip. *Enormous hands*, he thought. *A pianist's hands.*

"I don't suppose it's an everyday occurrence to find an accused murderer sleeping outside your door."

"Not quite," Rollie said, still not fully settled. They both laughed, and Rollie added, "But not a murderer. An innocent man. That's the point."

"Indeed it is. And to whom do I owe my freedom, possibly

my very life? I want to say thank you. *Tatenda*, in Shona," he said. Lovemore placed his hands together and bowed his head slightly, as though to pray, but instead clapped his hands softly. "This is our traditional gesture of gratitude."

"You applaud me? That's so cool! That's what a playwright lives for—especially a failed playwright."

"We will change that. Of this I'm *certain*." With his accent it came out like *satin*. "Has your sister mentioned the prospect to you?"

"What prospect? Which sister?"

"Oh dear—my memory for names…a tall, beautiful woman. She found me here last night and has offered me an audition for the part of myself." The infectious joy of his broad smile could have been part of the audition.

"Ah. That's Yolanda. No, I haven't seen her yet today. You were here last night?"

"Quite late. When I was released, I realized I had no particular prospects for employment. Of course I had read of your play; even that Sheriff Greer will be taking the role of himself, and so in one brainstorm I had the idea of doing the same myself."

"Holy cats! Talk about irony." He tried to keep conversing as normal, even though his mind was convulsing with this new development. There must be dozens of unforeseen consequences about to unroll. Most would be wildly beneficial, surely. But would they all?

"I, for one, have no grudge to bear. Perhaps Mr. Greer also will have none."

"Well, let's hope the fuck not." Rollie said. "But you know we're a troupe of volunteers. We don't get paid for it. This is totally small-time, more like a hobby."

"I was unsure about the arrangement." He rubbed his thumb and forefinger down the nerves in his neck as he thought this through. "If we are successful, and my presence is seen as instrumental, perhaps there can be a small allowance."

"Oh, sure. If that happens we can do something."

"At the very least, as the most recent entry on my updated résumé, 'Stage Actor' will look better than 'Jailed for Murder'."

"Ha! I suppose so! Let's go inside. There's decent coffee down there that I keep hidden from Yolanda."

"My benefactor is a man of taste," Lovemore said.

"I like to think so, although some might disagree." He unlocked the side door and led the way down the dim stairs. "How long were you waiting outside the theater?"

"Quite some time. Mrs. Crowell—my landlady—evicted me."

"Evicted you? That doesn't seem fair."

"Not evicted, to be precise. She wants to charge me a storage fee for the things I left behind."

"That's harsh. Do you have a lot of stuff?"

"Some nice fishing gear, several books with sentimental value, and a radio. A few clothes. That's about it."

"Passport? Green card?"

"Right here." Lovemore tapped his jacket pocket. "In point of fact, the dispute centers not on rent money. She simply wants to rid herself of me. In her home I'm a source of embarrassment. The neighbors, too, want me gone."

Rollie hit the light switch at the bottom of the stairs. "Down here, nobody wants you gone." With a sweep of his hand he indicated that there was ample unused space in three different directions. "You can see we have plenty of room right here, albeit filled with junk. Mostly old props we can't seem to part with. I know there's a shabby sofa from one of my less successful masterpieces. And a semi-broken down piano. Is it true you play?"

"After my fashion. How did you know?"

"My brother surmised it somehow. We can work that into the script. Musical interludes—could be a real crowd-pleaser. If it's okay with you."

"I'm happy to help in any way."

"Great. For now, let's fix you a space of your own. The men's dressing room is down that hall. There's a bathroom in there. What sort of things will you need for today? There should be clean towels in the janitor's closet. I'll ride over to Walgreen's for a toothbrush and so on."

"No need for that." He lifted the paper bag.

"Great. There's the sofa." It was tipped onto its back. Strips of a black gauze bottom cloth hung in tatters, revealing the wooden understructure and horsehair stuffing. "Help me set this upright and I'll find something to cover it with. I know what—I'll call my sister and have her bring over some bedding. Maybe a sleeping bag. This thing looks kind of ratty."

"Oh, my dear friend—if you knew how refreshing is your innocence. Compared to the prisons I've been in, it seems to me that now I have checked into the Ritz."

Rollie looked at him, not laughing, this time, at his joke, but taking in the totality of this man. The things he had seen! The torments he had faced! Rollie liked to think of himself as a man of the world—indeed, compared to most residents of Twisting Creek, this was true—but the man before him made him feel like a child of shelter and privilege. This man was more like some exquisitely upholstered vessel of experience. It was inspiring just to be in the same room with him.

Lovemore mistook the moment of awe. He said, "I know the question on your mind: Did I do it?"

"No…" Rollie tried to protest, but Lovemore's hand gesture of open palms showed his acceptance of the inevitable.

"It is only to be expected. You feel that before we develop any kind of trust you must know whether or not your testimony helped to free a murderer. I can tell you frankly, with all my heart, that your courageous step saved an innocent man from certain death."

"No," Rollie stopped him short. "It wasn't all me. Leo Akers did the heavy lifting."

"Leo is a fine lawyer, and there were other factors. But you saved the day. The DNA evidence would have been my undoing, and only you could cast doubt on that. You didn't have to dig from the closet your old affair with Sarah, but you did. And it saved me."

Now it was Lovemore who seemed cast in distant thoughts. Without speaking, the two of them bent to the task of clearing a space and righting the heavy sofa into it. Dust motes swirled in the light from the corridor. Rollie surveyed the walls for the light switch to this room. Then, without further prompting, Lovemore said, "I must tell you that in one way it broke my heart to hear you speak of it. Your conquest of my dear Sarah was so easy. It cheapened the love she shared with me. At one point I wanted to stand up in the courtroom and say, 'No! He's lying!' My heart wanted to do that, but of course my head is far ahead of my heart in survival skills." He laughed.

This time Rollie laughed with him, relieved at the last-second return to humor. "I think that's true of the human race as a whole."

"Yes, I think so too. But believe me, I didn't kill her. This means her killer is still at large."

"I'm sure the sheriff is already hard at work tracking him down."

"I wish I shared your faith in Sheriff Greer. But one thing I know—the real murderer, whoever he is, had better pray that Greer finds him before I do. I will strangle him with my bare hands."

"Yes, I'm sure. Either way, the guy's ass is grass." He waited for a response, but there was none. Maybe Lovemore didn't know *ass is grass*, but Rollie didn't pursue it. Instead he said, "In the meantime you should get some rest. On Monday morning I'll phone Leo Akers. After a word or two from him, old Mrs. Crowell will release your goods. We'll work it all out somehow."

"I owe you so much already."

"Let me run upstairs and print you off a script of *Stage Death*. You can start paying me back right away."

CHEA HUNNICUTT WAS the first cast member to bail out. She was gone even before the meeting where Lovemore Ngwenya was officially introduced as the newest member of the troupe. She came to the Odeon early that evening to pick up a bag of cosmetics she'd stashed in the basement, and to say goodbye to Josh and Yolanda. She'd prepared for them a little parting speech. She was so sorry, she would say, to leave them with no leading lady, especially as they had been so kind and encouraging to her, but the power of her lifelong dream of being an actress wasn't enough to convince her to let that man wrap a scarf around her neck and yank it. It was that simple. If they got huffy about that, too bad. It was her neck.

Her farewell remarks, however, went unspoken, because neither Josh nor Yolanda had yet arrived. Deedee was there nice and early, though, to let Travis in for some carpentry. She was sitting on the bottom step of the basement stairs, watching Brandon as he crawled around the premises in a posture she'd never before seen, or even thought possible for a toddler: his face pressed near the floor, his torso supported by his elbows, and his butt stuck way up in the air. He was busily sniffing the corners and crannies of the storage area, with its contents of broken chairs, tilting cabinets, water-stained boxes of old marquee bulbs, useless stacks of everything from plumbing fixtures to rusting newsreel canisters to rolled and moldy carpet. It had become one of Brandon's favorite places. He could spend limitless hours back in there, drawing god-knew-what pleasure from it, learning...what? That was Deedee's big question. What benefit came to her son through his ever-seeking nose? Did Brandon now know the 1930s and '40s from their smell in the same way that Rollie knew them from their films? And anyway, how could his stubby legs carry him in that awkward position, and for so long without pause? It was all beyond Deedee's insight into her surprising child. She watched him, wondered, marveled, and hoped.

She scooted aside to let Chea pass by comfortably on the

stairs. In a few seconds, Chea was back, carrying a bag.

"I'm just here to collect my stuff," Chea told her, then whispered, "He's not here, is he?"

"You mean Lovemore?" Deedee said. There was no need to whisper.

"Professor Estershear says he's moved in."

"Just until he can find a place. He's gone with Rollie now to meet with his ex-landlady."

"Good. I didn't want to run into him." Chea started up the stairs, noticed Brandon, stopped, and sat down beside Deedee. "What's he doing, you think?" She was watching Brandon's determined quest.

"Oh, he's...what do they call it?" She needed to make up something. "He's going through an olfactory phase."

"I don't think I've ever heard of that."

"They say it's quite common, for certain gifted children." She looked at Chea's bag. "You're not leaving, are you?"

And without any warning or preamble, Chea leaned her head forward against her knees and began to cry. Deedee placed a comforting hand to her back and asked what was wrong, but really there was no need to explain. Deedee had already thought it through for herself, and now saw her own thoughts made material.

"I just can't go through with it," Chea said, trying to control her voice. Her carefully crafted goodbye sentences were nowhere to be found. "Ever since I was a little girl I've wanted to do something with my life, something out of the ordinary. My parents want me to live some safe and secure way, get a degree and a husband. So okay, I understand their feelings, but to me...when I first heard about the Twisting Creek Players and the Sarah Lester story I said, This is it! This is me! I can escape my stupid little life and put everything I've got into being somebody else. Just to know how it feels to live at the extreme, even near the edge of death. But not *this* near the edge. Not with the actual murderer at my throat. I can't do it."

Deedee moved her hand to cup Chea's shoulder. She drew her closer, feeling small spasms of disappointment shudder across the muscles of her back. "I understand. Of course I do. Everyone will."

"No they won't. Even I don't understand. Not completely. The guy was found not guilty. Where do I get off treating him like this? When he hears I quit, he's going to know that this is just the first of many times he's going to be shunned, out of fear he really did what the court didn't prove he did. Maybe for his whole life. It'll be, 'Oh yeah, you're the guy who murdered that woman and beat the rap.'"

"Look, you're in a very different position than most people. Being friendly to him on the street is one thing, but letting him pretend to murder you is something else again."

Chea leaned her face into Deedee's hair. "I'm so thankful you understand. You're like the presence of grace and acceptance. You help to lighten my load."

"Not hardly," Deedee said. But she knew that's exactly what she was doing, knew it because she could feel the weight shifting directly onto her shoulders. She knew that this woman had thought it through, just as she herself had, only not nearly so intimately. She knew that what Chea really meant was, Suppose this man got off only because the investigation was shoddy and the prosecution over-shot its case? Suppose this man really is the killer of Sarah Lester? What will happen when he throws himself into his new role? Will he fall into a fresh fever? Will he experience the identical emotional run as before, complete with the euphoria of first love, with the interlocking drive to protect and be protected? And as the arc of their relationship flows with the unalterable destiny of a Greek tragedy, will the paradox of his heated temperament, stoked by a cooling Sarah, ignite, once again, his fury? And will the man so damaged in Magwimbi's torture chambers be able to remind himself, even while baring his teeth and straining the muscles of his arms until their veins protrude, *This is only a play. I am an actor and this woman means nothing to me.*

Deedee felt that weight, and not only that. She understood that without the real Lovemore, Rollie's drama would have no impact. She knew that without a Sarah Lester there would be no Stage Death, and without Stage Death her brother would return to his old life as the town loser. In fact, his loser status would be enhanced, for only a world-class loser could approach so near to

185

fame, only to watch it blow up in his face.

She held Chea's now-gently trembling body and wondered momentarily where this unexpected empathy had come from. She hardly knew this woman. Why was she sharing her disappointment? Why, in fact, did Deedee feel as though she'd turned inward, into the hollow of herself, where the darkness belonged not to this lucky college girl, this girl with caring parents still alive, still guiding; this girl her own age who had not lost the dice throw of sperm and egg, whose ties to any commitment could be severed with a simple decision? Why did she care so much about tears that were already evaporating?

Quickly she knew the answer: she had placed a comforting arm across her own shoulders. She was consoling herself. This Chea Hunnicutt, who in less than five minutes would be gone from her life forever, was in fact the bygone Deedee of endless possibilities, the Deedee who had ceased to exist, yet who would never leave her.

She also knew that the strength of a dream was laughably weak when pitted against ties of legacy and family. Deedee knew that now there would be no Sarah Lester replacement. She knew that no woman in Twisting Creek, or in Kentucky, probably no woman in this whole cesspool of a world, would willingly allow the real Lovemore Ngwenya at her throat. No woman, that is, who didn't love Rollie to within an inch of her life.

LATE THE PREVIOUS night Seth had slouched off to sulk in his own apartment after Josh informed him that the Lovemore role would go to Lovemore. Someday, surely, Seth would agree that it was a great idea, and that he was better cast as artistic director than as the South Zambezi Strangler, but in the meantime it meant Josh was sitting alone at home with nothing to do on a rainy Sunday morning. The day promised to be one of those long spells of persistent drizzle that form a quiet weekend blessing for lovers of books and old movies, and a bitter abomination for everybody else. Once Josh had flipped through the paper, he had nothing to do until the audition for a new Sarah, scheduled after Rollie's matinee. Since he would be having breakfast alone, he decided to splurge for a havarti omelet at the Carnegie, then get to the Odeon early to see if Yolanda needed any help.

This plan still left him hours to kill. He decided he might as well catch the film while waiting for the audition. He checked the top of the front page, where on weekends Rollie usually got a plug: Alfred Hitchcock's *The Lady Vanishes*. Beside it Yolanda had placed a promo box:

> Lovemore to portray himself
> in *Stage Death*.
> See *Community News*: B-1

Josh rarely made it to any of Rollie's classics, certainly never to a Sunday matinee, so when he turned the corner by the Odeon and raised his umbrella just enough to look up through the gray mist toward the welcoming glow of the marquee, he didn't know what to make of the dozen or so people standing at the box office window. Did people usually stream in like this after church? Did this small group comprise the day's entire crowd, waiting for a tardy ticket seller to turn up? Or maybe it was simply a random group of pedestrians taking shelter under the awning. But no— there was a woman in there selling tickets, and here came some more customers.

Josh waited to pay his four dollars like everybody else. The man in front of him turned to say, "Did you hear that Lovemore is going to play the murderer in the play they're putting on here?"

"Amazing, huh? How did you hear about it?"

"Saw it in today's paper."

By now a young couple was behind him in line. The woman said, "Where are they going to find a woman to play Sarah? That's my question."

"There's an audition later today," Josh said. When they kept staring at him he added, "I saw a sign around the corner." It was the first time he'd felt the need to distance himself from the play.

At the main door a high school boy in a maroon bellhop uniform took his ticket and Josh saw yet more lines of customers at the concession stand. The lobby was vibrant with bright colors, brisk chatter and the smell of popcorn. He still didn't know whether this was a typical Sunday afternoon turnout or not. He bypassed the snack lines for the moment. He needed to check out the seated crowd. He looked through the porthole doors to the auditorium and could hardly believe his eyes. There must have been three hundred people in there. Perhaps the Hitchcock name was a powerful magnet. Combine that with the threat of all-day rain—could that explain it? A lot of early-autumn picnics would have been cancelled, and not everybody watched the NFL all day long.

Another man joined him as he pushed open the door. Josh looked at him. "Nice crowd."

The man surveyed the full rows. "Huge," he said. "Great flick. Did you hear that Lovemore will play himself, right there?" He pointed toward the stage.

"Yes, I knew about that. What do you think about it?"

The man blew a sharp puff of air that seemed to say it all. He tried to think of an appropriate translation. "Wow," he said. "Just unbelievably wow."

"Yes," Josh said and turned abruptly. "Excuse me. I need some popcorn." He made his way past the drinks line and saw the idle popcorn machine.

The attendant, an older man whose face Josh connected

somehow with Pops Woody—maybe he'd done some work around the house or something—saw Josh looking at the empty machine. "We ran out," he said. "Never happened before."

"Does Rollie know?" He pulled his cell phone from a jacket pocket.

"Deedee's gone to buy some more." He looked at his watch. "She should be back in a couple of minutes. Rollie says he'll delay the start."

"Maybe he should announce that. Otherwise people won't know."

"Good idea. You're his brother Josh, aren't you?"

He pressed Rollie's speed dial, smiled at the man, and asked, "Is this a bigger Sunday crowd than usual?"

"Never seen anything like it. And you know what they're all talking about? Not the movie, but Lovemore."

Josh complimented Rollie on the big turn-out and suggested an announcement of the delay, then put his phone away and made his way into the auditorium. He wanted an easy exit in case he decided to ditch the movie, but saw that the only available aisle seats were either way down front or near the back, which is where he sat down.

He surveyed the crowd. People were joking back and forth. Nobody seemed cross about the lack of popcorn or the delay. There were all sorts of people represented. Some were young college-aged couples, some were much older, Presbyterian Homes old. Judging from their dress, many families had come straight from church and probably Sunday dinner out. Black people were interspersed with whites. He wished he could take the stage and make a brief statement to point out that it was his great-grandfather Delmon Shanley who had ended segregation at the Odeon, fifteen years ahead of the next eastern Kentucky theater to do so. He wished he could announce that, and add, "So please read the Guardian." But then all at once it dawned on him, these people *do* read the Guardian. They were here now because they connected the Odeon with Lovemore. They were here because *he* was here, or he soon would be. His presence would soon fill that stage—just as the man at the door had said—that stage right there. They had come streaming in today not because of Hitchcock, or the rain, but in response to the magnetism of celebrity. They needed to bind themselves to notoriety, to form a link with fame in order to feel their own lives had impact. That's what this was all about.

And what was the vector of this gratification? How did they even know about Lovemore and the Odeon in the first place? Through the Guardian, that's how. Josh nearly rose from his seat as the electricity of this realization circulated through him. The Guardian did this. No other news organ in the country had the story. Not so much as one Internet blog. Only the little last-minute piece Yolanda had tucked into the "Community News" page, with a teaser above the nameplate.

Again he wanted to make a stage announcement: *See what I mean? See how we are a community because we all have shared access to the same information? See what we'll lose if we get all fragmented?*

The great wall speakers brought the crackle of a microphone, and a strong voice boomed forth:

Good afternoon ladies and gentlemen. My name is Lovemore Ngwenya, and it is my pleasure to welcome you here today. We at the Odeon know that no movie would be complete without popcorn, and we apologize for running short. Frankly, we were caught out by the size of the crowd. Fresh supplies are on the way. We will delay the start of the film for a few minutes to allow for that. In the meantime, please enjoy this newsreel from the year that today's film was released: 1938.

Thank you for being patient.

And if I may be permitted to add a personal note, thank you for being proud citizens of Twisting Creek, Kentucky.

The place erupted. Not in applause, exactly, but in an excitement that wasn't overtly condemnatory. Everybody was talking all at once. People sitting alone leaned forward over the row of seats to say something to others sitting alone.

Josh asked himself, He's upstairs with Rollie? Are you *shitting* me? Immediately he texted Rollie, *He's up there with you?*

The reply came almost as quickly, *Yep.*

A hand grabbed Josh's shoulder and he heard, "Scootch over."

He moved to let Edgar sit down. "Did you hear that?"

"I certainly did. It seems our Big Bro has suddenly developed a genius for theater."

"And look at this crowd. You can almost smell the thrill in the air."

"Because Rollie's finally got his ghost."

Josh looked around at him. "What do you mean by that?"

"I've been telling him that every old theater needs a phantom or an ogre, some inhuman presence to haunt the rafters and stalk the aisles. Now he's finally got one."

"Jesus Edgar, are you thinking what I'm thinking?"

"What's that?"

"We could pack this place. *Stage Death* could fill these seats for weeks. And we're no longer talking five-buck community theater tickets, are we? We're talking real theater pricing."

"With both Lovemore and the sheriff, I think we'll do real well. But first we have to find a Sarah."

Josh texted Rollie. *How many seats here?*

Rollie's simple reply: *1350*

"Yeah. That Chea chick chickened out." Josh touched the calculator icon on his phone. "How did you know?"

"Deedee told me last night," Edgar said. "I think she's steeling herself to have a crack at it."

"At twenty-five bucks a ticket…every night for a month. Look at this number." He turned the calculator screen toward Edgar.

"Over a million bucks."

"Seth and I paid seventy dollars apiece for *La Cage* at the Belk in Charlotte. Not for the best seats, either. Even at fifty bucks a pop, we're looking at two million dollars a month."

"That's gross revenue, for best-case scenario. And what if Deedee doesn't work out?""

"For that kind of money we'll let Seth play Sarah. I wouldn't mind watching him get his skinny neck wrung every night."

GARDIANE LA CAMARGUE was one of Rollie's Sunday Supper favorites because it was easy—since he used beef in place of oxtail it was basically a glorified beef stew with wine and olives in it—yet everybody thought it was special because the name was French. Plus, of all the great good luck you could have in the Shanley household, it sounded like Guardian. They called it Guardian stew, and requested it often.

He was alone in the dimming kitchen. The day's drizzle had diminished to an evening mist. Soon he would need to turn on the lights, but for the moment he enjoyed the half light. Open windows on two sides allowed a crisp October cross draft to add the scent of moist dirt and dying leaves to the thyme and tarragon steaming from his pot of beef broth. The warmth of the stove was in comfortable contrast with the autumn air. Rollie had wedged himself into his preferred chopping position at the corner counter near his mother's old clock radio, a wood-grain table model with a needle dial that lit its space along the spectrum of wavelengths and cast an amber glow onto the countertop. The clock was generally stopped, although occasionally, for a reason that no one could discern, it ran a while and then stopped again, but the radio always worked fine. It had a row of six fat, indented buttons for pre-set stations. Each of the Shanley kids had claimed one. The other one was their mother's, set to a country music station that none of her children listened to, but there it remained, waiting, it seemed, for her return.

Set in the opposing corner of the counter was a set of faux cheese crock canisters even older than the radio. In descending size they were labeled Flour, Sugar, Coffee, Tea. The Tea one had never held tea. For as far back as Rollie could remember, it had been the household petty cash repository. He supposed the canisters had been a wedding present to his grandmother, maybe even his great-grandmother. He imagined a cheerful young bride dropping a silver dollar into the Tea crock, locking down the metal clasp, and telling her new husband, "There! Now we're secure. Thieves in these parts don't drink tea, do they?" And laughing with the carelessness of young love.

Rollie enjoyed cooking here, where almost every utensil had a history. He loved to note that the Shanley kitchen hadn't changed much over the years; that decades ago, on the day when one of his now-vintage films came to town, arriving fresh and popular, with posters and fanfare, its stars on the cover of *Photoplay* or *Movie Mirror*; that on the day when a boy would say to his best girl, "There's a new George Raft movie at the Odeon," this kitchen had looked and smelled, and its yield had tasted, much as it did today. It had not only survived history, it had preserved history.

He was happy to be alone in it, chopping sweet onions the way he'd been taught, with short, swift strokes that for some reason reduced eye irritation. His knife was sharp; heavy, but perfectly balanced. Held just so, it felt weightless. The bowl of potatoes at his elbow would offer little resistance. Chopping vegetables with a professional knife was almost a spiritual act, imbued with precision and delicacy.

He switched on the radio and pressed his pre-set, the Franklin College NPR channel. A classical piano piece was playing. It sounded familiar, somehow. It might work as a Lovemore interlude. He was trying to listen for the composer's name. He stopped chopping, wiped his hands on his apron, and found a pencil and notepad.

It was a nocturne by Ciurlionis, the announcer said.

Of course! The Lithuanian dude. He'd heard it at a recital in Vilnius with...what was her name... Salomeya? Something like that.

You see? he thought. You see how it works? You live your life in all these separate little compartments: this experience with this woman and that experience with another one. You live here, you live there. You're a vagabond, a dessert chef: you manage a theater and you write plays. It all seems entirely random. People say you're headed for trouble. God knows what will become of you. Yet maybe one time in your whole life something happens, and without planning it or even being aware of it, it all assembles itself into one great work of art. The way you've conducted your life becomes your masterpiece.

He was entirely sober. He hadn't had a toke or a drink all day. Or yesterday, come to that. Yet he was as at one with life as a person could be. He tried to sing along with the next selection, an Offenbach barcarole.

He started on the potatoes. *"Belle nuit, pa-di-pa-da,"* he sang. He couldn't remember ever being so at home in the world. And why not? Deedee—his beloved Deedee!—had not only agreed to have a go at being his Sarah, but the real Lovemore was now *his* Lovemore. The man who owed his freedom, if not his life, to the gutsy testimony of none other than Roland Shanley. His two co-stars were *both* devoted to him in their own ways. To *him!* Man, this was just amazing.

Edgar's entrance destroyed his solitude.

"You'll never guess who I just saw in the Kroger's parking lot." Edgar began removing things from the freezer. When he'd made room for a carton of ice cream, he stuffed everything back in and closed the door before it could all slide out again.

"What? Sorry, I was…"

"Guess who went driving past as I was walking to my car?" He took an apple pie from a plastic bag and pulled five dessert plates from the cabinet.

Rollie looked at him as at a ripple in the calm surface of his thoughts.

"Come on, guess."

"The Earl of Sandwich. I have no fucking idea."

"Sarah Lester's brother, Ethan."

A skittle of anxiety ran down Rollie's neck. "What's he doing in town?"

"I suppose he's here to settle affairs."

"What could that mean?"

"Sell the house, maybe? Apparently nobody would rent it. It's been sitting there empty."

"Shit. I hope that's all. As long as he's not here to mess with our play."

"I wouldn't be too sure. Guess who I saw in the car with him?"

He waited until he saw that Rollie wouldn't attempt a guess. "Josh and Yolanda. In a big silver Lincoln Town Car. Yollie sitting in the back seat like a queen."

"You must have been mistaken."

"Saw them with my own eyes."

"That can't be good news." His hands lost their precision. He put down the knife.

"Might not be horrible news. Ethan and Josh were buds in high school. And Yollie seemed fine. She spotted me and gave me a royal wave as they drove by."

Rollie didn't reply. He looked at his hands and slowly resumed slicing potatoes.

"So what's for supper?"

"Guardian stew."

"Sounds good. With noodles?"

"Rice."

"Fabulous. Okay, see you at supper." Edgar carried his plates into the dining room.

Now the knife felt clumsy and alien. Rollie watched his hands as they tried to regain control.

Ethan Lester chooses this moment to visit Twisting Creek? And as soon as he gets here he needs to see Josh and Yolanda? This could not be good news.

You see! Rollie thought. You see how other people simply ruin everything? It was all good, then Edgar walks in and now look.

He gave up on his potatoes. Better to have a drink than to slice off a finger. But before he could even grab a glass, Edgar backed through the doorway, the plates still in his hands. "Whoa! Have you been in the dining room yet??"

"I set the table about an hour ago."

"It's all moved around now. There's a laptop and projector set up. Looks like Josh has a big show for us tonight."

A sour effluence streamed up Rollie's chest and settled in his throat. It didn't wash down with whisky.

The Guardian stew drew its usual share of compliments, Josh's show was a series of grandly optimistic spreadsheets, and the news from Ethan Lester wasn't quite as dire as it might have been. Ethan had read that Lovemore would play himself and had quickly surmised, just as Josh had done earlier that same afternoon, that the box office receipts could reach into the hundreds of thousands of dollars, perhaps more. Ethan held that since *Stage Death* was based on the story of his sister's murder, and since now the entire Lester estate was in his possession, he was entitled to a portion of the ownership. He would willingly allow The Twisting Creek Players to use her story in this way if—and only if—he received half the profits.

This turn of events delighted Josh, because, as he explained to his perplexed siblings, Ethan Lester was a show-biz kind of guy. The role of a New Orleans club owner was essentially that of impresario. He had to understand public taste and know what would pull in a crowd, so if Ethan judged this play worth bargaining over, that meant there was money in it. Further, the intellectual property right to *Stage Death* and all its proceeds lay with its creator—one Roland Shanley—and he could parcel them out as he saw fit. If Ethan needed confirmation of this basic fact, they could have Leo Akers give him a call tomorrow.

However, as a gesture to an old friend and teammate, he would ask Rollie to change Sarah's name, change all the names for that matter. Everybody would still know who it was about, but legally, perhaps even ethically, they would be in the clear. He said that when Ethan had driven him home that evening, they'd parted as old chums, even leaving open the possibility of lunch in the next day or two before Ethan had to return to New Orleans.

Josh's Excel charts depicted various profit margins given this or that seat-pricing and attendance. He had even estimated concession sales with or without a temporary alcohol license for the Odeon. He asked for other ideas, such as a *Stage Death* logo that could be printed on T-shirts and similar gear. He asked opinions on selling *Stage Death* scarves. With winter coming on, would they sell like Hermes? Or would they be too, too crass?

He had a slide of the main processing plant at Lombard Paper Mill, with its complex web of conveyor chutes and smokestacks. It was still for sale and he believed controlling interest would cost even less today than when he'd first researched it two years ago. He had a bar graph showing how much they would save by selling newsprint to themselves at cost.

He showed the iconic photo of a delighted Asian woman as her clean white gloves retrieved a stack of color printing from the Coghlan Digital ImagePress. He showed a five-minute Coghlan instructional video, to which Josh had added a clip of himself assuring the current printing department that not one single person need be laid off. In fact, the work coming their way from other area publications could create new jobs.

It was all good. Even Rollie didn't mind it, although it was very much The Josh Shanley Show. At least Josh had acknowledged him as the genius behind the whole resurrection. Well, he hadn't used the term "genius," but that thought must have been in everybody's mind. He wondered if it wasn't exactly the thought in Deedee's mind when she agreed to "at least give a try" to portraying Sarah.

In AOB Yolanda reported that Mom was unchanged. Everyone thought, although no one said, Why do we bother with these Sunday drives to Richmond?

That's how Sunday Supper ended. Only a week ago they'd showed family solidarity in foregoing millions in order to stand up to injustice. Today they showed equal solidarity in accepting the opportunity that had come their way, and in meeting the challenges it brought with it.

After apple pie and ice cream, Rollie packed a supper for Lovemore and drove off to the Odeon, while Edgar cleared the table. Yolanda noticed that a sharp breeze had driven away the day's moisture. She went upstairs to remove plastic wrapping from a stack of quilts they would need tonight for the first time since last winter. Josh packed away his laptop and projector. Deedee got Brandon ready for bed. By eleven o'clock, the house was asleep.

Rollie returned soon after that. Someone had left the back porch light on for him. No other lights were shining. Open windows welcomed chill air into dark bedrooms. Except for some rustling leaves, Sycamore Street was silent.

By midnight he too was asleep under a warm quilt. They were all asleep. All except Brandon. He had kicked off his blanket and was standing in his crib by the open window. He sniffed leaves starting to wither under the assault of death. It was the odor of a mystery with no solution, yet its obscurity attracted him. He tilted his head and flared his nostrils to the breeze.

At two o'clock the rooms facing away from town picked up no sound. Rollie, Deedee and Josh slept peacefully on. Yolanda and Edgar, with their windows opening toward Main Street, were both awakened by arcing sirens as fire trucks pulled away from the downtown station. Both thought, *a possible story*, then checked their clocks. Each rolled over into fresh positions on cool pillows. Whatever the story was, it had happened too late for the morning paper.

Only Brandon smelled smoke.

IT DIDN'T SEEM fair to Victor Caraher that you could drive straight east the whole stinking night, fighting semis and fog banks all the way from Paducah, and still be inside the state of Kentucky. This was yet another thing his parents needed to understand. He couldn't keep making this drive again and again. Even less when he became Sheriff. So, he asked himself yet again, had his long-haul petition been successful? Would a fine home in Bedford Woods finally convince his parents to pull up stakes in Paducah and join him in Twisting Creek? He doubted it. They were embedded urban retirees. "Sugar," his mother had warned him, "the old man's day doesn't even *start* until he takes old Scoot for a walk down by the river. Then on the way back he has to stop and buy a newspaper so he can read his sports while he sits outside at Dunkin's with coffee and a strawberry cheese Danish."

"Listen at her," his father had said. "Like she don't go with me ever' step of the way. How do you think she knows ever' detail? Tell him about your muffins while you're at it."

"Well see, it's honey bran. It helps keep me regular."

Those two! How infuriating they could be at times. Like the whole of life revolved around a cheese danish and a muffin. And like Twisting Creek couldn't offer up so much as a crust of bread.

Victor exited the Interstate onto the state road toward town, then made the quick left onto County Road 61 for the last twelve miles of his journey home.

Only now, away from the main roads, did he notice that it was a moonless night. He followed the mineshaft of his headlights into the heavy darkness. The draft of his car disturbed the ditchweed. He lowered his window to let in the scent. The road was empty, and pre-dawn was the perfect time to drive it. Late-night revelers had already called it a night, and the Monday morning work crowd still had a few hours' sleep before their week began. Following his hours of continuous vigilance on Interstates, Victor felt his stress lift, as though a binding around his chest had been loosened. He felt at home in the solitude of the last hours before sunrise. It was a time of undiscovered treasure, of harmony in silence.

He passed his sleeping neighbors, their houses lit only by outdoor security lamps. Some roadside mailboxes named the residents in crooked, stick-on letters. Some only had numbers. By this time, Victor knew nearly all of them personally. He figured it was part of being a cop—getting to know, and to understand, the people around him. Most of them were white, but not all. A few of them were poor, but not many. Almost all of them were winning an inner struggle against the allure of racism's promise to elevate them past a whole bunch of other people; elevate them not because they had earned it, but automatically, by birthright. For generations this portion of their legacy had acted as a vaccine against feelings of inferiority, for no matter how low you were in the white world, you were still miles ahead of even the most successful black person. Yet new laws, and a lot of soul searching, had voided that gift of superiority, and most of his neighbors no longer saw this as an inherited treasure lost, but as a dishonest burden lifted.

Victor liked to think that by being a good lawman he had helped that process along, just a little. Maybe as sheriff he could nudge it a little further. He thought about this as he drove County 61 in the dark.

The farther out of town you got, the greater the distance between mailboxes. As much as he loved it way out here, he could understand how his parents might feel isolated, but now that he had presented them with new circumstances they needed to unbend a little.

He'd told them that the house he intended to buy in Bedford Woods was an easy walk from all the donuts they would ever need. He explained that Bedford Woods was the old-money part of Twisting Creek, where a century ago logging and commercial barons built houses with big rooms, high ceilings and narrow windows so tall you needed a hook-tipped pole to raise them; houses where the only black people inside were there to clean. This was where he, Victor Caraher, soon to be one of the youngest sheriffs in Kentucky, was about to call home. There was a house there going cheap. It seemed the real estate market wasn't exuberant about a big old house with a recent murder in it. With his new bump in income, he might just be able to afford it, but he needed to make a decision right now. The sole owner was driving in from New Orleans, and he wanted to unload it.

His headlights revealed his own safety-striped silver mailbox far ahead, where the road curved away into darkness. Every time he spotted it, a knot lodged in his throat. His little girl had strapped reflective bicycle tape around the mailbox flag, so that during any dark night, once he got this far, he would know he was home.

He stopped at the beginning of the long driveway. His house was set so far back from the road that his headlights didn't reach it. His first thought was to grab his mail quickly and drive on, but when he opened his door the silence of the countryside seemed to demand that he shut off the engine, so he did, and with it, his lights.

Now he could see his house. The sodium dusk-to-dawn lamp cast a snowy glow onto the spruce that by now reached his second floor bedroom window. The unexpected chill in the morning air made him think of Christmas—his second one out here alone. Though maybe not out here. And maybe not alone.

Now he was in absolute silence, a silence city people might never even know possible, yet here it was, as tender against his ears as the cheek of a sleeping child.

He reached for his mailbox. The snuffle of a horse almost made him jump. It was the little roan filly in his neighbor's field, her head stuck over the fence for a nose rub. As Victor's eyes grew accustomed to the darkness, he saw shadowy forms of other horses a few feet back, slowly moving his way. But the roan was always the first one to greet him. She loved Victor with conviction. When he mowed his lawn she would follow him on her side of the fence, up and back, step for step, until he finished. She seemed to want it clearly communicated that she was there, even if no one else was.

He rubbed her silky muzzle and then opened his mailbox. He couldn't see what was there, but by feel he knew he was carrying a couple of flat envelopes, probably bills; some flyers, no doubt junk; and a small air-insulated package. Once in the car, he could see that the package was from Yolanda. He smiled. Some little gift, maybe? A polite nudge?

He opened it right there in the car. It was sealed so well he used his teeth to pull the tape off the flap. Inside was more plastic wrapping. Whatever it was, she'd wanted it to get there in one piece. When he finally got that off he knew what he had—but it only deepened the mystery. Why would Yolanda send him the bones of a human finger?

There was a note stuck down in the envelope:

I found this in my nephew's pocket and thought it might mean something to you.

Yolanda

The ringing of his cell phone nearly lifted him off his seat. Against all reason, he knew it was Yolanda, that she was out here watching him. He snatched up his phone, but the screen said *Greer.*

"You back yet?"

"Just entering the driveway. Something must be up."

"I know you've had a long night, but I need your help right away. There's been a fire. They've found the body of one old lady. Now we're looking for Lovemore. If he's not burnt to a crisp, we may get a second chance to string him up."

Across the smoldering debris, Sheriff Greer saw a fire fighter moving toward him, holding something in both gloved hands. Greer lifted the yellow caution tape and walked into the bright frame of the searchlights to meet him.

"You know what this is, sir? At first I thought it was a pencil sharpener."

The twisted metal glob was still smoking, so Greer didn't take hold of it. But he didn't need to. He was a fisherman. "It's a casting reel."

"Yes, sir. When I figured that out, I knew you'd want to know."

Greer understood immediately. "Good eyes, son. I doubt old Mrs. Crowell was a fisherman." He also knew that Lovemore Ngwenya was, and if he had set this fire, he would have taken his gear with him. "Keep looking. He's buried in there somewhere."

A young officer approached him. "There's a woman over here, sheriff." He nodded toward the perimeter tape. "She says she'd like a word."

Greer saw a middle-aged woman standing in the semi-darkness, huddled inside a long wool sweater that she kept pulled tightly over a baggy exercise outfit. He lifted the tape and walked over to her.

With no introduction she asked, "Have you found him yet?"

"Found who?"

"Lovemore, that's who."

"Do you know something about him?"

"I live right over there." She pointed across her shoulder with her thumb. "Once you all released him, I told Portia Crowell not to let him back in. I have two girls, sheriff. A man like that's not safe to live around."

"I see. No, we haven't found him yet, but we're still looking. We did find Mrs. Crowell's body."

"I hate to say it about a neighbor and a Christian, but she had it coming to her. She was playing with fire."

"So to speak?"

The woman gave him an angry-eyed look. "None of us around here wanted him living there anymore. We warned her."

"How did you warn her?"

"I told her about my girls. They couldn't draw a easy breath knowing that a murderer was living across the street."

"And how did Mrs. Crowell react to your warning?"

"She said don't worry, she'd take care of it. Still yet, there he come."

"You saw him?"

"Sure I saw him. I watched him like a hawk. I got two girls…"

"Can you describe his movements?"

"What do you mean?"

"When did you first see him here? After the trial, I mean."

"Saw him that first day! Soon as you all let him out."

"You mean when the jury found him not guilty."

Again she gritted her eyes at him. "Same thing. He come back that night, and I saw him come and go a couple of times, carrying shopping bags with him. Then early yesterday…"

"Carrying bags which way?"

"Just carrying them normal like." She pulled a pack of cigarettes from her sweater pocket, offered Greer one. He declined, but took the lighter from her shaking hand and lit hers for her. She looked down at her feet. "Look at the mud on my shoes. I'm sorry. It's cold and I'm a little nervous. Me and my girls been out front with the water hose, wetting down our house, scared of them flying sparks."

"Very smart thing to do. Do you want to step inside your house?"

"I'm fine here. I want to see them uncover his body."

"So when I say which way was he carrying his bags, I mean, coming or going?"

"Coming in. Like he was out shopping for stuff, bringing it back. Where he gets the money I don't…"

"Then early yesterday. Please continue."

"Yesterday morning, just about daylight, he walked out of there with one little brown paper poke."

He smiled at her. "We called them 'pokes' too. I like that word."

She shrugged, and seemed to relax. "You know, hillbilly ways. They don't leave you easy." Greer's smile signaled empathy, and she continued. "Then after that, I didn't see him no more. But he must have come back, or else he wouldn't leave all his stuff behind."

They both looked aside as they heard Victor Caraher's footsteps.

"Victor," Greer said. "This is…I'm sorry."

"Mrs. Lyda Baldwin. I live right over there."

"Mrs. Baldwin saw Lovemore leave here with only a small bag at dawn yesterday morning, but didn't see him return. Maybe some other neighbors did. As soon as people start to wake up, put a couple of men on it."

"So you don't think he's buried in there?"

"It's possible. They found some fishing gear."

"I'll set up the inquiry," Victor said. "And then I think I have a lead or two of my own to track down." He started walking back toward his car.

"I hope you find him right there in that pile of ashes." Lyda Baldwin took a sharp pull on her cigarette and added another lungful of smoke to the night's surplus. "I hope he's burnt up right here and then burns a second time in hell."

Victor turned back to her and asked, "Did people around here hate him that much?"

"After Sarah, you're damn straight they did."

"Did anybody hate him enough to burn the house down?"

"I reckon some folks figure if the state won't do its job, somebody got to."

BY NINE O'CLOCK the sun had crested the nearest mountain east of town. The line of shade gave steady ground, and the morning haze was burned away until the Twisting Creek plain and the whole western valley was as warm and golden as a pan of butter cake. Yolanda watched the sharp line of sunshine cross her lawn while she ate an unhurried breakfast at the picnic table on the back deck. The leaves of the sugar maple blushed, and the yellowing leaves of the poplar turned on frail stems, the scent of their slow decay dispersing in the warming air. Against the back fence, Rollie's herb garden showed plenty of life, but his little vegetable patch was already fading into an undifferentiated shade of brown. A dulling green remained on the stalks of a few tough old leeks, and red raspberries sheltered under the trellis. Squirrels crossed the electric cables between oaks; a pair of robins flicked their tails and hopped in the grass.

The sun line reached the deck. Yolanda removed her fleece and turned her face to the sky, wondering if there was a happier place on earth to pass an October morning than in eastern Kentucky, or indeed in her back yard.

She scraped the last of the oatmeal from her bowl and turned her attention to a blueberry waffle with peanut butter melted into the crevices. She wondered if anyone else ate their waffles this way. She'd suggested it to several people, but had heard back from none of them. For the life of her, she couldn't understand why. Maybe it was like Brandon sniffing into corners. It was something nobody else did, but you loved doing it, so screw them all.

The back door opened and here came Edgar. "A visitor for you, your majesty."

She heard a man's voice say, "Can I heat up that coffee for you, ma'am?" It was Victor. He came out carrying a carafe of coffee.

"Sure," she said. "It's about time I got some service around here." Victor laughed, but had no follow up, so Yolanda quickly asked, "What brings you out this way so early?"

"Investigating last night's fire."

Edgar jumped in. "I heard sirens early this morning."

"Me too," Yolanda said. "What's up?"

"Lovemore's building burned right down to the ground, and old Mrs. Crowell with it. Maybe Lovemore too. They're digging through the ashes now."

"They're not going to find him," Edgar said.

"I don't think so either." Yolanda picked up her phone.

"Whoa!" Victor said. "What are you doing?"

She frowned at him. "I'm finding Lovemore for you. He's probably at the Odeon."

"Why the hell would he be there?"

She started to say *Rollie let him in*, but changed it to, "We're letting him stay there."

"You're what? Wait—don't phone anybody yet." Victor took out his phone and called Greer. "I've got a lead. He may be at the Odeon…I don't know why, but I'm about to find out . . . No, he doesn't know yet…Right. Let me know when they're in place."

He turned to Edgar and Yolanda. "He's sending squad cars over to guard each entrance, in case Lovemore tries to run when he finds out."

"Finds out what?" Edgar asked.

"That we know where he is."

Yolanda gave Edgar a confused squint, and he shrugged. "I don't get it either. It was no secret where he was. The five of us knew about it, maybe others. If Greer thinks he's likely to run, that means he suspects him. But if Lovemore had anything to do with the fire, he wouldn't be at the Odeon now, where he knew he could be easily located. He'd be long gone."

Yolanda held up her phone. "How about we see if he's there before we hash this out any further."

Victor nodded assent, adding, "Generic conversation. Don't tip him off."

She pressed a number. "Hey Rollie. Are you at the Odeon? . . . You working? . . . Just you and Lovemore? . . . Deedee's already there too? So they've met now. How did that go? Any sparks? Any chemistry? . . . Just assure her that after ten minutes she'll forget all about the audience … The piano is a great idea. So Edgar was right—he really can play … Doesn't matter. Any musical interlude will add something. Anybody else there? … I saw Josh as he left the house. He says he'll be there before long… Yeah, we're all excited. That must feel pretty good, huh? … Cool. Rehearse away. I'll be there in a couple of hours … Bye."

"Well done," Victor told her, "but I have to say—I'm confused. I drove all night from Memphis—and now this."

"You think *you're* confused," she said. "Why are you here if you didn't know about our connection with Lovemore?"

"Simple. Your testimony got him off, so he'd be honor-bound to find you and thank you. I just figured you were more likely to have seen him this weekend than anybody else I could think of."

"Okay. Let me explain it. But first, have you had any breakfast?"

Yolanda went into the kitchen, leaving Edgar and Victor alone on the deck. Edgar asked him, "Why would Lovemore burn down the place that took him in when he first came to town?"

"I guess people could have different opinions on that."

"And your opinion is?"

"My opinion is…private."

"Even off the record?"

"Off the record, I'm not surprised he's going about business as usual at the Odeon."

Edgar tried not to smile. "When can you give me something on the fire?"

"Early this afternoon, maybe. In plenty of time for tomorrow's paper."

"In that case I'm off to the scene and to interview the firemen." He pulled out his phone and headed for his car. He was about to drive away when he heard Yolanda come back out onto the deck. He held his phone up and told her, "I called the paper. Randy's already got pix of the fire scene. Front page stuff, he says." Edgar drove away.

Yolanda brought over a tray with fresh coffee, a pop-up waffle, a jar of peanut butter, and the single slice of apple pie left over from Sunday Supper. "Food is kind of catch-as-catch-can around here, I'm afraid. But if you've never had peanut butter on a blueberry waffle, today may be your lucky day."

"Maybe I'll tackle this pie first."

"It's store bought."

"Doesn't bother me one little bit."

For a while she watched him eat. He seemed immersed in the process. He ate with the concentration of someone with nothing to distract him from the pure pleasure of food. From his face you'd have thought that a slice of Kroger's apple pie was the ultimate attainment of life's great journey. This was not the exhausted and despondent man she'd seen a week ago. This was a man who'd laid his burdens down. But where? Where had he stashed them? Surely he hadn't gone to Paducah to get religion. Had he reconsidered the responsibility of being a law enforcement officer in a world with an infinite number of possible suspects? Yet where a single mistake could cost a life? Had he simply decided to dump his career over a cliff, as an over-packed hiker might shed a backpack?

No, the man sipping coffee in the sunshine of an autumn morning was not the man who had sat with her at Fifi's, pressing his lips into a thin line and fretting about becoming sheriff in a town with a murderer at large and an innocent man on death... *Of course!* Yolanda had finally worked her way to the explanation. There was no innocent man on death row. In a sense, when Lovemore was freed, Victor Caraher had been freed along with him. This new Lovemore chase was all on Greer's shoulders. As her mother used to say, It's your baby, you nuss it. This was Greer's baby. Let him block exits with squad cars and chase leads down blind alleys. I've got a breakfast to enjoy.

"I guess you want me to make a long story short," Yolanda offered.

"Make it any length you want. As long as the coffee holds out."

"Bottomless cup, Deputy. So, let me tell you about my weekend." She explained that Lovemore had, on his own initiative, turned up at the Odeon with an offer to audition for the part of himself, and that he had spent the last two nights in quarters she and Rollie set up for him in the basement there. She explained that if *Stage Death* made any money they would pay Lovemore a salary or a stipend of some sort, and if it didn't, at least he had free room and board while he thought out his next step.

"I think it's a great idea. It should be a huge hit."

"Do you remember, at the trial, when Reynolds put Josh on the stand about the Guardian's financial troubles? We had attempted to borrow a lot of money from Sarah's bank to make two purchases that might rescue us. Remember?"

"Some sort of new printing system, I believe?"

"That's right. And controlling interest in a paper mill. Those two things."

"Okay."

"Josh thinks that *Stage Death*, with Lovemore in it, might bring in enough revenue to secure that loan."

"I see. In that case, of course you should go for it. I don't see anything wrong with it. After all, the man was found not guilty."

"Do you still think he did it?"

"Hell, Yolanda, I never thought he did it. Or thought he didn't. Following Rollie's testimony, there was certainly reasonable doubt. That's all the jury needed to know. Not if he really and truly killed her."

"Why didn't you tell me this a week ago?"

"A week ago I didn't know your brother was such a French stud."

She laughed. "Or that he brought out the animal in Sunday School teachers."

"It just goes to prove..." He left the idea dangling.

"Prove what?"

"You never know. Where human beings are concerned, you just never know." He stood up and stretched. "My god, I feel like I've been up all night."

"You have, haven't you?"

"That would explain it. Mind if we walk around your back garden?"

They strolled past the herbs and the climbing raspberry vines. The mixed scent of lavender perfume and of berries going sour reached the border of her mom's old flower bed, now a sunken grave of weeds and gopher mounds. They paused over it, as over a cemetery plot. "She gave up," Yolanda said. "Little by little, she simply surrendered any will to be happy. It seemed she was attracted by the other end of the spectrum. Irresistibly drawn to it. Fighting it off exhausted her, so she let it pull her further and further into a kind of tormented vision of how we're meant to live."

"I'm really sorry," he said, and put his arm around her shoulder. "And the medicine?"

"It killed off all emotions. She no longer laughs or smiles. But she doesn't cry and scream either. It's like suicide for the heart. Medicinal suicide."

"But maybe worth it."

"No doubt. If you'd heard her…" She didn't finish.

Victor's phone rang. He answered it, listened, said, "Got it," and switched off. He turned to Yolanda. "Greer says the Odeon doors are guarded now, and he's five minutes away."

They completed their round of the back yard and returned to the deck. Victor showed no inclination to hurry. They sat side by side, not at the table this time, but on a wooden patio glider. Yolanda tucked her feet under her; Victor maintained a gentle to-and-fro. Nobody spoke for a long while. The only sound was a faint squeak in the glider and its louder counterpoint, robins calling in the oak trees. A sparrow fluttered to the picnic table, cocking its head abruptly between the people and the breakfast tray.

At length Victor said, "It's hard to imagine anybody living here and not being happy."

Yolanda, smiled, but didn't answer. Her sad smile was meant to say, You've got your evidence. I'm happy here. My mom wasn't.

"You'd think most women would love the Bedford Woods life, wouldn't you?" Victor persisted.

"I would think so, yes."

"Probably most women would prefer it to life way the hell out County Road 61."

A note of alarm entered her thoughts. What was he getting at? He wasn't about to ask her to choose, was he?

"I ask because I'm thinking about buying a house not far from here."

Now *that* was a surprise. Where had that come from? "Big decision. I thought you preferred the countryside."

"Yeah…in some ways, I did. But it's not so pleasant when the only one you can share it with is the little filly next door."

"I take it that's a metaphor?"

"No. It's a horse."

"Ah."

They left it there for a while. The glider moved up and back, while on the picnic table more sparrows gathered and grew bolder about the leftover bits of pie crust. Yolanda thought maybe he'd dropped the subject, but he continued, "My parents, in Paducah, maybe. They might join me."

"They certainly should like it here. Peaceful, yet not comatose."

"I'm all they've got."

She noticed that, in this telling, the sacrifice was his.

"Or maybe my little Sasha. I bet she'd love this neighborhood."

Yolanda tried to recall what he'd said at Fifi's. *Sasha loves the country life. It's her mom that gets bored.* Wasn't that it? And if so, did that mean he'd dangle Bedford Woods as a consolation prize for his ex-wife? You give up Hollywood, bring me back my child, and I'll move you way up the Twisting Creek social scale? There was always the possibility that her Tinsel Town fantasy had popped, elevating the prospect of an Edwardian house in the Woods to the status of a dream come true. Or was it more like, You stay where you are. Just send me my Sasha. I'll find another mother for her.

Was that what this was? A leisurely interview for the position of wife and mother?

"You'll know the house I have in mind. I think you said you'd been in it many times."

Initially she had no clue, but then the realization covered her like the shadow of a cloud. Still she didn't offer a guess. She would force him to say it.

Finally he gave up waiting for a reply, and said, "It's Sarah Lester's house."

"You've got to be joking."

"Why do you say that? It's perfect. The price has dropped steadily."

"Because…"

"Most likely because of…the history, which doesn't worry me

a bit. And when the sheriff retires I'll get a bump in salary."

"That should be very soon. Or with this fire...?"

"I expect he'll delay. I know I would. If Lovemore had been convicted, Greer would have stepped down right away, but as it turned out, and with all these new questions surrounding the fire, and the fresh murder..."

"Possible murder..."

"Got to be murder—collateral damage, so to speak. Surely somebody was trying to kill Lovemore. The neighbors wanted him gone, and they wanted it real bad."

"Okay, so you become Sheriff, your pay goes up, a fine house is going cheap, but..."

"There's no but. The owner's in town right now. I'm meeting him in the morning."

Ah, she thought. So that's why Ethan Lester is here: to off-load his devalued assets, not to sabotage *Stage Death*. But, since he's here, he might as well try to squeeze another buck or two out of Sarah's murder.

"I'm sorry, Victor, but there is a *but*. An important one. Isn't there a conflict of interest here?"

"I don't see how you mean." His feet stopped and the glider halted.

"Draw up any list of suspects for this morning's fire, and surely Ethan Lester's name has got to be on there somewhere."

"I don't see where you get that."

"I don't see where you *don't*, unless it's because you want that house so bad."

"That's got nothing..."

"A murdered woman's brother blows into town the same weekend her accused goes free? Then the house where almost everybody assumes he is staying burns down? Coincidences that strong need to be questioned." He didn't answer immediately. "Well, don't they?"

Victor again started the rocking motion. He looked all the way to the end of the garden, closed his eyes, then lifted his face towards the cloudless sky as though his main purpose here was to stock up on vitamin D. "I suppose you're right."

That was a phrase she'd never once heard her ex-husband utter, although she dared not tell Victor that. "Look at the bright side," she said. "Think how fast Ethan will drop his price if you walk in twirling a set of handcuffs."

"You reckon he'd throw in new carpets and kitchen appliances?" He rose to leave, but, rather than retracing his entrance through the house, he chose to walk down from the deck and around by the path at the side of the house, past another long row of dead flowers.

Yolanda walked him to his car. It was still an ominous sight to find his big black and silver Dodge patrol car there, all decked out with arrest lights.

"Oh, that reminds me," she said. "Remember Odessa Dean, the old lady with Alzheimer's? Your new neighbor, if your plan works out."

"I remember her."

"Well, I figured out what one of her riddles meant. Did she say to you: smoking black soldiers willies?"

"Did she ever! One of the most memorable phrases ever spoken by an old white woman."

"I found out what it means. A Willys was a Jeep made famous in the war. It refers to his car."

"Whose car?"

"Lovemore's."

"Lovemore doesn't even have a car."

"But I saw it."

"If he had a car, why was he hitchhiking out of town the morning he was arrested?"

"I don't...I guess maybe I thought he'd borrowed it or something."

"What are you getting at? You're as bad as Odessa Dean."

She tried to piece it together for herself, as she'd understood it before. "On Friday—the day of his verdict—I went to the Odeon. It was quite late at night. I remember seeing a black Jeep convertible there. It gave me a start, because by then I knew what a soldier's Willys meant. Then when I went into the basement I got a much bigger shock, because Lovemore himself was down

214

there. Later I put those two things together and thought, Oh, I see. Odessa had seen his car parked at Sarah's, like when he came over to do her yard work. So I dismissed it, except as a small riddle solved. But now…who in town drives a black Jeep?"

He considered it, and countered, "Who else was at the Odeon that night?"

"Nobody. Nobody that I know of."

"I'll try to find out about the Jeep, if you're interested."

"I am. But for now you'd better check in with the sheriff. Try not to let him arrest our leading man."

He laughed and got into his car. His smile held as he started his engine. He lowered the window on the passenger side. Yolanda saw that he was reluctant to say goodbye, so she stepped from the sidewalk and bent down to face him.

Victor said, "Thanks again for breakfast."

"Such as it was."

"No, it was…" he stopped. Something had come to mind. His face went serious, but clearly he didn't want the morning to end that way. He forced a joke. "Hey! With all this other business going on, I forgot to ask you: Why did you give me the finger?"

"Give you the finger?" She had certainly never flipped off any officer of the law. Not where they could catch her at it, anyway.

"That package you sent. I'm pretty sure it's the remains of a human finger."

"I forgot about that too! Oh my god! Do you really think it was a finger?"

"I do. I'll send it off to Frankfort to be certain. Where did you find it?"

"You know Deedee's kid, Brandon? It was in his pocket. Do you think it's significant? Like finding a murder victim or something?"

"It looked pretty old to me. Most of the flesh had been eaten away. More likely Brandon was playing in an old graveyard. Sometimes those wooden caskets rot away, and heavy rains like we had will raise the water table and push bits of the dearly departed to the surface."

"Maybe an old Indian burial ground or something?"

"I guess it's possible. Do you know where he found it?"

"No idea. I found it while I was doing laundry. You never know what you'll find in that boy's pockets. He loves things that smell. Deedee thinks he'll make a great lawyer, for some reason, but my money's on perfumer. Or truffle hunter."

"Might make a good detective."

"Police bloodhound, more like."

"Wait a second!" Victor thought back to the day he'd gone shopping for fishing gear. "I may know exactly where he found it. I saw him one day last week, out near the lake with Rollie. And he was sniffing something. Rollie told him it was gross and Brandon threw it into the weeds. I thought it was a chicken bone."

"Then he must have pocketed an extra one, the little sneak."

"If it's human remains, there'll be lots more where that came from. I wonder if he'd like to sneak back out there for another sniff sometime?" He looked at his watch. "Matter of fact, is he home right now?"

"I think he's upstairs."

"And how about you? How busy are you right now?"

LOVEMORE WAS RUMMAGING around the rearmost storage area of the basement. He called out to Rollie, "I've found something." It was an undersized trolley with a frayed rope handle, but it might do for moving the piano. Luckily it was only a console; old, though probably not a true antique. Rollie had the dimmest childhood recollection of an aunt or somebody playing a piano while a different aunt or somebody smiled straight into his eyes and sang "You, you, you." The whole of this memory consisted of three elements: the scent of a woman's face powder, the word "you" repeated three times, and a piano player laughing with her head thrown back. That woman was probably playing this piano—a post-war Story and Clark walnut model, with muscular, bowed legs, brass sconces on swivel braces at either end of the keyboard, and an intricate harp-shaped music rack. Lovemore tapped out a few notes of Rock of Ages. It would need tuning and polishing, but it wasn't a disaster.

They rolled it to the freight elevator and onto the stage, where they stood a while, thinking about the placement. Deedee came in through the curtain opening, stage right. She looked at Lovemore, then at the empty hall. For a moment it seemed she might bolt and run, but Rollie was ready for that. He had decided that the best way to get this morning started was with some practical instructions that, for Deedee at least, would require little effort. He introduced her to Lovemore as "the angel I don't deserve." Lovemore responded, "Nor I." They shook hands formally, and Rollie immediately began to describe Act Two.

At the set change, scenery panels would descend to make the entire stage-left a courtroom scene. The jury was Seth's formidable mural of twelve menacing heads, not people with bodies in a jury box, but a screen of floating, disembodied faces, eleven of them white, one black. Seth had fixed eleven glares toward the witness stand. The eyes of the twelfth juror, the lone black woman, looked out at the audience.

The attorneys' tables would line up against the far wall, giving the witness stand central prominence. The piano would act as a stage partition, with stage-right set as Sarah Lester's living room.

"Act One ends with the murder. The first murder."

Deedee looked puzzled. This was a new twist. "There's another one?"

"Bear with me. You'll see what I mean in a minute. The set for Act One is the back yard, back porch, and living room. That's it. At the end of Act One, Lovemore will strangle you in the yard, drag your body into the living room, and flee back stage. The curtain closes with you lying there on the floor. Then the good news for you is, for the rest of the play, you're dead!" They all tried to laugh. "But you're not completely finished. Wait until you hear my plan. You still have to deliver one line. One word, in fact." He was tempted to tell her that word immediately, but forced himself to wait. He wanted her to hear it as it developed.

"So, during the set change, Lovemore, you'll change from your gardener's jeans and t-shirt into a jacket and tie for the trial. Deedee, your only costume change will be to remove the scarf he strangled you with, and put a crucifix in its place. I'm having a big red one made, like an oversized version of the ruby one mentioned in the trial. It needs to be prominent enough to be noticed even from the back rows.

"In Act Two, the back yard is gone. Your living room basically slides all the way stage-right, and the courtroom replaces it stage-left. See what I mean? The piano will stand here, as a set divider. But here's the thing: when the curtains open for Act Two, Deedee, you will not be lying there on the floor where we left you. You will be sitting in a rocking chair right over there, reading a newspaper."

Rollie's face flushed and his flesh prickled. It happened every time he recalled the moment he received the inspiration to lift the dead Sarah Lester from her floor and place her, alive and gently moving, inside the soft circle of a reading lamp. He explained to Deedee that all she needed to do for the whole of Act Two was to rock back and forth, quietly, unhurriedly, as though she had entered a world where time had no meaning. Occasionally she should flick the newspaper as one might, turn the page; small movements to remind the audience that she was still there. The newspaper she held would of course be the Guardian, but the headline, printed large enough to be read even from the balcony, said, *LOVEMORE SWINGS*. And even if people couldn't see it well enough to read it, they would all know what it said, because they would have seen handbills of that front page distributed as Guardian inserts, and as posters in the glass cases outside the theater and in the lobby.

"Lay the paper down in your lap sometimes. Let people see the crucifix, let it register in their minds. You can even pretend to doze off for five minutes, if you want. Allow the audience to get completely absorbed in the trial, stage-left. Just be sure to wake up and pick up the paper again, to tell the audience, *I'm still here. This is still about me.*"

Rollie walked them through the final scene. Lovemore breaks down on the witness stand and makes a tearful vow of eternal devotion to Sarah. He leaves his witness chair and crosses the stage toward her, not so much charging as staggering at her, once again the rough beast in a determined slouch.

Now he approaches her living room, where all this time Sarah has been waiting, quietly marking time in her rocking chair, back and forth, back and forth, a metronome in the corner of every consciousness in the audience. This scene has overtones of ballet in it. When he gets to her side of the stage, to the door of her house, as it were, she stands. Still he trudges toward her, his glare becoming more pained with every step. She moves forward as he passes into the room. For a few steps they approach each other. Face to face, almost touching, they both pause. Sarah places her hands on his chest, sparking a period of sublime tension. At this moment the audience will understand that they have been led through the impenetrable veil of death, into a world where all things are possible. The sector of their collective mind that has for an hour registered the gently swaying Sarah in her chair, now throws the alarm: *We have entered a forbidden land.*

The actors hold that pose just long enough for the spectators to process what they are witnessing. Will the couple embrace? Is this some sort of forgiveness from beyond the grave? Or will a kiss signal that he was innocent after all? Has Lovemore's professed love been true all along?

"We've reached this tantalizing juncture," Rollie said, "but we will not fall to easy sentimentality or some afterlife voodoo. Now Deedee's hands are on Lovemore's chest. She tries to shove him toward the door. He takes her wrists in his hands and delivers his final line, a question: *What is my redemption?* Then Deedee says her only line of Act Two, the last word of the play: *Death!*

"At this point Lovemore will pause for a count of five, then—with his bare hands, this time, not a scarf—he will strangle Deedee. Again. A second time. This is like a confirming murder. In reality she may be dead, but he has to kill her memory. So Deedee, again you slump to the floor. Same spot and position. We'll try to block it precisely. And that's the end of you.

"But this is not the end of the play. Now all the lights are shut down. The theater goes completely black. We may need to install a strip of faint blue lights for you, Lovemore, so you can find your way to the gallows."

"Gallows?" Lovemore asked.

"Look up there." Rollie pointed to the rear of the stage. Lovemore looked up and for the first time saw a noose way up there. "That will be there throughout the entire drama, opening curtain to curtain call. I think maybe we need to put a soft spot on it, so people will notice it. I was also thinking, maybe we can secure a small rotating fan to one of those catwalks up there, let it blow back and forth to give the noose a swaying motion. That would help it register with the audience. It would coordinate nicely with Deedee's rocking motion. What do you think?"

Deedee and Lovemore just looked at each other. It was almost too much to take in.

"Don't worry," Rollie continued, laughing, "you'll have a safety harness. Deedee has a friend who is expert at this sort of thing. He's already worked out how it'll operate with no danger to you at all."

"No discomfort, even," Deedee added. "He told me you won't even feel excess pressure."

"That's a relief," Lovemore said, pretending to wipe sweat from his brow. "One prefers a pressure-free hanging."

Rollie's phone rang. He moved backstage to let those two get acquainted, and to take the call in private.

"Hello…Oh, hi Yollie . . . Yep, playing the early bird…Mostly explaining the set-up for Act Two… Plus Deedee…She seems nervous. That's all…I've been trying to reassure her. Oh, and the piano works. Just needs a little refurbishing…He can certainly play a little. I don't know how well yet…Josh is on his way? Great. It's really all starting to come together…bye."

After that, they began the hard part: Act One. It belonged entirely to Deedee and Lovemore. If they formed no bond that the audience could feel as growing love, the whole play would collapse. The scene is Sarah's back porch and back yard. It opens with a lot of cautious flirting while the two of them rake leaves and paint outdoor furniture. The back porch then becomes the setting for their deepening relationship. Buried in the dialogue is Lovemore's description of his life as a political prisoner of, then refugee from, Abel Magwimbi's so-called "Heroes of the Revolution." He tells her of the beatings and starvation he suffered in Sisimutsa prison, and of the white headmaster of a mission school who paid the bribes that freed him. She tells him of Kentucky's slave-holding past, and how the American South, once a sort of vast Sisimutsa prison in the land of the free, finally threw off the chains of racial hatred. He tells her he has never hated white people, that on the contrary, he shared with them a mutual respect…even love. He tells her of his education at an Anglican mission in Tuvingu, on the border with Mozambique. It was there, he says, that he was taught to question authority and to seek knowledge. The same culture that had tried to conquer and humiliate his people, had also educated him with enlightened humanism.

Yet Sarah soon grows bored with intellectual drivel on a back porch swing. She wants to know how he plans to better himself. She ridicules his current contentment, calls it a residue of third world fatalism. By the end of Act One she has grown imperious. She calls him a "natural born gardener." When he accepts this as a compliment, she responds, "That's what I might expect from your kind."

Act One ends with Lovemore's dismissal. Her final command

is, "And don't you ever darken my door again." That's when he says, "You are dead woman." He uses her scarf to strangle her, drags her body into the house, and exits. The curtain closes.

Josh had been watching this walk-through from the rear seats. He applauded and moved forward as Lovemore was fleeing. "Bravo Deedee!" he said. "You make one of the best corpses in the history of theater."

"Thanks," she said, sitting up and rubbing her throat. "I think he squeezes a little harder than absolutely necessary to look real."

"First run-through," Rollie said.

Lovemore returned from backstage. He was carrying a cup of coffee. "My apologies. I probably take my role too seriously. I'll back away."

"Lovemore, this is my—our—brother, Josh."

They shook hands. "You seem to be a natural for the stage. Great voice too. Even from the back I could hear every word clearly. And the mikes are dead, I think."

"No amplification," Rollie said. "Just a great larynx."

"How was I?" Deedee asked.

"Great. A little tentative, maybe. What anyone would expect from a first-timer. You're going to be splendid."

"Yeah, right," she said.

"Hey, I saw police cars outside. What's up with that?"

"When?"

"Just now, as I came in."

Rollie shrugged. "We didn't know anything about it. But look…" he nodded his head toward the auditorium, where Sheriff Greer and a couple of uniformed officers were making their way down an aisle.

"Are you here to rehearse, sheriff?" Josh asked.

He ignored the question, mounted to the stage and walked straight over to Lovemore. "What do you know about the fire?"

"What fire?" Rollie asked.

Greer didn't look away from Lovemore. "Your house burned down. Without you in it."

"My house? I have no house."

"Not now you don't. But you're still alive. Unlike some."

"What's this all about, sheriff?" asked Josh.

Instead of a direct answer, Greer, still staring at Lovemore, said, "Unlike your landlady."

Josh immediately pulled out his phone.

Greer asked him, "What are you doing?"

"Calling Edgar." Greer sharpened his look until Josh added, "I've got a newspaper to run."

"And I've got a possible murder investigation to run." Again he turned to glare at Lovemore. "The second one that's somehow connected with you."

Lovemore returned Greer's look, but didn't reply.

"Come on, sheriff," Rollie said. "I'm sure…"

Greer's raised hand cut him off. He still hadn't taken his eyes off Lovemore. "Maybe you'd like to tell me where you were all night."

"Of course. I was right here. From early evening. I took my dinner here."

"That's right," Rollie said. "I brought it to him myself. About eight o'clock."

"Until what time?"

Lovemore looked at Rollie. "Seven? Seven-thirty this morning?"

"At about seven-thirty I arrived and we walked down to the IHOP for breakfast."

Greer thought for a moment, then again addressed Lovemore. "Where were you between two and three o'clock this morning."

"I told you, I was right here. I didn't leave here all night."

"Can anybody confirm that?"

Lovemore was silent.

Josh cancelled his phone call to Edgar and said, "Sheriff, if it was murder, surely it was someone trying to kill Lovemore. He had no reason to burn down his own house."

"I've got men working on that angle. But right now I need an answer, Josh. You boys may see your big hotshot play going down the tubes, but if you think I'm heading into retirement with two unsolved murders on my record, and this guy thumbing his nose at me, you're in for a big shock."

Rollie spoke up. "I can vouch for him, sir. I was with him until at least three o'clock."

Greer shifted his attention to Rollie. For a short time he merely stared at him. Rollie felt blood rising to the surface of his face, but could do nothing to stop it.

"Now you be careful, son. If what you just said is a lie, then you're looking a felony square in the face."

He did his best not to hesitate. "It's true, sheriff. At least three this morning."

"You say you left here at three this morning, and returned at seven-thirty. You expect me to believe that you got, at most, four hours' sleep before you came back here? I may be getting along in years, but I'm not senile just yet. So I'm going to ask you again, one last time: what time did you leave Lovemore here on his own?"

Rollie hesitated.

Josh jumped in. "He's telling you the truth."

"You were here with them?"

"No…but I heard Rollie get home just after three. I heard his car pull in."

"You heard his car. That's kind of convenient."

"My room is at the back of the house, facing the driveway. It's a gravel drive. I slept with my window open, and I heard the crunch of gravel. That's all."

"And how are you so sure about the time?"

"I looked at the clock. I was impressed that he and Lovemore were putting in such long hours."

Rollie added, "We've got a play to put on, sheriff. You know that as well as anyone. You've got your part memorized, but Lovemore hasn't. He's got to go all out."

Josh's phone sounded. He looked at the screen, said, "It's Edgar," then answered. "Okay…and what did they say … Your sure? … and that's how it stands as of right now? … Thanks."

All eyes were on him as he clicked off and pocketed his phone. Rollie asked, "Well?"

"Preliminary reports say the fire was accidental, started in the kitchen.'

"That doesn't surprise me," Lovemore said. "She was always

cooking up something when she was half asleep. Or half drunk."

Deedee finally spoke. "You mean she had a problem?"

"A problem?"

"With alcohol, I mean."

Lovemore grimaced. "I wouldn't like to say that. She treated me well. She helped me find work with Sarah. Thus indirectly she afforded me the happiest moments of my life. But she was fond of late-night drinking."

"While cooking?" Rollie asked. Lovemore nodded.

Greer gave up. He put his hands in his pockets, but, still reluctant to let it drop, didn't move.

"Rehearsal tonight," Josh said. "You'll be here?"

Greer's only response was to turn to his men and say, "Come on, boys. Let's get out of here."

Josh, too, turned to leave, but through the rear exit. Rollie followed him off the stage and through the twisting corridor. At the door, Rollie, whispering, perhaps needlessly, asked his brother, "Is that true? You checked your clock when I got home?"

"Yes. Yes, that part is true."

"And it was after three?"

"It had to be after three. Otherwise…what if they take Lovemore? No Lovemore, no full house. Then where are we?"

"Then we got nothing, is where we are."

"And anyway, it was an accident. Edgar said so."

"The woman drank a lot."

"It's crazy to try to cook when you're in that condition. So yes. I heard gravel, checked my clock. It said 3:12. I'm sure it did. You're equally sure, right?"

"Of course," Rollie said. Curiously, he extended his hand. "I would never change my story on that."

"Good. Me either." Josh shook his hand. "Then let the show begin."

BRANDON SAT HAPPILY in the back seat of Victor's patrol car, playing Smell and Tell. Smell and Tell was a new game Travis had devised for him. It involved Brandon pulling a small plastic jar from a bag filled with them, opening the lid, sniffing, and identifying the contents. The idea was to nudge him in the direction of less unpleasant smells, as well to encourage him to make some attempt to talk to people.

"Orgon garlic," he told Yolanda and showed her the label.

"Correct!" she said, "Oregano and garlic." Yolanda was sitting in the back seat with him mainly because she'd been afraid he might flip out once he noticed that he was sitting in a caged back seat. "It'll be fun! Like riding in a taxi!" she'd assured him. Needlessly, it turned out, for once he started his game he didn't notice anything else. He didn't look out the window. He didn't clap his hands in rhythm to the kiddie CD she'd brought along, or react to the crackle of the police radio. He didn't ask where they were going. He just sniffed and identified.

"Pomzon and Targon," Brandon said.

"Parmesan and tarragon! Good job!" Brandon didn't react to the praise. Yolanda tried to fathom the precision of his concentration. She couldn't shake the feeling that there was a touch of the supernatural about her nephew. She felt a goose of a shudder run through her. To counterbalance it, she said to Victor, "He's got this enormous vocabulary for his age. Deedee says he's like a miser hoarding gold coins."

"One day he'll go on a spending spree and you'll wish he'd shut up."

"Santino," Brandon said.

Victor asked over his shoulder, "What's Santino?"

Yolanda read, "Santino of Paris. I think it's Josh's after shave. There can't be too many two-year-olds in Kentucky who can identify Santino of Paris."

"Let's hope the hell not."

When they turned off the main road and started the descent towards the lake, he was aware enough of his surroundings to start pointing in the direction of Archer's Bait and Boat. "Travis," he said.

Yolanda was watching him intently, alert for clues, as one watches a magician at work. She told Victor, "He didn't even look up, yet he's pointing in the direction of the store. How does he know where we are?" She could have addressed Brandon—the child wasn't deaf—but she had the impression he would have ignored her question.

Victor tried to make eye contact with her via his oversized rear view mirror. "Maybe he felt it when we started downhill."

Or, she thought, shuddering, maybe he can *smell* Travis.

He couldn't smell Travis personally, because Travis wasn't there. The store was closed, with a big GONE FISHING sign on the door. It didn't seem like a great idea for his fledgling business venture, but it made their task easier.

Victor drove around back. The garage door was padlocked. Yolanda peeked through a crack and saw that it was empty. Victor removed the plastic wrapping from the finger Yolanda had sent him and showed it to Brandon. "Do you remember where you found this?"

Brandon sniffed it, laughed, and pointed into the woods. "Go der."

"You go, son. We'll follow you."

The tops of weeds and bush leaves brushed his face familiarly, though dryer than before. The scent, too, was fainter now, but pervasive. There was no breeze to carry it. Brandon was forced to first try this way, then that, allowing the intensity of the chemistry to guide him.

Victor and Yolanda followed his every zig and zag. He never looked back to check for them. He dove headlong through thickets of rhododendron. Occasionally they lost sight of him and had to follow the sound of him pushing through the undergrowth. Once, when he stopped to take his bearings, they lost even his sound and called out to him, "Brandy! Where are you?" He gave no response, but soon enough started moving again.

They followed him into deep woods, onto protected wilderness land. Old growth trees all around meant a thinned out forest floor. The underfoot now was decaying debris in the process of becoming soil. Great hemlocks, beech, white oak, and basswoods, survivors of the logging slaughter and well over a century old, dominated the canopy. Yolanda had no idea how they would ever find their way back. She thought to herself, I hope the little gremlin can smell the car.

He came onto a marked trail, which he crossed, and stopped, his head thrown back and his eyes closed. He started turning slow, meditative circles, around and around, again and again, then stopped, dead still. He squinted toward where rays of sunshine splintered through branches of red spruce, lowered his gaze toward a disturbed section of the mossy forest floor, and broke into a one of his determined, swaying runs. For all his high-kneed motion, he covered little ground with each step, but the force that propelled him was relentless.

"Der!" he said. "Look der!"

Victor and Yolanda hurried to catch up. Ahead they saw a mound of branches covering ruts from tires and larger depressions. Brandon laughed and started ripping away at the branches, then fell to his knees and began to dig at the earth with his hands. The frenzy of digging continued until his face was below ground level, and the sound of his laughter carried the hint of an echo.

Victor and Yolanda knelt beside him. They too started in with their hands, until Victor said, "Hold on. I don't think we should disturb the scene any further."

But he did disturb it just a bit further. He cleared a layer of moist dirt from the face of a human skull. And then another.

An hour later, freshly showered but still shaken, Yolanda drove to the Odeon. She needed to get her mind off the shallow grave in the woods and into her part as Prosecutor Reynolds. She needed to infuse Reynolds' lines with the contempt and venom of the originals. She hoped the sight of those eyeless skulls staring through the mud would provide precisely the motivation she needed.

She turned down toward the Odeon's side entrance—and there she saw it again. This time the shock nearly overpowered her. She hit her brakes. The car behind her skidded to a panic stop. Angry shouts and horn blasts pulled her back. She steered her car to the side and ran into the theater. Here it was again, the source of poor Odessa Dean's unnamable terror: a black soldiers' Willys. And whoever its owner was, he was in the Odeon right now.

"WHERE ARE YOU, Deedee?"

The sound of Travis' voice, distant and hollow, told Deedee that he'd entered the Odeon through the basement. She hustled backstage and called down the stairs, "We're up here."

He appeared at the bottom of the stairs, smiling and carrying his tool box in one hand and a small duffle bag in the other. "You and Brandon?"

"Me and Lovemore."

His smile sagged. Deedee noticed, and compensated with a beaming smile of her own. The guy really liked her son! No other man was in Travis' league where her son was concerned. Again, as back at his cabin, she felt the urge to throw her arms around him. Who besides Travis would be disappointed that Brandon wasn't there? Or was this disappointment caused, not by Brandon's absence, but by Lovemore's presence? She tried to fix her broad smile in place. She so hoped Travis wouldn't display any alpha male signals. She said, "Let me give you a hand," and started down the stairs.

"I've got it. It's not heavy." He raised the duffle bag to eye level. "Just way more rope than it ought to take to hang one man."

"Shhh," she said, pointing upstairs. She took the bag, carried it up the back stairs and slid it behind the gallows they'd built there, center stage rear, then she pulled Travis by the wrist onto the stage, where Lovemore stood, alone, gesticulating towards the empty auditorium and quietly mouthing his lines. "Let me introduce you two. Lovemore *Un-gway-nya*," she began, over-emphasizing the correct pronunciation, "this is Travis Archer, my new friend. Travis, meet Lovemore, my co-star." She laughed.

"Her even newer friend, perhaps," Lovemore said, shaking Travis' hand.

"Travis is the man who's going to hang you." She had been planning that joke. It went down well, so she had a follow-up quip ready. "And not just once. Many times."

"Multiple hangings would be a great relief to me," Lovemore said. They only looked at him, until he added, "for they mean a long-running success."

It was all so effortless and smooth, yet…she watched their eyes. The mirthful introduction wasn't reflected there. And weren't they locking on at least a tiny bit more than necessary? "Well," she looked at Travis and rubbed her hands together in workmanlike fashion, "shall we start by showing Lovemore how this rig works?"

Lovemore didn't seem to hear. He was now staring hard at Travis. "I can't shake the impression that I've seen you before."

Travis shrugged, turned to open his bag, but then turned back and offered, "Fishing, probably. I saw you once out on Greasy Creek."

Lovemore rubbed the sides of his neck with his thumb and forefinger, a gesture Deedee by now recognized as characteristic. "Possibly," he said, not convinced.

"You had first-class gear." This time the lock-on was unmistakable.

For an endless time, it seemed to Deedee, Lovemore refused to look away, but finally he did, saying only, "Yes. Thank you. It was a gift."

"Is it all gone now? I heard about the fire." Evidently even in confrontations such as this, fishermen could find shared empathy.

"All gone. But not to worry. If Stage Death is a success, you'll have found a new customer."

"I sure could use one…"

"No! Hold on! It wasn't at the creek. Did you know Sarah, by any chance?"

Deedee was still watching their every gesture, still getting a lesson in male behavior, but this time the flick of the eyes was at her. Travis had clearly indicated that this conversation should not continue in her presence.

"Yeah, she was my loan officer. You probably saw me at the bank."

"But I never visited her bank."

Lovemore wasn't taking the hint! If I saw it, Deedee thought, then surely he saw it. Wait 'til I tell Yolanda about *this*.

Travis took a long coil of rope and a lifejacket from the duffle bag. "Let's get on with it. What we need to do is have you hanged in a way that doesn't harm you, but looks real to the audience. As I understand it, after you strangle Deedee the second time—which still seems weird to me, but hey, I'm just Mr. Fix-It around here—the theater lights will all shut off for about one minute."

Deedee said, "Seth will get some techie type from the college to handle the lights and sound system, from way back up there." She pointed toward the top of the back balcony wall. "When he sees me fall down, that's his cue to cut the lights. Once you have completed step number seven, the lights need to come back up. But the unusual thing about this scene, for the lighting guy, is that he can't see when you're ready."

Lovemore said, "Rollie mentioned that. His solution is to use an automatic timer to switch the lights back on. We must pinpoint the exact length of time to allow you to get harnessed, but not so long that the audience gets bored waiting."

"It shouldn't be a problem," Deedee said. "After the two of you practice the steps a whole bunch of times, we'll clock it in rehearsals, to get it exact. And you know that this noose will be hanging there, lit up, during the whole play. But for that final minute even the noose will be dark."

Travis told Lovemore, "With the lights off, you'll exit the stage through the back curtains. They're thick and black, so back there, whoever is your helper—me, I guess—but whoever it is will turn on a weak bulb for you. That's when you need to go through seven exact steps. Got that? In order, exactly seven."

Lovemore said, "One, two, three, four, five, six, seven—all good children go to heaven."

"If that helps you remember," Travis said. "Step one, take off the suit jacket you've been wearing in court. Two, get into this harness. I've made it from braided polyester line and a PFD—a lifejacket—and it's strong as hell. Here's how it works. You slip your arms through it, then fasten it by these three plastic buckles. See? Click, click, click. You're in. Now, step three, climb these stairs up to the gallows. Step four, knot the lifejacket rope around the metal cleat I've attached to this wooden beam back here. This will hold you airborne. You should use a cleat hitch. I'll teach you how to tie one. Once you know how, you can do it in two seconds, flat."

"I know how to tie a cleat hitch."

"Great. Now you're ready for step five. There'll be a suit coat there just like the one you had on before, but larger, to hide the life vest. Put that on. Step six, put the noose around your neck. There'll be plenty of give in the rope. Your helper will take up just enough slack so the audience won't see it hanging limp. Of course, your actual weight is borne by the vest and harness rope. You with me so far?"

"I think so. I must say, I don't like the idea of you having me by the neck."

Travis thought a moment. "I don't like you having Deedee by the neck either."

"Well. Too bad for all of us," Deedee cut in, "but that's the way the play works. And it works very well."

Travis turned from her to face Lovemore. "She's right."

"Of course she is," Lovemore said. "Please continue."

"Okay. You are in the noose and standing at the edge of the gallows. The entire theater is in total darkness. Now you take step seven, which really is a step. You step through the curtain and off the front of the gallows floor. Once you've done that, and you're dangling in mid-air, hanging there limp, or twitching, however you guys handle it, then the stage lights come on."

"No," Deedee corrected, "only a spotlight on Lovemore, and a softer one on me, still lying there dead on the floor."

"Anyway," Travis said, winking at Deedee, "you don't have to worry about that part. As the Bible says, your work on earth is done."

Deedee said, "Do you want to run through it now a whole bunch of times? Starting with when you leave the courtroom and walk into my living room? Right to the end. With lights on, I mean. We don't have anybody here to run the lights, but we can practice the rest."

"Oh! Now I've got it!" Lovemore said. "It's been annoying me all this time: where I have seen you before. What kind of car do you drive?"

"An old black Jeep. Why?"

"Then that's it! I saw you at Sarah's house. I was working in the garden. I saw you leave your car and enter the house. Then I heard raised voices. Were you and she having a row?"

"A what?"

"Perhaps you were quarreling."

"No. Never. I had to sign some papers, is all. For my loan. Maybe I was telling some silly joke. Sarah loved to laugh. I'm sure you know that."

"I do know that," Lovemore said. "Absolutely I know that. But I also knew I had seen you somewhere. I am so glad we cleared that up. For a moment you had me worried."

A commotion downstairs stopped the conversation. They turned to face the backstage curtain, toward the approaching thud of footsteps on the stairs. They watched as the curtain bulged all along its length, angry probes where a fist sought out the opening flap. Finally the fist found the gap, and Yolanda burst through. "Who drives that black Jeep outside?"

"What's the problem?" Travis asked. "No parking zone?"

EVERYBODY ASSUMED THAT Sheriff Greer would be the next person to leave the cast—as indeed he was—but nobody could have imagined the way he left. Edgar, who knew him better than the others did, expected a phone call saying something like, "Sorry, but when I signed on I thought the Lovemore case was sewed up tight and I could end my career in law enforcement on a positive note, and then start my retirement with some light-hearted fun in your troupe. But his acquittal leaves one murder unsolved, and this burned out house leaves another—I'm not buying this accident theory, I don't care what the FD shift investigator says—so I won't be leaving the department just yet, which means I have to pass on the Twisting Creek Players. Thanks for inviting me, though."

But that's not what happened.

Greer turned up smack on time for the first full rehearsal. He didn't have much to say, just grabbed a cup of coffee and a handful of the chocolate *madeleines* Rollie had baked to mark the occasion, and sat in the farthest seat along the front row of the auditorium, practicing his lines. He paid no attention to the unfolding Act One on stage. Even though this was his first chance to watch it, he displayed no interest in it whatsoever. The on-stage people took no notice of him either. They were absorbed in their own parts. It was easy to miss the quietly murmuring figure in the shadows. No one knew he had already resigned as sheriff. Yolanda had no way of knowing that hours later Victor Caraher would phone to say he was now Interim Sheriff of Buford County. Neither she nor Edgar could have known that come midnight they'd both be back at the Guardian office, remaking the front page.

What caught people's attention at that first rehearsal was the energy of Greer's performance once he hit the stage. He was more animated here than he had been in the actual courtroom. When he said, "She wore a wool scarf cinched tight around her neck. I mean real tight. That's what he used to kill her," Greer emphasized the *he* and pointed directly at Lovemore, his finger trembling with anger. And all through his testimony he fixed a lethal stare on Lovemore that even the greats of the stage might envy.

When rehearsal ended, Lovemore approached him, shook his hand, and said, "You are a marvelous actor."

Greer said, "I can't hold a candle to you."

As the rehearsal ended and everyone was walking out to their cars, he tapped Deedee on the shoulder. "Hang back one second, okay?" He looked around for Lovemore, saw him watching them from the bottom of the stairs. "Better let me drive you home."

"I rode in with Rollie," she said.

"Humor me," Greer told her, leading her by the arm to his old Scout. In the truck he said, "Listen, I know this whole thing has grown way bigger than anybody ever thought it would. I figured it would have all the impact of a high school drama club."

"If that," Deedee added.

Greer laughed. "At least with those things a few parents get drug along. I figured we'd get an audience of about twenty bored Presbyterian Homes residents. But now I understand that this thing is supposed to rescue your family's fortune and make a name for Rollie, and cure cancer for all I know."

He turned a smile on her as she watched him drive. She was starting to understand that there was more to this man than the stereotype allowed for.

"So what I'm getting at is, I know you feel like you've got to go through with it. With being Sarah."

"You can't imagine how frightened I was, even without an audience. Could you see me shivering?"

"You were fine. Maybe your stage fright even added to your performance. But that's not what I'm getting at."

They stopped at a traffic light on Central. She felt him looking at her and turned to face him. "Then what are you getting at?" Although by now she thought she knew.

"I'm going to tell you straight, because your young life may depend on this conversation. Lovemore killed Sarah Lester. Let's face that. He's walking the streets today only because I fouled up the investigation. And because Liz Reynolds wanted to make a name for herself as one tough crime bitch, and she over-reached herself.

The facts of the case pointed more to voluntary manslaughter or maybe second degree murder. We could have nailed him on one of those. But they don't carry the death penalty, and Reynolds wanted him to swing. So now he's free."

Deedee fidgeted in her seat. She pulled at the neck of her sweater, the turtleneck she would wear in each performance. "He's an innocent man, sir. I will consider him such. In this country…"

"In this country a whole bunch of criminals are out free, and I suppose the other way around too. I have no doubt you will resist what I have to tell you, but you are in real danger."

She tried to make light of it. "I'm in more danger getting hooted off the stage by the audience."

"No, Deedee. Lovemore has what polite people call 'anger management issues.' If he mistakes you for the real Sarah, loses control, and starts to relive his last moments with her, then you are in mortal danger. And I'm not exaggerating the danger one iota. I'm not saying he's evil and gets a charge out of it. Although that might be true, too. I'm just saying there's enough of a chance he'll go berserk that you need to take precautions against it."

"Like what kind of precautions? Short of leaving the show, I don't see what I can do."

"Here's one thing. One time when I was trying to subdue an angry drunk, I wrenched my neck, and they put me in a brace. A hard plastic piece that curved all around my neck. One like that could fit under your turtleneck where nobody could see it."

"Oh, I wouldn't know about those things."

"They're easy to get. I got mine over at Timmons Surgical. It didn't cost a lot. You don't need a prescription or anything. The audience will never even know it's there."

"But he'll know."

"I thought of that. What we can do is get Rollie to tell him the strangling doesn't look real enough because he has to go too easy on you. Rollie can suggest it, for the good of the play. That'll work, don't you think?"

"Maybe." She wanted him to drop the subject.

"Let me run you over to Timmons tomorrow and get you fitted. Okay?"

"If Rollie's willing to explain it, I guess it's okay."

"Great. And here's another thing. I may not be here to look after you for much longer, but you're going to need a protector nearby, somebody you can signal if things go wrong."

"Nothing's going to go wrong."

"Maybe not. But just in case—you seem to be kind of fond of that Archer guy with the ropes."

"Travis."

"Yes, Travis Archer. He's a big, strong fellow, and he's right there backstage. Let's get him in on this. He could be your guardian angel."

And so the next day, his first full day as a civilian in over forty years, Greer phoned Rollie to tell him that from down in the front seats the strangling scene looked fake. He explained his idea for correcting this. Then he drove Deedee to Timmons Surgical Supply, described what they needed, and put it on his credit card. On the way back to town they stopped at the bowling alley to roll a game and enjoy a lunch of chili beans and beer.

Deedee hadn't bowled since high school. She felt like a girl again, complete with a father to watch over her, and to hang out with. For a while she almost forgot that soon she would have to stand up in front of a thousand people and get murdered. She told Greer, "We should do this more often."

"I wish we could, Deedee. I really do. But I took half my pension as a lump sum and I'm going fishing. The fishing expedition of a lifetime."

"But when you get back…"

"That might be a long, long time."

She didn't ask him why. The answer was on his face. Even after the beer and the bowling, his sad eyes spoke of a shining career marred beyond salvation by a botched ending.

"Where are you going?" she asked.

"Africa."

EDGAR SAT WITH Lovemore in the basement of the Odeon, rehearsing Lovemore's scene on the witness stand. Upstairs over four hundred people were watching a double feature of *Hangmen Also Die!* and *Hitler's Hangman*, Rollie's cynically rush-ordered, but inspired, pairing of World War Two propaganda films, both based on the massacre that followed the assassination of "Hangman" Heydrich, Gestapo chief in Prague, both made in 1943 by German exiles in America, and both—despite every slur he'd ever made against Rollie's films—on Edgar's must-see list. For lately Edgar had become interested in fascism.

Edgar didn't often try to analyze his own inner workings. If he'd ever bothered to think about his lack of introspection—which by definition he never did—his response to Socrates might have been that the over-examined life is a pain in the ass. One incident, however, had prompted even Edgar to self-reflection. It started with a comment from a Franklin College sociology professor. Edgar was interviewing her about society's fondness for the death penalty. The interview itself had stemmed from the Guardian's attempt to spin the Lovemore case as many ways as possible. He hardly expected to get anything more from it than a few column inches of generalizations and dry statistics. Yet in the middle of it the woman brought up Nazi death camps and turned the interview around. "What do you think defined fascism, anyway?" She paused long enough to let him realize he didn't know the answer, then said, "One grounding tenet, and one only: a belief in the cleansing and regenerative power of group violence. By killing off the weak and the outsiders, we make ourselves strong. That was all they had to sell, and people bought it like hotcakes."

And then later, out there at the scene of the fire, all those people pressed up against the caution tape, standing there for hours, some of them still in their bedclothes, hoping to see Lovemore's charred remains exhumed. Was it a simple desire for justice? A murderer slips the noose, so look what happens? Was it base revenge?

Or would these good Americans, raised on the Declaration of Independence and the Beatitudes, feel regenerated, redeemed, empowered, just like good Germans steeped in victimhood and bile?

These thoughts troubled Edgar all the more when he recalled that he had never really questioned the sheriff's assertion of Lovemore's guilt, or the consequences of a guilty verdict. Put all this together and Edgar found himself eager to learn more about organized violence and the individuals involved, both the brutes and the bystanders, and eager to see the two movies showing directly upstairs from where he sat. Of course they were Allied propaganda movies, not documentaries, but propaganda could be instructive in its own right.

However, right now he wasn't free to watch movies with the folks upstairs. He had a job to do. He, portraying his Leo Akers character, had to prep Lovemore for his courtroom scene in Act Two. He said, "Did she offer you money?"

"She gave me that ruby cross. She claimed it was worth several hundred dollars."

"And you accepted it?"

"Sir, I am very nearly broke. But I swear before you and this court and before my almighty God: when I left her I did not steal any jewelry, and she was as alive as you and I are right now. I would like to get my hands on whoever did it. I still miss her so much."

"And the last sentence you spoke to her—the sentence that some in this courtroom have characterized as a death threat—how can you explain that?"

Lovemore started laughing. "I must say, it's a lucky thing I didn't say that in court."

Edgar checked his script. "Sorry. Where are you?"

"No, I mean, what I just said: *I would like to get my hands on whoever did it.* It's lucky for me I didn't say that in the real court."

"Oh, I see. Didn't you?"

"Of course not. What must the jury have thought if I had? Rollie has embellished my words for dramatic effect. He's very clever that way."

"Right. But may I caution you—not that I'm an experienced

pro on the subject—but it's probably not a good idea to exit character in the middle of a rehearsal. Unless you have a serious question about a line. If it happened in performance you'd have a hard time getting back in. Better to stay in character. Make it a habit. Make yourself believe that you and the character are one and the same."

"Right you are. Shan't happen again."

They picked it up from there, but now Edgar's head kept slipping out of Leo Akers. He was thinking, But…but you *did* say that. Didn't you? Seems to me…but he's right. It would have been a foolish thing to say. Jurors might think, See? The man's prone to violence. Got to be wary of this one.

Late that night, back home, even as he was practicing his lines, pacing back and forth across the living room rug, it was still on his mind. When Rollie got home, Edgar asked him, "Did Lovemore really say he'd like to get his hands on the guy who killed Sarah?"

"Sure did. He said he'd strangle him with his bare hands."

"No, he didn't. He said, *I would like to get my hands on whoever did it.*"

"No. He said *strangle.* It struck me as a bit strong for somebody I'd just met. I thought, man, this dude's up front."

"Hang on. What are you talking about, 'Just met?'"

"At the Odeon that morning, the very first time I spoke to him."

"No. I mean at the trial. In your script he says, *I would like to get my hands on whoever did it.* Those are the exact words. Look." He held out the script.

"I know that's in the script. What are you asking me?"

"Did he really say it in court? Or did you add it for punch?"

Rollie thought for a moment. "Shit, Eddie, I don't remember. I tried to stick to my notes. Don't you think it's a good line?"

"It's fine. It's just that in our work this evening he denied saying it. Said it would have been stupid."

"Yeah, well, he's a free man today, so what's his problem? Doesn't he want to use it?"

"Oh, he's got no problem with it. I was just curious, that's all."

Edgar dropped it and soon went off to bed, but the next

morning it was still there, stuck in a corner of his brain. At lunch time he drove down to the courthouse, where he found Karolyn Burton at her desk, trying to spear pieces of corkscrew pasta with a toothpick. She didn't look up from her exacting task until she heard his knock on her doorframe.

"Well," she said. "Howdy, stranger."

"Don't you have any silverware?"

"It's a dieting tip. You'd be surprised how quick you give up on pasta if you have to spear it piece by piece."

"You could probably starve to death eating spaghetti."

"I should try that. You want to try a toothpickful?"

"I wouldn't want to deprive you of your lunch."

"How do you manage to stay so skinny, anyways?"

"Constant fear of going broke, Karolyn. That's my dieting tip."

She laughed. "What brings you down into the bowels of our great justice system?"

"Just that…I don't guess you've transcribed the Lovemore trial."

"I'm sorry. It's all still in machine shorthand. Probably it'll stay that way unless somebody pays for transcription service. Why are you asking? Something for the paper?"

"No, not really." Edgar put his hands in his pockets and leaned against the door. "To be honest, it's for the play." Edgar thought, Semi-honest anyway. "It's just one line. How much would a transcription service for one line cost me?"

"Can you be specific about day and time? I can locate it by the time stamps."

"I know it was during Lovemore's own testimony, on Tuesday, the twenty-eighth."

"I think we've still got the printout rolls here in the office files. I'll tell you what. Take this." She handed him her container of pasta and a toothpick. "Eat half of this for me and we'll call it even." She rolled her chair over to some filing cabinets.

Edgar laughed and took a couple of bites. "Delicious," he said.

"Here, I've located it. What was the line?"

"It was right after Leo asked him about the ruby necklace. Lovemore says he took it because he was broke. Right after that."

"Next he said, *She was as alive as you and I are right now. I would like to get my hands on whoever did it. I still miss her so much.* That part?"

THE OLD GREEN Scout belonged in a museum or in a junkyard, one or the other; not on I-64, barreling east through West Virginia. That's why Allard Greer was all cramped up in a tin can called a Rio, the cheapest thing he could rent in Twisting Creek. The steering wheel rubbed against his belly, he couldn't figure out how to turn the heater on or adjust the passenger side mirror, and now he remembered that his GPS was in a suitcase in the trunk. The blinding sunrise had him squinting his way to a nasty headache, and might well slam him into the side of a semi. That, he figured, would be one hell of a way to cure a headache. He decided a better way was to pull over as soon as he could. It seemed silly to make his first pit stop less than an hour after he'd left home, but it seemed even sillier to keep on driving. In fact, the past few weeks had been nothing but silliness; silliness distilled and refined to its purest form. Grain alcohol silliness. Crack cocaine silliness. Enough silliness to overbalance and topple a lifetime of achievement.

Coffee, at least, was never silly. In the parking lot of a restaurant in Barboursville, he played with the controls until he got the heater working. He found a lever that caused the steering wheel to release his belly. He got the other adjustments under control, took a pair of sunglasses and his GPS from his suitcase, and went inside.

Nobody looked up at him. It was a strange feeling, not being noticed. He didn't exactly dislike the anonymity. He didn't yearn to go put on his uniform so people would look up and think, Oh shit, the sheriff. He felt different, that was all. It was one little sign among many that he'd crossed over into a new phase, and he noticed it.

He sat at the counter and ordered coffee. According to his GPS, Falls Church was six hours away. He had plenty of time.

Apparently *St John's Episcopal Church, Falls Church* confused his GPS. He would have to dig the street address from his notebook, which was back in the car. Until that moment he'd never considered what a curious name for a city Falls Church was. Like the whole town was one big church. He supposed it referred to some church near a waterfall, not a church you fall into. He drank his coffee and imagined dozens of sinners tumbling down a hill and rolling into a church. Fall off the wagon. Fallen women. Fallen angels. He would have to ask what's-his-name at St. John's about that.

What was that guy's name? That, too, was in his notebook. In the car. And what was his title? What did Episcopalians call their preachers? They weren't priests, were they? Vicar, maybe? What the hell was a vicar, anyway? That was another question he could ask later today. Maybe, for him, that would be the whole point of retirement: ask a lot of strange questions, learn a bunch of new stuff.

He was on the wrong side of a divided highway from St. John's Episcopal. Normally he would do a U-turn, but he wasn't sure that the Falls Church police would honor his Twisting Creek badge, so he had to do a few good-citizen right turns before he found the entrance to the church parking lot. Arrows led him around back, where a slender and—he couldn't help noticing—strikingly attractive black woman was raking dead leaves from a row of shrubbery that fronted tall stained glass windows. Greer asked her where he might find the church office. Her answer caused him to stare even closer at her, not for its content, which directed him around a corner and through a door, but for its accent, which was African.

That was not to be his last surprise of the day. The church "rector"—so it said on his door—heard his footsteps and met him outside his office. The guy wore two gold rings in each ear, a sleeveless, army-green muscle shirt, trousers that stopped just below the knee, and Jesus sandals. He had hair down to his shoulders, a US flag tattooed on one bicep, and a different flag on the other. Greer had heard that Episcopalians were relaxed about homosexuality, but he hadn't quite prepared himself to be met by a church official in semi-drag.

"Ah," the rector said, extending his hand. "You are Sheriff Greer, aren't you?"

"I am. And you are Mr. Anderson, I believe. I recognize your voice."

"Come into my office. My wife is downstairs making coffee. I hope you'll join me." He was already picking up the phone.

"Sure," he said, but was thinking, *A wife?* A real, female version of a wife, or is "wife" just modern terminology? Either way, he knew, he had already started his late-stage educational project.

"So! We were extremely pleased to hear from you that Lovemore was acquitted, and has already found a job."

"Not exactly a job, but something like one. He's joined an amateur acting group."

"Really? He's got the voice for it."

"Don't I know it. He's got talent, too."

"Are they into Shakespeare? He'd make a perfect Othello."

"He makes an even more perfect Lovemore." Anderson tilted his head at him. "He's playing himself in something they call Stage Death. About the trial."

"You're joking!"

Greer heard a door open and a woman's voice saying, "He isn't joking, darling." He turned as she circled him with a serving tray, and got yet a new surprise: she, too, was African. With Lovemore's polished accent.

"My wife, Privilege. This is Sheriff Greer, from Twisting Creek."

"Does he show promise, our Mr. Ngwenya?" she asked.

"Promise? Oh, you mean as an actor?'

"Yes. I found the website."

"No question. He's a natural."

"That is excellent news." She turned away, and as abruptly as she had entered, she was gone.

Anderson said, "I suppose that where you come from the idea of a mixed marriage still carries a certain stigma." He spoke in the lowered voice of one who is accustomed to receiving confidences from those who've strayed.

"Oh, no." Greer gave him a chummy laugh. "Not one bit." As evidence he started to cite *My deputy*…but quickly recalled that Victor was no longer in a mixed marriage. Nor was he his deputy.

"In the world you grew up in, my marriage to that wonderful

woman would have been illegal. Funny to think that you'd be here to arrest us, not share our coffee."

"You mustn't take me for a redneck sheriff."

"Loving versus the State of Virginia. Isn't that just too perfect?"

"I don't get it."

"That was the Supreme Court case that undid all those laws. A Virginia white man and black woman fell in love and went to D.C. to get married, where it was legal. They came back home and were arrested. His last name—hers too, by that time—was Loving. Isn't that great?" He laughed and shook his head. "It's enough to make you religious, isn't it?" He laughed again.

Greer laughed with him. "Loving versus Virginia. You couldn't make it up." He let the humor hang there between them, let it ebb and evaporate, then asked, "You don't think there was a racial angle to the case against Lovemore, do you?"

Anderson's eyes met Greer's. "I don't know. Was there?"

"None. I can assure you of that."

"Good."

"He's a free man today. If you need proof."

"Good," he said again. "I'm glad. Very glad. As is my wife."

Greer didn't respond. After forty years as a cop, he didn't know how to interview as a civilian.

The lady from the flower garden came in, wheeling a large green trash barrel on a trolley. Anderson noticed her, turned to peer down into his waste basket, and waved her off. She left without a word.

"In that case, what are you doing here?"

"Oh…I suppose I'm trying to put my own mind at rest. See, it was my last case. As of two days ago, I'm an ex-cop."

"My official affidavit was good enough for you when you were a cop, but not now? I don't get it. Is this some kind of extra-legal pressure? Maybe you've morphed into some kind of self-styled vigilante?" He was smiling like he didn't mean it.

"No, whoa, whoa!" Greer held up his hands, tried to chuckle. "You've got me all wrong. I only figure there's a lot more to Lovemore than I've yet understood, and I'd like to know more. That's all."

"What could I possibly tell you that wasn't in my affidavit?"

"Well, for instance, the process. How he got to this country. It seems like he doesn't know a soul here. How can that happen?"

"That's easy, and not nearly as suspicious as you seem to think. One of the callings that this parish takes very seriously is upholding the human rights of our brothers and sisters in countries that aren't—shall we say?—quite so concerned about legal niceties. Like due process. Or a fair trial."

"Like he got in Twisting Creek."

Now Anderson really smiled. "Exactly like that. So occasionally we get word from one of our missions that a person needs...assistance...in a rescue. As you well know, good old Abel Magwimbi, 'liberator' of South Zambezi, has turned out to be a monster. The kind of fascist that poor Africa has had more than her share of. You don't toe his line, you can spend the rest of your life in prison. Sometimes we find a way to free some of his victims."

"And your assistance takes the form of...?"

"Money, basically."

"You bribe the right people?"

"It's unfortunate, but that's the way the world works. Then we help them enter this country."

"Like an immigration agency?"

"We may be a small congregation, but we do have some ties to Washington."

"So your money gets them out. Your Washington connections get them in."

"Sometimes we make it work. Such was the case with the dear woman whom you met earlier."

"You mean your wife?"

"I do."

"And the janitor lady? With the trash barrel?"

"Her too."

"It must get expensive."

"God doesn't keep account books."

"Not the money kind, anyway." Greer laughed and Anderson joined in. They were back on common ground.

"Mind you, it's not always so costly. With Lovemore, we didn't have to bribe anyone. Someone had already taken care of that for us."

"Do you know who?"

"No. My guess is it was someone connected with the mission school where he grew up. The headmaster was our contact. Ex-headmaster. Ex-mission school, as a matter of fact. Magwimbi moved in his thugs and they run it now." Greer thought through his file on Lovemore. Yes, he had the name of the school. He didn't need to tip his hand to Anderson.

"So if you didn't fork out the cash, what was your role in the Lovemore case?"

"We just helped him get in, then let him stay here at the church until…well, until he came to Twisting Creek. You know all about that part."

"Did you have any trouble with him while he was here?"

"Why do you ask?"

In these cases he was always tempted to say, *Because I want to know the fucking answer, asshole.* "Just trying to get a fuller picture of the man. That's all."

"I answered that question long ago. I see no reason to repeat myself."

Jeez, the guy's got a short fuse. Do southern cops bring out the guard dog in him? Or will day after day of fighting sin with tattoos and earrings turn you downright cranky? No wonder his wife served coffee and got the hell out. "So if I understand you, you don't really know much about these refugees before they arrive here. Have I got that right?"

"In no way have you got that right. We have full confidence in our contacts on the ground. And by the way, I resent the implication."

"Sorry. I didn't mean to imply anything. Implying isn't really up my alley. I'm more into saying it out loud."

"I wonder—is listening up your alley? If so, then listen up. If you think you can dig up dirt and still nail your man, you'll run smack into double jeopardy. In this country…" he knotted the bicep with the American flag…"you can't try a man twice for the same crime. So I'm afraid you're wasting your time."

"Wasting yours, maybe." Greer stood up to leave, shook the rector's hand. "Not wasting mine."

On his way out, he spotted the cleaning lady stalking him at the periphery of his vision. She followed him out the main door and to the parking lot. Greer thought maybe she was going back to her flower garden, which indeed was where she stopped, but not before saying, so quietly that he nearly missed it, "You put Lovemore in jail?"

He turned toward her. "Yes. But he's out now. Why?"

She averted her eyes. She bent to shake the leaves from the branches of a red huckleberry. "He good man or bad?"

"Maybe you know more about him than I do." Her only reaction was to give the bush a quick bash with the handle of her rake. Brown leaves rained down. Greer watched her rake them away, then said, "Mr. and Mrs. Anderson seem to like him."

She exhaled a derisive sigh, as though the observation didn't merit comment. Greer kept staring at her, trying to force a response. Finally he saw that she had given him one, he'd simply missed it. With her eyebrows she was inviting him to come closer. She lifted one branch of the huckleberry bush loose from the rest. A few berries, stubborn and desiccated as cinders, refused to fall.

"Look here." Greer bent in closer and heard her whisper, "*Baas* think him good man, but no speak Shona."

"Who? Oh, the boss? Mr. Anderson?"

She nodded. "I speak Shona. Lovemore speak Shona, he say bad bad things."

"To you?"

"He want my sex. I say no. He say me whore."

"Mrs. Anderson speaks Shona, right? What did she think of him?"

"Oh, she like him okay. She like him too much."

"Ah, I see. It's like that, is it?" So that's why the rector packed him off to Twisting Creek, with a little pocket money and a useless job application.

The woman cocked her head at Greer. "He have my cat?"

"Your cat? I'm sorry...?"

"I have cat here in garden, give to eat. When you catch him, he have cat?"

"No ma'am, we didn't find any cat."

"He say cat mean sex. In English. This true?"

"Cat means sex?"

"He say he can't have my cat—you know I mean?" Greer felt red heat fill his face. She nodded. "Yes. He say I not give my cat, he take my other cat. I never see that cat again."

Greer thought, *Cats have nine lives. They come and they go. And sometimes they come back to haunt you.* He buckled himself into his little car and set his GPS for Dulles Airport.

ETHAN LESTER HELD the door open for Victor as they walked out onto the front porch of the old Lester home on Dogwood. Victor was in uniform. Ethan was wearing baggy black shorts with big pockets, and a slate gray cashmere sweater that matched the color of the chest hair curling over the low neck line. He didn't seem to have a shirt on underneath. Just the thought of it made Victor itch. Ethan, too, perhaps, since he kept his left hand underneath, slowly rubbing his chest. To Victor he offered his right hand, saying, "Congratulations, Chief Deputy Caraher. You're now the proud owner of a fine old Bedford Woods Edwardian."

Victor smiled. There was still a lot of red tape to go through, but they'd agreed on a price—an unimaginably low price for a house in the Woods. They "shook on it," as people around here said, and the deal was done.

Ethan assured him that there would be no glitches in securing the mortgage, but if there were, he said, just notify him. He still had plenty of pull with First Security. He handed Victor a set of keys and invited him to poke around the house to his heart's delight, even to start painting or yard work—whatever he had in mind. He apologized for having to rush off. He was to have a quick lunch with Josh Shanley before hustling back to New Orleans. He checked his watch and called back into the house, "Adriana! No time to waste now!"

They heard a yawning reply, and footsteps on the landing. Soon a barefoot young woman in a pink satin chemise joined them on the porch. She said nothing. She blinked at the sunlight and entwined her arms for a long stretch that nearly lifted the hem of her gown to her crotch. She curled up against Ethan and lay her head on his shoulder, much as if they were still in bed.

"Say, 'Good morning soon-to-be-sheriff Caraher'," Ethan instructed.

She started the phrase, but let it trail off into a sleepy sigh.

"Now run along and get dressed. We'll have lunch and then

start the drive back." He eased her toward the door and slapped her on the butt. She giggled and sped away.

"These pretty young things," Ethan said. "They stay on Facebook all night, then want to sleep all day."

"She's your…"

"My employee." Ethan lifted his eyebrows, man to man, then shouted into the house, "And I'll fire her ass if she's not back down here in ten minutes!"

"Lucky, though, she was here with you. It's always good to have a corroborated alibi when arson investigators start asking questions."

"Oh, she's good for a lot more than that," Ethan said, and rubbed his chest some more.

"Yes, well. You need to get going, and I do too."

"We'll be in touch. Again, welcome to the Woods."

When Victor reached his car he turned to wave goodbye, but Ethan was gone.

He'd left his phone in the car, on purpose, and now saw three missed calls from Yolanda.

She instantly answered his return call. "Guess who drives a black Jeep?"

Victor said, "Um…Travis Archer. Guess who just bought a house a few blocks away from you?"

"Jesus that was fast. How did you know?"

"Know what?"

"About the Jeep."

"It was an educated guess. I had somebody check it out."

"So?"

"So what?"

"What are you going to do about it?"

"Look, Yolanda…I know that this incident has got you…" He found himself searching for a polite term for *fucking nuts.* "… got you feeling personally involved, but I've already initiated an investigation and we need to proceed methodically."

"He's got my sister!"

"Just because you think you've deciphered one poor demented old woman's garbles about black willies, doesn't mean I can arrest a guy for driving a Jeep."

"I'll bet anything that it smokes when his engine is running."

"Proves nothing. Anyway all cars send off steam when it's cold."

"But we found corpses right by his house."

"We found corpses—old, decayed corpses, remember—on public land. Land that anybody can access. A good half-mile from his store. A store, let's also remind ourselves, that he opened only a few weeks ago. Just because we got to the grave site by starting from his property doesn't mean the actual corpses started from there. That's a false assumption."

"And here's a correct assumption—my little sister is falling for this crazy man." She pulled herself up short. "Okay, *crazy* may be an assumption. True or false, we don't yet know."

"Are you prepared to accept a level-headed suggestion?" She didn't answer. He'd always heard that silence implies consent, so he continued, "Then here it is: take Deedee aside and find out what she knows about Travis. That'll be your job. Your sisterly job. And my job will be to investigate this possible incident..."

"*Possible* incident?"

"It could have many explanations. An old family graveyard. A bear or cougar attack. A suicide pact. You yourself said it might be an ancient Indian burial ground. Right?"

"That was before I knew about the Jeep."

"There are many more facts we need to know. So, as I was saying, you question your sister, discretely, and I'll investigate in a professional manner. How does that sound?"

Again she was silent for a long time. Victor started his patrol car and turned from Dogwood onto Spruce. A distant movement caused him to look up at the house across the way, where he saw the spindly ice-blue figure of Odessa Dean cringing on the floor of her front porch. Her aide was bent over her, trying to coax her up. Victor slowed, lowered his window. Maybe she needed his help, but she saw him, shook her head, and waved him on by.

"Are you still there?" he asked Yolanda.

"I can't believe you bought that house. Did you even ask him about the night of the fire?"

"Of course I did. He said he was home asleep, just like most people were."

"Do you believe him?"

"He had an alibi. A woman stayed with him."

"Oh sure, like she's totally believable."

"Usually for a late night crime that's all the alibi anybody's likely to have. People who live alone don't even get that." He knew she knew that, but he also knew she was in no mood to say so. "So now how do we proceed?"

"I'll find out what Deedee knows."

He could hear the undertone of exasperation in her voice, but overlooked it. "And I'll investigate in a professional manner. That's how we get at the truth. If we ever get at it."

And I've got a profession too, Yolanda thought as she hung up. I'm a journalist. An investigative journalist. I guess I can question anybody I please.

She was sitting alone in the staff room in the basement of the Odeon. Deedee was still upstairs, rehearsing the hanging with Travis and Lovemore. Yolanda wondered how long they would be at it, but decided it didn't matter. She would wait. She sent Deedee a text saying, *When you finish, meet me downstairs—alone.* She made herself a cup of coffee and sat down, trying to decide whether Victor's systematic mind was the hallmark of the trained lawman, or the root of a pervading monotony that sent his ex-wife packing. She had to admit that the points he made were, on the surface, valid. But goddamn it she wasn't exploring the surface here. Couldn't Victor see that? Her little sister was gullible. One man had already duped her into a grave mistake, and now here comes another one. She thought back to her conversation with Deedee after she'd first met Travis, recalled Deedee's prediction: *he could be either super-nice, or way creepy.*

Yolanda tried to remind herself that the Nazi clique in control of all human affairs must be delighted to find her so vexed. She drank her coffee and allowed her mind to search through the whole mess for one scrap of humor. Was it funny that all this got started when hapless Rollie got stoned and had an idea about a play? Was it hilarious that the whole town suspected Lovemore, who had Deedee by the neck, while Yolanda alone suspected the man who had Lovemore by the neck?

No, was the answer to that. *Hell* no. It wasn't the least bit funny, and the Nazis who ran the human condition were laughing their asses off.

Deedee came in and closed the door behind her. "What's up?"

"Nothing much, really. I'm just curious about something. Maybe you can help."

"Sure." Deedee sat down.

"How much do you really know about Travis?" She saw that the question caused Deedee to flinch, nearly to stand up.

"Why do you ask?"

"You seem to be spending a lot of time with him."

"So? You're trying to say he's not our kind, just because he's a little rough around the edges?"

"Not at all. I don't even know what his edges are like. It's just—you and I have both made some bad choices. We need to watch over each other."

"Be each other's mom?"

"Sort of, I guess."

Deedee smiled. "You tell me about Victor and I'll tell you about Travis. Your African-American and my Redneck-American."

Now Yolanda could laugh. Here at last was the humor she'd been searching for.

"Well," Deedee thought about it. "I don't know very much. He has a brother studying law at Wayne State University. That's in Detroit. There's an uncle he seems fond of. He's evasive when I bring up his parents. And he's never even asked about mine."

"Maybe he knows already."

"Maybe so. He doesn't like 'outsiders', as he puts it. He couldn't believe they acquitted Lovemore, but when they met today for the first time I didn't see any sign of racism or whatever."

"Did he know Sarah?"

"Travis?" Deedee stalled as she thought back to the signals Travis had tried to give Lovemore. Signals which Lovemore ignored. She thought of the locked stares.

"Yes, Travis."

"Through the bank, yes."

"Has he ever mentioned visiting her at her house?"

"Why do you ask?"

Yolanda shrugged. Smoking black willies would sound insane. She said, "A hunch, that's all." She knew it was lame, but Deedee's reaction stunned her. She rushed over to the chair next to Yolanda and put her arms around her. She seemed ready to cry.

"All I know is..." She was having trouble being coherent. "All I know is he loves Brandon. I mean he really loves him. Sometimes I think he hangs out with me so he can be with Brandy. They're playing together upstairs right now. Do you know how incredible that is? A man actually enjoys being with my little freak? He even thinks about him when we're not around. Travis is the one who invented smell-and-tell, did you know that? He's like a godsend."

"I know. I know. But what about Sarah?"

"Maybe he had a crush. Who knows? Who cares? He loves my son."

Yolanda held her tight. She said nothing more. Nor did Deedee. But they both knew the next words, heard them hanging unspoken in the air: *So please don't ask the questions that will take him away from us*

But it might not be that simple. Yolanda went to her office and put through a call to the registrar's office at Wayne State. She identified herself as a reporter for the Twisting Creek Guardian in Kentucky, and explained that a group of local attorneys awarded an annual scholarship to a deserving local student. She said this year's choice was Joseph Douglas Archer, a student at Wayne State. The secretary said they were not allowed to give out contact information. Yolanda said she understood and completely agreed with that policy, and would never dream of asking her to violate it. All she needed was for Mr. Archer to contact the Guardian for an interview. The secretary asked for the name again.

She was gone for a long time. When she came back she said, "Are you sure you've got the name right? We don't have a Joseph Douglas Archer. In fact, we don't have any Archers at all."

SATURDAY'S PREMIER PERFORMANCE was sold out in advance. That morning's Guardian was able to run a front-page story, not too self-congratulatory, or so Josh hoped, on the surge that Stage Death was creating in the local economy. There wasn't a vacant motel room in all of Buford County. By early Saturday evening there were lines outside most restaurants, and when the show was over, bars filled up and excess patrons spilled out onto the street.

Seth chewed the scenery with the sheriff's part. He pounded his fist and stood up in the witness stand to stare down Lovemore. Josh knew he would have to tone him down, but the audience didn't seem to mind.

A sense of unease filled the auditorium when Lovemore took the stand. And when the lights came up to reveal the climactic hanging scene, great cheers resounded, from the front row to the rafters. It was hard to tell if people were thrilled with the play, or with the sight of Lovemore swinging from a noose.

The evening's real climax, however, came with the curtain call. Deedee took her bows to thunderous applause, but when it was Lovemore's turn, all that changed. He was booed lustily, and long. The catcalls continued even after he'd retreated behind the curtain. Someone yelled "Murderer!" Others followed, until soon it seemed the call for blood would erupt into violence. Backstage, Edgar looked at Josh, who looked at Deedee. Nobody knew how to calm the situation. Would there be a lynching in Twisting Creek after all? It seemed they needed to get Lovemore the hell out of there.

Lovemore himself had other ideas. Amidst the hoots and jeers, he stepped through the curtains and calmly walked to the very front of the stage. He smiled, calmly surveyed the audience from front row to back balcony and from wall to wall, and then raised his arms for quiet. Into the clamor he said, "Good citizens of Twisting Creek!" His powerful voice penetrated and ordered the developing chaos. Within moments every voice in the hall was stilled, every ear expectant. "Please allow me a moment to thank all of you for coming here tonight. Even as you have enjoyed the entertainment that we did our very best to provide for you, let us never forget that we dedicate all our efforts to the memory of a dear friend and neighbor. Please join me in a moment of remembrance for our absent sister, Sarah Lester."

The reverberation of his voice faded, and all was silence. He bowed his head, as did most of the audience. After half a minute, Lovemore continued, "Let us remember also that Sarah's murderer is still out there, somewhere, a free man. We pray that he is brought to justice. But for now, please remember that, here, we are all friends." He pulled back the curtain and motioned for the others to join him on stage. He took Deedee's hand, held it high above their heads. She took Yolanda's. Josh, Edgar, Seth, and all the rest did the same. Travis emerged from backstage, hoisted Brandon onto his shoulders, and joined them in one long, triumphant line.

Lovemore turned to the cast. "Do you know the words to 'Abide with Me'?" They all looked at each other. He addressed the audience, "I will play us out with one of my favorite hymns. If you know the words, please feel free to sing along."

He positioned himself at the piano and sang:

Abide with me; fast falls the eventide;
The darkness deepens; Lord, with me abide;
When other helpers fail and comforts flee,
Help of the helpless, oh, abide with me.

Rollie, watching from his perch on high, saw women dab their eyes as the entire crowd of over one thousand exited the theater as quietly as they might have left a church. He knew he would be wanted downstairs for pats on the back, but first he had to do a couple of things. In his little office he opened the safe to get a joint and to look at all that money. Never, perhaps, in the history of the Odeon, not even in its glory years of Gone with the Wind and The Ten Commandments, had this safe sheltered such a stack of dollar bills. And this was only from the cash customers! Less than half the take! Rollie, my man, he thought, you are living the dream.

He poured himself a whisky and sat there, sipping, smoking, and counting out one thousand dollars in fifties and twenties. He sealed it away in an envelope. He wasn't being sneaky about this. He'd already discussed it with the others. Lovemore was broke, and he had earned it.

Downstairs he found the cast in high spirits. He called Lovemore to one side. "Here's a quiet gift for you."

"*Tatenda.*" Lovemore clapped his gratitude. He took the money out and counted it then and there. "This amounts to… what? Twenty seats in the front row?"

Surprised, Rollie didn't know how to respond. "I'm sure there'll be more, if the crowds hold up."

"Oh, yes. There will be more. Of this I'm *satin.*"

THE NEXT MORNING the cast met at IHOP's glassed-in garden room for breakfast and reviews. Josh was the last one to arrive. He rushed in, waving tear sheets over his head. "Listen to this," he said. "This is from the *Lexington Herald-Leader*:

> '*Morally, of course, it's an abomination, perhaps the most cynical theatrical stunt ever pulled. But as theater, it quite literally takes your breath away. There on the stage, a few feet from where you sit, stands an exquisitely vulnerable young actress as she rejects the actual man whom nearly everyone in the house believes to be the real-life killer. We can't take our eyes from his massive hands as they grip her slender neck. For two hours he has revived his old passion for her and relived their days of bliss. We witness her brave, futile struggle against his attack. She slumps to the floor. The theater goes as dark as death. When we can once again see the stage, it is to view their two corpses, hers on the floor, his suspended from a noose.*
>
> *The curtain closes. And now—unlike with any other play you've ever seen—the closing curtain actually increases the tension. There's a question banging in your brain. You don't want it there, but there it is: Is the actress dead? Has her costar really killed her? Did the revisited love capture him so completely that he forgot it was an act?*
>
> *For the next two minutes—or is it a century?—when at last the curtains open again and we see the murdered woman and the hanged man standing there on stage, hand in hand, taking their bows—for those two minutes no theater experience in the world has ever crackled so loudly with the brutal tension that you will soon witness for yourself in Stage Death, at the Odeon in Twisting Creek.*'

Josh said, "Brutal tension, baby! High-fives!"

Rollie beamed as the others slapped his hand. IHOP's other customers looked around to see what all the commotion was about. There followed a lot of nudging and pointing. With Lovemore sitting there among seven white people, it wasn't hard to figure out who it was.

Josh held up another notice. "Here's the lady from the *Cincinnati Enquirer*.

'If the story doesn't mesmerize you on its own, you cannot escape the spell of the eyes of the villain, facing you from the stage as he faced the real jury but days ago. Then you will know the power that infiltrated a sequestered jury for one solid week, held them in thrall as they produced a unanimous miscarriage of justice. And you will know, just as surely as you know he's guilty of murder, that had you been on that jury, you too would have set him free. It's as though Dostoyevsky had come to life in Kentucky, creating characters too god-like for prison. But this Raskolnikov is not in Crime and Punishment. *He's in* Crime Without Punishment, *aka,* Stage Death, *in Twisting Creek. The tickets may cost as much as your hotel room, but you will soon forget the cost. The play, however, will stay with you forever."*

The celebration that followed this review was more subdued than before. They'd started to understand how this blatant accusation of guilt must sound to Lovemore. Rollie told him, "You mustn't take this crap too seriously, man. You know how newspaper people are."

Josh backed him up. "Nobody's going to buy a newspaper that says, It's a decent little play. Overpriced, but the bad guy is a real hunk."

Yolanda said, "It's true. We're all totally full of crap, a bunch of intellectual lightweights."

Lovemore turned his back to his table. He seemed to know that a restaurant full of customers was paying attention to their private conversation, and looking straight at him. Facing them, he said, "I think I'm starting to figure that out."

THIS TIME THERE were a couple of fading red pick-ups parked in front of *Archer's Bait and Boat*. Both had two-tiered gun racks in the rear windows. Deedee checked out them carefully. One truck carried a shotgun and a rifle, the other only a rifle. For the first time ever she thought about the risk Travis must be running out here all alone, with ready cash, a stock of valuable merchandise, and mostly well-armed customers. She wondered if he kept a handgun tucked somewhere beneath the cash register.

She paused at the screen door long enough to locate the occupants of those trucks. She saw a middle-aged couple in plaid parkas inspecting the rack of lures, very much as Brandon had done. Up near the counter were two younger men wearing olive drab knit caps that didn't quite cover knotty threads of greasy hair. Was their truck the one with the empty gun slot? Did they have a shotgun trained on Travis right then? Even as Deedee tried to chide herself for seeing evil in every human transaction, she made sure the door slammed hard enough to make everybody look around at her. This would give Travis a chance to grab his pistol from under the counter.

"Hi!" he called out. "What brings you out here on such a gloomy afternoon?"

The boys at the counter turned and nodded a brief greeting. The older couple didn't look up. Nobody was brandishing shotguns. She laughed at how ready she had been to overreact, how she'd burst through the door to rescue a Travis in distress, when it turned out that the only crack of gunfire was her slamming the door. Wait until she told Yolanda this story! In the telling maybe she'd have everybody dive to the floor when the door slammed. Yolanda would howl at that. Maybe she would assure her that with all the recent murders and hangings and dug-up skeletons, it was a perfectly understandable reaction.

Travis held his grin steady while she rounded a table of winter clothing, then he asked, "What are you laughing at?"

"At your question, I suppose. What *am* I doing here on such a gloomy afternoon, anyway?"

"Beats me," he said.

"Checking up on you, I guess. Just wanted to know if you're working hard or hardly working. As my daddy used to say."

The older couple looked at her and smiled. They carried a small handful of purchases toward check-out. The man paid, winked at Travis and said, "You're working hard, ain't you?"

"Shoulder to the wheel, nose to the grindstone." Then he asked Deedee, "Where's Brandon?"

"He's with Rollie."

"Oh. You should have brought him."

She shrugged. What she'd come to say, she didn't need to say yet. But whenever she said it, it wasn't for Brandon's ears.

One of the long-haired boys said, "We was just checking on the price. Be back in a week or two."

"Any time. Remember what I said about them saugers. They're already starting their upstream migration, and there's no better eats in this world. You want to impress the girls, you invite them over for pan fried sauger fillets rolled in corn meal. Ain't that right, Deedee?"

"My knees go weak just thinking about it," she said.

The boys looked back and forth at each other and seemed to come to a silent agreement. "Why don't we go ahead and take 'em right now."

Travis reached behind him for the two matching rods and reels he had been showing them. "You won't be disappointed, I promise. Remember to work it like I showed you." He demonstrated again, flicking the rod gently. "Try a bucktail jig. Here, take a couple of these. I tied them myself. You bring it all back if you're not happy with it. I'll be right here. I'm not going anywhere. Am I, Deedee?"

He had taken her by surprise. "Rock of Gibraltar," she said.

The boys paid and walked away. One practiced his flicks on the way out. Travis called out, "Look for deep eddies over sandy bottoms. You'll fill your creel in no time."

"Got it," one called back, and they left.

With the store empty of customers, Travis said, "Thank you. I do believe you sealed that deal for me."

"I didn't do anything."

"Don't kid yourself. Dangle a pretty girl in front of these boys and they'll bite like a sauger on that bucktail."

"You said you were one hell of a fisherman."

"But you were the key."

"Hey, I'm the Guardian ad lady. Selling stuff for customers is what I do."

"Maybe not usually in person."

"Let's call it community outreach. But that really wasn't my purpose for being here."

"What was, then?"

"Put up your *Gone Fishing* sign. I need to get outdoors. Let's walk down to the lake. There must be a path down there. How about it?"

They walked the gravel driveway around behind the cabin, past the padlocked garage, through the brush and weeds, between the pair of hemlocks and along the ruts of the old logging trail, until Travis turned up toward a steep rise covered in juniper and thistle. He led Deedee by the elbow around some grass-hidden root outcrops and over to a gradient of rough cobblestone stairs. Once they had climbed those, the land slopped sharply downhill toward the lake, and they were in virgin forest. They left behind the scrawny evergreens and scrabbly floor of the old clear cut, and entered the region's only remaining patch of old-growth, a final redoubt of the massive hardwoods that had once covered half a continent. It was like stepping from the street into a Gothic cathedral. Suddenly you felt like yourself in miniature, gazing in wonder at a ceiling too high and heavy even for those great pillars. The temperature dropped, the sound of their footsteps was muffled, and the contradictory scent of age and timelessness filled the air.

"I don't think people appreciate this place, right here so near home," Deedee said, her eyes scanning the canopy in search of an eagle's nest.

"But if they did, they'd be out here more, maybe ruining it."

He took her hand as she climbed a complicated monkey's puzzle of exposed basswood roots, and did not release it when she reached the ground again. They walked without speaking, lazily descending the last slope of the land until a whiff of lake water reached them. Deedee released her hand and began a hell-bent charge toward the lakeside. If the day had been warmer, and she'd been dressed for a swim, you'd have thought she would finish with a headlong dive into the lake, but she knew this stretch of lake shore, knew that at the bottom of the hill there was a bench anchored to the ground on metal legs. She raced down past the tree line and onto a stretch of weeds where the hillside started to flatten out. From here she could see the bench at the bottom of the hill, could see that it was unoccupied. With her final step she leapt onto its backrest and, arms pinwheeling, there she perched.

"Wow! Look at you!" Travis said.

She turned, a gymnast on the balance beam, and challenged him. "Let's see you do that."

"No way," he shouted, galloping toward her. With his final step he propelled himself up and over the bench and hit the ground at such speed that he barely managed to stop his momentum at the water's edge. He walked back to her, panting. "Holy shit, did you see that? I nearly pitched straight into the lake. I bet it's ice cold."

Deedee bounced pertly down to the seat and to the ground. She sat down, patted the seat beside her, and said, "Okay, Travis. The fun's over. We need to talk."

"Do we?"

"I think so. Don't you?"

"I guess so. If you say so."

"That's such a male answer. Sort of nice-guy male, but very male."

"Thanks—I think." He still seemed to think the joke might not be over, that there was a punch line just around the corner.

"So tell me about your parents."

His changing face told her he didn't see the least bit of humor in that.

"Why do you ask?"

"Because I'm interested. Of course. You never mention them."

"You never asked me."

"I'm asking now."

"There's not much to tell. And what there is ends in tragedy."

"Tell me anyway."

"Well…they came up here from Tennessee before I was born. We lived here at the cabin until about the time I should have been starting middle school."

"Should have been?"

"They were sort of…well…peculiar, is what they were. I may as well be honest about it. They both avoided contact with other people as much as they could. My father did odd jobs around town. My mother seldom left the cabin. My brother and I were being 'home schooled,' which in our case really meant unschooled. Luckily we had an uncle up in Michigan. He had given up on Tennessee too, but not to hide out in these hills. He went up north to work in a Ford factory. Then one Christmas he came down here for a visit. He wasn't invited and he sure wasn't welcomed with anything like the Christmas spirit. Later he told the story and laughed about it, but at the time it must have hurt. He saw how far behind in our education my brother and I had fallen, so he just up and took us up there to live with him and my aunt. They took care of us like their own sons."

"Your parents let you go, just like that?"

"Let's put it like this: I don't think it broke their hearts."

"You poor little guy." She put her arms around him. He gave a quick laugh. Even Deedee wasn't sure how seriously she'd meant the comment. She quickly released him. "Okay, I'll admit it's a sad situation, but in fact it turned out for the best, didn't it? I don't see how the ending is so tragic."

"No, that's a happy one. But my parents, I guess they ran completely out of money, and one January they started driving up to Michigan to see if my uncle could help my father get on with Ford. Or anywhere, really. But just north of Toledo their car hit a patch of black ice, and they were both killed."

"Oh. I see. I'm so sorry." She laid her head on his shoulder and maneuvered toward him until he put his arm around her. Was she manipulating him? She asked herself that. No, her sorrow was sincere. She could be sure of that much. But wasn't she also luring him into a false calm before her final question? She had to admit the possibility. "So the cabin sat empty all those years?"

"Yep. I never came down here even once." He stopped there.

Deedee waited for him to pick up the story, but he said nothing. "Okay," she said. "So you're up there in Michigan. Go on."

"It's not very interesting."

"Continue, *por favor*." She pressed her head against his shoulder.

"Well...my uncle loved fishing. He taught me most of what I know. I took a job in one of those big Outdoorsman Pro shops while I worked on an associate degree in business. That's pretty much it."

"No, it's not. What brought you back down here?"

"The new road."

"Keep going."

"Keep going where?"

"How did you even know about the new road?"

"I often read the Guardian online."

"See there? I knew I liked you for some reason."

"I said the magic word, didn't I?"

"Continue."

"So when I realized there would be lake traffic running right by the cabin, which was already mine anyway, I thought maybe I could make a go of it down here as a small businessman. So here I am."

"Wrong. There you were at Sarah Lester's desk, applying for a loan."

"Okay..." he offered warily. "That was one of the steps."

"Did you have a thing with her?"

"No. Not really."

"It's okay with me, either way. I just want to know the truth. In case you haven't figured it out yet, I'm pretty big on truth. You get burned once like I did, you get cautious."

"In that case, yes. I guess Sarah and I did have a little fling, but it never did get serious. And it didn't last very long. Satisfied?"

"Sure am. I have no reason to distrust you. Yet." She sucker-punched him one, right in the stomach.

"Shit, Deedee! You could hurt somebody like that."

"Just keeping you on your toes." She laid her head back on his shoulder. She wanted him to expect anything—anything besides her final question.

The sky was entirely obscured, but a less dense patch of clouds moving toward the crest of the western hills meant that afternoon was quickly moving toward evening. Soon dusk would threaten and they would have to abandon their bench. They would walk back to the cabin in the day's waning light, then it would be time to head back to the Odeon and the nightmare of Stage Death. But first she had to ask him one question.

"So why did you lie to me about a brother in law school?"

"What do you mean?"

"You don't have a brother enrolled at Wayne State."

"How do you know that?"

"Yolanda phoned the registrar."

"Why the hell would she do that?"

"For a feature story, I suppose. That part doesn't matter. There's no Archer at Wayne State."

"Not now, there isn't. Not this semester."

"What does that mean?"

"He's taking a year off to work and save up enough to help pay for next year. Do you have any idea how much law school costs?"

"That's the whole story? That's all there is to it?"

"It's that simple. We're not rich people."

She held his hand as they retraced their way back along the path. They were feeling their way through the deep virgin forest. In places it was already dark enough that they could have used a flashlight. In fact, somebody else had one. The sight of it startled Travis. Almost nobody came this far out into these woods at the best of times, certainly not near dusk on a gray October evening. He stopped dead in his tracks.

Deedee said, "Oh, that's probably a policeman."

"A what?"

"They've uncovered a couple of corpses there."

"Corpses? Are you sure about that?"

She thought she heard a quiver in his voice. "Yolanda told me about it. Maybe an old Indian burial site or something like that."

"Shit!"

"Do old graveyards spook you?"

"No, not at all."

"Are you worried it'll frighten away customers?"

"No. No, I don't think so. I'm not frightened of anything," he said, but seemed to pick up the pace until they had reached the hemlocks.

Deedee noticed tire tracks and recalled the afternoon she'd peeked into his ramshackle garage and seen a mud-covered Jeep. "Do you sometimes drive your car back here?" She indicated the ruts.

"Sometimes I pick up fallen branches to use for firewood."

"You have a wood stove?"

"An old fireplace. Upstairs." He pointed toward the roof of his cabin, where a gray stone chimney was hardly visible against the gray sky.

"How about when it's muddy?" She tried to sound vaguely curious, as though mostly she was making conversation.

"You're such a town girl. How much sense does it make to collect wet firewood?"

They didn't talk the rest of the way, until Travis caught sight of red and blue lights that gave a Christmas-like glow to his parking lot. A Twisting Creek Police patrol car was waiting there. He saw a man at the wheel but couldn't make out who it was until the door opened and Victor Caraher stepped out.

"Hello, Victor. Are you here to do some more shopping?"

He tried to show a sense of humor. Deedee gave him credit for that. But she also noticed that the quiver was back in his voice.

"No, Travis, I can't say I am. I'm here to ask you for a swab. For DNA testing."

IF THERE WAS one change Allard Greer could effect in the world's travel industry, it would be to remove all full-length mirrors from hotel bathrooms.

It was his first morning in Africa. He had endured thirty-one hours of airplane confinement and a fitful night in an overpriced hotel in Tuvingu, where he didn't sleep so much as fall into a brief coma. He woke up confused, irritable and overmatched by the challenge of being awake. He wondered if Lazarus hadn't felt the same way. *Where am I and what's the big idea anyway?*

He stepped out of his overheated shower. In a hot, humid, starving, third-world country, he might have expected a cold shower, wouldn't have complained about it, even at three hundred dollars a night; but no, here the cold water didn't work, and when the steam cleared he found himself facing a squat red pouch of a human being, furred about the belly in curling white tufts, and with the law of gravity on proud display in every body part.

So he had to admit it: *It all comes down to this.* It wasn't so much a thought, as a phrase pinging around in his head. *It all comes down to this.* To this thing in front of him; to this pink sponge of a wineskin filled with some sort of jellied substance; to this lone, failing creature, stained, drained, surviving on the remnants of precious, non-renewable resources laid down years ago. It all comes down to this. Young women in a nondescript town half a world away need protecting, and it comes down to you.

So fuck it, he thought. Let it come. He and this thing in the mirror would face Africa together.

The taxi shuddered over disintegrating tarmac. The driver talked non-stop about something—anything and everything, as far as Greer could make out—although, with that impenetrable accent, and with the way he drove, selecting his lane based on his assessment of the depths of potholes, and not relinquishing his claim until the lines of oncoming trucks were right on top of him and flashing their lights, Greer wouldn't have been much interested anyway.

Finally they turned up a steep hill, onto an even more pitted road, though one with almost no traffic at all. "There, *baas*," pointed the taxi driver. "You can see from here."

Far up the mountain at the end of this road, a set of low buildings on a rocky plate nestled against a sandstone cliff. "That's the school?"

"Ya. Before."

Nearing the top of the hill he spotted a granite slab standing like an oversized tombstone beside a white-pillared gate. If you looked closely at the granite slab you could see Woodhurst College for Boys in ghost-lettering. On the opposite side of the gate, a metal sign said, Chimurenga Heroes Academy.

The place looked dead. Greer asked his driver to wait for him and went off in search of somebody—anybody who could tell him what might have happened to the one man he'd come all the way to Africa to meet: Daniel Grevint, former headmaster of the former Woodhurst College, and one-time benefactor of Lovemore Ngwenya.

The single-story buildings were all constructed on the same design: a wide loggia with wooden floorboards leading to a series of simple stone walls. Everything was white, or had once been white. Now the dominant colors were chipped brown and derelict gray. A couple of young men in tattered jeans and t-shirts sat on the loggia floor, smoking and playing checkers using pop bottle caps. Greer noticed a machine pistol with magazine lying on the floor beside them. A small pack of dogs, their coats sand-shaded enough to nearly camouflage them in the dirt, shook themselves awake at Greer's approach and began to bark. Greer walked toward the checker players.

"Excuse me, gentlemen. Could you tell me where the office is?"

The boys looked at each other. The taxi driver, who had been watching from his car, called out something in Shona. One boy answered in Shona, then to Greer said, "That side."

He walked until he found an open door. A brass plate attached to it said "Library", although when he peeked inside he saw no books, no shelves, no tables. He called, "Hello?"

A woman's startled face appeared from behind the door, startling him just as much. It got worse when her hand came into view. He jerked his head away from the barrel of a gun…but no. That machine pistol out front had made him twitchy. It was only the handle of her broom. She was the cleaning lady. He laughed and put his hands over his heart.

"I'm really sorry," Greer said.

"Good gracious God!" the woman said. Her smile revealed a wide row of silver teeth, but when the boys appeared behind Greer, her smile disappeared, her voice dropped an octave, and she asked, "What do you want?"

His every instinct told him she was the one to ask. The lively eyes and smile he had glimpsed belonged to a woman who knew things about the people around her. If she'd worked here more than a year, and if Daniel Grevint wasn't the kind of boss who disdained contact with his lessers, she would know what had become of him. But Greer's instincts told him just as clearly that with those boys standing behind him, she wouldn't say another word. "Sorry," he repeated. "I get so lost." He walked away from them and down the open walkway.

He paused at each room, pretending to look for something specific. He read, "Biology Laboratory", "Maths," "Form Room 1." Pausing, moving along, pausing. He heard footsteps behind him. He turned, and the boys were right there.

"You looking for?" one asked.

"It's my son's idea." Greer laughed, to show how inconsequential the search was. "He went to school here, and wanted me to take a picture of his old classroom."

"No photos," one boy said. "Not allowed. Not allowed to be here."

"Ah. My mistake. Forgive me. I'll leave right now. Is there a toilet I can use before I go?"

They said something to each other, then one said, "Go behind there, anywhere."

"Ah, thanks. I'll be off then."

They didn't follow him. He watched them as they moved around the corner, eager to get back to their checkers, then he retraced his steps back toward the library.

He was elated to find her waiting for him behind the door. With nothing more than a glance and a bit of human discernment they had outsmarted a couple of self-important teenaged thugs. He felt the urge to hug her.

Her silver smile returned. "You want?" she asked.

"Did you know the old headmaster here, the one they drove off. Name of Daniel Grevint?"

"Now in Angels of Mercy Nursing Home." Her face hardened again. "They beat him so bad!"

"Thank you," Greer whispered, and thought to add, "God bless you."

"Tell him Jamaica Rose never forgets. He will know."

The Angels of Mercy Nursing Home was way the hell across the wide Tuvingu plain and across another mountain and valley, at the foot of a small stand-alone hill they called Jacob's Kopje, so Greer had another hour of daredevil thrills and spills on South Zambezi's highways. He caught himself thinking that it was a damn good thing these people were so poor, because the roads were deathtraps. What would they be like if people could actually afford cars? It was an unworthy thought, one he knew he would feel guilty about later—just as soon as they got off the road.

They stopped in front of what Greer thought of as a plantation manor. What they called it here he had no idea, but it wouldn't have looked out of place surrounded by live oak trees in Georgia or South Carolina. Here it was surrounded by jacaranda trees in full purple flower. A sweet fragrance, like honeysuckle jam, seemed to float on the humid air as he climbed the stairs to the main entrance. Once on the veranda he noticed what lay hidden behind a thick border of climbing rose bushes: a long row of drooping, dozing patients, already as silent as they would ever be in death. They sat interspersed, blacks and whites, a piano keyboard of lives nearly as extinct as the world they'd lived through.

Inside he found an attendant and asked for Dr. Grevint. He

was led directly back outside, to a side porch, where the former headmaster sat with a book in his lap. He was younger than Greer had envisioned him. Compared to the other residents he probably was young. He might still have been a working headmaster if the "heroes" hadn't closed his college. Even at that, rather than sitting in a wheelchair, deformed and drooling onto the pages of his book, he might have been playing a round of golf, if the heroes hadn't bludgeoned his neck with a shovel. As it was, he sat up as best he could. He curved into himself, with his head cocked as though listening to some distant alarm. He was smaller than Greer had imagined him, his leathery round head covered with only a horseshoe rim of hair.

Greer bent down to where Grevint could see him. "Are you awake, sir?"

"I am. Who is this?"

"I bring you greetings from one of your old students. Can you spare a few minutes?"

"I can spare all I have left. They may be very few indeed."

Greer noticed that the man didn't laugh when he said that. Maybe by custom headmasters weren't a chuckling breed. "I also bring you greetings from Jamaica Rose."

"Please sit down. We've discovered that the best position to converse with me is from a seated position on the floor. If you can manage."

Greer heard some crackling sounds, but he made it to the floor. "Is that better?"

"Much. Dear Jamaica Rose. I miss those days so painfully; her cheerful smile as generations of young boys scrambled along the corridors."

"She's still got it. The smile, I mean. The corridors are mighty quiet, though."

"No money, they say. I would submit: no heroes. But I'm in enough trouble already." Still as solemn as a schoolmaster.

"Do you remember the boy named Lovemore Ngwenya?"

"Oh, indeed I do. I paid the bribe that got him released."

Greer looked around to see who might be listening.

"Nobody here cares about that. We all know what goes on.

And I choose not to be so cautious this near the end. So yes, I remember Lovemore Ngwenya. A scholarship lad. Fine musician. I lost touch with him after he fled. Where is he now?"

"In America. He's pursuing an acting career."

"How fitting. He had a real presence."

"Was he your only black student?"

"Oh, no. My goodness no. When he came along we were as mixed as mixed can be, with Indians too. Even a few Portuguese still turned up. Their families had fled the war in Mozambique. Now of course the Mozambicans have a responsible government which welcomes refugees from our great leader."

"The world is just too backasswards for its own good."

"Backasswards," the headmaster repeated. "Yes. Well put. Backasswards."

"Do you have any specific memories of Lovemore Ngwenya?"

"Do you ask for any particular reason?"

Greer said, "Not really. Not now. A little over a year ago I tried to contact your college about him. We were trying to put together some background on him. He had landed in some trouble in my hometown. Unfortunately that was at a time…" Greer paused to choose his words gently.

Grevint helped him. "A time when the heroes were looting everything they could carry, including our library. Illiterates hauling away lorry loads of Voltaire and John Locke. Books that a week earlier had been the homework assignment for young black and white Africans. There's our revolution in a nutshell. But just as the Zimbabweans finally woke up to the truth about Mugabe, we will wake to Magwimbi."

"I'd love to discuss this with you sometime," Greer said, "but right now I need to get going. There's a taxi waiting for me."

"Wait. You said he was in trouble?"

"It's all over now. As I mentioned, he's on the stage. All I wanted to know was if he had ever shown signs of violent behavior."

"Well, I could tell you a few stories of our Lovemore on a rugby pitch! He terrified our opponents."

"I don't suppose that's so bad. A penalty here and there is part of sports."

"He had a temper, that one did."

"Off the field too?"

"I have to say that occasionally he ended up in my office. Nothing too serious, though. Playground fisticuffs. We managed to handle it in-house. I'm pleased that he's a success, and am gratified that he asked you to stop by and see me. Does he know I'm the one who 'sprung him,' as you Americans say in old films?"

"I don't think he knows who it was."

"No matter. Tell him when you get back. Tell him I felt guilty for giving him lines. In fact I felt sorry for him and several black lads like him. They didn't know who they were. They were torn between cultures. Both sides viewed them with suspicion."

Greer didn't feel it was his place to comment. He remembered the days when his own neighbors believed America was composed of "sides."

"What brings you to South Zambezi, anyway?" Grevint asked.

"Oh, I've just retired. Thought it was time to see the world. Take a safari. See Victoria Falls. You know—the usual."

"I'm sure you were disappointed not to find Weeks here."

"I'm not in any great hurry."

"What do you mean? Ah!" He finally laughed. "Yes, that's a good one. Of course I mean Owen Weeks, Lovemore's old music master. At one time he lived with Weeks and his daughter. That was before he got into political trouble. I'm sure you knew that."

"Oh, yes! Mr. Weeks. The teacher he stayed with." Greer thought he faked it well enough.

"They opened their doors to him. And not as a houseboy, you can be sure."

"You mean Weeks isn't here?"

"Not here, but not so far. For you it's not so far. For me it's another planet. After the heroes seized his home, he and his family fled into Mozambique. Soon after that Mrs. Weeks was murdered. And a year or so later, his daughter."

277

ON WEDNESDAY EDGAR'S story broke the news of a third corpse, this one a young boy, found buried near the lake. It appeared that he, like the woman already exhumed, but unlike the adult male, had died from a single gunshot to the head. The man had been riddled with shots to the chest. The article laid out the logical possibilities in a quote from Interim Sheriff Caraher.

"Either one person killed all three victims, and perhaps others we haven't found yet, or else one of the dead killed the other two, then committed suicide. That makes it a possible family murder-suicide, which is pretty common. But if that's what it was, it turns probability on its head, because in the overwhelming majority of such cases the killer turns out to be the father. Yet this man could hardly kill his wife and child with a single bullet each, then pump seven rounds into his own chest."

On Thursday Edgar reported police had found the murder weapon, a 9mm semi-automatic Browning with four of thirteen rounds still in the magazine.

Newspapers hadn't sold mid-week like this since the peak days of the early eighties. The story of the fire at Lovemore's old house had arrived with precision timing for the Guardian, and the discovery of the first two corpses had bolstered business even more. And now, a young boy and a military weapon. Small-town newspapers survived on stories like these—stories with intense local interest but too confined in scope for the wider media to take up. Newsstand sales blew right past the downturn expected to follow the conclusion of the Lovemore trial, and subscribers had no news lull to prompt cancellations.

Lovemore, too, continued to be a regular Guardian reader. He was reading it at IHOP's breakfast counter when he saw Edgar's piece on the identification of the two dead adults. They were believed to be Randell and Martha Archer, who had lived nearby. Their son, Travis, was "cooperating with the investigation."

Lovemore finished his coffee in two gulps, paid up, and walked out to the street. Such was his celebrity by now that he barely had time to stick out his thumb when a driver not only stopped for him, but offered to drive him directly to his destination.

"Dogwood, in Bedford Woods."

"But that's..." The driver caught himself.

"Yes, you are right. The house of my beloved Sarah. But now it's the home of Sheriff Caraher."

"Oh, I see!" said the driver, sounding relieved and impressed. "Is it a social call?"

"Police business," Lovemore said in a tone that indicated it would be indiscreet to reveal more.

"Oh, I see!" the man repeated, and didn't have much to say the rest of the way.

For the first time since the day of the murder, Lovemore walked down the familiar sidewalk. It was covered, just as it had been the first time he'd seen it, with broken branches and crumpled yellow maple leaves. Perhaps no one had cleared that lawn since he himself had been Sarah's gardener, a million years ago.

The Guardian was still on the front porch. Lovemore picked it and rang the doorbell. He didn't really care if Victor was still in bed or not.

Victor opened the door almost immediately. He was dressed to go jogging. "Good morning," he said. "This is a surprise."

"This isn't." Lovemore held out the newspaper and pointed to Edgar's story. "I'm glad you got him for killing his parents, but I'll tell you one more thing. He's the one you've been looking for. He's Sarah's killer. I'm sure of it."

"Whoa! Lay back a minute. What are you talking about?"

"I saw him here, at this house. I heard them quarreling. I can show you exactly where I was standing when I saw him drive up. I was pruning the hydrangea right around that corner. And I'll show you the open window directly behind it through which I overheard their argument."

"What argument?"

"She was finished with him. By that time she was mine, you see. She didn't want to see that Boer anymore, so he strangled her. There's your motive."

279

Victor did not point out it was exactly this motive that Greer had attributed to Lovemore. He merely said, "It is a common enough motive for murder."

"And soon enough it will be Deedee."

"Deedee Shanley? What do you mean by that?"

"It's precisely the same scenario. Deedee will soon part ways with him and take up with me. The process is already under way."

This was news to Victor. Yolanda's anxiety was all directed toward Travis. Wouldn't she have told him if her sister was developing feelings for Lovemore? Yes, certainly she would—providing she knew about it herself. But did Deedee tell her everything?

"You and Deedee?"

"Getting stronger every day. When she professes her love for me, she means it. I can see it in her eyes."

"You're talking about during the play?"

"You have no idea how close the bond between co-stars can be. It's real. There's no mistaking it."

"So, according to your analysis, this puts Deedee on Travis Archer's hit list."

"He's the seething type that finally explodes. They're hard to spot—but spot him you did. Hardly a week on the job, and you've got your man. You are to be congratulated, sir."

"I'm afraid congratulations are premature. In fact, we don't have our man. We had no evidence to link Travis Archer to any crime, so late last night we let him go."

BEFORE HE HEADED for Mozambique or anywhere else, there was one stop Greer needed to make in Tuvingu. His driver from the previous day was right there, as promised, at eight o'clock.

"To the police station this time."

The man seemed reluctant to go there. "You sure, *baas?*"

"Yes, of course I'm sure."

"You already had trouble, *baas?*"

"No, not exactly. Not me personally. And you don't have to call me boss. I'm nobody's boss anymore."

"What I call you, *baas?*"

"Most people just call me sheriff. Because I used to be one. You know what a sheriff is?"

"Oh, yah! Big man! So we go Central Police Station."

That was where Greer met Inspector Prosper Moyo, and soon he didn't feel quite so alone in Africa.

Prosper Moyo was a trim, slight man. In Kentucky he would have been laughably petite for a lawman, and in fact wouldn't have met the height and weight requirements if they hadn't abolished those as discriminatory toward women. Moyo's bright eyes, his crisp movements and show of willingness to please soon told Greer that the loss would have been Kentucky's. He led the way up three flights of stairs—the elevators were temporarily out of order—"temporarily since last May"—into a long, dark room lined with green filing cabinets around long wooden tables. Every surface was covered with tilting stacks of files in beige folders and lock-down notebooks. Stray papers flapped up at the corners when rotating fans blew their way. The only evidence of computers was a haystack-shaped pile of tobacco-stained keyboards, laid out as though ready for a bonfire. Moyo stepped across their trailing cables and picked up an armload of individual folders.

He told Greer, "I remember the Weeks case well. When a closed case sticks in your mind for months on end, there is a cause for that. And the cause is always something...can I say...minor?

Am I right? A small incongruity. Often seemingly unconnected with the case itself. Do you find that also?"

"I sure do. Like what in this case?"

"Mrs. Weeks was murdered by a vigilante militia. I'm sure of that. One bullet in the back of her head. On a dark jetty on the Sabie River. They took her boat and fled."

"Her boat?"

"After Woodhurst was…let us say…repositioned, Weeks sold up everything and bought a shabby little tourist resort on the Sabie, in Mozambique. Well, I say shabby. I have never been there. But even on the website it looks derelict. You can find it on the Internet. What is it called?" Moyo flipped through the file. "Here it is: *Weeks' Cabins and Cruises*."

Greer wrote it down. "Wasn't anyone with her?"

"Not that we know of."

"Doesn't that seem strange to you? A woman out on the river at night, all by herself?"

"Indeed it does. Word was she was smuggling."

"Smuggling what?"

"Officially, *dagga. Mbanje,* we call it here. Marijuana."

"But unofficially?"

Moyo glanced around the empty room, but even then leaned in close to whisper, "Anti-Magwimbi propaganda. Photographic. From a recent state visit to China. Quite possibly of a…," he smiled, "…a salacious nature."

"Oh yeah? Well, you know, these great leaders have to engage in international relations."

"All in a day's work, my friend."

"Do you know who turned her in?"

Moyo shrugged. "Anonymous tip, I was told. That could either mean it really was anonymous, or that it's none of my business."

"So you searched her boat?"

"I did not gain access to it. I merely located it—in a military yard that was loading Chinese military equipment to be sent to Zimbabwe. Of course mixed in with that was an assortment of booty for private profit. And of course I couldn't get close to the assailants, who in any case were underlings of someone far more powerful than I. So far, there's nothing unusual about this."

"I have to say that in my hometown we would not count this an ordinary day at the office, but you go ahead."

Moyo laughed. His face showed a delighted pride that his everyday cases could appear exotic to an American cop. "The victim left behind a husband and a daughter. A beautiful seventeen-year-old daughter."

"Sorry to interrupt, but these people are all white?"

"Of course. It is not legal to marry interracially in South Zambezi. The government eagerly adopted the old colonial law."

"'Loving versus the state of Virginia'."

"Sorry?"

"Never mind. I'll explain later. Please continue."

"So now the family consists of only the husband and the daughter. However, the daughter was not by this husband, but by a former one who died in the war of independence."

"How old was the husband?"

He didn't have to look in the case file. "Fifty-six."

"So we have a middle-aged man living with a young woman, not blood kin to him. Not the best circumstance, but these things happen. You don't think he killed his wife to set this up?"

"No, it was militia."

"So where's the little detail that doesn't sit well?"

"The husband was a music master. His star pupil was a young black man—Lovemore Ngwenya. After the wife's death, do you know who he invited to live with him?"

"Lovemore?"

"I don't know how society is where you come from, but here no white man with a teenage daughter would ever encourage a young black man to move in with them."

"Not black or white or any color. I wouldn't. Would you?"

"My point exactly. Yet it happened."

"So how did Lovemore end up back here in prison?"

He shrugged. "That was the political bureau. Maybe you need to ask this chap."

He opened the file to a photo of Owen Weeks, and Greer got his first look at the man who would, over the next month, become his near-constant companion. It was a posed photo of Weeks standing on the bank of a wide river. In his right hand, at full arm's length, he held an upright fishing rod. The tip of the rod, extending far above Weeks' head, made him appear shorter than he really was. For the moment Greer merely thought it silly, this rigid posture, formal but for a wry smile, this pudgy, red-faced man in his bush shirt and short khaki trousers. Later Greer would have to revise his initial impression, as he came to recognize the pose as mimicry of the stance of an African spear-carrier. By then he would see that it was a glimpse into the soul of Owen Weeks.

Inspector Moyo asked, "Are you planning to visit this man in Mozambique?"

"I came here to fish, didn't I?"

Moyo threw back his head and barked a surprisingly resonant laugh for a man of his size. "Well said! In that case you need bait. For that I advise you to visit one particular *n'anga*—a wizard. Or you might call him a witch doctor. We call him *Chirombo*. It means *Powerful*. If you are willing, I will explain what you must do."

IN CHURCH-GOING EASTERN Kentucky it is considered seemly to schedule Sunday events in the afternoon, so that pious folk can keep their evenings open for a second worship service. It makes no difference that come evening all the churches are nearly empty while living rooms are packed with people watching Survivor or 60 Minutes or their third NFL game of the day. What matters is conforming to standards, and standards dictate Sunday matinees for the likes of Stage Death. Which was just fine with the Shanleys, because the Odeon was packed anyway, and the evening was free for Sunday Supper.

The day had been too busy for anyone to prepare a proper Sunday Supper, so on his way back from Eastern State, Josh stopped at Kroger's and grabbed an assortment of deli items and set them all out on the dining room table and sideboard so people could dig into whatever they wanted. He bought a cheesecake for dessert, and that was that.

He was able to report that Mom had smiled, although not exactly at him, and had even seemed to hum a little tune, or perhaps it was more of a melodic purr, while he brushed her hair. Her doctor had told him that it was too soon to tell how well she would react to her new meds, but if she showed no signs of a relapse they would titrate down the dosage and watch the results. With a little luck, by Thanksgiving they could let her try a day at home.

Good news like this merited more than this slapdash meal, with its little plastic trays of raw vegetables and cheese dips, tubs of macaroni salad and baked beans, cold cuts on butcher's paper, but it went down well, and when Josh announced the take from the first week—over half-a-million—their plain Sunday Supper became a feast.

Josh raised a glass and said, "How long can these numbers hold out? Another week? Two more weeks? We're already booked that long. How about…into November? As of right now we can't know the answer to that. But what we do know is that if they hold up for a month, or, if we dare hope, until Thanksgiving, we can secure our loan without mortgaging any of our properties, and the Guardian will be saved. So let's raise a glass to Stage Death, to Crime Without Punishment, and to our own Dostoyevsky, Mr. Roland R. Shanley."

The rattle of plastic jars meant Brandon was playing smell-and-tell alone in the back seat. To be precise, he was playing smell-without-tell. Rollie adjusted his rear view mirror. "Don't forget to say the words."

"Too easy," Brandon said.

"But you have to say the words. That's part of the game." Ever since smell-and-tell came along, Brandon had absorbed hundreds of words on first or second encounter.

He slammed his fist into the bag and drew one out. *"Pine and lemon!"* he shouted.

"That's better," Rollie said, but thinking, A little less volume might be even better.

A gentle wind, moist and cool, filled the air with swirling leaves. They fell like great overbaked snowflakes, brittle and burnt, swirling down past telephone cables and skittering in brown streaks across Rollie's windshield. It was like driving through a tickertape parade to celebrate mass death.

"Coffee and milk! Too easy!"

"Sweetened or unsweetened?" This was one of his.

"No sugar," Brandon said, but with a bit more humility.

Ha! Rollie thought. The little dude responds to a challenge.

They drove past Buford Chevrolet. "Hey, look over there." A flailing air-pumped stick man proclaimed a sale on last year's models. Red and green plastic pennants flew along a web of wires that stretched from the street all the way to the showroom. "Isn't that pretty?"

Brandon stopped playing. Had he actually stopped smelling to look at the stick man? Rollie checked his mirror. Brandon was pointing. Soon he said, "Der!"

That's when Rollie spotted Lovemore. He pulled into the lot. "What are you doing way over here?"

"Ah! You startled me."

"Me too. I didn't expect to see you out here."

"I am hatching a plan to purchase a new car."

"How did you get out here?"

"I hitchhiked, as usual."

"Aren't you afraid?"

Lovemore shrugged.

"Want a lift back to the Odeon?"

He got in the car. "Hello, Master Brandon." But Brandon was in no joking mood. He pulled a jar from his bag, sniffed, and said nothing.

"So…" Rollie said. "Any great deals back there?"

"No, none. Not on my salary. I'm afraid that even the cheapest new car on offer would cost nearly twenty of those envelopes you give me."

"Prices have really risen lately," he said. But he wondered if that wasn't a hint.

He didn't have to wonder long, for Lovemore said, "Perhaps I need to consider moving on to a more permanent solution to my financial crisis."

Crisis? The guy goes from prison to a thousand dollars a week, and he calls it a crisis? Wait until Josh hears about this.

Rollie hadn't said a word, but it was as though Lovemore had heard his thoughts. "I wonder how many reservations would be cancelled if I left the cast?"

"People seem drawn to you, that's for sure, but your stage career is barely a week old. Maybe you should put in a few more weeks here with us, build your reputation as an actor, and give Hollywood a try. You remember that movie they made here last year? Somebody in Twisting Creek surely has some contact with the director. I know Yolanda interviewed him. There's a start."

"I don't know, Rollie. It seems very speculative. And I wouldn't feel right abandoning you at this point."

"Well, we're certainly glad to have you."

"However, I'm also beginning to understand that my talents here are insufficiently appreciated."

"You're the only one who even gets a stipend. We told you from the start that we're only a little amateur outfit."

"Yes, that's true." He rubbed his forefinger and thumb along the nerves of his neck. "It's true as far as it goes. But there's a lot of ticket money coming in. Where does it go? That's my question. Am I not being exploited?"

"I can't speak for everybody…"

"I risk my life every time I walk on stage. You do realize that."

"How do you figure that?"

"What's to prevent anyone carrying a gun into the theater? They could shoot from the darkened gallery and remain anonymous."

"Don't you think you are being a bit melodramatic?"

"Someone tried to kill me once before. Think of that so-called accidental fire. Surely you don't believe that cover-up story."

"You yourself said she drank."

"Speaking of the fire--here's another thing that may require putting right. Do you remember the alibi you provided me with on the morning after the fire? Which, by the way, was a completely unnecessary alibi. You told then-sheriff Greer that you had been with me at the Odeon until three o'clock in the morning. Do you recall making that claim during…what shall we call it? … an official police inquiry?"

Oh, shit, he thought. *This cannot be happening.*

"And Josh supported your statement. Remember?"

"I remember," Rollie said. He did not add, I'm not likely to forget saving your ass a second time.

"I wonder if I shouldn't contact the new sheriff, Mr. Victor Caraher, and put that right. For the sake of accuracy, of course."

YEARS OF LAW enforcement in the Kentucky hills had taught Greer to value superstition, because superstitious people leave trails. He left the hotel just as dawn broke through the heavy clouds crossing the Bvumba Mountains from Mozambique. His regular driver knew the way to the village of the *n'anga* called Powerful; he even knew the *n'anga*, by reputation.

"Do you believe he can see things we can't?" Greer asked him.

"Of course. If he could not, he would not be a *n'anga*."

It was a logical deduction he found impossible to counter at six in the morning. Even now the road was dominated by open buses overloaded with passengers and by huge trucks overloaded with goods tied up in enormous burlap sacks. They all seemed to change lanes at a whim, as a school of fish will swerve all at once. Mixed among them were cars, motorcycles, bicycles, donkey carts, pushcarts, and lines of pedestrians trying to walk the precarious mud-berm between the highway and the road cut. Everybody was walking everywhere. If Allard Greer had learned one thing in Africa, it was that the lines of walkers never ended. Day and night, single-file or double, people walked and walked and walked.

After an hour, the driver turned onto a dirt road. Potholes gave way to dust. The sky was thick with dark clouds, the air laden with humidity, yet the earth was ashen dry. Greer looked behind him at the solid wall of red dirt thrown up from their passing. "When's it going to rain?" he asked.

"This is our question. We are all expecting rain, praying for rain, but no rain coming. Now is called the suicide season. Then the rains come, and everybody singing. Look ahead. The *kraal*."

It was a wall of intertwined tree branches surrounding a village. Through the fence he saw a grouping of a dozen or so round mud-walled houses with conical thatched roofs. Near the wall a small boy with a stick was driving a bony cow. The driver asked him something and drove on.

"Powerful lives outside the *kraal*. Soon there."

Powerful had a house identical to the others, but inside his own wattle fence. The gate was elaborately decorated with colored streamers, animal bones, dried gourds strung together like a giant necklace, and the hide of a hyena. From here Greer acted according to Inspector Moyo's instructions. He carried a plastic bag with four bottles of beer—South African Castle Lager to show he was serious—and hung it across the gate, facing the *n'anga's* house. That was all he was to do today. They turned around and drove back to Tuvingu.

The next day Inspector Moyo drove him to the kraal. He parked his police car, got out and sat under a *msasa* tree. Greer hung eight bottles of Castle on the gate, then went over to sit with the inspector. Now all they could do was wait. If the beer hung there all day, they were not to be admitted. If the beer disappeared, Powerful would soon send someone to invite them inside.

They waited over an hour. A knobby-kneed and barefoot boy came as far as the gate and waved them inside. Powerful was already seated outside his house on a platform surrounded by bare earth under a baobab tree. Even shriveled and bent he seemed tall enough to tower over most of his countrymen. He wore only a sort of loincloth and a knit cap. He had the gristly limbs of a man who had worked the fields all his life and would live forever. His elevated seat was covered with layers of cloth, originally of many colors but by now mostly various shades of dust. Greer and the inspector sat on a reed mat some feet away from him.

Powerful made a sign with his hand and Inspector Moyo spoke. After a short conversation, Moyo told Greer, "I've explained that I am here simply as a translator. I've told him you need his help to explain the disappearance of a white woman."

"Really? Is that why I'm here?"

"Perhaps. I think you would like to know what happened to the wife of Owen Weeks."

Greer looked at the old man silhouetted against the trunk of the baobab. He almost seemed an extension of the tree as he sat before them, perfectly still, evidently not the least interested in what they were saying.

"Fine. But first, can you tell him that I too am a *n'anga*, at least in my own land?"

"Is this true?" Moyo asked

"It's true enough."

Moyo translated. Powerful's gray eyes widened and he said, "Please tell me how you came by your power."

"It was automatic. I inherited it."

This was clearly fresh news to him. "How can this be?"

"My father had six brothers before him, making him the seventh son. And I have six brothers before me, making me the seventh son of a seventh son. Therefore I have supernatural powers." The story wasn't true, exactly. As a child Greer had heard it from a Holiness faith healer who claimed he could rid his grandmother of a neck goiter. Unsuccessfully, as it turned out. But Greer suddenly remembered the incident and knew instinctively that it would create a bond between himself and the *n'anga*.

"Is this a rule in your land? Seven sons?"

"My grandfather was the son of an American Indian mother. That makes my medicine more powerful. But it doesn't work here."

"No. It doesn't work outside. How were you initiated?"

"When I was eight my father took me to the bank of a river and covered my face with black mud, then he pricked his thumb with a thorn and made the sign of the cross on my forehead in his blood. He quoted scripture where the Lord grants the gift of prophesy to some chosen few, and that was it."

The *n'anga* said that in his case the process was entirely different. He had been working in his field, stopped for a lunch of *sadza* and bean stew, then fell asleep here, under this same tree. Here he dreamed that his father had taken the shape of a hyena and had entered his body. While so inhabited, the father-hyena spoke through Powerful's own mouth, "I am the *n'anga*, I am called Powerful." And when he awoke, he had second sight.

"Fine," Greer told Moyo. "Now let's see what he knows about Weeks. Ask him if a year or two ago a white man came by here, seeking his services."

"I know one did," Moyo said. "Weeks did. It's in his case file."

"Ask him why."

Powerful said that the man had simply asked how long his

wife had to live. "I threw the *hakata* and read the results. They said her natural death would come many years after his death. This did not please him. Then he asked me if I had the power to overrule the *hakata*. I told him, yes, maybe I do, but I do not use it. To use it would make me a *muroyi* and a murderer, not a *n'anga*."

Greer asked, "That was it? Weeks left it like that?"

"No," Powerful said. "He said that if I didn't commit the murder myself, but used someone else to bring it about, I would have no blood on my hands. So I thought he made a good point, and I gave him this advice: to rid yourself of an enemy, create for your victim another enemy even more ruthless than you are."

Greer asked, "You mean like President Magwimbi?"

"I can't ask him that," Moyo said.

But Powerful said, "Like Magwimbi. Yes."

Rollie led Josh into his little broom closet at the Odeon. "It's blackmail," he said. "I don't know what else we could call it." He opened the safe and moved stacks of cash around until he found the cigar box.

Josh said, "But still . . . he's right about the economics of it. Sometime this week we'll top the one million dollar mark. What would it have been without Lovemore?"

"Even so…" Rollie's mood wasn't the kind a financial statement could ameliorate. He felt duped and betrayed. "Can you believe the…the *audacity* of the man! To threaten us with perjury!" He flicked aside baseball cards to uncover his Band-Aid box of joints, lit one, passed it to Josh.

"No thanks. Not perjury, I think. More like obstructing justice or something."

"Whatever. He's still a prick. After we saved his ass—twice!"

"So we pay him more. It's not that big a deal. Relax. There's a hot new rumor going around town that will cheer you up."

"After a stab in the back like this? I don't think so." He blew the tip of his joint to a bright orange glow, then drew in a deep, slow breath. He knew he could always count on this to blunt the pain. He took care to widen his ribs as far as he could. He tried to imagine he had climbed the tallest peak in eastern Kentucky to fill himself with the dense, clean fog of the Cumberlands. He tracked the progress of this benign new presence within him as it penetrated his chest, his bloodstream, and, soon, his mind.

All this time Josh watched him, saying nothing. He looked around at Rollie's office. He'd never been up here before. At last he noticed what a dreary little rat hole it was. When Rollie exhaled, Josh said, "Jesus, Rollie—is this where you spend all your time? Smoking that shit?" With his foot he lifted a flap from one of the Johnny Walker cartons. Five of the six bottles were empty. "This place is like the epicenter of alienation."

"It's also where I wrote Stage Death, which is saving your

fucking paper, so take a hit of this and get off my case."

Josh ignored the offer and the insult. He found an empty envelope and started counting out cash. "Aren't you interested in the hot new rumor?"

"Okay. Sure."

"You know that movie they filmed here last year? I hear from the manager of the Carnegie that the director has booked rooms for himself and some staff. That could only mean one thing: he's here to scout Stage Death."

"Whoa! You think?"

"Maybe for a movie, maybe Lovemore himself. The guy's got stage presence, there's no denying that. And with his back story, you never know. He may soon be richer than all of us." He stuffed one thousand dollars into the envelope, sealed it, held it up between them like an offering, and said, "Let's call this an investment. It sounds so much nicer than a bribe."

EAGER THOUGH GREER was to get across those misty mountains into Mozambique, he knew he needed to take some time to think strategy. If Lovemore's relationship with Owen Weeks was key to the investigation, Greer needed to learn what Weeks knew. That much was clear. What wasn't clear was how to accomplish that. He didn't know how to do it. For thirty years he'd known how—you bring the guy in, put him in a hard chair under harsh lights, and interrogate the living shit out of him. But that was then. He was in a whole new world here. This was more like undercover work. He had no experience at all in this line. In all his years in law enforcement he'd never gone under cover.

Well, Sheriff, he told himself, you're going under now. Do it smart.

Smart in this case meant taking time to think it through. After breakfast at his hotel he stopped at the desk to book an extra night, and then spent most of the day drinking coffee at a patio café on Independence Avenue. He tried to alternate his thoughts between practical issues and drifting reverie. In this he was helped by the constant scissoring of feet and lower legs of pedestrians passing beyond the thick border of yellow cassia. A white-coated waiter faced the street at the garden entrance, his hands locked behind his back. Occasionally he spoke to a passerby. He turned to Greer only when called. He seemed to understand that his odd white customer had serious considerations to attend to, and for the moment a waiter's job was less to serve his customer than to protect him from interruptions.

Greer's first big revelation was that Weeks might have been following the Lovemore case online. Which meant that Allard Greer couldn't be Allard Greer anymore. He couldn't be a retired sheriff from Twisting Creek. Okay, a fake name was easy to come up with, but it meant he couldn't use a credit card. Could he get Mozambican cash from ATM's over there? And what if he needed to present his passport when he registered? The hotel here in Tuvingu asked for it. They even made a photocopy of it. Would Weeks also do that, and connect his client with the man who'd led the Lovemore investigation? He sure as hell couldn't get fake papers here, and would probably get arrested if he tried. He'd have to wing it on that one.

And psychologically? How could he get into this man's mind and learn what secrets lay there? If Weeks had delivered the anonymous tip to Magwimbi's militia that ended his wife's life, if he had arranged to be in sole control of a beautiful young girl way the hell out in the Sabie River wilderness, the only possible way Greer could ever learn about it would be through Weeks himself. Maybe he wouldn't have to confess it, exactly. But he'd have to skate perilously close to a confession.

How can I win him over? Find out his weaknesses, for one thing. Figure out his needs, then fill them. Lucky thing Inspector Moyo was an honest cop. Greer's two bribe bottles of Wild Turkey were still unopened. With a little luck Weeks would be a drinking man.

Trouble with women—that was important. I need to distrust and loathe women. I cannot be a widower who still misses his wife eight years after her death. I need to be a widower, and glad of it. Maybe one who, shall we say, nudged the process along. He remembered the old joke about the man who prayed for his wife to die, then killed her to prove the power of prayer. Get Weeks drunk and tell him that one. And laugh like you mean it.

He emailed Weeks that he was coming, caught the Beira bus down the main EN1, got off at Chimoio and hired a driver to take him to *Weeks' Cabins and Cruises*, which turned out to be less resort than shantytown. The land here was more arid than on the South Zambezi slopes of the Bvumbas, and the cabins looked at home there, unused and ready to blow away.

It was already evening when he arrived. From a distance he spotted Weeks, standing on his veranda, smoking a cigarette and watching for him.

"I saw your dust trail. In this humidity it settles on the trees." He looked off into the sparse stand of fever trees before bringing himself back to the business of receiving a guest. "Oh, I'm Owen Weeks. You must be Mr. Green."

Greer shook his hand. "You can call me Lou." Lou Green was the solution Greer had hit on to fudge his identity in case Weeks asked for a passport. *Louis* was his middle name. He could say he'd always gone by that. And *Green* was close enough to *Greer* to be explained by a typo or a misreading.

"How ever did you find me? Most of my guests are Zimbabweans or South Africans. Never American. And never anyone this time of year."

Under the cigarette breath there was the smell of whisky. That was very good news.

"No big mystery. I just googled. This is my big retirement safari, I guess you might say. And I love to fish." As evidence he held up his rod case and his new blue tackle backpack.

"My word!" Weeks said. "I've never seen one like that."

"Inside there are all kinds of nooks and crannies. When we get time I'll open it out for you."

"I look forward to it. And I'll show you my gun collection. Are you also a hunter?"

"Have been known to hunt. Fishing's more my game, though."

So they fished together. For nearly a month they were each other's main companion. They motored upriver on Weeks' pontoon boat as far toward the South Zambezi border as they dared, then glided downriver as far as the little town of Felicidade, where they tied up and drank *Manica* lager on the wooden plank benches of a riverside bar called Os Abrigos. They sat there, often saying nothing for long minutes at a time, just smelling the putrid river, breathing the sodden, suffocating air, watching the black clouds form huge inky blobs over the Bvumbas, and listening to the low threat of thunder, a lion's warning call.

"Is it ever going to rain?" Greer asked.

"That's what we all want to know. Some years it doesn't. It builds and builds like this, getting nastier by the day, and then the clouds just go away without so much as a farewell. Then everybody starves. They call this the suicide season. Did you know that?"

"Yes. I heard that. And when it does rain?"

"The thunder is explosive. Rain comes down like iron rods, in drops so big they hurt your skin. But everybody goes out and dances in it anyway."

"I hope I'm here to witness that."

"I hope we all are."

After a couple of beers at Os Abrigos, they would walk the pressed dirt path that served as Felicidade's main thoroughfare, where women sat on plastic sheets amid their piles of cassava, red peppers, potatoes, cashews, and pots of cornmeal mush and peanut stew.

They didn't buy much during these market visits. Weeks had servants to do that, but he liked to flirt with the young women in the village.

One day he said, "Let's take a couple of these punkies home."

"These what?"

"Punkies. Chippies. These young hookers. They're all for sale, you know."

"Count me out for now, Owen. Where women are concerned, I'm kind of off my feed at the moment."

Weeks stopped walking, and looked away from the market women. "Really? What happened?"

"Long story. Maybe I'll get drunk enough sometime to tell you." That was a technique Greer had hit on: make it seem *you're* the one with the hidden depths. The guy might be willing to trade you secret for secret. "By the way, didn't I hear you playing the piano one night?"

"Why? Did it keep you awake?"

"Not at all. I enjoyed it. I'd like to hear more."

Weeks waved a dismissive hand.

"No, really. I'd love to just sit and drink and listen. I don't play any instrument myself, but I can contribute a fresh bottle of Wild Turkey. You like Kentucky bourbon?"

They'd always eaten the same meal, but not together. Veronica did the cooking in Weeks' big kitchen and then sent Greer his share. Tonight though, Weeks invited him to have dinner with him. Never before had he made it past the veranda. Now he would see the interior of a Portuguese manor house built a century earlier. He handed Weeks a bottle of bourbon and was invited into a vast room with polished teak floors, mahogany walls that seemed tall enough for two stories, and a great staircase with banisters in the form of anacondas.

A shiny ebony piano dominated the music room. Greer headed straight for it, and for the framed photo it held of a hard-eyed young woman in a white satin dress. She held her arms folded across her chest. Her bright chestnut hair was flipped up at the sides, and her impudent red mouth puckered as though ready to spit out something sour.

"Is this your wife?" he asked. It was a ridiculous question. It was a picture of a teen-aged girl. But Greer liked the way "wife" implied sex.

"My step-daughter," he said. "Alas, no longer with us."

"Where is she now?" With Weeks staring at him, he soon realized what he'd meant. "I'm so sorry. She was very beautiful."

Weeks said nothing else. He turned to a mirror-faced cabinet for two glasses. Greer poured them each a drink. Their first of many that evening. There was wine with dinner, followed by more bourbon. Weeks' eyes took on a liquid glow Greer hadn't seen before. He decided to open the taboo topic.

"You've told me you're a widower, like me. And you're a fisherman. But beyond that I don't know much about your life. Oh, and I know you play the piano."

"You're the silent one, mate. Silent and mysterious. Did your wife put the clamps on?"

"You may be on to something there, Owen. Let's put it this way: she wasn't a woman who appreciated good conversation."

"I knew it! I can always tell when a man's had an unhappy marriage."

"Let's drink to that." He poured each of them more whisky. "Hey, speaking of that, there's an old joke where I come from. A man prays for his wife to die, then kills her, because God always answers your prayers."

Weeks didn't laugh, he nodded. "Yes, that's good. I like that."

"So did you marry a harpy too?"

"Let me tell you! You've never met a nutcracker like my wife. And do you know what kind of life I saved that bitch from? The Heroes had killed her first husband. You know who the Heroes are, right?"

"Magwimbi's henchmen?"

"Exactly. They killed him and drove Linda and Sabella off their farm. That's Sabella, her daughter." He pointed to the picture on the piano. "Linda had nothing. No money. No skills. Nothing!" He stopped there. He seemed to have lost his place.

"She had one thing." Greer said. "She had a beautiful daughter."

"Ha! You think she's so beautiful. You should have known her." He walked to the piano and picked up the picture. "Look at those eyes. Just like her mother's. Do you know how she was making a living when I met her?"

"Daughter or mother?"

"Mother, goddammit! The daughter didn't do a fucking thing. But Linda was a nanny! A nanny for *bleck* people!"

"For…oh, for black people?"

"Fucking right. That's what I rescued her from. And you see what I got for my pains." His hand swept around the empty room, and he stopped talking.

Greer took the photograph back across the room to the piano, and remained there, hoping Weeks would follow. For a while he stayed where he was, standing by a leather wingback chair, one hand on it for stability.

Greer said, "How about playing me something."

"What do you want to hear?"

"Anything would be fine. Chopin, maybe?" It was the only piano composer he could think of.

He weaved his way to the piano bench. "How about a nocturne? Something pleasant to take our minds off everything."

He played a couple of minutes. Something melodic and tinkly. Greer had no idea what it was, didn't really listen. He needed to get Weeks back on topic. He knew he needed to be careful with a man as secretive as Weeks, a man who would seal himself off after one probe too far. Yet already precious time had been spent gaining the man's trust, while in distant Twisting Creek the peril increased with each passing day. Greer closed his eyes as though to appreciate the Chopin, but what he saw was Deedee's Sarah professing her love to Lovemore, and then her scorn, while Lovemore circled her throat with his powerful hands.

Weeks finished playing and looked up at him, eyes wide, seeking approval.

Greer said, "Hey, you are good! Not that I ever doubted it."

"Thank you. How about something American? Gershwin?" He arranged his fingers on the keyboard for an opening chord.

"Actually, Owen, I'm more interested in this wife of yours. So you rescued her from poverty. But who rescued you from her? That's what I want to know."

Weeks stopped playing and jerked his face up to Greer's. "You're an interesting one, you are. Most of my guests only want to talk about themselves. You only want to talk about me."

"My story's just boring, that's all. Though maybe not quite so boring at the end." He made what he hoped came out as a concealing giggle.

"What?"

"I hope it gets boring again soon, so I can go home."

Weeks turned on the piano bench and said, "Okay, mate. Spill it."

"It's just that—my wife died in an auto accident. Did I tell you that? No? Okay, she did. Thanks to a blown tire on a mountain road. And just before I left the States there was some question as to what a bald tire was doing on her right, front wheel. Hopefully that question dies down before I get home."

Weeks stood up, grinning and pointing his finger. "You did it, you bastard! You changed that tire!"

Greer smiled. He'd once investigated a case much like this, only it was a broken ball joint, but he didn't want to have to explain the working of a car's suspension system to a music teacher. "Now Owen, that's a crock of shit, and you know it. Some clown down at the Goodyear store made a little mistake, that's all."

"As a liar you're bloody miserable, you know that? You'd better camp down here for a long, long time."

"So I had Goodyear. You had Magwimbi."

"I needed more than Magwimbi, I can tell you. Magwimbi was the easy one." He staggered toward a liquor cabinet. "Let's have some port. I always like to switch to port after a meal, don't you?"

Greer knew nothing at all about port, except that it was strong. "Perfect," he said, and waited. "So…Magwimbi was easy?"

"Nutcracker Linda had it in for him. No surprise really—his Heroes killed her husband. So she started ferrying anti-Magwimbi literature to some stash point along the river. I guess somebody must have grassed on her." He winked. "Somebody down at the Goodyear shop, I shouldn't wonder!"

Greer indicated the young woman in the photograph. "Was this one with her?"

"That little bitch? She wasn't the least bit political. She took a while. Tell me something, Lou. Have you ever truly given your heart to someone? I mean *all* of it? Maybe you had to plan it far in advance, to sacrifice everything for it? Even do things you wouldn't normally do, to make it happen? Yet they reject you like you were a piece of rubbish? Absolute stinking filth? Has this ever happened to you?"

"I know exactly, Owen. I've been there too. And you know what? In the end they get what's coming to them."

"That's it! You've put a finger right on it. They deserve exactly what they get."

"So, it wasn't Magwimbi's Heroes. Let me guess. A boating accident?"

"Not even close, my friend! Any sort of accident might lead to an investigation. You see what happened in your case. Sorry to offend."

"It's okay. I'm just not as clever as you."

"Next time, if it happens again, here's a little piece of advice. If you want to be rid of an enemy, make for that enemy an enemy even more ruthless than you are."

"And how can I manage that?"

"If you could find someone…this is merely a hypothetical case, mind you…you could find someone volatile, a real nasty piece of work, and convince them this girl loves them. Convince the boy that she's ready to fall. Black or white makes no difference to her. She likes him just as he is. All he has to do is make the play. Then sit back and enjoy the show."

A crack of thunder seemed to shake the walls. It was as though the whole of the Bvumbas had exploded. Weeks drew back a set of drapes and pressed his face to a bay window. From somewhere outside they heard Veronica singing a hymn of thanksgiving to the mountains and the sky. Sheets of rain drumming on the roof blended into the roar of thunder. Through the window Greer could see raindrops fall as streaks onto the window sills and spray like fountains against the glass.

With Weeks' back to him, Greer took a camera from his pocket and snapped his last photo of Africa. It showed a hard-eyed young woman in a white satin dress. It was everything he'd come for, the ultimate treasure of his African quest. He joined Weeks at the window. "This may be the culminating moment of my life," he said. "Can we watch it from the veranda?"

LOVEMORE'S EYES NARROWED as he crossed the stage toward Deedee. He wrapped the hanging strands of her scarf around his hands and pulled with the full might of his arms. The audience was so quiet, and his effort so muscular, that Deedee could hear threads in her scarf snapping under the strain. He pulled her close enough to rest his mouth against her cheek, on the side of her face away from the audience, and whispered, "If you trusted me you wouldn't wear a neck brace."

He was making a habit of this—of whispering into her ear when there was no way she could respond without the audience noticing. One night he said, "You know I love you, don't you?" One night he simply said, "Sarah." That soon progressed to, "I know who killed you." Even while she pretended to struggle for air, her eyes searched his face for a clue. He jerked the scarf to him, placed his mouth by her ear, and said, "The Boer."

Tonight he had said, "Come out with me. I have money now."

So she went out with him. Maybe it was foolhardy, but the man intrigued her. Far from the simple thief-murderer the town had once pictured him, he was a tangled set of interweaving, shifting components. Locally, Stage Death had transformed his notoriety into celebrity, but that was too simple for Deedee. With every performance her feelings toward him were becoming more and more conflicted. An unexpected tenderness for him had found its way into their bitter love scenes. She'd heard of women whose fear of dangerous men gradually gave way to a submissive gratitude for restrained danger. Could his withheld power became for her a zone of safety, and gratitude grow into love?

Was this happening to her? Was she starting to crave off-stage the vulnerable safety that came with being Lovemore's on-stage lover? Was this why she sat in her dressing room before every performance, contemplating the neck brace in her hands longer and longer each time before she strapped it on?

She needed an answer. She needed to know how the

compartments that made up Lovemore Ngwenya had been created, and how they worked together. What's more, she knew "the Boer" meant Travis, and as much as she would like to think she could remain outside the pissing contest those two seemed bent on, she needed to know what evidence Lovemore had on him.

After that night's play she drove him out to the Lakeside Grill. During the drive he didn't say much—he never did immediately after a performance—but eventually he said, "Soon I will have a car and I can drive you."

They were passing the bait store. Deedee wondered, Is it a coincidence that he waited until we reached this spot before he mentioned buying a car? Or had he planned it? Did he even know exactly where Travis' store was? Had he spotted Archer's unlit road sign?

"A car, huh? Around here you sure need a car. We used to have public mini-buses, but their budget got axed."

Apparently municipal fiscal woes didn't measure up as a topic of conversation.

The Lakeside Grill was crowded, confirming the opinion that Stage Death contributed to the local economy. A murmur went through the room when they entered. It was the first time Deedee had experienced the buzz of celebrity. She ordered a margarita and Lovemore ordered a Kentucky breeze. Deedee had never heard of it, but the waitress was unfazed. Then she looked closely at them both and said, "I saw you guys! You are so talented!"

"Thank you," Lovemore responded simply. His eyes followed her as she weaved her way between tables and to the bar. He winked at Deedee, leaned back in his chair and stretched his long legs as far under the table as he could. "Yes!" he said. "This is more like it."

"I guess you feel cooped up in your basement room."

"Not at all. It is far more spacious than many of my previous residences."

Deedee laughed. "I just meant, with no car."

"Soon. Very soon. You've heard the rumors."

"About Hollywood?"

His eyes grew alert and he held his wide hands high, in a

gesture of surrender, "We must face it, my dear. We are destined to be stars!"

"Don't get your hopes up. My mom used to say, High hopes have steep slopes."

"In my country it is the opposite. We say the dreaming hunter eats his fill."

"Listen, I want to talk to you about something. When you whisper things to me during the play, off-stage things, it…it bothers me. I mean, it throws my timing off."

Lovemore said, "Again to the contrary. I say them to deepen your performance. You are such a fine actress, the perfect Sarah."

"Well, thank you, I guess. But please stop."

"You must try to imagine the two of us in Hollywood. That's our ticket out of here."

"But it isn't helpful." Deedee made sure her tone of insistence was impossible to miss. "So please stop it."

He didn't reply. The waitress arrived with their drinks and seemed on the verge of asking for an autograph when she caught Deedee's look and left them alone.

"Here's one other thing I want to ask. What is it with you and 'the Boer.' I guess that means Travis. What do you know about him?"

"I don't trust him, that's all. He reminds me of an Afrikaner racist."

"And you think he was in love with Sarah?"

"There is no question in my mind about that. And with you."

"You think he's in love with me?" She tried to sound surprised, but she knew that it was probably true, and it meant Lovemore had a perceptive eye.

His smile meant it was too obvious to merit comment. He sipped his drink and glanced around the room at people glancing around at him. "My dear Deedee, thank you for coming out with me at last. I asked you primarily to be in your company."

She felt herself mirroring his smile.

"But, secondarily, I wanted to say two important things. One, I admire your acting ability and the way you channel your stage fright to enhance your art. And the second thing is, if I may be frank, I find that neck brace offensive."

She mirrored his smile no longer. "But it's for the performance. I thought Rollie explained…"

Lovemore put up his hand. "I don't accept Rollie's explanation, or yours. I suspect that the real reason you insist on wearing it is you think I am dangerous, and I further suspect that the idea came from Sheriff Greer."

"That's absurd."

"You're not a very competent liar."

She thought, So much for my acting ability.

"Deedee, don't you understand what an insult that thing is to me? I respectfully request that you stop using it—unless you yourself distrust me."

She could feel the pinprick threat of tears around her eyes.

"Do you distrust me, Deedee?"

"No. Of course I don't, Lovemore. You are my co-star. I won't use it anymore. I was thinking of stopping anyway."

He seemed satisfied with her response. He relaxed into his chair and drained his glass. "Delicious. Far superior to the tepid gin-and-tonics of our colonial masters. Do you know who taught me to drink this?" He didn't wait for an answer. "Sarah, that's who."

"It seems our famous local teetotaler really knew her wines and spirits." Deedee was surprised by a sudden urge to irritate Lovemore. She wondered where it had come from.

"Ah, yes! Indeed she did. There were so many surprising aspects to her. Her hidden passions."

"Or maybe not so hidden, if Rollie knew about them." This surprised her even as it came out of her mouth. Why was she provoking him? Because he dared her to dream of a bigger life? Because he had divined her conspiracy with Greer? Surely it couldn't be jealousy?

He sat forward.

She added, "And now the whole town knows."

"That is an unkind remark," he said. "But I forgive you. It stems from a woman's natural jealousy."

Again he seemed to read her mind. *Goddamn him!* Insults are always so much more painful when they ring true. But she brought herself under control. A restaurant full of people who recognized them was not the place for a shouting match. Maybe she should reach across the table and strangle him. Someone would surely video it for YouTube. But then she had a better idea, something Josh had told the family last Sunday Supper. She laughed aloud at the thought.

"You amuse yourself," Lovemore said.

"Sometimes. I've just remembered another rumor going around town. Ethan Lester will be here next weekend. All the way from New Orleans, just to watch us on stage."

GREER FINALLY FOUND a working Internet connection at Johannesburg airport. Three days and about that many hours' sleep later, he picked up Deedee and together they went to his old office, where Victor now sat behind his old desk. He showed them a photo of a young woman with an impudent red mouth, her hard eyes staring at the camera. "I have a plan. Deedee, how are you with accents?"

Peeking through the curtains, Deedee watched tonight's audience file in. She spotted an older, shaggy-haired man with an out-of-date goatee, leading a small line of younger people into the second row. She recognized him as Hugo Messer, the director of No Senator's Son, and she supposed the others must be talent scouts, or maybe potential investors. Ethan Lester wasn't among them. She looked around the auditorium for him, but couldn't spot him.

Greer came up behind her. "You're sure you know what to do?"

Hesitantly, she nodded.

"Good. Don't worry. I'm stationed just off one wing, and Victor is in the other. We've got our eyes on every move." He looked around for the chair where Travis would wait, off-stage, until the hanging. Lovemore's security harness lay there now, neatly folded, its complicated web of ropes sorted in a fisherman's systematic pile. The hangman's rope was looped onto a chair leg, where it would secure the noose over the gallows right through the entire play, until the hanging, when Travis would take it in hand to make it appear taut.

Deedee asked, "Who knows about this plan besides you, me and Victor?"

"Not a soul," Greer said. "The more people that know, the more chance of leaks. You didn't tell anyone, I hope."

"No." This level of deception was foreign to Deedee. She looked away from Greer, peered once again through the gap in the curtains, toward the hundreds of people settling in for the show of a lifetime. She wished she could make them all go away, make the whole nightmare disappear.

Greer spotted something beside Travis' chair. It looked like an electric cable. "What's that?" he asked, more to himself, not expecting Deedee to answer.

"It's the cord for that fan up there." She pointed up into the catwalks. "Travis switches it on at the beginning of the second act. It makes the noose wave back and forth a little bit. Just enough to catch the audience's eye every now and then. At least that's the idea.

Greer pressed the switch, watched the fan start to undulate, and switched it back off. "Okay. I'll take my station now. Don't worry about a thing. Just go out there and deliver the performance of your life."

She didn't like his turn of phrase, but he seemed not to catch it. He moved into the shadows, out of sight.

The first act went along as normal. By now she'd now done it often enough that she was confident of her lines and marks. She tried not to think of the talent scouts in the crowd, or of Act Two. Only one unusual thing happened. In the scene where Lovemore steadies her as she nearly topples over while attaching a bird feeder to a tree, where she turns to him, brushes seed from his hair and shoulders, and they have their first kiss, she felt his hand slide up her back and into her hair, where he squeezed his fist enough to tug at the roots. It didn't exactly hurt. In a more sexual mood she might not have minded. Was that the point he was trying to make? *This is the kind of man I am? Sample this foretaste of pleasures to come?* Or could it be just another technique to put her in character?

She smelled lust on his breath. This was definitely not stagecraft! Even the greatest actors in the world couldn't fake pheromones. Could they?

He pressed her face into his chest. If he was this rough already, how hard would he pull on her scarf? She regretted her promise not to wear her neck brace.

As it turned out, the first strangling was no worse than usual. If he really meant it when he said he deliberately instilled fear in her only to improve her performance, she had to admit it worked. Especially without the cervical collar. Every time the scarf tightened around her throat to end Act One, he could end her life. She knew the audience believed it; she believed it herself.

The second act started with a now-expected bit of comic relief, when, on his way to court, Lovemore stops for a moment at the piano to play a few measures from Chopin's Funeral March. A month earlier, when he'd first inserted it into the act, the intent was to be dramatic, to infuse the audience with Chopin's trudging march of doom, like steps to the gallows, but at the last moment Lovemore had the inspiration to look up from the keyboard and flash his audience an arch, wicked leer. Initially there followed a sprig of laughter, no more than a garnish for the tragic meal. Soon, though, people anticipated it. On stage you could almost hear a drawn breath as the Chopin ended. You sensed they were thinking, *Watch this now. He's going to do it.*

So now he did it, every time, and laughter resounded around the hall. It was funny because they knew he wasn't going to hang. Not really. In real life he'd been freed, to entertain them with his defiant sneers.

At this point, on this special day, things had to change. Normally in the second act Deedee sat quietly in her rocking chair, reading an oversized Guardian with the headline *LOVEMORE SWINGS*. But not tonight. Tonight she dropped the newspaper to the floor, and left the stage. Were there whispers in the audience? Was Lovemore watching her as she slipped through the curtains and out of sight? Or was he too busy with his trial scene to glance her way? She would never be able to answer these questions.

By the time his trial ended, she was back in place, slowly rocking, as though nothing had happened. He left the courtroom and turned toward her, making his ponderous march to her final death scene. Now he saw. His face twisted with the bewildered terror of a witness to the supernatural, for what awaited him was not the blond and innocent Deedee Shanley in a turtleneck sweater, nor even a resurrected Sarah Lester. It was a hard-eyed woman in a white satin dress and high heels, her arms folded for a challenge. Her bright chestnut hair was flipped up at the sides, and her impudent red mouth puckered as though ready to spit out something sour.

"Not you again," she said. "I thought I told you to feck off."

At the sound of her voice, he stopped mid-stride. "Who do you think you are?"

"I'm the woman you killed. Or I should say, one of them."

He moved in closer. "Sabella?"

She jeered in his face. "You look like you've seen a ghost. You really thought I was dead, didn't you?"

Almost in her face now, he repeated, "Sabella?"

"You and Owen both thought I was dead. Ignorant bastards, the pair of you."

"It can't be you."

"I don't die so easy."

This was the last line she'd memorized. After this, she was instructed to spit in his face. But she didn't have time. He was on her in an instant.

"Bloody Boer bitch!"

His hands went to her throat. She felt a stricture seize her neck like none she had ever felt before. She grabbed at his wrists, struggled for a breath, and sank to her knees.

From either wing Victor and Greer charged toward her. Travis saw them run on stage and couldn't understand what he was seeing. His first thought was that maybe he'd missed some new stage directions. As soon as he moved toward them, the theater went completely dark. The noise of desperate scuffling was everywhere, but nobody could see anything. The audience watched in silence while on stage men shouted and scrambled. They heard the thud of bodies hitting the stage floor. They heard a cacophony of piano chords, as if someone's head was being slammed into the keys. They heard Sarah scream, and they heard her stop. In the audience, a lone woman began to shriek, and others, as though awaiting their cue, joined in.

At last the automatic timer put a spotlight on the gallows, where Lovemore was swinging like a pendulum. His legs kicked, his hands groped for the noose, and then his whole body went limp. The audience jumped to its feet. They cheered. They called out, "Bravo!"

"Lights! Now!" Victor shouted, but there was no one in control. The automatic timer would have to tick away the seconds.

Travis moved to the gallows stairs, where the harness lay, untouched. He looked at the rope tied onto the metal cleat and called out, "He tied up the wrong rope!"

Greer said, "No. He tied the rope he meant to tie." He and Victor moved closer and lifted Lovemore by the legs, while Travis unhitched the cleat. Together they laid him across the circle of light, where Greer could see into his lifeless eyes.

Travis saw Deedee still lying on the floor. He ran toward her and cupped the back of her head in his hand. When she opened her eyes, Travis sat her upright in his embrace.

The applause continued.

T HIS TIME D EEDEE didn't even stop by the bait store. She sent him a text: *Be at the bench at 2:00 if you ever want to see me again.*

She was ten minutes early. From the top of the tree line she saw him down by the lake, not, as she'd expected, sitting motionless on the bench, as still as a fisherman, but practicing a leap from the bottom of the hill onto the backrest of the bench. She paused to watch as with each attempt he overshot the mark, failed to establish his balance and was forced to step down onto the seat of the bench. She ducked behind the trunk of a tree as he circled back up for another try. With each modulated attempt it seemed her own heart modulated, until he had calibrated his speed and timing just right, and stood there, perfectly balanced on the backrest, gazing off to where the distant gray water merged with the layer of gray cloud to create a solid gray backdrop of lake and sky, a vast but intensely personal cinema screen for the scene that would determine the direction of their lives.

The breeze freshened as Deedee moved toward the lake. Straight overhead a small break in the overcast sky, like a gash in the earth's quilt, meant a cold night was ahead. Deedee knew enough science to understand that the cold of a clear night was due to the earth's heat escaping to the upper atmosphere, but emotionally she saw it a different way. She saw it as the protective barrier of clouds in full retreat from the assaulting ice of the universe. She knew it was wrong to see it that way, but she couldn't help it.

She approached him and said, "Do you feel it getting colder?"

Travis bounced down from the bench and looked up at the widening streak of blue. "Looks like it's going to be a cold night. Better bundle up."

"It's going to be a cold afternoon unless you can explain everything in some way that I haven't even imagined yet."

Travis sat down. He patted the seat beside him, but she didn't respond. She started pacing back and forth like a sentry.

"But you already know what happened. It's been all over the

news by now."

"I know the police report—your younger brother Jason murdered your parents and then himself. What I don't know is why you lied to me. Lied right through your teeth. Wayne State my ass!"

"Maybe it would be better if you sat down here and sort of calmed yourself."

She quickened her sentry's pace and pointed a finger at him. "Don't tell me to sit down and don't tell me to calm down. There's only one thing I want to hear from you—the truth."

"Okay."

"And no more lies. Not one single fib, you hear me?"

"Of course. From now on, I swear." His head moved back and forth as he followed her pacing. "Deedee, you're going to make me dizzy."

"Start now or I'm gone."

"Okay. But where do I start?"

"Your younger brother was weird, like my Brandon. Start there."

"He wasn't weird, exactly. Well, he was, but only in the sense that we're all weird, only maybe a little more so."

"Murdering his parents counts as way weird, if you ask me."

"They were the weird ones, Deedee. Like a lot of these outsiders, they thought they could come out here and lose themselves among a bunch of hillbillies, but they brought who they were with them. It was them that drove Jason over the edge. You should have seen how they treated him. Like a dog. Literally like a dog. They'd find him sniffing something, and they'd rub his nose down in it, hard. And then they'd take a switch to him, or a strap, and say if he wanted to act like an old hound they'd beat him like one until he learned his lesson. I saw my mother kick him—a full, hard kick, like at a football. My *mother*! Listen Deedee, I've heard psychologists say that if one parent is abusive, most kids can survive that, provided the other one offers love and comfort and some prospect of protection. But when both father and mother take turns berating you and beating you, what kind of chance do you have? He had no one to turn to. Not even a grandparent or somebody. He was stuck out here in the woods with two people who beat him senseless. That's what made him weird."

"That didn't make Brandon weird."

"But that's what I'm saying. Brandon or Jason neither one was all that wacko to start with. That's why I say he wasn't much different than you or me or anybody. None of us is strictly by-the-book standard, are we? We all follow roads a little bit different from everybody else. Maybe Brandy and Jason followed roads a little more different than most, but that's okay. In fact, I admire them for it. It's one reason I love Brandy so much. I know it sounds unlikely, but I admire him."

"You *admire* him?" she repeated, even though in fact she was starting to understand him.

"How can you not admire a person who goes whole hog in the direction he chooses, screw the consequences? Personally, I think Brandy should be a role model for us all. I felt the same about Jason. It was Jason's example that made me come down here and open up this hopeless little bait shop of mine."

She stopped pacing now and sat beside him. "But still—for a boy to kill his own parents, he must have been…" She stopped. She didn't want to say the word.

Travis said it for her. "They drove him insane. If ever a killer was innocent of murder, Jason was innocent."

"Can you tell me about that morning? Can you talk about it?"

"Sure—I promised you total honesty, so here it is. It happened when I was thirteen, and Jason was eleven. I was out on the lake fishing and heard gunshots, several of them. I've never been really sure of the number. The sound didn't come from up by the house, but a lot closer, it seemed like. I rowed over to the bank and started searching around to locate where they came from. The first body I found was my mother's. She was lying on a bluff not far from the lake, in a shady spot where they used to dig ginseng root. I looked around and saw my father's body about twenty feet away, surrounded by blood. And right near him was Jason, with a hole in the side of his head and our father's pistol at his side. But you know all of this, don't you? It was in the paper." He tried to smile, to show that it had all happened a long time ago.

"I needed to hear it from you. Why did you bury them? Why didn't you contact the police?"

"I've asked myself that question so many times. For one thing, I suppose I was kind of messed up myself. I wasn't abused as much as Jason was, because I guess I wasn't quite so…unique. But even with me they didn't spare the rod until I grew to the point where my size sort of protected me. For another thing, I didn't want my brother to be known as a crazy murderer. We'd led such completely private lives, walled off from the outside world—taking it on myself to bury them all seemed like the normal thing to do. It was no more than an extension of the life they'd brought me up to."

"But you did break out of those walls."

"What I told you before about my uncle visiting here, and being angry about our education—that was the truth. That Christmas, as he was leaving, he slipped me his phone number and a note saying if I needed him, call him. That note became like some precious treasure to me. I hid it in a crack between the roof beam and ceiling in my bedroom. So after I buried my family, I pulled that note down from its hiding place and I hitchhiked into town where I could find a pay phone. I told my uncle that my parents had decided to look for work in California, and Jason would go with them, but if the offer still stood of a home with him and his family in Michigan, I'd sure like to take them up on it. He sent me bus fare, and north I went."

"They're not going to prosecute you now for covering up a murder?"

"It seems not. I know it was a mistake, but I was pretty much a child myself. I think the court will understand why I made it."

Deedee understood too, but she wasn't ready to forgive him just yet. There'd been too much anxiety over the missing brother at Wayne State for her to let him off so soon. "I can sort of understand why you lied to your uncle, but why did you lie to me? That whole law school business was totally unnecessary--unless you were trying to bullshit your way into my pants."

"Jesus, Deedee! Is that what you think?"

"Let's say it's a hypothesis you need to disprove."

"I was just trying to give you some hope, that's all. I couldn't very well say, Your son reminds me of my little brother, who killed his parents then himself. Could I?" He waited. "Well, could I?"

"Well no, obviously not. But you could have kept your mouth shut."

"But didn't it make you feel better, imagining Brandy going off to college? I remember watching your face light up when it sank in."

"Sure it cheered me up, but it was a lie!"

"Let's say it was an alternate version of the truth."

"It was a *what?*" Even as angry as she was, she had to laugh at that.

He laughed with her and put his arm around her. "It was a possible truth that could have happened if Jason had been brought up in a loving home. And before you say *Why didn't you say that at the time*, I think you know the answer to that, don't you?"

She did. It had been far too early in their relationship to be talking about bringing up children. Even with a single mother, when the topic must come up far sooner than it normally should, it had been too early. Deedee leaned her head onto his shoulder.

Travis said, "And you see that Brandy's already doing better, right?"

There was no denying that. Everybody remarked on it. "Thank you for inventing smell-and-tell."

"I only wish I'd invented it about twenty-five years earlier."

With that thought in the air, the possibility of molding a better future against the impossibility of turning back the clock, they sat silently for a long time, watching the widening streak of blue in the overcast sky. Deedee felt the bitter invasion of the universe as it overcame the earth's fragile defenses.

"Excuse me a second." Travis stood up, removed his coat, sat back down and spread it over both of them. Deedee leaned in close. They enjoyed a shared warmth, and listened to a loose formation of honking mallards approach over trees behind them. The gabbling stopped, there was a random splash, and the ducks began to probe for minnows under the lake surface.

Deedee said, "I wonder if they know hunting season is right around the corner."

Travis knew it wasn't a question about ducks, not exactly, so he said, "Deedee... he's a tremendous kid. A truly special little guy. If you love him right down the line for exactly who he is, he'll turn out great. And you, and anybody else close to you, can count it a privilege to watch him grow up."

"You're going to make me cry."

"Ha! I don't think crying's what you're all about. You laugh too sweet to cry much."

She punched his stomach and laughed.

He told her, "Listen, I've been wanting to tell you how brave you were to capture Lovemore like that. You took a huge risk."

She shrugged it off. "It had to be done. They had no grounds to extradite him, and they couldn't try him again for Sarah's murder. It didn't seem right that a man could kill two women and walk free. Still, I didn't expect him to kill himself. I thought maybe a confession..."

"The whole town is proud of you. It took true courage. You're tough as nails."

"So now you know to watch your step, right?"

Travis laughed and pulled her closer. "Indeed I do. So...have you forgiven me yet?"

She took his cold hand, tucked it inside her sweater pocket, and asked, "Do you have any plans for Thanksgiving?"

ON THE SURFACE it might have been a Thanksgiving like no other, with gratitude abundant, a day when every person at the Shanley table could have recited blessing after blessing. Significant ones too; recent, and, in some cases, against all odds.

Stage Death had grossed over three million dollars, most of it straight profit, and auxiliary sales of posters, t-shirts and the like were still going strong; were, in fact, likely to increase in popularity following the dramatic final curtain. Negotiations were already under way to purchase a paper mill and a modern print facility. In two months the Guardian had evolved from a tottering twentieth century relic to a model of twenty-first century entrepreneurship. Last week Josh had finally agreed to return an ICNA phone call, simply so he could chuckle in someone's ear at the very idea of selling out.

Former Twisting Creek loser Roland Shanley was now known throughout the area as the brains behind Stage Death. And if Rollie was the Guardian's archangel, Deedee was its Joan of Arc. She need never compose another classified ad as long as she lived.

She and Travis were reconciled.

Brandon was progressing, albeit on his own terms, but even that might someday be counted a blessing.

Mom's shrieks of terror hadn't returned in spite of Haldol withdrawal, and her doctor believed she was well enough to go home for the day.

Sheriff Greer had made an extraordinary journey to Africa to nab his man and rescue his reputation.

The town's demand for justice had at last been granted, and this without anyone dirtying their hands or consciences with an electric switch or a hypodermic loaded with pentobarbital. The murderer himself had redressed the balance of good and evil, when he placed the rope around his own neck.

The "interim" was now officially removed from Victor's title. And the now-Sheriff Caraher had another announcement up his sleeve, but one he would keep for later in the day.

So everyone might have been in a festive mood as the aroma of turkey and stuffing filled the house. However, as abundant and momentous as those blessings were, Thanksgiving Day found the assembling group more pensive than triumphant. Nobody present was able to completely ignore that one man was missing; a man who in one way or another had been central to their lives, and to the blessings they were loathe to tabulate. The whole Lovemore episode had shaken their faith in mankind's capacity ever to be certain about anything. On a deeper level, their faith in a bedrock reality now had a crack in it, for even after they'd learned the answer to the simple question of who murdered Sarah Lester, they faced a more unsettling question: Why did he do it? And what might change a *why?* into a *why not?* What caused some couples to part in peace, even as friends, and others to part bitterly, with lethal consequences? Could some small difference in a person's life shift their path from good to evil, or from evil to good? If so, what? And if not, why not?

The sense of not knowing and not possessing the ability to know was highlighted when Seth arrived early, dragging boxes and a toolkit, and took over the dining room. He went inside, made a show of rolling up his sleeves and getting into a white smock, closed both the door to the living room and the one to the kitchen, and that was it. No one would be allowed in the room until Seth gave the go-ahead, and the wait seemed endless.

Everyone working in the kitchen and waiting in the living room could hear him; that was easy. One of those boxes must have contained a stereo, for soon the sound of a Renaissance mass penetrated to those outside. They heard a chorus of polyphonic chants give way to one lone voice, a boy's, that faltered and fluttered high above the choir like a young bird attempting to fly on unsteady wings, an eaglet lifted and dropped by its mother, then caught mid-air and dropped again, until at last it gains control of its wings, catches an updraft, and soars.

Seth hammered for a while, and rattled things around a lot longer. There was a shouted conversation through the door, to the effect that only Josh was allowed even as far as the kitchen, but

Josh argued that there were too many dishes for one person to prepare, so finally Seth relented on that one point. Even then he insisted that the kitchen door should only be opened as wide as necessary to admit trays of food, and he would take them from there.

Travis was the first guest to arrive. He heard the music and carpentry noises coming from the sealed dining room, and asked Deedee, "What's going on in there?"

"Seth is in there doing something very hush-hush. Nobody has a clue."

Travis called a greeting through the door and offered Seth a hand, then he and Deedee took Brandon out back to toss a nerf football around. Old Sheriff Greer and new Sheriff Caraher drove up together, but in separate cars, in case Victor got called away on some emergency. Yolanda poured mugs of mulled apple cider for all of them and they, too, went out back. Even from the patio they could hear Seth whacking on something.

A car horn out front drew everyone to the porch, and there in the back seat sat a woman the guests had never seen before. Edgar was bent into the trunk, retrieving his mother's wheelchair. He could have maneuvered it into the house himself—there were only two steps—but with everybody lifting she seemed weightless.

Her unfocused eyes didn't acknowledge the circle of arms around her. Her hair was bright silver. She was hunched in on herself as though trying to form a sphere with her body. In outline she seemed ancient, late for the graveyard. A stranger might have taken her for Deedee's grandmother. Only her taut skin, though tinged in a sickly gray, gave her age away.

Rollie was the last one into the living room. He wiped his hands on his apron and asked Edgar, "What did her doctor say about this?"

"He says she hasn't uttered so much as a word in months, but she's taken a few bites of food on her own, and he can't see that a short visit home will do any harm."

Josh rapped on the dining room door. "Seth? Mom is here. When will you be ready?"

Seth opened the door just wide enough to show his face. "You and Rollie go to the kitchen and start handing me the food."

From the kitchen all they could see were Seth's arms as he took one platter after another.

"Careful with this turkey," Rollie said. "She's an eighteen pounder."

Once the food was all in place, Seth instructed everybody to file into the dining room via the living room entrance. They could now see a traditional Thanksgiving table setting, with a fat turkey centerpiece, bowls of oyster stuffing, sweet potato casserole, green beans and caramelized potatoes, and silver trays of cranberry sauce, olives, and gherkins. Light from tall red candles reflected off green wine bottles and crystal glasses.

The fireplace was glowing, and the aroma of black cherry logs mingled with the Thanksgiving scents of pepper, sage and basted meat drippings. The only incongruity about the room was a white bed sheet covering the mantelpiece and the entire wall on either side of it. With everyone lined up behind the table and facing the covered wall, Seth pulled the sheet away. "Ta-da!" he said.

It took them a moment to figure it out. When they did, they gasped, and applauded.

What they saw was a pastiche of Leonardo da Vinci's The Last Supper, with the table laid out exactly like the Thanksgiving table in front of them, complete with a centered turkey, long red candles, and bottles of wine. The place settings were all the same blue-and-white Meissen dishware that the Shanleys had used for decades on formal occasions. The top of the fireplace cut into Seth's painting to simulate the doorway that had been cut through Leonardo's original.

Seth's innovation was that, except for Jesus, all of his subjects were the people in the room. Yolanda gesticulated wildly from the right of the canvas, Travis leaned in to whisper something to Deedee on the left, and Josh held the bag of gold coins—greatly exaggerated here from Judas' meager purse. Brandon sat on the floor at Josh's feet, sniffing the draped table cloth. A young pastel Mom, painted from an old photograph, sat at Jesus' proper left, in front of Greer and his raised finger.

Only it wasn't Jesus.

"Who is it?" Travis asked, pointing.

"It's Leonardo. Taken from a self-portrait," Seth said. "Did you know he was gay?"

"Yes, I heard about it," Travis answered, as though it had come about as the result of some event, an accident perhaps, or a conversion.

They all laughed and sat down. Deedee situated her Mom's wheelchair beside her, where she could feed her. It seemed a good plan, except she hadn't figured on Brandon. As far as Brandon was concerned, that was his spot. He tugged the wheelchair away from the table to give himself room to climb up.

"No Brandy, today that's your grandma's place," Deedee said, but neither Brandon nor her mother paid any attention.

Mrs. Shanley offered no help, but no resistance. Brandon climbed onto her lap and made himself comfortable.

Greer spoke up. "You know what I'd like to ask? This may sound funny, but...do you think we could set another place at the table. In memory of Lovemore."

"Well...sure," Josh said. He moved toward the china cabinet. "But why? I thought that of all of us, you liked him least."

"I don't know why, exactly. What I saw over there...it seems to me if a few things had been different he might have turned out to be a fine man. In fact, in a way he did turn out fine. He saw that his murderous rage would keep happening, and he put a stop to it."

Deedee jumped up. "You know what? Up in my room I have that big crucifix I wore in the play. How about if we put it in his plate, like a memorial?"

Seth looked at his painting. "I'll have to redo that side, with an empty chair for Lovemore. But I'm pretty sure I can work it in." He nodded his head.

Brandon slid from his grandmother's lap and ran after his mother in his stiff-legged fashion. They returned together, Deedee carrying the imitation garnet-studded crucifix, Brandon with one hand in his pocket. When Deedee placed the crucifix on Lovemore's empty plate, Brandon produced a velvet drawstring bag.

"Brandy...what is that?"

"Lovemore."

"What do you mean?"

He lifted the bag to his nose, then to hers. "Lovemore," he repeated.

She took it from him. "Oh my God! Look at this!" She pulled out a handful of jewelry. Not garnets this time, but real rubies, and emeralds and diamonds. "They must be Sarah Lester's stolen jewels."

Travis walked over to her and held up black pearl earrings. "I recognize these. Where did you find them?"

Brandon said, "Basement."

"In the basement?" Rollie asked. "You mean at the theater?"

Brandon nodded solemnly.

Everybody had to get a closer look, no matter that food was getting colder and colder.

"Sarah had great taste in jewelry," Seth said.

Edgar asked, "What do you think? A few thousand?"

Nobody knew. They sat, silent and stunned. Brandon climbed back up into his grandmother's lap and picked up a spoon. Into the quiet room Greer said, "You realize what this means." No one ventured a response. "It means he loved her. It wasn't a premeditated murder-theft. If it was, he had almost two months to figure out a way to sell all that stuff. He kept it because it reminded him of her."

Deedee set the bag beside the cross on Lovemore's plate. It seemed a much smaller version of the bag of gold Josh held in the painting.

Edgar turned to Victor. "One other thing remains unclear, to me anyway. Who burned down Lovemore's old house? Any clues?"

Rollie spoke up. "Lovemore himself had a motive. Mrs. Crowe was trying to make a case for back rent. He hated her for that."

Victor said, "But plenty of people who wanted him dead thought he was asleep there at the time. Or maybe the accident theory is right. Neighbors say she really did get like to get drunk and cook up midnight snacks. I think this is another one of those things we'll never know for sure."

Once again the tragedy of recent events pervaded the room.

A snapshot taken of this moment and shown to a stranger would be misinterpreted as a Thanksgiving gathering at prayer. But the thoughts around this table were not prayerful. They were full of sorrow for the murdered Sarah and her tortured killer, and for a crapshoot pattern of life and death.

With Lovemore's silent presence acknowledged, Josh, in his formal way, stood at his end of the table and raised his glass. "We have a great deal to be thankful for this year." You could tell by his opening tone that he'd thought in advance about what to say. "First and foremost, our mom is here to join us."

Everybody raised a glass. Deedee clamped her mother's hand around a water glass and lifted it. Mrs. Shanley watched it rise and fall, as though it were some act of magic. Brandon watched her eyes as she watched her hand.

Josh continued, "Many of us know the Guardian has been a Shanley family responsibility for six generations."

"Is that all?" Rollie jumped in. "Seems the last count I heard was more like since the dawn of time."

Rollie could get away with that kind of thing now, and Josh laughed. "No, Rollie, only six. Beginning with Orval in 1882 and on down through Mom and Woody, and now it's us. We're number six. And Mom, today's very special news is that it seems we have secured the future of the Guardian for another generation. Special kudos go to Rollie."

"No, not really," Rollie said. "It was a total group effort."

Greer raised his glass, "Here's to group effort."

They toasted each other all around.

Still standing, Josh said, "And Mom, do you know what this occasion marks? With both you and Brandon here, it's the first time these three generations of Shanleys have ever been together."

Everyone put on a happy smile for the toast. Deedee lifted her mom's water glass for her. They drank, grew quiet, and began to pass food around.

Into the silence Victor said, "I think I have something to be thankful about, and I can announce it now. My wife—my ex-wife—and my little girl will be returning to Twisting Creek. I'm not sure if Hollywood didn't work out, or whether my move into Bedford Woods did the trick. But they should be back by Christmas." He looked at Yolanda. "I'm not sure that this is the time or place to tell everybody, but I just learned it myself."

"It's perfect," Yolanda said. "I think I've started to figure out that I'm happy to stay exactly where I am."

"Ha! Not me," Deedee said. "Travis and I have a little announcement to make. See this?" She lifted her left hand and now for the first time everyone noticed an engagement ring there. Travis drew the hand toward him and kissed it. She smiled at him, then turned back to Rollie and said, "But don't you worry—I'll come back for Sunday Suppers."

There followed more congratulations and toasts.

In a quiet moment Greer held up a forkful of stuffing and said, "This is delicious. I don't think I've ever tasted any better."

Rollie said, "It was Mom's recipe. In fact, Mom…" He tried, without success, to catch her eye across the table. "Mom, this is all your meal. Everything here is exactly as you made it."

Brandon lifted a spoonful of the stuffing to his nose. "Smell-and-tell!" he said.

Rollie said, "Okay little dude, smell-and-tell."

"Sage!" he said.

"Correct! And…"

"Nutmeg!"

"Correct! There's more."

Brandon sat quietly in his grandmother's lap, his nose right up against the spoon of stuffing. He crinkled his forehead. There was something in there that puzzled him, a scent he hadn't encountered before. He looked into his grandmother's face and lifted the spoon to her nose.

She seemed to notice him for the first time. A pink flush gave expression to her face. She closed her eyes and inhaled. "Oysters," she said.

"Oysters?" Brandon asked.

"Correct!" Rollie said. "Way to go, Mom!"

"My turn," Brandon said, sniffed, and said, "Celery!"

Very softly, almost to herself, Mrs. Shanley said, "Correct."

"Your turn," Brandon said.

"Onions," she said.

"Correct! My turn next."

"Yes," his grandmother said. "Next, it's your turn."

Also by RJ Huddy . . .

No Senator's Son

"... the perfect balance
between engaging writing,
fascinating character development,
and a twisting plot that explores
political intrigue, collective and
individual motivations, and
beautifully intricate global scenery."

Learn Thai with Me

" ... the way RJ Huddy slips
deftly between four cultural settings
(Saudi Arabia, Afghanistan, Thailand
and Kentucky) is both fascinating and
informative. For expatriates, it is also
completely plausible. Above all, *Learn
Thai With Me* is a good story: laugh-
out-loud funny, provocative, insightful,
and human."

The Verse of the Sword

"... observations about life
in North Africa will bring a
smile of recognition to the lips of
those who are familiar with that
part of the world, and enlighten
those who are not. This is great
storytelling, rendered compulsive
by sudden and totally unexpected
twists and turns in the plot."

All proceeds from the sale of these books go towards research
for a cure for CMT Neuropathy, a form of muscular dystrophy.